CW01117908

For Steve Westby

The Plotting

John Lucas

*with kind regards & in
recall of a memorable
evening in Ilkens 28 April '23
John Lucas*

**GREENWICH EXCHANGE
LONDON**

Greenwich Exchange, London

The Plotting
©John Lucas 2016

First published in Great Britain in 2016
All rights reserved

This book is sold subject to the conditions that it shall not, by way of trade or otherwise, be lent, resold, hired out or otherwise circulated without the publisher's prior consent in any form of binding or cover other than that in which it is published and without a similar condition including this condition being imposed on the subsequent purchaser.

Printed and bound by **imprint**digital.net
Typesetting and layout by Jude Keen Ltd., London
Tel: 020 8355 4541

Cover design by Narrator (www.narrator.me.uk)
info@narrator.me.uk
Tel: 033 022 300 39

Greenwich Exchange Website: www.greenex.co.uk

Cataloguing in Publication Data is available from the British Library.

ISBN: 978-1-910996-06-5

> Some are temporary heroes.
> Some of these people are happy.
> *W.H. Auden,* 'Dover'

> A perturbation of pulse:
> and a word your body is trying to make you hear
>   … It is so much like
> the twist in the plotting of things that she should pass here …
> *Bernard Spencer,* 'In Athens'

for the Burgundy Street Five

1

It *was* her.

Wasn't it?

He should have been able to tell, because there weren't many in that evening. There never were in the weeks immediately after Christmas. The dead time of the year. A few of the regulars huddled round their usual tables. One or two he didn't recognise, whose faces meant nothing to him, listened attentively to the music or muttered to their companions. As for the woman at the back, who'd entered unobtrusively as the last set began, she was on her own, sitting as far away from the low stage as she could get. So, anyway, it seemed. Once or twice he thought he noticed her looking in his direction, perhaps even wanting to meet his eye, but under the room's lowered lights he couldn't be sure, and although there were features and gestures that reminded him – the oval face with the fringe of dark hair above those strong, arched eyebrows, the way she lifted the glass to her lips, supporting her right elbow with left hand as she sipped her drink (which wasn't often), nothing told him for sure whether it was the woman he thought – but wouldn't dare to hope – it might be.

Then, as the quartet moved into the their closing number, the landlord abandoned his forlorn attempt at a jazz atmosphere by throwing up the dimmer switch and under fluorescent strip lighting the back bar of the Three Tuns became once more part of a lacklustre pub on a wet Wednesday night in late January.

Eyes closed, he concentrated on the music. Coda. Decelerando. Final chord held through four bars. That was it. Thank you and good night.

While the others began to stow their gear, Terry ran through his usual spiel. "Loved playing for you good people as always, and whatever you lacked in numbers you more than made up for in apathy." Pause. "Sorry. Slip of the tongue. *Appreciation.* And remember, if you want to hear more from the Terry Marsden Quartet, come earlier next time. That'll be two weeks from now, if we're still alive." Further pause. "Meanwhile you can listen to our latest CD, available at all good record stores or free from your local waste tip, and featuring" – pointing to them in turn – "Al Stocking on guitar, Si Colston, bass, Geoff Cousins, tenor, and yours truly on keyboard and Beta Blockers."

There was a thin scattering of applause, the hollow thunk of beer glasses as they were set down on the formica-topped tables, a scraping of chair legs.

The crowd, such as it was, was already making for the exit as Norman came from behind the bar to collect glasses and push some readies into Terry's hand. "Very nice, lads. Loved that last number. What's it called?"

"Satin Lady," Terry told him for the umpteenth time. "Not to be confused with Sophisticated Doll. Don't want you singing along in the wrong key."

"Would I ever." Norman laughed uneasily. Then, moving away, his hands steadying a leaning tower of empty beer glasses, "So we'll see you gents in a fortnight's time. Unless you fancy a bevy in the front bar. Always welcome."

The soul of generosity, old Norman. He always asked, safe in the knowledge that they'd say no. Not worth the risk of being caught by the boys in blue after one too many.

The bar was virtually empty by now, and soon the four of them would be heading in separate directions. Routine farewells, promises to sort out the chords of one or two numbers that weren't yet in the book, half-agreements on the need for a practice session that they knew wouldn't happen.

Only after he'd snapped the locks shut on his sax case could he nerve himself to look toward the table where she'd been sitting. She was still there, but standing now, face averted as she pushed her arms into a long, dark-red duffle coat. Then, reaching a hand to free the hair at the back of her neck from its collar, she turned to him and under the full lighting let her eyes meet his, a faint smile on her lips.

Well, well.

Toting his case, he pushed a way past the scattering of tables and chairs to where she stood. The smile, he could now see, was unsure, but she was looking at him steadily, almost expectant.

Not yet able to speak, he put out his hand. For a moment she hesitated, then took it, shook it – moved it up and down once, rather – and let her own hand fall back to her side.

"So," she said, after scrutinising him for a few seconds. "How are you, Geoff?" And now her smile was gone, and her eyes searched his, shifted to look past him, then once again locked onto his. Concern? Apprehension? A challenge?

"I'm fine," he said.

See, I *can* speak. And, as she waited. "And how are you – Helen?"

"I'm fine."

To his left he was aware that Terry, having paused in the act of manoeuvring his keyboard and amp toward the great outdoors, was calling out a fare thee well, no doubt taking the opportunity to clock a good view of the woman his tenor man was chatting up.

"Yeh. See you, Terry," he said without taking her eyes off her.

She moved her shoulders as though to ward off the blast of cold air that hurtled into the room from the now wide-open door through which Terry prepared to steer his equipment.

Something about the way she followed the other man's movements made him glance over his shoulder in time to catch the look – puzzled, enquiring, almost as though he was trying to decide whether he knew her or not – that Terry was directing at her, but when he turned back to Helen she was concentrating on smoothing the fingers of the woollen gloves she'd pulled on.

At last she raised her eyes, met his gaze. "Winter in Longford," she said. "It could be Siberia." And she laughed.

Hunching up his own shoulders, he grimaced in a display of mock-sympathy. "Winter in Longford. Doesn't have the ring of Autumn in New York, does it?"

"Nor of Moonlight in Vermont."

"Ah, you can't beat the old numbers."

Then, when she looked at him without speaking, "Fancy a drink?" he asked, not certain what else to say. "One for the road."

She stared round her. "Well," she said, "there's no one in the place, but the barman isn't called Joe, and it isn't quarter to three."

"There's a bar further down the street."

She seemed to consider his offer. "If you're sure."

"Sure," he said. So tight was his throat, so dry his mouth, the word sounded more like a squawk.

He stood aside to let her pass through the door he held open for her and, as she brushed by him, that scent she used, its dark, musky aroma, long forgotten, so instantly familiar, assailed him.

Damn.

2

But inside the bar he'd brought her to, his tenor case stowed beside his feet, propped on stools with their drinks in front of them – he'd risked a white wine, while she accepted a vodka and ice – talk gradually became easier. The only other occupants were a few teenagers, sprawled on a leather sofa marooned on the bar's bare boards, open bottles of lager or coke on the low table in front of them. And the music – music! ha! – was turned down.

"So," he said, as they clinked glasses. "What brings you here?"

"Must be the atmosphere," she said, the smile revealing her deliberate misunderstanding of his question. "The heady excitement of it all." She looked around her, then back to him, enquiring. "This used to be a straightforward town pub, didn't it? What happened?"

"It's called progress. The vertical drinking experience. Kick out all the furniture and ensure it's no place for the infirm. Surely all that had happened before you left?"

She shrugged. "If so, I don't remember." Then, finishing her brief inspection of the occupied leather sofa, "Anyway, I'd say that this looks decidedly post-vertical."

"From what I hear it'll soon be post-post-vertical. There's a rumour that some restaurant chain's put in a bid. This could soon become Longford's number one Eaterie."

"Really? I'll give it a try, then. Strike while the oven's hot."

He left a moment's silence, before his next words. "You're not just passing through, then?"

From the way she looked at him, then away, he wondered whether she'd heard the tremor in his voice. "No," she said, serious now. "I'm back here because I have work."

"Teaching?"

"F.E. The local college lost its Head of English midway through the autumn term." She paused. "He was diagnosed with some illness that required immediate retirement – so they advertised for a new Head, I applied, and here I am." A brief pause. "Happily in post since the start of the year."

She was watching him and he wasn't sure what came next. Trying to feel his way, he raised his glass, said slowly, "In that case, congratulations. Assuming they're in order."

"Well, it's definitely not a death sentence," she said. And when she smiled, a wry, self-deprecatory smile, he felt confident enough to put on a cod interviewer's voice as he asked, "So, perhaps you'd care to tell our viewers what it feels like to be back after all this time? What is it – ten years?"

As though answering a question he hadn't asked, she said, "I knew you'd be playing tonight. Janey Macpherson told me you were still – what's the phrase? At it? On the road? Blowing? But with a jazz group now."

"Janey Macpherson?" Then he remembered. "That'll be the Janey who used to be in the Alleyn Players? With red hair and the all-cheerful manner?"

"That's her. A good friend of mine. She keeps me up to date."

"What – with the life and high times of Longford? Must be quite a task."

"There's not much Janey doesn't know about this old town. Anyway, about the Players. Did you know that this year's play will probably be *Measure for Measure*?"

When, without looking at her, he shook his head, she added, "Janey was hoping I'd audition but I had to explain that I'll be too busy, settling in."

He set his glass down. There were questions he wanted to ask, none of them the one he now did. But he raised his eyes to meet hers as he said, "So the Players still exist? I lost contact with them years ago." Had Janey mentioned that a certain production of *Much Ado about Nothing* had put an end to his time as an amateur luvvie? Perhaps, perhaps not.

"Janey Macpherson," he said after a pause. "We sometimes met at her house for read-arounds. Had a husband, a much older man, in banking."

"Very good. Your memory is clearly in perfect working order. Yes, that's Janey, although her husband's now dead and she no longer lives in that vast place out in the country. We did an open-air production there one summer, remember? You were Snug."

"And you were Helena."

"But naturally. Type casting, you could say. The love-lorn maid, abandoned by her paramour. Story of my life."

She spoke lightly enough, but the smile on her lips failed to reach

13

her eyes. He couldn't prevent himself looking at her unadorned ring-finger and then, raising his eyes, found that she was looking steadily at him.

"I'm sorry."

Sorry for me, sorry for you.

She inclined her head, though whether in acceptance of his word of sympathy, or for some other reason he couldn't know; nor could he find a way to break the silence as he watched her hunch over her glass, stare abstractedly into it. Age had slightly thickened the flesh around her jaw, grooved the skin on either side of her strong, straight nose, its arched nostrils, but her dark, wide eyes were, he saw as she raised them and looked into his, still clear, the emphatic eyebrows above them reaching almost to the raggedy fringe of hair she'd kept as when he'd known her a decade earlier, and, now that she'd slipped the coat off her shoulders, he could see the firm figure beneath her dark-green, long-sleeved jumper. In what had to be her late thirties, she was not merely an attractive woman, but one whose allure was strong as ever, or so he now felt, alive to how her proximity made the blood flush through his veins.

What he couldn't see or understand was why she'd come to the Three Tuns that evening. A stray line from *A Midsummer Night's Dream* came back to him. Helena to Demetrius, the lover whom Puck has deluded into falling for her friend Hermia: "I am sick when I look not on you." Its sheer inappropriateness caused him to choke back a laugh in which there was no delight.

She lifted an enquiring eyebrow.

But he couldn't tell her. Instead, he wondered aloud how come Janey Macpherson knew about the existence of the Terry Marsden Quartet, "given that we're not headline news, not even in the *Longford Free Trader*," and when Helen said, smiling, "Perhaps your reputation spreads wider than you know," he switched to asking her about the college. Did she think she'd enjoy being there, had she come across colleagues she could feel at ease with, what were the students like?

No doubt guessing that his questions were prompted more by routine politeness than genuine curiosity, she made perfunctory remarks about a change being as good as a rest, told him that she'd had enough of Wolverhampton where she'd been ever since leaving the town she'd now come back to, and although more than one colleague there had told her it would be a mistake to return to old haunts and faces, so far she'd found no reason to regret being here.

"And I really enjoyed hearing you play," she said, sounding as though she meant it. "When did you make the leap into jazz?"

"Not much of a leap," he said. "More a way of crossing the street. The Blues band folded a good few years ago and Al – the guitar man – told me of a mainstream to modern quartet he was also with. Their tenor lead had left and they needed a replacement. I like the music, the group were prepared to put up with me. So," he spread his hands, "Java Jive. Here I am."

"I'm glad."

The smile seemed genuine, the words too. He said, perhaps with too much emphasis, "It's good to see you again, Helen."

As though to undercut his words, the teenagers got noisily to their feet, and relieved not to have to register the effect of his words, he followed their slow exit into the winter night.

When he eventually turned back to her, he saw she'd risen from her stool, and, as she shrugged herself into the duffle coat, settling her hair over its collar, she was looking at him enquiringly. "I'm hoping you can do me a favour," she said.

"At your service."

Her eyes met his, unsmiling now. And the words, when they came, were cool as the night air that drifted in from the door the teenagers hadn't bothered to pull shut as they left the bar. "I'm in temporary digs but looking for a suitable flat. Janey tells me your landlord owns several properties around town. She thought he might possibly have the kind of place I'm after."

So that was it. Cut to the chase.

Feeling the familiar sense of disillusion, he asked "Suitable? What's that?"

"Oh, you know," she said with apparent indifference. "A bachelor girl's place. One bedroom. Living room. Kitchen, bathroom. A place big enough to swing a cat. Where I can feel comfortable on my own."

"You're not thinking of buying then?"

"Not when I don't know how long I'll be here."

She reached into her coat pocket, drew out a bulky purse, and, having prised off the thick red rubber bands by which it was bound and let them dangle from thumb and first finger, found the card she was looking for. "So far I'm enjoying the new place. But that may be because I'm so glad to be away from … from … "

She stopped, coloured slightly, but didn't speak the name that had forming on her lips.

15

He dropped his eyes, looked at the fingers holding the card. Her almond-shaped nails were as shapely as he remembered from ten years ago and it was all he could do to control the tremor of his own fingers as he held the card up to read the words printed on it.

Helen Birdlip BA, B.Ed. Lecturer & Educationist.

Underneath was a mobile telephone number and her email address.

She watched with a faint smile as he pushed the card into the breast pocket of his cord jacket, then she resealed her purse, and, having drained the last of her drink, stood. Mission accomplished.

There was no suggestion of another round.

But outside, in the gusty, wet street gleaming like coal-tar in the blurry headlights of a few, late cars, she said quickly, "Next time, it'll be my shout." She held out her hand. "Good to see you again, Geoff, and to have the chance to catch up."

She turned and walked briskly away toward the town centre. No suggestion he might walk some of the way with her. He watched her retreating figure as it passed under street lights, the assured, unassuming grace that carried her away from him. Next time, it'll be my shout. Here's hoping.

* * *

Norman stood in the doorway of the back entrance to his now darkened pub, dragging on a cigarette as he watched Geoff unlock the small Fiat and lay the tenor in its case across the car's back seat. If the landlord had noticed him duck behind the boot to fish the car keys from out the car's exhaust pipe, he didn't let on.

"'Night, Norman."

Settling into the driver's seat, he was about to slam the door shut when the publican, in the act of grinding his cigarette-stub into the yard's asphalt, called over to him, "Who was the lady, if you don't mind my asking. Don't remember having seen her in here before."

"That was no lady … " But he didn't finish the remark. "An old friend," he said, "from before your time."

Then he did close the door, flipped a hand in farewell and backed out of the yard.

Norman, he reckoned as he pushed the gear stick into second, had been at the pub the past half-dozen years, the same time the quartet had been in existence. So, no, he wouldn't have seen Helen before tonight.

But old friend. Yeh, yeh. Last seen ten years previously. *Every time we meet ...*

Driving through Longford's now deserted night-time streets, he played back her remark about it being good to catch up. *I get that old feeling ...* Catch up with what exactly? I'm not an old friend, not for her, am I? I still don't know why she went off all those years ago. Old friend. Who are you kidding? She didn't ask anything about my work, wasn't interested. Or had Janey know-it-all told her? Fascinating, my dear. I had really no idea the life of a town librarian could be so exciting. Or is risqué the word I need? Spending your days slipping the covers off books and peering into their depths. It sounds desperately sexy. Or is chirurgic the more appropriate term? Yes, well. Dream on.

There'll be no new romance for me ...

He laughed derisively into the dark, remembering the fabled 'Don't let's say au revoir, let's just say goodbye.' Billie? Peggy Lee? Mildred Bailey?

... it's foolish to start ...

The plane trees lining each side of Ewing Avenue, many of them pollarded the previous autumn, loomed against the cloud-ragged night sky, ungainly, gaunt, like encrusted pillars of some ancient, underwater city exposed to air by a retreating sea, beyond them the tall reefs of darkened houses. Pure poetry, what? And so we say farewell to the legendary land of Longford.

Steering through the open wrought-iron gates of no. 27, he rolled his car up onto the shingle forecourt ... *when that old feeling ...*

Baw was waiting for him in the porch. He opened the front door and at once she pushed ahead of him, then, tail erect, turned to face him while he locked up and pushed the bolt across.

"I suppose you want a nightcap," he said, reaching down to scratch her black head.

As though to confirm his words, the cat turned and stalked down the hall toward the kitchen, snaking around and between his legs as he stood at the sink.

Watching her lap from the full saucer of water, he thought of Helen's remark about not knowing how long she'd be staying in Longford, and said aloud, "The dame's playing you for a sucker, Marlowe."

... is here in my heart

17

Baw lifted her head, blinked slowly at him, then ducked back to her drink.

3

The following Monday, after a dull, lonely weekend, he drove home from a dull, lonely day at the library and, as he turned in at no. 27, his car headlights caught Frank Alexander emerging round the side of house.

"Evening, Geoffrey," Frank said, stepping up onto the porch and watching as his tenant levered himself from the Fiat. He waited while Geoff retrieved a bag of groceries and his briefcase from the car boot and crunched across the gravel to where Baw prowled around Alexander's old grey flannels, rubbing her head against leather slippers the landlord habitually wore when "doing the domestics," as he called his household chores.

"Help you with those?"

Geoff shook his head, tucked his briefcase beneath the arm holding his grocery bag, and opened up his door. As usual Baw marched in ahead of him.

"Mind if I come in for a minute?" Alexander asked. "I was going to leave you a note but seeing that you're here … "

Without bothering to reply, Geoff motioned the older man through into the hall. As he shouldered the front door shut he watched Alexander run an accustomed proprietorial gaze over the interior, no doubt looking for stains in the tan carpeting that ran the length of the hall, smears or scuff marks on the cream walls with their several framed prints. Unable to peer inside the two rooms to the right, whose doors were both closed, he made do by tilting his head for a quick once-over of the ceiling. Nothing to worry about. Geoff could almost hear the sigh of relief.

There was, he noticed, no sign of a note in either of Alexander's liver-spotted hands.

Should he invite Alexander into the front room? That was the one he kept for what his mother would have called "best". But without the gas fire having been lit to take off the room's chill it was inhospitable, and for all Frank's fussy ways Geoff liked his landlord well enough to feel he owed him the chance of warmth.

He gestured toward the kitchen and the older man preceded him down the hall.

"Cup of tea? Or something stronger, perhaps."

"A cuppa would be very welcome," Alexander said, as he sat upright at a kitchen chair, one of the four grouped at the scrubbed-wood table on which Geoff rested the groceries. "Nice table, this."

One of the advantages of renting unfurnished accommodation was that you could suit your own tastes. One of the disadvantages was that, in Geoff's experience at least, landlords felt under less pressure to attend to matters of household maintenance. It wasn't after all *their* furniture that was being affected by rising damp, nor *their* bedrooms that suffered under loose roof tiles. Still, in this respect at least Alexander was an exception. He was always prompt in carrying out necessary repairs. But then he lived above the shop.

As though to confirm the satisfaction he felt over this arrangement, Alexander said, as he stirred sugar into the mug of tea Geoff had placed at his elbow, "I thought I should warn you that I have some work starting upstairs tomorrow. I have decided to have the bathroom modernised, and to put in a shower. There could be some noise, I'm afraid. Drills, banging, what not."

Geoff finished forking a sachet of salmon into Baw's saucer before, straightening and turning to his landlord, he said, "Well, I doubt it'll bother me. I'm out all day. But thanks for letting me know." Then, as the possible import of the landlord's words hit him, "You're not thinking of moving out, are you?"

"Me? Good lord, no. Not at my age. I'd prefer to see out my time where I am. And that being so," Frank added, with the odd formality which was braided through his talk, "I have rather come round to the idea of installing a shower for my comfort. It will, so everyone assures me, suit me better than clambering about in a bath."

Clambering?

"Naturally, I intend to be here while the alterations are being made. The men could be working late. Poles. I mean the man in charge is English, but the workers themselves are from Poland, so he tells me. They're supposed to be reliable chaps." He took a mouthful of tea, swilled it round his mouth, then swallowed noisily. "Catholics I shouldn't wonder. Still, you can't have everything." He sighed, shook his head.

Frank Alexander attended the nearby United Reform Church. Of a Sunday morning, if Geoff was in the front room, he would see his landlord marching across the forecourt, workday flannels and check shirt exchanged for a black suit with neat white shirt and dark-blue tie, grey cap atop a virtually bald head which was full of the non-sequiturs he regularly handed out as if they were considered views of the world. Catholics I shouldn't wonder.

"Anyway," Alexander said, setting down his mug and grunting as he got to his feet. "Forewarned is forearmed, as they say. I'll leave you to get your supper, Geoffrey."

He stood there, a lonely man, a widower of many years.

"As you're here," Geoff said, and saw the light of expectancy in the landlord's eye. "There's something I've been meaning to ask you."

Alexander sat down again, all too plainly eager for any chance to extend the conversation.

"A friend of mine," Geoff said. "She's looking for a place to live. A flat."

"Someone at the library?"

"No." Geoff began unpacking his groceries, stowing chops, butter, cheese and milk in the fridge, loaf and rolls in the bread-bin, filling Alexander in as he did so. "She's a teacher – lecturer at the FE College in town."

"And she isn't enamoured of her present accommodation I assume."

"It's not that. She's in temporary lodgings. She's only just arrived. We ran into each other a week ago." He wondered whether to say more, decided against.

"A friend, you say?" Alexander was puzzled, or pretending to be so.

"Sort of. We've not seen each other for a long time. Ten years." Should he mention the Alleyn Players? No, forget it. That would require further explanation. "She left for foreign parts. Wolverhampton, to be precise. Got a post at a school there, and we lost contact. Now, she's back, living in digs while she finds somewhere more permanent."

That was as much as he was prepared to say.

It was enough to satisfy Alexander. Scratching the side of his grey-stubbled cheek, the old man said, "I'm afraid I have nothing available myself at the moment, but I will of course keep my ear to the ground. What kind of place is she, this friend of yours, looking for? Family size? Near town? Or does she prefer to live where there's less hurly-burly?"

"Not sure," Geoff said. "Whether she has any strong preferences about location, I mean. But I should think something about the size of my place would do her nicely." Helen had wanted a bachelor girl's flat, hadn't she? "She's on her own." No, he didn't know that, couldn't be sure. She might have a part-time lover. Something for the weekend. Yes, well.

Frank was once again on his feet. "I'll ask among my acquaintances," he said, making for the kitchen door. "And I will, of course, let you know as soon as I have anything to report. One or two of my fellow-worshippers are, as you probably know, situate similar to myself. No, I'll see myself out," as Geoff made to accompany him. "And I hope the noise from upstairs doesn't prove to be an affliction."

Situate. Affliction. Where did Frank come by such words, Geoff wondered, as he heard the front door close behind his landlord.

* * *

An hour later, changed from suit into sweater and jeans and having grilled and chomped his way through two lamb chops accompanied by the remains of some salad prepared several days earlier and now, as Frank might have said, showing distinct signs of deliquescence, though a glass of red plonk did its best to assuage the hint of fetor, he was heading out of town toward the converted farmhouse where Terry Marsden lived.

It was Terry's new wife, Lorette, who, as he was about to bring the wrought-iron knocker crashing down yet again, finally opened the door. Her face, its tan illuminated by the bracketed carriage-lamp, wasn't especially welcoming.

She stood aside as he edged past her into the large, square, parquet-floored hall. Scent, at once expensive and discreet, filled the air.

"I hope I'm not late?" he said.

Without bothering to answer the implied question, she said, unsmiling, "You know where to find them, don't you." No question there.

"Yes, thanks." And, as she turned away, he added, "How are you?"

She looked back to him over her shoulder, her carefully made-up eyes studying him as though she suspected him of some satiric intent. Then, deciding he meant to be civil, she said coolly, "Well enough, thanks." A pause as she flicked a strand of long, blonde hair away from her mouth. "Perhaps the country air suits me." There was a flicker of a smile in which irony played its part, and her slim body in its floor-length dark blue robe disappeared through a door beyond which he could hear the sound of canned television laughter.

In the built-on conservatory at the rear of the large house the others were ready and waiting.

"You got the message then." Terry raised his head from the back of the keyboard where he was fiddling with some wires. "Sorry it was a bit eleventh-hour. Blame Al for that."

"Knew you wouldn't mind," Al said, ear to sounding board as he tweaked the pegs on his Gibson. "Anyway there's nothing on telly. Course you could have been out with your bride." Al used the local argot for girlfriend, partner, wife, but Geoff decided not to understand him.

"Who?"

"That lady waiting for you last gig at the Tuns."

Geoff pretended to think. So many women to choose between. Ha, ha. "Oh, Helen. Helen Birdlip. An old friend. I'd not seen her for years."

"Blimey," Simon said. "I wouldn't have let her slip through *my* fingers." And he shook his head to indicate his appreciation of Helen's looks.

"Tut, tut, and treble tuts," Al said. "Don't let Barbara catch you talking like that. You've got nothing to complain about."

Simon's smile was all complacency. "Who's complaining?" he said.

"Birdlip. Helen Birdlip." Frowning, Terry was trying out the name, as though trying to fire up his memory. "I've seen her somewhere before, I'm sure of it, but I can't, you know, place her. And the name doesn't ring a bell."

"Not one of your exes, then." But seeing Terry's look, Al added quickly, "Only joking. OK lads, let's get to work."

And as Geoff, having unpacked his case, was fitting his horn together, he explained, "It's this golf club gig. Terry won't be around much between now and then, except for next Wednesday at the Tuns, and I don't fancy using that gig for trying out anything not in the book."

Terry lifted a crystal cut-glass brandy glass to his lips. "Don't know about that," he said. "A new number or two might wake the punters from their doze. Still, probably not to be recommended. Might bring on a stroke."

"Business brisk, then."

"Mine?" Terry looked sharply at Geoff. "Never brisker. In, out,

23

shake it all about."

"I picked your message off the answerphone when I got in last night," Geoff said. "And phoned back. Left a message for you." The sense he had of being blamed for something not his fault gave a slight edge to his voice.

But Terry was indifferent. "Like I say, I'm busy. Busy, busy. Anyway, s'lright, you're here, that's what counts. Simon, unzip a beer for Geoff."

"Better not." But before he could say that he'd already drunk wine with his food the bass player thrust a can of lager into his hand. Ex-policeman though he was, Simon had a way with alcohol that suggested he wasn't over-concerned with the letter of the law.

Al handed round some sheet music. "Took all day doing these," he said. "Had to put the stiffs on hold. Joke."

Swallowing a mouthful of lager, Geoff asked, "This golf club job. Is it black-and-white?"

"Nah," Terry said, who was responsible for all the outside gigs the group came by. "It's not like it's their annual ball. Still, let's be sure to make a good impression. Get one golf club dance, it could lead to a whole lot more. You never know. So scruff order's out. Smart casual, I suggest, lads, is what we're looking for. Jackets and ties, and leave the jeans in the wardrobe. Right, what have we got here?" He riffled through the sheets that Al had propped on his keyboard. "*Drop me Off in Harlem?* What's that when it's at home?"

"Ellington," Al said. "Medium tempo. You've all got the chords and I've written the dots out for Geoff."

"Fair enough," Terry said. "Let's see what damage we can do to it. You want I give you four in?"

The practice began.

* * *

Two hours later, driving back to Longford,, Geoff thought, as he often did, about Terry. What exactly *was* the business that kept him so busy. "Financial adviser," his business card said. But what was that? What did such a person actually *do*? Simon's reply, when Geoff had once put the question to him, was "Tell other people where to put their dosh and pull in a wad for his own use." And then, as Geoff had looked at him, he added, "Well, I don't know. Nobody knows about El Tel, do they. He's fly. A mystery man. To be straight with you, if someone told me he'd done time for murder, I can't say I'd be surprised."

That was on an evening when they began their first set without him. A few minutes before they were due to launch into action, Norman had brought them a message phoned through from their leader to the effect that he'd been delayed by business. It wasn't the first time, not by a long chalk. Nor did it faze them. They had plenty of numbers in the book that suited bass, guitar and tenor. But that night they'd finished the first hour-long set with a lengthy run-round of 'Rose Room' and the three of them, Terry still having failed to appear, were standing at the bar nursing interval drinks and wondering whether they'd have to get through the entire evening without him, when Simon made his remark, one the other two decided to treat as a joke, though Al had said, "I dunno about fly. Way he carries on, he's more likely to sink." But when the others looked to him to explain his remark, he merely shook his head. "I mean, he takes on too much. All this rattling up and down motorways when he should be at home looking after the Blonde Bombshell. He doesn't want *that* blowing up in his face." Which left Geoff, at least, wondering whether Al knew more than he was prepared to let on about Terry's affairs, however you played the word.

The group's leader finally arrived as the three of them were about to begin the second set.

"What's this beauteous vision," Al asked Simon and Geoff. "Looks a bit of a Hooray to me," as Terry, assisted by Norman, lugged his keyboard and clobber through the crowded bar and up to the waiting trio. "Do we know you?"

"Sorry lads," Terry said. "A multiple on the M1. This is the best I could do." He was in pin-stripe suit with dark blue shirt and cut-away collar that allowed a good view of the striped, black and red tie he now undid and pulled free.

"So what school were you at?" Simon asked, nodding at the tie as it vanished into a pocket of the jacket Terry draped over his chair. "Eton?"

"You mean what's the Regiment," Al said. "Nottingham Irregulars, I shouldn't wonder. Regimental mascot a three-legged tape-worm."

An undertaker by day, Al favoured garish wear for their gigs. Mustard-coloured trousers and a maroon sweater contrasting vividly with Geoff and Simon's jeans and black-leather jackets, he himself looked something of a Hooray. But he was one of the best guitarists in the region, in demand among jazz groups who knew his worth as a Mr Rhythm with huge repertoire and solo skills in advance of most of his rivals.

"Right, what's first up?" Terry said, ignoring the banter.

"'Flying Home'?"

Ignoring the hint of possible satire, Terry nodded at Al's suggestion. "OK. Nice and bright, don't let it slacken."

Yes, a mystery man, all right, Geoff thought as, home once more, he eased the Fiat onto the forecourt, gravel under his wheels sounding like cicadas waking from a mid-summer siesta. That look Terry had shot him when he'd asked whether business was brisk. As though he'd suspected Geoff was – was what? Asking an out-of-order question. That was Terry for you. An edgy customer, one you didn't get too near. Still, no doubt about it, El Tel, as the others sometimes called him behind his back, was adept at finding them outside gigs, not the Big Ones he claimed to be after, but good payers, even so. Business Dinner-Dances, Medics' Balls, support band at the regional RAF. Station's annual shindig, and now this golf club social.

And, he thought, as he stood in his kitchen, making himself a late-night cup of tea, someone who, as his father would have said, wasn't short of a bob or two. That farmhouse must have cost a packet, and the two divorces would have set him back a tidy sum. Nor did the recent acquisition, Lorette, look as though she was ready to slum it. If Terry was a mystery, so was Lorette. But though she might be all lacquer she wouldn't have come cheap.

Unlike himself, he thought, using a teaspoon to squeeze his teabag against the side of his mug before hoisting it out and flicking it onto the draining board. Lie there, my art. He became aware that Baw was watching him from her basket beside the washing machine.

"Sorry, cat," he said. "Not the sort of thing I'd do in public. But when it's just you and me, old pal, manners go to pot."

Carrying the filled mug, he was about to leave the kitchen when he saw his answerphone light winking red.

Hello? Geoff? I hope I've got the right number. This is Helen – Helen Birdlip. I'm wondering whether you've had an opportunity yet to speak to your landlord about vacant flats he might know of. A brief pause, followed by a sigh that changed to a laugh. *I have to tell you that my digs are driving me mad. The wallpaper in particular. Have you ever seen a purple palm tree? There are twenty of them clustered on my bedroom wall. As Oscar said, one of us will have to go and I fear it may be me. Although in my case for fear read hope.* Further pause. *Perhaps you can give me a call sometime, I'd really appreciate that, especially if there's anything you can tell me about possible accommodation. Hope you're well. Do get in touch. Please? Bye.*

He switched off the kitchen light then, standing in the dark, played the message once more. Neither her voice nor her words gave anything away. Even the way she said "please" was more requirement than entreaty. An old friend. You could have fooled me.

Anyway, it was too late now to call her back. He'd do that tomorrow.

And then he thought back to Terry's remark. "I've seen her somewhere before. I'm sure of it." *Where* had he seen her? The question nagged. Could he, Geoff, find a way to ask her about that? And then, suddenly remembering the look she'd directed at Marsden the other night in the Tuns, he thought, and why, Helen, might you know Terry?

4

But in the event he didn't call her.

Because next day, as soon as he arrived at work, he discovered that Josie, one of the two assistant librarians, was off ill. "And so," Colleen said, as she gave him the news, "we've got nobody to chair tonight's meeting."

"What meeting?"

Colleen, in her customary dark-blue cardigan, white, unadorned blouse and grey-pleated skirt, turned from the photocopying machine from which issued sheets of paper, the look on her face midway between exasperation and concern. Stapler in hand, she turned back to her task of sorting the papers before clipping them together and dropping them onto the desk beside the machine.

"*Your* meeting," she said over her shoulder. "The meeting of the committee *you* set up."

Groaning, Geoff placed his suitcase on the slatted wooden chair beside a desk strewn with books and papers, and went over to the sink unit. The implied rebuke was unmissable. This is *your* fault, so *you* can sort it out. Staring out of the window at the forecourt from which he could see down to the High Street, he poured coffee from the machine into his mug and sipped. Weak, as usual.

As though she'd heard in his sniff of disapproval an attempt to challenge her unspoken accusation, Colleen straightened up and turned to face him. "I put a good three heaped spoons into the filter. Any stronger and we'd levitate."

"Perhaps we're buying the wrong coffee."

"We?"

"All right, I'll get the next bag. And something other than these arrowroot biscuits."

He bit into one and she watched his theatrical shudder of distaste, a slight smile relaxing her severely pretty face.

"Those papers are Agendas, right?" And when she nodded, he said, "Surplus to requirement, then. We'll have to cancel the meeting. Or postpone."

"We can't," Colleen said. "Some of them will be coming from far corners of the county. And we don't have addresses or telephone numbers for all of them. I know. I checked." Now get out of *that*.

"Emails?"

"Not all our older citizens own a computer. No, the meeting can't be called off."

He opened his mouth to protest, but before he could speak, Colleen shook the agenda papers at him. "It was your idea. The Library Users' Consultative Group." There was more than a hint of scepticism in the way she pronounced the words.

"You'd have preferred 'Customers'."

Colleen turned to finish arranging the papers before she said, "You know I wouldn't. But I *would* have preferred to do without one more committee."

"It isn't a committee."

"It may not be called a committee, but it certainly quacks like one." She watched him as he swilled his mug out under the cold tap and, having dried it and returned it to its place, settled at his desk and began to drag papers from his brief case. "Once you set these things up, Geoff, you have to abide by the consequences."

"Yes, miss." But his smile was intended to disarm her. And really, he thought as he prised the day's silver-foiled wrapped sandwiches from inside his briefcase, she was right. His idea of having the group as a form of *vox pop* to put pressure on the Council, an idea which, when he'd stitched it together a few months previously, had seemed such a good one, so certain to appeal to officialdom as evidence of the existence of a Vibrant Public Sector Interest with Proactive Thrust, had already begun to come apart at the seams. Too many of those who had volunteered for the group turned out to be opinionated philistines whose ideas of library use ranged from removing any book more than five years old, unless the book happened to be written by someone "people" *wanted* to read – which on enquiry turned out to be Jeffrey Archer; or denying access to anyone not suitably dressed – which on enquiry turned out to be "people" (aka men) who were "down-at-heel" and, as one attendee boldly stated, likely to bring the library into disrepute because "to be perfectly candid they emit an unwholesome smell." *Emit*. What kind of person used that word? Answer, the kind of person eager to join Longford and District's Library Users' Consultative Group.

Josie's indisposition could have been the perfect opportunity to bring the LUCG to an end. But Colleen plainly wasn't going to allow that to happen, not yet, anyway. "You're enjoying this, aren't you?" Geoff said "So why don't you chair the meeting?"

"You know I can't," Colleen said. Then, as he looked enquiringly at her, "I'm off early. It's Tuesday, remember."

"Oh, of course." And he did.

Every Tuesday Colleen, leaving her husband for that evening to look after their two small children, drove up the M1 in order to spend some hours with her widowed mother in Chesterfield, the diagnosis of whose Alzheimer's had been recently confirmed. The old lady was now in sheltered accommodation and Colleen's weekly visits were not to be neglected. "Sorry, Geoff, but it's down to you."

Right again. Following recent budget cuts, the library's staff was 'rationalised'. If Geoff had hoped the LUCG might protest, as he did, he was soon disillusioned. The most vocal of the Group – an aged, choleric grocer from Newark called Gleat, Gerald Gleat – was of the opinion – humble of course – that libraries couldn't expect to be cushioned against what Gleat referred to as "the realities of real life out where real people live," and that speaking personally he welcomed the thought that this provided the ideal opportunity to force some lazy buggers to do a day's honest work, work which ought to include the turfing out not only of books that weren't written by authors people wanted to read but of also turfing out so-called users – emitters to a man – whose overriding need was for compulsory fumigation or prolonged immersion in Lysol, or both. Others of the Consultative Group had seemed too cowed to offer alternative points of view, and the one man Geoff could have looked to for support, old Arthur Stanchard, wasn't able to attend that particular meeting.

Not that even Arthur's presence would have made for a different outcome. County Hall proposed, County Hall disposed, and as a result only Josie, Colleen and Geoff himself were now permanent, full-time librarians. The others, four in all, were part-timers. And even supposing the money could be found to pay for extra duties, you couldn't ask a part-timer to chair a meeting which, while not perhaps high-profile, was, in the kind of management-speak he had anticipated officialdom would adopt for the LUCG, nevertheless an important part of what it was indeed delighted to support as "establishing and maintaining good relations with our client-based approach," especially as no money was involved.

"How the blankety blank do you have relations with an approach?" Colleen had asked, when the officially embossed Mission

Statement arrived from County Hall, accompanied by instructions that the Statement was to be circulated among "all relevant staff members". Then, relaxing into mild imprecation, she added, "Bloody illiterates."

Now, her stapling chores completed, she pushed the papers into Geoff's hands. "Here," she said, "there are more than enough copies to go round. You know the ropes. If Squires doesn't turn up someone else has to be deputed to take the Minutes." She smiled mock-reassuringly at him. "Only six items on the agenda. You'll be home and tucked up with a good book and mug of Horlicks long before midnight. Anyway, the building has to be cleared by 9 p.m., remember. Union rules, by which I've no doubt you'll be keen to abide."

* * *

In fact, the meeting was over and done with well before 9 p.m. This was partly because Gleat, the one member who could be guaranteed to speak to every item, was not in attendance, though he made sure to send his apologies, handwritten on embossed notepaper; partly because the only substantial item that evening was about book supply, and beyond lamenting the cuts in buying that new budgeting entailed, there wasn't much that could be said. The group's unhappiness about cuts to opening hours had been minuted at the previous meeting (Gleat's enthusiastic endorsement almost certainly caused less by any thought of the inconvenience such cuts would bring to users than by his fear that once again librarians might escape from doing an honest day's work). 'Consequent' on the LUCG's expressed views, a letter had been sent to County Hall, and a reply received, which Geoff now read out under 'Any Other Business'. He knew it should have come under 'Matters Arising' but saved the letter until last, in the hope it would send the committee members home more determined than ever to do battle for the cause.

"*'At this point of time, therefore, the Libraries and Leisure Services Sub-Committee, having taken note of your suggestions, wish to thank you for them and inform you that the main thrust of the suggestions will be laid before the next full Council meeting, and the results of any deliberations consequent upon discussions will be communicated to you.'* Emollient," he said, as he laid the letter down.

"Emetic's more like it," Arthur Stanchard growled. A union man, a boilermaker who'd been left, as he said, on the scrap heap when the factory where he worked unexpectedly closed down, Stanchard was at first reluctant to join the LUCG, but Geoff, who knew and liked him, had eventually persuaded the old man that, as someone whose own education, as he often said, was entirely owing to the existence of public libraries, he ought to be on the group. After all, Geoff said, uncomfortably aware that he sounded like a spouting head but determined nevertheless to pursue his argument, given that Arthur loved quoting the lines of a poem that began "Much have I travelled in the realms of gold,/For which I thank Westminster and Paddington Public Libraries," Stanchard must surely realise that it was now more than ever necessary to save such realms from being put beyond the reach of those who most stood to benefit from them.

"Won't do any good," Stanchard had said. "You'll see." But, professional pessimist though he was, he came to relish the chance to remind younger members of the group of what they all stood to lose. For Gleat Arthur had a contempt he hardly bothered to conceal and which was fully returned. The two men loathed each other.

"Would you care to animadvert?" Geoff asked Stanchard, who smiled briefly in acknowledgement of the parody of chairman-speak.

"Over a pint, yes."

"Then, in the absence of any further business, I declare the meeting closed. Discussion can, of course, be continued in the Plough."

And it was, to such effect that Geoff didn't leave much before closing time. By then he was left alone with Arthur, listening to the old man's reminiscences of a time when the WEA had still been a force for good. "All gone now, though. That's what them toffee-nosed boggers couldn't stand. The likes of us knowing as much or more'n the likes of them. It's not *their* reading 'abits as'll be done for by all these closures."

"Don't suppose they read much more than their bank statements," Geoff said, getting to his feet as he swallowed the last of the pint he'd been nursing for the best part of two hours. "And for all we know they get their servants to do that for them. Well, Arthur. Fight the good fight." Then, fearing that sounded more flippant than he intended, he added, "You know I sometimes get the feeling that the way things are going, nearly every library in the kingdom could be closed down without anyone saying a dicky bird."

The old man also stood, buttoning his raincoat and, from an

inside pocket taking and shaking out an old cap, which he jammed onto his wispy grey hair. "It won't come to that," he said, looking steadily at Geoff. "Plenty are protesting. I'm an old socialist, I still believe in the power of the people. Never despair, comrade. We'll do for the boggers yet."

The words, Geoff realised, were vibrant with an intensity that shamed his own more casually uttered opinion.

"What you readin' at the moment," Arthur asked, as they made their way to the pub's front door.

"Me?" Geoff had to think which book was beside his bed. "Oh, a history of West Coast jazz. I don't suppose you'd approve." He held the door open for the older man, then followed him out into a damp, blustery night. "How about you?"

Arthur turned to face him, his eyes, glittering under the street lighting, offering a challenge to Geoff. "Why wouldn't I approve?"

"I always thought old socialists gave jazz the thumbs down as decadent music, not fit for a new society. And as for America ... "

"Well, you're wrong," Arthur said, pulling up his coat collar of his coat against a sudden blast of cold wind. "Me, I like most kinds of music. Know what Armstrong said when someone asked him if what he played was folk music?"

"Louis Armstrong?" Geoff knew what was coming.

"That's the feller. He said, 'It's all folk music. Leastways I ain't never heard no horse make it.'"

They both laughed before Arthur said, "Ever heard of the Clarion Singers? Yes, so you should've done. I sang with 'em for years." He shook his head. "Anyway ... "

He looked about, as though wanting what came next to be confidential. "If you want to know what I'm reading, I'll tell you. A pile of books on ornithology. Most on 'em from the city library."

"Is that a long-standing interest, then?"

"It is." Arthur smiled at the surprise Geoff couldn't keep out of his voice. Got you there, the smile said. He stood aside as a group of teenagers, hoods pulled down, veered uncertainly across the pavement to where the two of them stood. But they were drunk, not menacing. One even said "G'night" as he swerved past.

"I go off whenever I can with a group of bird-watchers," Arthur said, watching the youths' retreating figures. "Not twitchers, mind, we're watchers. Twitchers are a daft bunch. More money than sense." He turned back to Geoff. "All a watcher needs is a good pair of binoculars, a twitcher can't leave 'ome without a load of fancy cameras, light meters, the lot. Don't suppose they ever see what they're supposed to be looking at. Too busy pointing a camera at it."

And with that he lifted his hand in a farewell salute and stumped off into the night.

Turning in the other direction, Geoff made his way back to the library car park. Arthur Stanchard, that man of surprises. He'd known nothing of the old man's interest in ornithology. But the Clarion Singers. He ought to have guessed at *that*. Many-angled Arthur. It was like listening to a piece of music you'd known for a long time, thought you knew perfectly, until, quite suddenly, you realised that a phrase, perhaps a single note, wasn't as you'd always heard it, but was subtly different, shifted from sharp to flat, or fell just short of the bar line.

He stopped, the night wind chill on his back. He was passing the bar, now in darkness, where a week earlier he and Helen had sat in awkward conversation. No, that was wrong. It was more that after so many years they had to feel their way back to their former friendship. Wrong again. *He* had to feel his way. She was far more at her ease. But then she obviously hadn't felt for him what he had felt for her, a great wave of emotion which had come back, full force, as soon as he saw her again. Or rather, as soon as he made himself admit that the woman in the saloon bar of the Three Tuns was her, *was* Helen, was the woman whom, years earlier, face it, Cousins, you were crazy over and who you hoped might ... Until one day she disappears ... And, well, after that who wants this year's kisses?

He should have phoned her. He shook his head, exasperation mixed with regret, and as he did so saw that on the glass door before which he stood was a notice whose wording, as he stepped across to it, he could just make out by the light of the nearest street lamp.

FURNITURE STORE OPENING SOON.
WATCH THIS SPACE

Not a restaurant, then. The rumour had been wrong, as rumours so often are. Ah, well. The moving finger writes. Time to move on. The phone call would have to wait.

5

"Hello, is that Helen? Helen Birdlip? Hi. Yes, yes it is, Geoff. I'm sorry not to have replied sooner to the message you left the other night. *Slight pause.*

I wanted to phone you yesterday evening but then I got trapped at a library meeting that kept me out until late and didn't think you'd be grateful if I disturbed you at some unearthly hour. What? Oh, no I never go to bed until about midnight, either, but not all people are the same. *Slight pause.*

Anyway, I thought you'd like to know that I've managed to talk to my landlord, Frank Alexander is his name, and he's going to keep an eye out for any accommodation – any flat that might suit you. *Slight pause.*

He did ask me, though, whether you had any preferences. Not so much Des.Res. as in the town or out of it. You have a car, don't you? I mean, if an otherwise ideal place comes up but it's not near the town centre, would that matter? No, you're right, Longford isn't a large place. Where I am is on the outskirts but I can walk into the main shopping drag in about twenty minutes. Yes, I use the car for work but then the library is on the far side of town. *Pause.*

Anyway, Helen, this is, as they say, a courtesy call. I didn't want you to think I'd forgotten my promise to speak to Frank about you, that's all.

Well, yes, a drink on some future occasion would be nice, would be grand. No, of *course* you don't owe me. But if you're free, I'd love to. *Slight pause.*

Though we shan't be able to use that bar we were in the other night. It's gone. I mean, it's closed down. I passed it last evening and saw the evidence with my own eyes. A vast congregation of disconsolate drinkers howling for admission. No, all right, nobody. It's due to reopen as some sort of furniture store. Yes, I quite agree. Longford needs another of those as much as it needs another Chinese takeaway.

No, I don't know exactly how many there are. Twenty? About the same number as there are Pizza Parlours. Still, all is not lost. There's a bar I sometimes use called the Black Cat. New. Well, newish. After your time. I mean after you left Longford. It opened about five years ago. Before then it was probably a Chinese takeaway or a Pizza Parlour. Or, yes, you could be right, a furniture store. It's bearable, though. A bit more *soigné* than your average vertical drinking experience, but not fatally dependent on upwardly mobile fifteen-year-olds. The drinkers are mostly beyond the acne stage and their deodorants less full-frontal. *Pause.*

Sometime next week, perhaps. *Slight pause.*

No, I suggested that because I guess you're busy at weekends. *Really?* Well, in that case we could try for Saturday evening. But are you sure? Yes, I can quite see why marking essays isn't the ideal way to spend a Saturday evening. *Pause.*

Tell you what, instead of a drink, why don't I make so bold as to invite you round here for a meal? No, honestly, I had no plans. Besides, I like cooking. People have died for my marinara. I said *for* not *of*. And of course it would give me the chance to introduce you to Frank. He lives upstairs so I could ask him to drop down for a drink before we eat. How would that suit? It *would*? Brilliant. You've got my address? 27 Ewing Avenue, that's it. Take the main Nottingham Road heading east and at the first major roundabout go right. The road is second left, can't miss it. No, I don't advise the bus. They disappear from view once the sun goes down. Taxi? Oh, sure. *Pause.*

Dunno. *Slight pause.*

Would 7 p.m. be OK? *Slight pause.*

No, I don't mind what I drink as long as it's Merlot. Only joking. If it's going to be marinara – and it is – we could be awfully proper and drink white. I'll leave the choice to you. *Pause.*

Until Saturday evening, then. *Slight pause.*

Bye."

Yeesss!

6

The tail-lights of the taxi were disappearing as he opened the front door.

"I asked them to come back at 11 p.m.," she said, stepping past him into the hall. "I hope that's all right."

"Perfect," he said. "Carry your bag, miss?"

She handed him the carrier bag she was dangling from her left hand and shrugged herself out of the dark-red coat. Watching him drape the coat over his free arm, she said, "The coat may be hung, the contents of the bottle are to be drunk."

"Thanks," he said. "Should it go into the fridge? Or do we drink it *chambré*?"

"Chilled, definitely."

He tried not to let his glance linger over the green, halter-topped, long-sleeve shirt, thin band of gold round her neck, eyes momentarily meeting hers before he turned to lead the way towards the kitchen, and said, "May I recommend a fortifying drink, and then, if you feel up to it, a tour of the premises?" The deliberately fake bonhomie sounded to his own ears merely awkward. Get a grip, Cousins, stop acting the clumsy schoolboy.

"Whatever you propose." Her smile suggested she felt more at ease than he did.

In the kitchen, she stooped to scratch the cat's head as it purred around her legs then rolled over and lay across the black boots that set off her trim, dark grey jeans.

"This is Baw," Geoff said, "and this," to the cat, "is Ms Helen Birdlip. Teacher and Educationist."

"Why Baw? It's not short for Barbara, is it?"

"Have you ever heard of a cat called Barbara?" And, when she shook her head in mock apology, "No, I thought not."

"Well, it can't be short for Tiddles."

"Very true. Three guesses."

Helen studied the cat, who stared unblinkingly up at her, its pink tongue protruding tinily but startlingly from black lips. Then, having satisfied itself that the guest was an unthreatening presence, it rolled off her boots, adopted an at-ease sitting posture and began to wash a white forepaw.

"Oh, I know," Helen said. "Baw. Black-and-white. Yes?"

"Got it in one. And your reward is a glass of the house's finest." Placing her offering in the fridge, he lifted out an already-opened bottle and poured for them both. When he handed her the filled glass, he was so near that the scent she used came to him, and momentarily he felt himself shake all over, could not speak.

But a few minutes later, filled glasses in hand, they stood in the front room as she gazed around at the old but serviceable three-piece suite – acquired when he had the task of clearing out his parents' house, he explained – his ancient hi-fi, the equally ancient TV.

"Don't you worry about these being nicked?" she asked. "Or do you draw the curtains when you're out?"

"No. For one thing, Frank is around most of the time. For another, drawing curtains probably means you've got something to hide, and that encourages a prospective tea-leaf. For a third, as Simon so astutely observed, no self-respecting villain would be caught dead hoping to flog the kind of rammel I have."

"Simon?"

"Bass player in the group. He's an ex-cop, I trust his advice."

They left the room which he'd spent some time earlier that afternoon dusting and vacuuming, though apart from using it for practice he was in there so infrequently that it bore few signs of wear. The one spilled glass of wine on his sea-green carpet was hidden by the carefully-positioned sofa, and any markings on the pale cream walls were kept from view by large black-and-white photographs of jazz heroes – Pres, the Duke, Getz, Art Kane's wide-angled picture of all those he'd been able to assemble that morning in 1950s Harlem.

By contrast, the back room, study cum-bed-sit, where he spent most of the spare time he wasn't in his kitchen, was, he had to admit, shabby. Standing beside Helen, and seeing the room through her eyes, he winced inwardly. It had been given a hefty going-over with the Hoover and, following his brisk ministrations in the front room, he'd spent a good hour in here hanging shirts and trousers in the wardrobe that occupied one alcove – the other held the head of his single bed which extended along the wall dividing study and front room – stowing underwear and socks into its two drawers. But the wardrobe was old, its inset mirror fly-blown, from the cracked leather arms of the sagging easy chair over which he'd draped Helen's coat, strands of stuffing protruded like wisps of etiolated mould, and the desk, now that he'd cleared away a litter of papers and music manuscript, looked battered, scarred, and, frankly, overdue a journey to the scrap heap.

It was the desk that drew Helen's attention, in particular his open laptop, the small pile of books beside it. She seemed about to speak, but at that moment there was a peremptory rap on the front door.

"That'll be Frank."

The landlord stood in the porch, both buttons of his check sports coat done up, dark tie carefully centred in the collar of his white shirt, caught in the act of raking down the remnants of his thin grey hair with the fingers of one liver-spotted hand. In the other he held the beret he sometimes clamped onto his head as he made his way to town on shopping expeditions. "Cold out," he said, stamping his feet before stepping inside.

"Come far?"

"Now, then, no call to be sarky." But he grinned amiably as he waited for Geoff to close the door. "Where are we?"

"I thought we'd go through to the kitchen," Geoff said

"Helen", he called through the open door of his study-bedroom, "Mr Alexander is here."

But she was already standing in the kitchen, glass in hand, an expectant smile on her face as Geoff ushered his landlord in and made the introductions. "Helen Birdlip, an old – old acquaintance. Frank Alexander, my landlord. Take a seat, Frank. We're drinking wine, would that suit you?"

"A modicum of whisky if you have it."

Frank had put on a posher than usual voice. Given that he'd changed out of his grey flannels, that his feet were encased in polished brown brogues, and that there was a distinct whiff of Old Leather coming from the region of his shining, recently-shaved cheeks, it was clear he was out to make an impression, and it wasn't Geoff on whom the impression was to be made. Fee, Fi, Joy to me. I smell the cash of a new lessee.

Having shaken Helen's hand and watched her sit, Frank dropped into a chair across from her, smoothing his beret as he laid it on the table beside him. Geoff found an appropriate glass and, as the landlord grunted approval, plonked it on the table together with the whisky bottle and a small water jug.

Keeping his eyes on Helen as he worked the cork free from the bottle, Frank said, "Geoffrey gives me to understand that you are looking for accommodation to rent. Is that so?"

"It is."

"And this would be for yourself. Or is anyone else involved?"

"Me, myself and I. Alone."

"I *seeee.*" Frank's way of drawing the word out made it sound as though he'd stumbled on the secret of the universe.

He poured himself a generous amount of whisky before asking, "And are you particular as to location? I am aware of there being property in town, some of which indeed I own, though I appreciate that there are those, like Geoffrey here, who prefer to be less city-centred. I should add, therefore, that I have one house well into the countryside. The land around us is considered very fertile. And good for game."

Fertile. Good for game. What on earth was Frank going on about? Did Helen look like a hunting, fishing and shooting type? Or was his landlord establishing his own credentials? The kind of man who provided for the gentry?

Without shifting his gaze from Helen, Frank said, "I have, I think I can say, a wide portfolio." He took a sizeable glug of whisky and settled back in his chair. "Suppose you tell me what exactly you're looking for … " – the hesitation was caused, Geoff was certain, by his decision not to call her young lady.

While Helen ran through her short list of requirements and preferences, Geoff turned the heat down under the marinara sauce and set to simmer a large pan of boiling water into which he was waiting to plunge spaghetti. Frank, he noticed, was now leaning forward, elbows on the table, tips of fingers to his mouth in what was surely an unintended parody of the concerned physician or, conceivably, deep thinker.

"I shall have to ponder this," he said eventually. Oh, so thinker.

"Geoffrey, might I trouble you for a splash more whisky before I venture out into the night."

"Feel free," Geoff said, as his landlord reached for the bottle.

In total innocence Helen asked, "Are you going anywhere interesting?"

"No," Frank conceded, sipping his whisky. "As a matter of fact, I shall be returning to my own apartment." He paused. "I live directly above Geoffrey, as a result of which I had only the other day to forewarn him of possible disruption while a new shower was being fitted in my bathroom." He looked enquiringly at Geoff.

"Didn't hear a thing," Geoff said. "I assume all was done and dusted while I was about my business."

"As I predicted," Frank said, smiling complacently, "they were remarkably good workers. Poles, you know," he added for Helen's benefit. "Catholics."

It took another ten minutes to prise him from his chair and get him to the front door. Even there, he made something of a production of saying farewell, first putting on, then doffing his beret to Helen who stood in the kitchen doorway as he told her to rest assured that he was mindful of her needs and would do his utmost to provide a commodious place where she might rest her head.

"Blimey," Geoff said, as he rejoined her in the kitchen and refilled their glasses. "He's not usually like that. It must have been the proximity of pulchritudinous femality."

"Stop it."

But the landlord's would-be gallantry had relaxed them.

Though, "Don't let his manner fool you," Geoff said. "He's as sharp as glass."

"And as easy to see through. Still, if he finds me what I want," she said, "I'll forgive him his manner."

"Speaking of which, should you need the facilities, as he would probably call them," Geoff said, who in his afternoon tour of duty had made sure to provide fresh towels, "you will find them by exiting from the room where you are now sitting and locating the second door on your right."

"I think I will avail myself," Helen said.

While she was gone, he lowered the spaghetti into the now boiling water, checked the sauce and added another sprinkling of basil, removed the clingfilm from a bowl of green salad he'd earlier prepared, and by the time she was back had positioned two large candles on either side of the table where they threw a softening light over the by-no-means new tableware.

As they sat across from each other, forking up the spaghetti marinara, he told her about the local greengrocer and fishmonger he relied on for what they were eating – "One lesson my mum taught me, never buy supermarket gunge when you pay only a bit more for food that actually tastes" – and poured the last of what he called the house white before reaching for her bottle. "Ah, Chablis."

"Difficult to avoid Pinot Grigio, but I managed it."

"Odd, isn't it. A few years ago it was all Chardonnay. Now, nobody drinks it. Do you remember those discussions about how heavily a Chardonnay should be oaked? Instant connoisseurship. 'I venture to suggest this could do with a splinter more of holm.'"

She laughed obligingly. "Now here's a puzzle. I seem to remember that at least one girl at school was called Chardonnay. But that was before the wine became Number One, Top of the Pops. Explain that if you can?"

"I can't." With a piece of bread he wiped his plate clean. "Waste not, want not," he said, noting the quizzical smile accompanying her study of his movements.

"Another of your mother's lessons?"

"You said it." Then, reaching for the corkscrew in order to open her bottle, "Well, at least no one will want to name a child of theirs Pinot Grigio."

"Not in England, no." She laughed, openly this time, candle-light reflected in her eyes as she said, "By the way that bottle is a screw top." And, watching him drop the corkscrew as though it had stung him, she added, "Screw tops are no longer *infra dig,* are they? Another thing that's changed. A few years ago nobody who claimed to know their Chablis from their Chambertin would have dared to buy a screw top. Screw tops were for dossers and alkies. But now even the best wine comes without a cork. Well, the best that falls within range of my purse. Which doesn't, as you notice, include Pinot Grigio."

"Why don't you like it?"

"Not sure. I think it's the name. It sounds like a Mexican outlaw. Bring me the head of Pinot Grigio."

"Or a fascist dictator. General Pinot Grigio. Generalissimo Grigio have many gold teeth he flash so as to attract the laydees. And he drink hees wine from hees moustache cup."

"What exactly *is* a moustache cup?"

"Where you keep your moustache overnight. What else? Soused in a preparation of liquid dye and termite repellent." He poured wine for them both. "Bet they don't have moustache cups in Chablis." Then, holding his glass up to the light, he asked, "Have you by chance met the Chardonnays of Chablis?"

"No. Are they related to the Dubonnets of Deauville?"

"A cadet branch. They went their own way centuries ago. Built a chateau on the south-facing slopes under the commodious gaze of a particularly lovely Pyrenee. 'The Chardonnays' Chateau of old Chablis.' Bing Crosby used to sing it. Or was it Dean Martin? Though many preferred the cover version put out by Embassy records. As I recall, it featured Manuel and his Music of the Misty Mountains, or was it the Misty Music of Mountainous Manuel. I can't remember."

"And I'm baling out," Helen said. "Too much laughter makes me hiccup. Especially when I'm drinking wine."

When their eyes met, neither of them, he thought, wanted to look away.

After what seemed a long moment, he said, as though searching for words, perhaps trying to re-establish a certain equilibrium, fearing to push too far, "It's like fours, though, isn't it?"

And in response to her look of enquiry, he added, "Fours. A jazz routine. Each instrument takes four bars in sequence and you try to leave a hook for the one coming after. Perfect for a quartet."

"Why?" The question suggested a genuine interest.

"Because," he said, as he gathered their plates and took them over to the sink, "so many numbers are in thirty-two bars. Two eights, a middle eight, a closing eight. With four of you to play that works out perfectly."

"Isn't it a bit – well, mechanical. Thirty-two bars. Doesn't it get to be a habit? The same old routine. I thought jazz was against such things?"

There was now a faint disapproval in the way she spoke, a tone of voice which left them as far apart as ever.

He brought the cheeseboard across to the table, set beside it a plate of biscuits and a bowl of fruit.

"A sonnet is a routine," he said. "But I'm told on good authority you can still do something with the fourteen lines that hasn't been done before."

"Who was the authority?"

"A poet we had reading at the library not long before Christmas. Someone asked her where she found her inspiration – the kind of question you always get after a reading, which is at least preferable to 'When did you first realise you were going to be a poet?' – and she said that she often stumbled on what she was looking for by playing around with a particular form."

"Oh, tennis with the net," Helen said. Then, helping herself to an apple, she said, frowning slightly as she began to pare it, the peel uncoiling from under her knife, "Tell me about the library meeting that kept you out on Tuesday evening. It must have been unusually interesting to have gone on for that long."

She stopped, blushed faintly, or so the flickering candle-light suggested. "I'm not prying, am I?"

He said, "I wasn't finding an excuse for not phoning you, honest."

"You could have emailed." Was there a faint hint of reproof in her voice?

"I prefer the sound of the human voice," he said.

"Soft," she said, laughing.

"*Soft?* Ought I to be offended?"

"I hope not. S.O. F. T. Sweet Old Fashioned Thing."

"Now I *am* offended." But he wasn't.

She opened her mouth as though to deny that was what she had inadvertently suggested, but he spared her. "Although I admit that when the meeting finished one or two of us transferred from library to pub and carried on the discussion there."

"If only we could do that at college. I dread our after-hours meetings. A chance for every humanly challenged creep to keep the rest of us tied to our chairs while they bang on about 'procedural matters' or 'bending our minds to expedite this issue.' Quote, unquote." And she shuddered extravagantly.

"Our meetings aren't all sweetness and light. Far from it. In fact, I've begun to wish I never set the damned committee up." And, taking in a mouthful of what seemed to be an excellent Chablis, he told her a little about it. "Sorry," he said, as he finished, "I make it sound as though I'm trying to start some sort of uprising. I genuinely thought that bringing together people across the county who cared about their libraries would be a good thing to do. But I was on my own. No other librarian did, or at least nobody else spoke up in favour of my idea. I don't say I blame them, they've got their own lives to lead."

He paused, thinking of all those colleagues who'd warned him that what he was proposing would turn out to be one more example of pissing into the wind, or who, like Colleen, could foresee the difficulties, sensed that however well intentioned, the setting up of the Group would only bring him enemies, earn him a reputation as a trouble-maker. But at least Colleen helped out.

He said, surprising himself at the vehemence that invaded his words, "I guess that there are those who think the idea was a kind of self-promotion. Geoff Cousins, Saviour of the Library Service. Fat chance. But I thought, I *think,* we owe it to libraries to do what we can for them, don't you? What's wrong with drawing attention to why they're needed, what we'll lose by shutting them down or cutting their hours and the services they provide."

He paused, emptied his glass. "I suppose this sounds like a Mission Statement being delivered by the perfect Mission Creep."

But encouraged by the emphatic manner in which she shook her head, he went on, "Not that we have any clout beyond speaking up for libraries as good things. It's all strictly voluntary and more or less without rules, let alone 'procedural matters'. We're a talking shop. Anyway, that's the idea. To give a voice to the punters."

"All I have is a voice," she said, "To undo the folded lie."

"If you say so."

"Not me. Auden. He was talking about the lie of Authority."

"Meaning?"

"Oh, you know, the liars in public places. Government. Men in Suits. Or military regalia. The Pinot Grigios of the world." She raised her eyes, met his. "So that puts you in the other camp. Down among the unwashed. A better class of person than the power-mad." Her smile, when it came, lingered, as, once more, her eyes did on his.

Their conversation, he thought, was like a series of waves, bringing them closer, pushing them apart. How near to each other were they?

Perhaps trying to find an answer his own question, he forced himself to look away, lowered his eyes and found himself staring at the hand with its almond-shaped nails that lay beside her empty plate, a hand he could so easily have reached out to touch.

"Mad enough though."

And although it wasn't what he wanted to talk about, he dragged himself back to safety by explaining about Gleat and others like him, before telling her of Arthur Stanchard, and his recent discovery that the old man numbered among his many interests bird-watching and music, including jazz. "He's a wonder," he said, by way of conclusion.

"Speaking of jazz," Helen said, relieved, for all he knew, to turn the talk in a new direction, "which after all was a subject that cropped up some paragraphs back, tell me about the group you play with. Or rather, about that man who seems to be your leader. The keyboard player."

"Terry Marsden?"

"So *that's* his name. Yes, that sounds right." She nodded as though in confirmation of some idea or other. "I'm sure I met him once," she said.

In the act of raising his glass, Geoff lowered it again without drinking from it. "Really?" he said. "When? Where?"

Helen looked for a moment startled – was it? – by the eagerness of his questions. Toying with a slice of apple, turning it between her supple fingers, she eventually raised it to her lips and bit into the white flesh, chewing slowly as though to gain time, as if she were considering whether to say more or wondering whether she should have chosen some other topic of conversation.

"Well," he said slowly, and after what seemed a silence that threatened to take hold, "it couldn't have been … " How to say it? "It couldn't have been when you and I knew each other all that … all that time ago."

What was that expression in her eyes? Watchful? Foreboding? Knew each other? He shouldn't have said that. He hurried on. "I mean, it couldn't have been me that introduced you. I've only been with Terry's outfit for the past six years. Before then I played with a quite different group."

She said, smiling now, "The Blues Botherers."

Was she grateful for the chance to deflect further questions about Terry Marsden?

"Yes, The Blues Botherers. Sorry about the name, but it wasn't my idea, I promise. Did you ever hear us?"

Taking another slice from her apple, she said, "I came once or twice, with friends from school. Can't remember where it was, though. An upstairs room in one of the town pubs, perhaps?"

"What the management of the Crown called their function room. The drummer reckoned he was due a hernia from having to lug his kit up and down all those stairs. Given the average age of our present audience we'd need a Chair Lift if we played there." A pause. "Shall I make coffee?"

And when she accepted he said, as he stood, "While I'm doing that you can tell me how you met Terry. El Tel, as we call him." Even if she didn't want to tell, he wanted to hear. Besides, it was she who'd started the hare.

"If it *was* him." Then, briskly, as though rebuking her own show of uncertainty. "But no, it was him all right. Of course it was. 'Terry.' That was the name. And he looks more or less as I remember. Dark, short-cut hair, a bit fatter in the face, perhaps, but yes, it was him." She seemed ready now to pursue the topic.

He was intrigued. "And where did you … where did this meeting take place?"

She laid her last slice of apple down, untasted, frowned into her glass, concentrating on the memory. "In a hotel bar in Nottingham. It must have been a Friday or perhaps Saturday. He was playing the piano. Cocktail music, I think it's called. Show tunes with elaborate runs up and down the keyboard. You Must Remember This. And during the interval, or 'tea-break', so he said, he came over to join us. He knew the man I was with."

Back turned to her, he could feel his heart constrict.

Man? What man?

But he knew.

He carried the tray loaded with cafetière, milk and cups over to the table, concentrating on not allowing his hands to tremble as he did so. Carefully, he set the tray down, carefully he sat, carefully he poured for them both, carefully he managed to push a filled cup over to her without liquid slopping over the sides. And only then could he say, "If you don't mind my asking, how did El Tel know the man you were with?"

She hesitated.

He sipped his coffee, not looking at her.

"Peter Cadogan," she finally said, "I was with Peter Cadogan." A pause. "You remember him."

Oh, yes, he remembered. He remembered. But all he said was, "The director? The man who ran the Alleyn Players?" And he nerved himself to lift his eyes to hers.

Did she register the note of false surprise in his voice? Yes. She knew he knew.

But she, too, could play the game. "The one and only," she said. Another pause. Then, "It was the time we were rehearsing for *Much Ado*."

"Ah, yes," he said, putting down his cup. "The last time I bent my knee at the shrine of Thespis." Then, abandoning the camp accent, he said, "And the last play *you* were in. I mean as far as the Alleyn Players were concerned."

"The very last. After that I was off to pastures new. Though any pastures in Wolverhampton were built over long ago."

A smile briefly flickered, and as quickly disappeared. She, too, was fiddling with her cup. "Janey Macpherson told me that you'd hung up your sock or buskins, or whatever they're called."

After a moment or two, she set her cup back in its saucer, looked at him.

He could feel the heat rising to his cheeks. "The Macpherson Journals, eh? An Everyday Story of Am. Dram." Then, before she could reply, he said, trying for a Hollywood voice which even to his own ears sounded ridiculous, "Somehow it didn't seem the same without you."

He saw the guarded look in her eyes, her understanding of what his words implied.

"No," was all she said for some moments, then, "Oh, dear, is this awkward?"

"It was a long time ago."

But Cadogan, he thought. I was right. That bastard.

Pouring the last of the wine for them both, relieved he could do so with a steady hand, he said, risking her gaze, and at the same time wanting to pull back from the brink they seemed to be approaching, "Tell me what you remember about Terry Marsden. I'm interested."

Did her apologetic smile include a grateful acknowledgement of what lay behind his question? "Well," she said, speaking more lightly now, "I don't remember much. As I say, Mr Cadogan and I were having a drink." Pause. Oh, the venom she put into pronouncing that name. And now her voice once more shifted register. "If you want to know why we were there, the answer is that we were 'romantically involved'."

The satiric edge to the cliché only helped the knife to slip further in.

She pushed the remains of her uneaten apple to one side. "Though something tells me that may not be news to you." Without waiting for his reply, she went on, as though now resolved to tell the whole story, and with this new-found determination lifting her eyes briefly to his, "Romance? No, the usual grubby affair. I thought it was serious ... " She paused, studied his expression, then, resolution wavering, ducked her head. "Turned out it wasn't. Not for him, at least." She moved a hand as though brushing away a bothersome fly. "He was careful about where we met, *naturally.*"

Again, the loaded venom. "But as business took him to different cities – or so he could tell his nearest – we seldom used the same place twice." Her attempt at a smile was more of a grimace. "You've no idea how many hotels I visited in the course of a few months. If it's Tuesday it must be Ipswich. Though not of course in term time."

"Which is why you were in Nottingham with Cadogan on a Friday or Saturday. Teaching week over."

"You missed your vocation. Cousins of the Yard." She paused, the laugh thin, mirthless. "But yes, that's it. Sordid confessions of a teacher. This isn't what you want to hear, is it?"

And when he opened his mouth to speak, she said, cutting him off, "No, I don't mean about PC" adding, and this time the laugh was as short as it was sharp, "PC. *Him* PC? He should have been PG. Peter the Great. That's how he liked to think of himself. Great lover, great solicitor."

"Great director?"

She laughed, a short, contemptuous bark. "That, too."

"But about Terry Marsden?" Let her believe that it was El Tel he wanted to hear about, as, in a way, it was.

Sorry, her smile said. "Yes, him. *That's* who I'm supposed to be telling you about. Well, on the occasion I'm trying to remember, PC and I were having an *après* drink, and to be honest I wasn't aware of much that was going on around us, because that was the evening he told me we'd have to see rather less of each other in the future."

She emptied her glass, set it down and then said, "Oh, he was going to leave his wife. *Of course* he was going to leave his wife, but first of all he had to plan for his children's future, and while that was happening he felt that he and I mustn't be selfish."

She stopped, looked directly at her host, soliciting sympathetic agreement. "I love it, don't you, when you're asked by some selfish bastard whose concern is entirely for himself if you wouldn't mind being a bit less selfish." Another pause while she studied the ringless left hand lying upturned on the table, as though trying to scrutinise its fortune lines.

"SB," Geoff said.

He was still trying to absorb what she'd told him, that she and Cadogan had once been lovers. So that was it. His suspicions finally confirmed. Until this moment he'd been able to suppress them, or, no, since he couldn't suppress them, not entirely, since they'd been there, like a constant, dull ache, he'd nevertheless been able to tamp them down. Pain management. Ha. But the pain had flared up again when, after ten years, he'd seen her in the back room of the Three Tuns; and now, with each word she spoke as she sat facing him in the flickering candle-light that made her face, in the shadows playing over it, look so vulnerable, her hand so close to his that without effort he could reach out to cover it, he wanted to tell her all that he had never before been able to say.

Without effort? No, even with the wine they had drunk caution held him back.

She was watching him. She was, he thought, on the verge of asking him some important question.

"SB," he said, trying to smile, "Selfish bastard. Son of a bitch. Sugar baddy."

"Call him what you like," she said, studying his face. You have the right to do so. The words, unspoken, hovered he thought between them.

For some moments there was silence. She seemed to withdraw her gaze, and her voice, when she next spoke, was conversational, even brisk. "At that Nottingham meeting Terry called him Mr C. As in 'fancy seeing you here, Mr C.' After which he looked at me and said something like 'Here for the music?' And so I had to be introduced. Naturally I was a friend, a member of the Players, someone Peter had met quite by chance in the bar and so had invited me to join him for a drink. As for me, I was on a shopping spree. It was the agreed excuse we'd worked out in case anyone we knew spotted us together. How plausible can you get? 'Yes, Mr Cadogan is directing me in our latest venture into Bardom, so when I saw him in the hotel lounge into which I'd dropped for a pick-me-up after a day's window-shopping, what could be more natural than that I join him for a cocktail or several?'"

She stopped suddenly, as though she had forgotten what came next.

"What indeed?" Geoff said, trying to help her, or was it simply to bridge an awkward pause. Then, feeling the need to add to his bare prompt. "I can just see Terry swallowing *that*. He's got form himself, you know." And when she looked enquiringly at him, he added, "He's into his third marriage and Simon knows of one or two affairs on the side." Should he tell her of the evening when Simon, according to his own account, had been called out to investigate a 'domestic' and found himself confronted by an irate husband who ... Well, no, that could wait, perhaps, for some future occasion.

Helen said, "That's as may be, but it didn't stop him having a dig at PC. Asking after the wife. 'Mrs C. well, is she? And the kids?' A bit pointed, that. I was on the verge of telling him he shouldn't worry about *them*. *They'd* be looked after. It was me who needed some TLC. But next second, he was gone. 'Duty calls,' he said; something like that. 'I'll give you a bell tomorrow, Mr C. Got a little problem,' And off he went. End of meeting." A pause. "I remember, though, what Cadogan told me about him."

"Which was?"

"Oh, that he was one of those who sailed close to the edge but never went over. His 'little problems' usually needed the professional advice of a solicitor. A rough diamond. But that we needed people like him. *He* needed the man you call El Tel, was what he meant. Peter the Solicitor kept the Boys in Blue at bay and Mr Piano Man helped to keep PC in fees. Payment by results. And, so he said, the money helped to keep the Players afloat. 'The ladder to art is propped on a dung-hill.' You wouldn't forget a remark like that, would you? Especially when the man who made it was at the same time telling you that he didn't, after all, love you. That he was going to cut and run."

This time she paused to looked away, said, "I'm not sure why I'm telling you all this."

Was that true, or was she trying to find a way of clearing troubled territory between them? Or could she have been unaware of his own feelings? No, he didn't think so. She knew, she must have known, how he felt about her. This evening's talk, its evasions, its silent communications, proved that much.

He said, "Marinara clears the way for candid confessions. It's a well-known fact. I've told you about the LUCG and now you tell me about El Tel and PC. The Italians could make an opera out of all this."

She stared unsmilingly at him, ignoring his clumsy attempt at humour.

He said, "I don't mind, I really don't." And, when she still said nothing, he asked, desperate now for some response, "Did you ever meet Cadogan's wife?"

The look on her face was rueful now, abashed even. "At a few of the parties he threw at their house," she said. "I didn't want to go, not after we'd begun our … " She paused, abandoned her search for the word she wanted. "But he insisted. It would have looked 'odd' apparently if I'd not shown up. And she was always in the audience for production night. But I don't think we ever exchanged more than a few polite words. Why? I mean, why do you ask?"

"I always thought she seemed a poor, timid creature. But I heard that not long after that production of *Much Ado* she threw him out."

"Who told you that?"

Startled by the sharpness in her voice, he said, "Can't remember."

He pretended to search for a name, then shook his head. "Longford's a small place. I'd quit the Players but I still bumped into quite a few of them about town. It may have been one of them, perhaps one of several who used the library. Does it matter?"

Lifting her glass and studying the inch of wine that glowed saffron in the candle flame, she said, her voice now back under control, "No, I suppose not. Sorry. Anyway, it's true. His wife put an end to their marriage."

He risked it. "But you didn't want to be thought of as the scarlet woman who was responsible for that?"

"No," she said, with renewed vehemence. "I didn't. Because it wasn't true." Pause. "But I *did* want to get away from Longford."

"Well, you don't need to worry, your name wasn't part of the story."

"Which was?"

"Which was pretty vague, as I recall. Wife discovers husband has been cheating on her for years so tells him to clear off. That's about it. If your name had come into what I was told, I'd have remembered. Anyway, it was only a rumour."

"Oh, she threw him out all right. And guess who told me?"

"Janey Macpherson?"

"Wrong. I was the recipient of a letter sent to the school where I taught. From a Mr Peter Cadogan." She wrinkled her nose as at a bad smell. "His version of events was that he'd finally had the courage to tell his wife he was leaving home and that he was now free to love me as I deserved. Words to that effect."

"What a shit."

A wry smile. "As you so rightly say. Naturally, I asked Janey what she could tell me about PC's domestic arrangements – she knew of our affair – and in exchange I got several chapters and many verses on his dealings with women, ending with the tale of how his wife, long-suffering though she might be, was finally moved to action when she came home one afternoon and found hubby shagging an unknown bimbo in the parlour. Anyway, that was the gist of it. Divorce was quick to follow. Janey hadn't wanted to tell me about any of Cadogan's extra-marital activities while my own affair was in progress, hoping, she said, that this time he might perhaps mean it. I wish she had let me in on the truth. I was the simpleton."

"I'd no idea he was so ... well, so keen to play the field."

"He was clever, I'll say that for him. A smiling, damned villain. A model solicitor, perhaps. He let me believe I was number one. But from what Janey finally told me, I was some way down the line."

He thought about that. "If he fooled some of the people all of the time and all of the people … etc., then how come Janey knew what was going on."

"Oh, he'd tried it on with her," Helen said, eyeing her empty glass, "but she didn't fancy him. After that, though, she noticed the tell-tale signs. Apparently to the trained eye there are *always* give-away signals. In my case, the fact that I began *not* to look at him at rehearsals whenever he gave me directions. Not wanting to meet his eye was clear evidence of a guilty secret. Ditto, the fact that he came all over formal whenever he gave me directions. You know, 'Miss Birdlip, could I suggest you take that line more slowly?' So when I finally told her – I felt I had to confide in someone – she told *me* that she already knew what must be going on between Cadogan and me. I yelled at her, I'm afraid, made a fool of myself and wound up by accusing her of not being a friend. A friend would have warned me. Though" – she shrugged, sighed, shrugged again – "I don't suppose it would have done any good. She *has* been a good friend, you know. Still is."

As though to break the mood, at all events wanting to put an end to this, she looked abruptly at her watch, as she did so placing her two hands on the table and pushing herself up. "The witching hour of eleven approaches."

Geoff too stood, facing her across the table.

"Sorry to take so much of the evening up in talk about a man I never want to see again."

She looked at him enquiringly and when he said nothing, added, "But don't think it's taken away the taste of a lovely meal. It hasn't." She opened her mouth as though about to say something else, or so it seemed. Then, with a smile that could have been one of the purest relief, "Was that a taxi horn?"

It was.

At the door, as he helped her into her coat, he said, "Perhaps I'll see you again at one of our gigs," to which she replied, "Perhaps, although I'm no great jazz fan," following which remark, and as though to suggest he shouldn't take it personally, she pecked him lightly on his cheek, repeated her thanks and, without a backward glance, crunched her way over the forecourt and out to the waiting cab.

* * *

To help him in his chores of clearing up, he went into the front room and selected a favourite CD. He had a speaker fixed on a shelf in the kitchen and before Helen's arrival briefly wondered whether he ought to offer her the chance of listening to something while they ate. So many of his friends took for granted that this was civilised behaviour, though not him. If the music was good you ought to listen, which meant you couldn't talk. If the music wasn't good, why bother. But Pres and Teddy. Who'd want to talk while they played.

Having watched Baw chew daintily at the saucer of food he put down for her, he set about washing the dishes, trying as he did so to listen out for the discreet subtleties by which the great tenor man and pianist matched each other on the up-tempo opener, 'All of Me'. But he found that, despite his best intentions, he was playing back the evening's talk. Why? What was it that nagged at his mind? Leave aside her looks, which, like the scent she used, her voice, its slight huskiness, the breathy intonations, the low, soft laugh, all of her … There was something else …

Pres and Teddy were now into 'Prisoner of Love'. He listened as they moved to the middle eight. Ah, now. The first note of the second bar *was* flatted. They'd argued about it over practice at Terry's, Al claiming that his transcription of Colombo and Robin's number was spot on and there was no such note. Maybe not. But that's what Pres played, and as it came round again and Pres played it again, with the piano in accord, it came to him that so apparently slight an inflection was proof, if proof were needed, of their genius. At that point a blue note turned a sweet tune into one of the tenderest melancholy, gave it a depth its composers couldn't have glimpsed.

And as he listened so he realised what had been nagging at him. Not the revelation that Helen and Cadogan had been lovers, even though he'd hoped against hope that it wasn't so; no, it was that she'd chosen to tell him, had almost gone out of her way to do so. Yes, that was it. She'd manoeuvred the telling, hadn't she, deliberately dragged the conversation to a point from which True Confessions could begin. "Speaking of jazz … " For sure his mention of fours had unwittingly given her the opening, but it was one she'd realised could lead her to where she wanted them to go.

'Love Me or Leave Me' came swinging its way into the kitchen. Some weeks earlier, he'd borrowed Simon's DVD of the 1950s film, enjoyed Cagney's reprise of his customary gangster role, the ritual smashing of glasses so appropriately to hand for the big scene when he discovers Doris Day is about to leave him, had winced at her inability to get anywhere near the dark energies of Ruth Etting, the night club singer she was meant to be playing, but loved the Donaldson–Kahn title number, its minor-key, klezmer-ish edge. He had most of the lyrics by heart. "Love me or leave me, and let me be lonely … I'd rather be lonely than happy with somebody new." Ah, they don't write them like that any more. "Night time's the right time for just reminiscin'."

"How very true," he said to Baw who was studying him as he paused from putting away the newly washed plates and concentrated on the diminuendo with which the two great musicians brought the number to its close. And then he thought, but why choose this night for such reminiscence? What had she said? "Oh, dear, is this awkward?" Well, yes, it is awkward, having to face the truth that while I was longing for you, you were in love with the great PC, were his paramour, had no time for me. Yes, I'd say that having to acknowledge this is quite awkward. And I might add it has been awkward for the past ten years although until I saw you again the other week I thought I'd learnt to cope with it.

Wilson was now leading the group on 'Taking a Chance on Love'. God, what a pianist. The sheen of his playing, its *clarity*, its ability to honour the bar lines while, just occasionally, venturing across them as though to say, I can go anywhere I want but I'll never get lost, listen and you'll find me.

And yet, he thought, Helen couldn't, surely, have planned to use the evening in order to spring her surprise that was no surprise. Or could she? And if so, why? To set the record straight?

'Our Love is here to Stay', Lester now taking control. He began to wish he'd chosen some other CD. One thing was for sure. Assuming she hadn't told him about Cadogan in order to twist the knife in his reopened wound, neither could she have intended to make amends. Amends? What amends? Amends for what? Even if she'd known of or suspected his hapless love for her, it wasn't after all *her* fault. She'd given him no encouragement. Nor was she offering it now. The kiss she'd planted on his cheek as she left was friendly, sisterly even, but that was as far as it went.

* * *

When the music finished, he said goodnight to Baw, already curled up in her basket, snapped off the kitchen light and went through to his study, where he lay, fully clothed on his bed, thinking his way back, as so often he'd done in the past years, to all he could remember of that production night of *Much Ado*. The Alleyn Players deliberately didn't run to full performances, they went in for rehearsed readings, in which dressing up was kept to a minimum, as were props, including sound effects. This left them free to concentrate on the text, so Cadogan, who'd set the company up, insisted. No distractions, What we attempt is for the ear far more than the eye. The eye, according to Cadogan's Law, being a fatal distraction. Still, a few movements were permitted, the occasional handshake, an arm round a shoulder, people moving together or apart. But the spoken word was to predominate. A row of chairs was supplied for the cast who filed on at the beginning of the performance, actors rose to speak their lines as and when required and returned to their chairs once the scene in which they were involved was completed. The invited audience were attuned to the need to listen for two-hour stretches – there were no intervals – and, if they wanted, to follow the performance with open texts, much as some concert-goers have open scores on their knees.

Propping himself on one elbow as he gazed into the dark, he thought of how Cadogan liked to interpret and explain to his cast the play's 'inner meaning,' as he called it. The war of wits between Benedick and Beatrice was a way of attaining to 'reasonable love.' No starry-eyed romantics, these two. Instead, disenchanted, reluctant but, in the end, committed lovers. And what was the final proof of commitment? "Kill Claudio." Beatrice's demand of Benedick after her friend Hero has been left at the altar by the callow youth, Claudio, Benedick's comrade-in-arms.

Getting to his feet, he undressed and, standing barefoot in the dark, recalled how in the weeks of rehearsal, they'd discussed Beatrice's command "Kill Claudio." Amateur luvvies at their task. How serious *was* Beatrice? Was it spur-of-the moment anger? Possibly. A joke? No, that could be ruled out. A test of Benedick's readiness to forswear raffish masculinity? Perhaps. Though Helen, playing Beatrice, argued that the line shouldn't be pressed too hard. She wanted Beatrice to retain an element of collusion with Benedick. And as evidence of this, in the lead-up to the public reading, having given her order, she'd always turned away, a smile on her lips, no sooner come than gone.

Which was what made her utterance on the night of the actual play-reading carry such an impact, at least to him, Geoff. "Kill Claudio." She'd not turned away, had instead locked eyes with him, Geoff, a mere attendant lord, and one who wasn't even involved in the scene, had been an onlooker sitting with the rest of the cast. But she'd spoken the words with such intensity he felt they had a meaning for him alone. Might it even be that she understood his feeling for her, was signalling that she returned it? The words bore a message, one that left him almost dizzy with hope.

But an hour later, his hope had washed away. Helen didn't appear at the post-production party. Someone – Janey no doubt – let it be known that she had sent her excuses, was nursing a headache and had gone home. And a little later he heard she'd left Longford, news which, together with the information that Cadogan and his wife had gone their separate ways, had been enough to end his relationship with the Alleyn Players, especially as his informant implied that she herself, outraged at the way Cadogan had treated her friend, had slipped the wife some news about Cadogan, anonymously, of course.

Better that Helen didn't know that. He got into bed, pulled the duvet up, closed his eyes.

* * *

He must have dozed off, because he came to with a jerk, alerted by wind buffeting his window. *Kill Claudio.* Who had read that part? He couldn't recall. Oh, but he could. Some mooncalf of a teacher, but not one at Helen's school, a rather shadowy figure whose name wouldn't come although he thought it started with a P. Paul? Peter? Patrick? Yes, that seemed right. Patrick. But surely there'd been nothing between Patrick and Helen, nothing to justify the intensity of the words she'd directed at Geoff. *Kill Claudio.* And then, *then*, he remembered. Of course he did.

7

He woke late the next morning, walked in a chill wind to the local shop for his newspaper and a carton of milk, and on his way back met his landlord, who in full Sunday regalia was on his way to church.

"Morning Geoffrey." The words, uttered with brisk affability, were accompanied by a grin and mock salute as Frank touched the peak of his cap with the fingertips of his right hand.

Geoff smiled a greeting and was about to go on his way when Frank, holding up his hand like a traffic policeman, stopped in front of his tenant, working his shoulders as though in some callisthenic exercise of his own devising. "I enjoyed meeting that young lady of yours. I thought she seemed very – civilised."

"I'll tell her. But she's not 'my' young lady. A friend, merely a friend."

Frank took this information in, said enigmatically, "Well, you could do worse," and proceeded on his way.

Thinking Frank's remark over as he chewed breakfast toast, Geoff mouthed an imitation of Frank's words. "I thought she seemed very – civilised." In contrast to your last, he meant. And certainly, on the few occasions Frank and Jade had happened to meet, friction was in the air. Jade, with her art school looks, her green-lacquered nails, gel-spiked, flame-red hair, nose ring, and invariable uniform of black jeans, black sweatshirt, black bomber jacket, hadn't been, as Geoff guessed Frank would have phrased it, at all his cup of tea. Any more than he was Jade's.

"Who's that old bloke?" she'd asked Geoff after her first encounter with Frank, a Sunday morning when, as on this occasion, Frank had been on his way to church, while Geoff, with Jade beside him, was bringing home a bagful of shopping for their breakfast. "Looks like he's got a poker up his arse. He's not your sort, is he?"

"He's my landlord," Geoff told her, looking over his shoulder as Frank, after a momentary pause to exchange formalities, continued his stiff-backed march along the avenue. Then, feeling the need to defend himself from what sounded like an accusation, added, "There's no harm in him."

"What's he dressed up like that for?"

"He's on his way to church."

"*Church?*" It was a squawk. "Bloody hell, you know some weirdos."

The affair hadn't lasted. Geoff wasn't Jade's sort, either. Their meeting and then coming together was pure chance. She'd been at a gig the group played for an office party and during a band break they fell into talk at the bar. "I sort of like jazz," she said, "it's sort of not comin' at you. Lets you find your own way." He'd nodded, pretending to understand what she meant, and many hours later, after far too many drinks, they'd taken a taxi back to his place. It was that simple.

And it was equally simple for her to tell him some weeks after she'd begun sharing his bed, mostly at weekends, that she was moving on. No hard feelings OK? OK. The woman about whom he knew hardly anything apart from her name, her age – she was at least a dozen years his junior – and her occupation – assistant salesperson at a stationer's in town – left him as abruptly and as painlessly as she'd arrived. On the whole, and all things considered, he was glad to have Sunday mornings to himself once more. No Empty Bed Blues.

* * *

Thanks 4 meal. Hope U OK. See U soon. H X. The text message he read as he dressed for work had been sent the previous day. Brief and to the point. He wondered whether to text back, decided he'd do so later, from work, then, having fed Baw, picked up his old leather briefcase, tucked the cat under his other arm and deposited her on the porch mat, locked up and, heater going full blast and wipers working to dispel the overnight frost that crusted his windscreen, was soon on his way across town.

Monday morning traffic was never as heavy as the rest of the working week. St Monday still had His – or should that be Her – worshippers. At this hour only a few shops were open for business, steel shutters up, although the two Indians who owned the town's ironmongers were already arranging a pavement display of galvanised buckets palisaded by racks of stiff-bristled brooms and garden implements, forks, spades, hoes, and next to them Gerald Harbin, greengrocer, stood outside his shop, smoking as he lifted an arm in response to Geoff's wave.

At the end of the High Street, and with time to spare, he took a right turn before pulling into the small car park behind the library, where he brought his Fiat to rest beside the only other car, even older than his but in a far better state of repair, no scrape marks visible, no dented fender, no scatter of papers on the back seat.

Josie was already in the staff room when he pushed through the door.

"Feeling better?" he asked her.

"Yes thanks." Then, as though she owed him an explanation, she added, "It wasn't anything serious. More of a stomach upset. That time of the month. But two days in bed set me to rights."

"Not SAD, then."

"I'm never sad," she said. And looking at her face as it broke into a candid smile, he could believe it. Josie, with her no-nonsense air, her trim figure set off by the dark green calf-length skirt she wore with a succession of what looked to be hand-knitted sweaters, red, green, blue, straight black hair cut to frame her round cheeks, had the conventional prettiness that went with the conventional partner to whom she'd introduced her 'boss,' as she called Geoff, on a social occasion some months back.

"SAD," he said to her, as he busied himself with the coffee machine, "the illness that afflicts many of us post-Christmas. An acronym for Seasonal Affective Disorder, or something like that. Anyway, Josie, good to hear that you don't suffer from it."

"Don't suffer from what?" Colleen, entering in time to hear the last words, was muffled in heavy scarf, her coat collar pulled up round her ears.

Geoff explained.

"I should hope not," Colleen said. "Can't afford to be down in the dumps with your wedding coming closer every day. But by heck, as they say oop North, this morning's a cowd 'un. I'm in need of a warm-up. Is the coffee on?"

"It is. And this time," he said, "it should be good and strong."

"So you remembered to buy."

"I'll have my usual tea," Josie said. "Coffee upsets my stomach." Then, seeing Colleen's sudden, enquiring look, she laughed with the pleasure of guileless daring. "No, it's not *that*. We're not planning for children yet. We'll know when we're ready."

No unforeseen circumstances were to cloud Josie's clear view of life.

* * *

By the time he left the security guard to shut up early that evening, Geoff and the other two had, with the assistance of one of the part-timers, filled the working day with undemanding routine work, the small change of daily life, issuing and checking in books and, rather more often, solving computer problems for those who sidled in and hunched over the machines from the moment the library opened its doors, and who, some of them at least, showed no signs of leaving until they were reminded that closing time was fast approaching.

What kept them there, he wondered? The cold outside? The illusion of company, of being with others in a warm, well-lighted place.

"As if," Colleen said when, *sotto voce*, he suggested that one old man, a regular who as always was assiduously staring at the screen in front of him, might be tracking his stocks and shares. "He's reading world news," she whispered back. And later, in the privacy of the staff room, she added that once, when she helped the man, a long-time widower, to log on, he'd confided in her that keeping up with the events on the other side of the word made him feel he was somehow in touch with a daughter, his only child, last known address Melbourne, Australia, from whom he'd heard nothing in years.

The sadness of that added to the depression that gripped him as, with the doors finally shut on the last of the day's users, the three of them looked over the library's programme of forthcoming talks. Of the SPRING SEASON OF CULTURAL EVENTS grandly and misleadingly promised on the A 4 posters Josie had run off, only two of the six interested Geoff. He volunteered to chair both meetings. One was by a university historian, whose chosen subject was 'Radicals at War'. Arthur Stanchard would certainly want to know about that. The other, due in three weeks' time, was to be given by a moderately successful novelist, James Padgett. The event was billed as a chance to share with 'A Leading Writer' his thoughts on Contemporary Fiction.

Geoff could hardly say no to that one. It was after all his suggestion. As he and Padgett were old university acquaintances, he'd said, Padgett might be persuaded to come for the modest fee which was all they could afford. Acquaintances? Stretching it, rather. He didn't know Padgett at all well, wasn't even sure he'd any longer recognise him. They'd not crossed paths since student days, and even then they'd met half a dozen times at most. Having submitted work

61

to the university literary magazine, the two came together over drinks while their contributions were subjected to so-called critical scrutiny by the editorial team and an invited audience of friends and scroungers, a confrontation which required them to respond thoughtfully to such remarks such as "Yeh, I sort of empathise with that" or "I didn't feel it had anything to say to me personally, not as a person."

Over the years, Geoff had become aware that Padgett was James Padgett, the novelist. He had listened to the truncated version of the man's second novel when it was made a Book at Bedtime. *Masked Owl* was about a woman who escaped from a conventional marriage into a feral, hand-to-mouth existence. One reviewer called the novel "fiercely poetic", another found it "hauntingly evocative," although in a radio discussion which coincided with the book's paperback publication, Padgett, while complimented for his "powers of imagination", had nevertheless been disbelieved when he told his interlocutor that the story owed nothing to his own experiences, that he'd invented it.

Now, Geoff's offer to take the chair for the forthcoming meeting having been accepted by the other two – *nem. con.* as Colleen said with a wicked grin – he realised he'd have to read more of Padgett's novels before the writer made his appearance. His compensation for this was that the budgeting arrangements, as agreed with County Hall, included a post-event meal for the Chair of each Event and the guest speaker. Permission was also granted for the purchase of a bottle of modestly priced table wine. A full receipt, countersigned, was required before expenses could be refunded. Such largesse.

Thinking about this as he drove home in the wintry dark, rain smearing his windscreen, he found he could remember very little about Padgett apart from a lingering impression that as an undergraduate the man was an awkward, even reluctant conversationalist, an impression the radio discussion had done little to dispel, marked as it was by pauses, abrupt starts, lapses into half-finished sentences. What had he let himself in for? Two hours of lockjawed boredom?

But as he steered the car onto the forecourt of no. 27 and brought it to a halt, an idea came to him. He grinned at his reflected self in the rear-view mirror. "Now that," he said aloud, "is not half bad. If I were you, Cousins, I'd go for it."

8

Helen's reply to his text message was brief and not especially encouraging. **Padgett Who. May be busy. Will let you know asap Hx.**

A week later, he'd heard nothing more. Nor did she show for the group's next gig at the Three Tuns, the date of which he'd decided not to mention. Enough is enough. Enough is too much. Besides, she was probably busy in her new post and, again besides, where's the fun in sitting in the back bar of a run-of-the-mill pub nursing a lonely drink and listening to less than wonderful jazz, even supposing you like the music, which he rather suspected Helen didn't. Put that way, Cousins, the reasons for non-attendance are unanswerable.

But still. In the days that followed, his mood varied between a kind of dank despair and one of mild disappointment. Sometimes it was a winter of icy discontent, at other times misty melancholy. He'd emailed her the programme of the library's SPRING SEASON OF CULTURAL EVENTS – how overblown that title now seemed – but along the electric wire no answering message came. Which, however you turned it to the sun, clearly meant No. *No.* Or, to spell the matter out, I find the invitation to sit in a draughty room on a hard chair while listening to a novelist about whom I know nothing explain the travails of authorship is, how shall I put this, somewhat lacking in appeal, even though, as bonus, it would offer me the chance to admire your suave skills as chairman. So no. No! Got it? **NO.**

During several fretful evenings he read Padgett's latest novel, *Away*, which according to a prefatory note was intended as a follow-up to *Masked Owl*, although this time it was the man who chose to walk out of a life of respectable duties, preferring what the blurb writer identified as "day-to-day existence spiced by hilarious misadventures," before he eventually discovers love and redemption with a younger woman, a free spirit who shows him paradise in a grain of sand. Every middle-aged man's dream, in short.

On the last of these evenings, apologising to Baw who, curled on his lap, woke to shake her head irritably each time he turned the page, he closed the book and as he did so allowed himself to wonder whether he could seriously imagine a life spent foraging for out-of-date food in supermarket skips, of humping a damp, malodorous sleeping-bag from bus-shelter to railway vaults, of learning to avoid the attentions of what Padgett's hero called "the underground army of winos, druggies and derelicts," let alone of enjoying an hour in some church hall where "women in pinnies and pearl necklaces offered all who entered a sandwich and cup of tea and hoped you would be led by their ministrations toward the Kindly Light." Hilarious or what?

No, he thought, not hilarious at all, tipping Baw onto the carpet and, having lobbed the novel onto his cluttered desk, knelt to riffle through a pile of CDs until he came on Ben Webster with Oscar Peterson. 'The Touch of Your Lips'. This is where redemption lies. Not some clichéd dream of recovered youth but a yearning for fulfilment in the present or the future. Nostalgia is a disease that kills.

* * *

The Golf Club bar was packed, hot, noisy with braying laughter and the honking voices of men and women, sounds which, as a writer he admired and had once tried to emulate said, combined a sort of heaviness and richness with a fundamental ill will – people who, one instinctively feels are the enemies of anything intelligent or sensitive or beautiful. Some words, like some faces, like some songs, you never forget.

"Doesn't matter what we play," Al said, as though wired to Geoff's mood, "these berks aren't here for us."

They had closed the first set on an upbeat 'Avalon' and been rewarded by an indifference deeper than contempt. At least contempt would have been *some* sort of response.

"Thank you, ladies and gentlemen, and now the orchestra will take a well-earned rest."

No response. No one clapped, no one so much as looked in their direction. Even Terry's heart, usually pinned to the shiny lapels he sported for what he called Top Jobs, wasn't in evidence. Though "Look at it this way, lads," he said; "if they're not complaining then we're not doing anything wrong."

"We should put that on our band cards," Simon said. "The Terry Marsden Quartet. *The Punters Did Not Complain*. Bound to go places with that."

"Don't forget the money," Terry said, raising his glass of gin and tonic. "Top whack, this is. And don't forget who got us the job. Do the business, tonight, lads, there could be more in the offing."

"I'm not sure I can stand the excitement." Al was studying the crowd that spread across the wide room, curtained windows to one side, to the other a well-stocked bar behind which the three women bar staff, in uniform frilly-blouses with black bow ties, supplied drinks to men who were, as he observed to the others, dead ringers for Edmund Heep or, at the younger end, seedier versions of Jeremy Clarkson – if that's possible, Simon said – most of them clutching beer mugs to their chests while they took possession of smaller glasses no doubt intended for partners whom they could be trusted to refer to as "the fairer sex," or "my good lady," or "my better half."

"How's this for a trip down memory lane," Simon said. "Bet you haven't seen anything like it for a long time. England as she used to be. When we were a force to be reckoned with and everyone knew their place."

"And my parents couldn't find one."

"One what?"

"Place. Digs. No Irish. No Blacks."

"Well, you've done all right," Simon said.

"Yeh, and I don't even have to dress up to be in black. Perfect for an undertaker."

Simon laughed obligingly.

Leaving them at it, Geoff wandered over to the bar to relinquish his empty half-pint glass.

He was about to return to the others when a voice behind him said, "Well, well. I do believe it's Mr Cousins."

That voice. Even before he turned, he knew who had spoken.

"Not the sort of occasion at which I'd expect to see you," he said unsmilingly to Peter Cadogan's smiling face.

"I was about to say the same to you."

Oh, me. I'm with the band. On business, you could say."

"And so, I fear, am I. Business far more than pleasure." He paused to let the implied insult sink in. "But," and he sighed, "when a client extends a pressing invitation it is, as I'm sure you can understand, unwise to say no."

By no more than a lift of chin and half-turn of his head he indicated a couple standing on their own some way behind him. The man was tall, at the far end of middle-age, grey-haired, his rumpled suit suggesting a relaxed at-easiness. In contrast, the woman, while younger than her husband – their loosely linked hands suggested that they were a married couple – looked as though she was somehow on guard, the severe lines of her well-cut linen dress at one with the steady, unyielding gaze with which, he saw, she was looking across at him and Cadogan.

The gaze made him uneasy and he shifted his attention back to Cadogan in time to hear him say, "Though it's a pleasure to see you again, Geoff, after all this time. You're looking well. How's tricks?"

Trying not to meet Cadogan's eyes, to acknowledge his look of pretended concern, Geoff said, "Much as usual. Life in the fast lane, otherwise known as Longford Library."

"And this?" Cadogan gestured in the direction of the quartet. "Music keeps you busy, I imagine."

The smile, instant and meaningless, was as he remembered, the handsome face a shade fuller than it had been, but the blue eyes still managed their unshadowy innocence , the skin smooth, tanned, and the shoulders, encased in a smart tweed jacket, held high. Had the hair line receded at all? No, Geoff reluctantly accepted, the blond, wavy, well-barbered head was as it had been. The very model of a model solicitor.

"Busy enough."

"You've never thought of rejoining the Players?"

Geoff shook his head.

"Pity. We could do with you."

"I had heard you were still in existence."

"There have been fallow periods," Cadogan said, "but I'm calling for auditions anent *As You Like It.* An especial favourite of mine, and now that I can cast an ideal Rosalind it seems too good an opportunity to miss."

"Oh?" Something about the way Cadogan was smiling at him made Geoff's skin begin to prickle. "I'd heard you were thinking of *Measure for Measure.*"

The smile broadened, the eyes met his in innocent, bland enquiry. "I was. But it's all change. Perhaps you hadn't heard? Miss Birdlip is back in town."

"Yes, I know," Geoff said, too quickly, before turning half-sideways and pretending to stare round the crowded room at people, the majority of whom he didn't recognise. Anything to avoid Cadogan's face, his smile.

But he wasn't about to escape the voice.

"I wouldn't want to cast her as Isabella, you see," it said. "Hysterical virginity? Not Helen. Not our Miss Birdlip."

Furious, Geoff forced himself to face his tormentor, found himself fixed by the enamelled glitter of Cadogan's eyes.

"I thought good acting meant taking on any roles … "

But he stopped, not knowing what to say next.

Cadogan said smoothly. "Oh, I've no doubt Helen could manage, but Rosalind is an altogether more sympathetic part. A wiser woman, more aware, is how I'd put it … " He paused, as though searching for the word he needed. "More *magnanimous*," he finally said. Another pause. "Wouldn't you agree?"

Before Geoff could think of a reply, he felt his elbow gripped and Terry said in his ear, "Time for the next set, tenor man." Then, to Cadogan, "Good to see you, Mr C. I'd value the chance to talk over a few matters when you've got the time."

"At your service as ever," Cadogan said, making an elaborately theatrical gesture of acceptance. "Phone my secretary and book a visit." He looked once more at Geoff. "So *As You Like It* it's to be. Everything comes to him who waits," he said, the smile at once a challenge and smugly triumphant. "Well, good to see you, and to exchange a few words about the Bard. Not often *that* happens in a golf club, I imagine." The smile, inviting complicity, broadened. "*Do* think over my offer," he said. "Even if you could only find time for one of the smaller parts. Corin, perhaps."

And then he was gone, balancing several glasses on a tray as he shouldered his adroit, unhurried way through the crowd.

* * *

As they packed up at the end of the evening, Al said, "You seemed a bit out of sorts, Geoff."

"Meaning?"

Perhaps disconcerted by the terse challenge, Al's smile was intendedly reassuring. "Nothing the punters would notice, but you were a bit late in on a couple of entries, plus the wrong key for 'Indiana', though you got it sorted out pretty damned fast."

It was true. He *had* fluffed at least two entries and he *did* come in on E Flat for a number they always played in F. "Just making sure you lot were on your toes," he said, as lightly as he could. "E Flat for F, it happens. Even Lester did that once."

But you aren't Lester, Al didn't say, though his quizzical smile spoke the words for him.

* * *

But driving home, it was Cadogan's smiling face he saw, Cadogan's words that whispered in his ear, "Perhaps you hadn't heard. Miss Birdlip is back in town." And, more disturbingly, "Everything comes to him who waits." The bastard. What was he up to? Oh, of course. Helen as Rosalind, the magnanimous heroine. Easy to know what *that* meant. Forgive and forget.

But in that case, he thought as he turned into Ewing Avenue, what exactly was *she* up to?

9

"Hi, Helen? Yes, it's me. Geoff. *Pause.*

I haven't called at a bad moment, have I? Why do I ask? Well, you sound ... a bit brisk, shall we say. Oh, sorry, I didn't realise. Jogging? No wonder you're short of breath. No, I don't do that kind of thing myself. Even the thought of running makes me dizzy. Well, since you ask, I'd have to say that I tend to exercise from the sitting down position. Oh, you know. Raising a glass so as to lower a bottle of wine while reading a book and listening to good music. My version of multi-tasking. Think it could catch on? No, I guess you're right. *Slight Pause.*

I'll keep it brief. The reason I'm phoning is that Frank – my landlord, you remember – has just dropped in to tell me that one of his flats is about to be vacated and he thinks it might well suit you. He's hoping you'll contact him, if you're interested, that is. *Slight Pause.*

I'm assuming you haven't found somewhere? No, I don't know the exact location. Frank didn't mention an address, but he did tell me to let you know that although it's near the town centre it isn't noisy. He was insistent on that. 'Do tell Miss Birdlip that the apartment is pleasingly secluded.' Standard house agent's language, for all I know. Meaning not situated adjacent to a metal grinders or a sewage treatment plant. Noisy as in noisome. As 'mature garden' means overgrown cabbage-patch. Yes, true, it all needs deconstructing. I've always liked Ripe for Redevelopment. Meaning that the bloody place is falling down. And then there's Charmingly Old-Fashioned. Code for the rats have been forced out by damp rot. But to be fair to Frank, he takes good care of his properties. *Pause.*

Well, anyway, that's the message. He wants you to phone him, 'as a matter of urgency.' And now my tale is told. Sure, now would be perfect, he'll be in. His number is the same as mine bar the last but one digit. Land line, that is. I'm pretty sure he won't have a mobile. Instead of 6 you need 5. Yes, it confuses a fair number of people. You've no idea how many phone calls I get from renters wanting me to replace a loose tile or mend a dripping tap. And from time to time

Frank gets asked to dig out his tenor and dep. with the Spondon Swingtet or, for all I know, Misty Manuel and his Mountainous Music. *Slight pause.*

The other reason for calling is to thank you for your text message. Excellent that you can come to hear Padgett's talk. I've no idea what it'll be like, of course. I knew him at university, but since then we've gone our separate ways. *Slight pause.*

Yes, I'm chairing it. Oh, you know, keep order, and if necessary interpose my body between him and hordes of hysterical groupies. I've been doing my homework, reading what turns out to be his latest. *Away***,** it's called. No, like the title it's on the short side and it slips down easily. I can lend you the library copy although, as you say, it's probably still on sale in the local Waterstone's. It's mainstream enough. No, no, I'm not knocking that. Far from it. Basie was mainstream, the Duke, Pres, Goodman … *Pause.*

By the way, I was wondering … I have to take him for a meal afterwards, and I was wondering … I mean you'd be very welcome to join us. Nothing grand, one of the pizzerias, I guess. Sure, go Dutch, if you'd prefer, but the drinks at least are on me – that is, they're on Library Expenses. We top executives get to wallow in wine at the taxpayers' expense. *Slight pause.*

OK. I'll put the phone down now, let you get to your dinner. Oh, of course, Frank can wait *that* long. No, no need to thank me. I was happy to oblige, as the actress said to the bishop. *Pause.*

Well, great to talk. *A bientôt.*"

But it wasn't *that* great was it, he thought, as he stood at the sink, cleaning fish for himself and the cat. She'd have heard him straining for what he could never seem to achieve when he was with her and which the distance imposed by a telephone made even harder to attain. Why did he sound so … so … Gawky. That was the word. *Gawky.* "You're gawky, Cousins," a teacher had once told him. "All fingers and thumbs." Then the infuriating smile. "Metaphorically speaking, of course." He was returning an essay which the boy could see at a glance bore few indications to show that the teacher was impressed by the long hours that he had put into the essay. Plenty of red ink, of crosses and signs of disagreement, but very little by way of approval.

So how would Helen have rated his recent performance. Five out of ten at most. Could do better. You're gawky, Cousins.

10

"So according to you, almost anything the novel can do film can do better." Helen speared one of the tortellini and turned it round on her fork before popping it into her mouth. The two men waited while she chewed, then swallowed. "That's a bit sad, isn't it? What about all those people who can't get to a cinema. Or who don't want to go. What's to happen to them?"

The mild irony was lost on James Padgett. Laying aside the knife with which he'd been sawing at his pizza, he reached for his glass and downed the wine in one go. "No, that's not what I'm saying. I don't mean novelists should chuck it in," he said, his eyes gleaming with the light of battle as he swivelled his gaze from Helen to Geoff and back again. "But take description, for example. all that elaborate 'scene-setting' novelists once saw as crucial. Why bother, now that the camera can do it so much better. And quicker."

He paused, speaking slowly as though thinking his way but, Geoff thought, more to ensure he made his case an open-and-shut affair, he said, "Let's say there's a rainy city street. Panoramic view, tracking shot, zoom close up." Another pause, to satisfy himself they understood. Then, speaking more quickly, "Three or four seconds and you know all you need to know about the place, the state of the weather, the time of day, even the day of the week." He looked at them in turn. "Think how many words – how many *paragraphs* – you need to give the reader that amount of information."

He put down his knife, leaned back in his chair. I rest my case.

"But how do you let readers know what's important? I mean, what do you give them that the camera can't."

Padgett answered Geoff's question with a single word. "Dialogue."

"As you said in your talk."

"As I said in my talk."

"But films use dialogue," Geoff said.

"And sound effects," Helen said. "Mood music and all the rest of it. Closing doors, dogs barking, dripping taps. Blop, blop. All part of the atmosphere. All things novels can't do – or can't do nearly as well. 'Somewhere a dog barked.' Dreadful."

Padgett nodded in silent agreement. Then, pushing aside his empty plate, "And just think how much time a novel has to spend on providing what's called the back story," he said. "How did X come to be in a certain city working in a certain job at a certain time when he or she met Y? It all has to be supplied. In a film, it's no bother. 'Of all the bars in all the world.' Enough said."

"Sounds to me as if you're talking yourself out of your career," Helen said.

Again, Padgett ignored the flicker of amusement in her voice.

"No, because prose has its own pleasures, its own rhythms, its own *pace*, effects that film can't replicate."

"But aren't you arguing against yourself?" Helen looked puzzled. "I don't see what dialogue has got to do with such pleasures."

"It depends how you handle the dialogue. Interior dialogue, especially. Film's bad at that. Voice over. A clumsy device. That kind of thing gives me no pleasure, at all. Not as a writer, not as member of the audience. But finding the rhythms of thought, ah, now."

He picked up his refilled glass, drank, then, as he replaced it, said, "I'm not suggesting it's the be-all. But there's a real pleasure in discovering the words, the rhythms, that will communicate what I suppose is the psychological make-up of the people you're writing about. And I do mean pleasure. I don't go for all that stuff about the agony of creation. What's wrong with delight?"

"Fair point," Geoff said, "although to be honest I don't suppose what interests you is why most readers pick up a novel."

"It may be why they put it down, though," Helen said. She was frowning into her wine glass, serious now. "Most readers would settle for a good story, wouldn't they, rather than what you call the pleasures of prose. At least, if that means what I think it means."

"Which is?" The light of battle was still in Padgett's eyes. "And when you say story, do you mean plot?"

"I might," Helen said, meeting his gaze.

"Because the trouble with plot," Padgett said, as though she hadn't spoken, is that it isn't like life. 'It's not … it doesn't have a plot, It's history.' I'm quoting an American poet. He fought in the Second World War. His experience, I'd say, persuaded him that narratives of good and bad are a kind of lie. Things are never that simple."

"Perhaps not," Helen said, flushing. "But that's not the end of plot. And anyway, I've no time for a novel where from page one you know that the writer makes no bones about who's in charge, telling you what to think, that this is all fiction, that the 'plot' doesn't matter and that if you think it does then you're some inferior form of being. Anyway, that's how it seems to me." She laughed, more a defensive snuffle, adopted a fake pompous expression. "Why, dear readers, do we read? That's what we want to know."

Geoff shared out the last of the wine. "And what I want to know," he said, " is whether I should order another bottle. On me, of course."

* * *

He felt a modest elation with how the evening was going. It was proving to be a success, and had been from the moment when Padgett, arriving by taxi some half-an-hour before the talk was scheduled to begin, shook Geoff's hand with what seemed genuine warmth, reminisced smilingly about their university days and various student acquaintances, and, when out of his raincoat, showed himself to be wearing nothing more challenging than a sports coat over an open-necked shirt and dark pullover, with, below, a pair of dark brown cords and old suede boots. Though why *should* any writer be identifiable through their dress, let alone demeanour? Ah, but according to newspaper interviewers through whose columns Geoff had been trawling, Padgett was known to come on grand, often turned up in suit or, if at home, wore pyjamas and dressing gown.

And yet meeting the writer's friendly grin, the dark-eyed gaze behind what looked to be reading glasses, taking note of the stubbly face, a bit rounder than he recalled, but then the best part of fifteen years had passed since they last met, Geoff could see nothing forbidding in this man whom interviewers characterised as stern, unforthcoming, even uncooperative, or, on the other hand, maddeningly flippant. Perhaps he simply didn't like being interviewed.

A fact which, after his talk, and in answer to a question from a woman in the full audience of all ages who had turned out on this misty winter's evening, Padgett confirmed. "Have you noticed," he said, not so much replying to her hesitant enquiry about whether he used his own life as the basis for his work as addressing the room at large, "that most broadsheets have replaced serious reviewing with interviews. That's bad enough. Worse, though, is the fact that the interviewer is supposed to be the star of the occasion. By comparison the interviewee is a kind of fall-guy or stooge." He waited for the nods of agreement, and when they came, said, with added assurance, "Anyway, not even the most sympathetic interview, whatever it tells you about the writer's views on life, can tell you whether his or her novels are worth reading. The best talkers are often the worst writers. Padgett's First Law."

"Is there a second?" Geoff asked.

"Certainly. Padgett's Second Law is that interviews are a curse of contemporary cultural life."

"Then why give 'em?" Arthur Stanchard shouted out from his favoured back row seat.

"Good question." Padgett smiled ruefully. "The honest answer is that I give interviews because my publishers ask me to. It's free advertising, a way – they hope – of selling copies of a novel that might otherwise go for shredding after gathering a month's dust at the rear of your local, friendly bookshop."

The self-deprecating grin accompanying his words succeeded in disarming further questions and allowed Geoff to bring proceedings to a close. Padgett signed copies of the three novels his publishers had sent for the occasion, all of which, Geoff noticed, were bought by the audience, one by Josie who asked him to sign for herself and Mark – "my fiancé," she explained holding out for inspection her engagement ring, her eyes sparkling with the excitement of meeting a real, live author – and then, renewed thanks to their distinguished speaker having produced genuine and prolonged applause, they were free to leave.

As they strolled to the nearby Italian restaurant where a table waited for them, Helen, whom Geoff had introduced to the novelist as lecturer in English at the local FE college – a professional acquaintance, he implied – asked Padgett whether, if he didn't enjoy interviews, he found any pleasure in the kind of talk he'd just given. "Oh, yes," Padgett said, seriously. "I'll take any chance to talk *properly* about writing. But that's not what interviewers want, is it?"

Standing aside for Helen as Geoff pushed the restaurant door open, he added, "It's a bad mistake to despise your readers. Or audience."

"Because it affects sales?"

"No, because, as the audience this evening showed, they're serious people and they deserve to be taken seriously."

And, after they'd been shown to their seats, and their glasses had been filled, he raised his to Geoff. "Thanks for this evening, Geoff. It's been a pleasure. Made me think again about what I'm doing as a writer."

Which led to an over-the-meal discussion about how writers could reconcile their own interests with what readers might be expected to want; and that led to Padgett's claim about some of the advantages film enjoyed over writers of descriptive prose.

* * *

It was still several minutes short of ten o'clock when they left him at his hotel. He had an early train to catch, he'd explained, adding with a wry smile, "Nothing exciting. Work routine. I need to be at my desk by nine o'clock each morning. What you could call a psychological imperative." And with that and a farewell flick of his hand he disappeared into the hotel lobby.

As they turned away, Helen said, "Well, I enjoyed that. Enjoyed talking to him. Was he as you remembered?"

"From student days? On the whole. Success certainly hasn't spoiled James Padgett. Perhaps he'd need more success to run the risk of that." Then, looking at his watch, he asked, "Fancy a drink?"

"Where? Now that the den of vice you took me to last time has closed what's left?"

"We could try the Black Cat".

"I'll try anything once." The smile hovered between mocking challenge and inviting warmth.

And a few minutes later, as they found themselves seats in the bar's low-lit atmosphere, she said, looking about her and speaking with a conspiratorial grin, "A marked improvement on the other place. I do believe some of the drinkers here are of a legal age."

Their drinks, for which Helen insisted on paying, were brought by a young woman in black trousers and a T-shirt bearing the stylised image of a cat's whiskery face. Geoff watched Helen shrug herself out of her coat and drape it over the chair beside her, managing the action with movements so casual and yet of such fluid grace that he had to lower his gaze. When he dared once more to raise his eyes he found that she was studying him above the rim of her vodka and ice.

In the soft light her face looked sculpted, the high cheekbones almost on a level with those eyes made luminous by the lanterned candle at her elbow.

He saw her mouth open and close but had no sense of her words.

"Sorry," he said, "What?"

She raised an enquiring eyebrow. "I said, do you agree with what he – with what your friend said about novel writing. That's your starter for ten."

"Oh." He thought about it, once more averting his eyes from her steady, enquiring smile, and staring at his scuffed leather boots, as though they might have the answer to her question. "I don't know. Perhaps. But," and he stared into his drink, "I don't remember there being much dialogue in that novel you lent me, the recent one. But I *do* remember a good deal of the descriptive prose."

"Agreed. As well as a good deal of plotting he also told us the contemporary novel ought to deny itself." She laughed. "'Ought to deny itself.' It sounds terribly stern, doesn't it. The novel as entertainment? Off with its head. Though I have to say he wasn't at all like that." And when, able now to look at her, he nodded agreement, she said, "My guess is that he was telling us not to expect any more novels like his last. Betcha the next one will be all dialogue."

"And no plot? Could be. Watch this space."

He was going to add to the remark but before he could do so a hand was on his shoulder and, turning, found himself staring up into a face he knew.

"Hi," Jade said, "I saw you come in. I'm with a group of mates over there" – gesturing in the direction of a far corner of the bar. "How are you?"

"I'm fine," he said, startled. Then, recovering, "And you?"

"Yeh," she said. "Cool." She was in her usual all-black gear but her hair was now straw-blonde, and a diamond-shaped silver stud glittered beside her upper lip. "Well, you going to introduce me?" Then, to Helen. "Men," she said. "No bloody manners."

Helen said, "Hi, my name's Helen. Helen Birdlip. An old acquaintance of Geoff's."

"And I'm Jade. I guess I'm a more recent acquaintance. Now you see me, now you don't." But the laugh was without malice or hidden meaning. "Well, I'd better get back, but good to see you, Geoff. Take care. You, too, Helen."

She reached over to shake Helen's hand, green nails gleaming in the candle-glow, patted Geoff on the shoulder, flipped them a wave, and was gone.

Helen's enquiring look had him reaching for an explanation. "Jade's a good 'un," he said. "She turned up at a gig where the group was on parade. A party. She works in a stationer's in town. Or did when I last asked."

Then he stopped. Jade had shared his bed for a few, semi-drunken, giggly occasions, ones that, while he took pleasure in them, as, he was certain, she also did, meant nothing much to either of them. Difficult, if not impossible, to find words to describe what was after all hardly an affair, at all events find words that wouldn't make him sound at best callous, someone prepared to exploit a girl years younger than himself. It wasn't like that, he wanted to tell Helen, not like that at all. "Cool," Jade had said. That word did as well as any to describe the few weeks they'd been together. But "cool" wasn't a word he could use. It didn't belong in his vocabulary. Did it belong in Helen's? Or was he now registered as a cradle-snatcher? Sod it. Of all the bars in the world ... But this was Longford. Of course, Jade would be likely to use it. Of course. He'd been in there himself with her. Of course, he should have thought of that before suggesting to Helen they go there for a drink.

To his relief, though he expected to find it short-lived, Helen did not seek further information, and her momentarily sceptical look as he spoke about Jade had gone. She said merely, "She reminds me of more than one of my women students. Lively enough, but you wouldn't get much dialogue out of *them*. It's all mutter and monosyllable. Ah," she mock-grimaced, "showing my age, I suppose."

To me, dear friend, you never can be old, he wanted to say. Instead, and to get back to where they'd been before Jade's intervention, and perhaps obliterate it, he said, "What the novel can't do. That's what we were talking about. Or does the subject bore you?"

"Bore me?" Helen asked. "No. I want to know whether you think I'm right."

"About James – about Padgett's next novel? I don't think there'll *be* a next novel. Not for some time, at least. My money's on a play script. Unless he's going to turn one of his books into a film. But on the whole I'll go for a play. A play's *all* dialogue."

He was trying to work round to something else he wanted, needed to say.

"Plays have sound effects." She paused, sipped at her drink, then added, "And some action. It isn't only jaw jaw."

Her words gave him the opening he needed. "But rehearsed readings are. Jaw jaw, I mean." Pause. "Which reminds me. I saw Peter Cadogan recently."

"Yes, he told me. At a golf club do."

The words, like the look she now directed at him, like her slight, untroubled smile, were candid, open, unfazed. "He said your group played well."

Taking a deep breath to steady himself, he said, his eyes locked on hers, "He asked me to rejoin the Alleyn Players. Apparently he's thinking of doing *As You Like It*. With you as Rosalind."

"Apparently he is." She laughed, but under the low lighting he couldn't get the measure of her look. "He takes rather a lot for granted." Then, glancing at her watch, she said, pulling a face, "Geoff, I'd better be going. Us working girls, you know." And, draining her glass, she reached for her coat.

Had she meant to wrong-foot him? Whatever, she'd certainly put a stopper on further talk about Cadogan.

Following her out of the Black Cat, still reeling from what she had so calmly revealed, he said, "Frank tells me you like the flat he showed you."

She turned to him, her face relaxing into its smile. The accord between them, if it had been lost, seemed to have been restored.

"Yes," she said, almost eagerly. "It's pretty well ideal. I'll be moving next weekend. It's all arranged."

"Need any help? I can manage a bit of lifting and heaving. And my tea-making skills are not to be underestimated." See, I'm still standing.

"Now, *that* is an offer I can't refuse." Her laugh was lost in the rumbling of a late bus as it headed for the town's depot. Turning up her collar, so that her face was almost lost to sight, she said. "Most of my stuff's in storage and I've arranged for it to be delivered by van, but I can always use an extra pair of hands, even if it's only to pour cuppas."

"In that case," he said, buttoning his jacket against the wind, and making a slight bow, "consider me at your service."

"I will," she said, and, laying her hand lightly on his sleeve, "Thanks for tonight, Geoff. I really enjoyed it. And if I *do* decide to take up Cadogan's offer I hope you will, too."

And with that, and having given his arm a squeeze, she turned and walked away. There was no repeat of the kiss, slight though it had been, which had accompanied her previous goodbye. A meal is worthy of a peck on the cheek. A social evening gets merely the friendly touch of a hand. Ah, well.

* * *

Watching Baw as she lapped up the last of her late-night food, he played back Helen's words. "He takes rather a lot for granted." Exactly *what* did Cadogan take for granted? That she'd play Rosalind. That she'd return to his bed. "Everything comes to him who waits." The words jabbed at him, a long needle of pain, especially now he had proof that Helen was back in touch with that smug bastard. "Yes, he told me." *When* did he tell you? When you were tucked up in bed together?

Come on, he told himself, snap out of it. You've no claim on her. To her, you're a friend and nothing more. *You* might have been embarrassed when Jade hove into view, but Helen wasn't in the least concerned. The state of your affairs, emotional or otherwise, is of no interest to her. It never was. Why should it be? Baw stopped her washing to look up at him. But shutting his eyes it was Helen's face he saw, her eyes, those dark eyes, glowed in the bar's low lights, her fingers touched his arm, her voice filled his head …

And after all, he thought as, reopening his eyes, he bent to scratch Baw behind the ears, Helen had agreed with him about Cadogan, shared, so it seemed, his assessment of the man. SB. Smug, Selfish Bastard. But if that was so, how come Cadogan seemed to be once more in favour? At the very least, he was in contact, and knowing Cadogan that could only mean one thing. You play Rosalind and I'll supply the director's couch.

Going to switch off the kitchen light, he said aloud, "Kill Claudio."

Now you come to mention it, why not?

* * *

A few minutes later, fresh from a shower, he stood in front of the bathroom mirror remembering Jade's remark, made early one Sunday morning as he returned to bed after a pee.

"You're not bad for an old feller," she'd said.

Putting on his best Jeeves voice, Geoff had told her, "We endeavour to give satisfaction."

"I'm not complaining." Jade's candid laugh provided some sort of reassurance.

"Which proves there can be life after 35."

"How old are you, then?"

"Add three."

"Really?" She propped herself up on an elbow, let her eyes and then her fingers roam about his naked body." It's the first time I've been with anyone that old," she said, as though he was some sort of brontosaurus.

Now, daring to study his face in the mirror, he said aloud, "Well, you'll have to do." Hair, dark brown, in need of a trim, but still thick on top, face, on the long side with deep-cut lines either side of a nose that ended in blunt disregard of the flat upper lip that most reed-players acquire over the years, though, pinching the flesh under his jaw, he was glad to have got rid of the moustache and beard he'd grown during his student years and kept for too long afterwards; he preferred to let his chin show its rounded ordinariness.

"See, nothing to hide," he said as he stared into the brown eyes meeting his. "What's Cadogan got that you haven't?"

Then, turning to inspect himself in profile, confirmed that, although his legs were too thin, if he straightened his shoulders he didn't need to suck in his stomach to look in reasonably good shape.

"But nothing to write home about, either." And he snapped off the light.

What *had* Cadogan got? Money. Power. And now, possibly, Helen.

Climbing into bed, he recalled the question Jade put to him on the last Sunday, as it turned out, they'd been together. "You ever been married?"

Guessing the reason for his hesitation in answering her, she added, giggling, "Don't worry, pet. I'm not about to ask you for a ring. I was wondering, that's all."

He shook his head, relieved. "No, never been married. Not once."

"How about love, then?"

"Ah," he'd said, "that's different."

11

Struggling into consciousness, Geoff realised that the knocking wasn't after all part of his dream.

Frank stood in the porch, dressed as if for business. Buffed brogues, neatly pressed grey trousers, collar and tie, and mackintosh folded over the sleeve of his tweed jacket.

"Come on in, Frank. Be ready in a minute. What's the weather like?"

"The weather is, I am happy to report, satisfactory. Dry." Alexander looked Geoff up and down, taking in without comment the old grey T-shirt which was all that protected his tenant from culpable indecency. "No need for removal men to be treading wet mud into the carpets."

"Good. Make yourself at home and I'll be with you."

A few minutes later, hair still damp from his hasty shower, Geoff was dressed and in the kitchen boiling the kettle as he washed out a thermos – "I may have oversold my tea-making skills to your new tenant" – while Frank, seated at the kitchen table, veered between watching his tenant's actions and meeting Baw's unblinking stare. The landlord did not ban the keeping of pets, though dogs were discouraged. "Their presence has in the past led to complaints from the neighbours," he mentioned as Geoff signed the contract on which they had agreed, "so if you *are* thinking of keeping one I shall have to ask you to ensure that it is well-behaved."

No crapping in next-door's garden, no keeping locals awake with all-night barking, and above all, no taking lumps out of postmen's legs.

"You're safe with me," Geoff told his landlord. "I've no interest in dogs." Nor had he any interest in cats, or so he'd thought, but returning from a gig late one night he found a black-and-white kitten curled up in the porch, took pity on her – she seemed little more than a ball of matted fur and bone – scooped her up and, in the kitchen, gave her a saucer of milk before depositing her back in the porch. So long, and been good to know you.

But she was there again the next night, and the next; and a few evenings later he accepted the inevitable. From that time forward she belonged, as the disc he eventually had made for the collar he affixed to her neck proclaimed, to Flat 1, 27 Ewing Avenue, and she answered to the name BAW.

As though sensing that Frank wasn't entirely *simpatico*, Baw now turned her back on him and began the morning's elaborate ritual of cleaning herself all over, left rear leg thrust out as she worked her way through a tangle of fur on her inner thigh.

"Not fleas, I hope," Frank said with mild distaste.

"Not live ones, anyway," Geoff said, "not after Baw's done with them. Don't worry, Frank. She keeps herself spotless."

Frank looked dubious. "Is Miss Birdlip keen on pets?" he asked.

"Dunno. Shouldn't think so. She's a working girl." Geoff screwed the lid onto his thermos flask, dropped it together with a carton of milk and a packet of biscuits into a carrier bag. "Right," he said, "all fit and raring to go."

Frank levered himself up from his chair, looking at his watch as he did so. "I told Miss Birdlip we would meet her at ten o'clock," he said, giving her name full phonetic value. "She will, I understand, be arriving in the removal van." He paused, waiting for Geoff to agree by a nod or smile that this was a decidedly eccentric mode of transport. Then, "We should still be in time, if we are not delayed by traffic." He sighed, professionally anxious. "But on a Saturday morning, who can tell."

It was 9.15.

* * *

Fifteen minutes later, in a flare of early spring sunshine, Geoff brought the Fiat to a halt outside the house Frank indicated.

"OK to park here? No chance of a ticket?"

Having received the landlord's reassurance, Geoff locked the car and, Frank standing beside him, turned to scrutinise Hutton Lodge, the name picked out on the stone lintel above the house's wide central porch. A substantial, double-fronted, red brick building, partly shaded by a monkey puzzle tree which occupied a large share of the front lawn, it had a curved gravel path which led from porch down to gates now wide open, awaiting the arrival of the new tenant. Helen was to have the upper floor, reached by an outside staircase at the back of the house.

In showing her around, Frank had assured her that she need never see the other flat dwellers. So at least she told Geoff when phoning to check that he was still prepared to help her move in. He was. "Good," she said, "I'm glad about that," before adding that according to her landlord the tenants she need never see were "a professional couple. Ideal neighbours. You wouldn't know they exist."

"The English dream of neighbourly perfection," Geoff said. "You may be living above a pair of murderous psychopaths but at least they keep themselves to themselves."

She laughed, said, "If they *are* psychopaths I'd rather they *didn't* come calling."

But in fact as he and Frank walked up the drive the front door opened and a man called out, "Mr Alexander. Can this be our new neighbour? I thought we were to expect a female of the species."

He was tall, his affable smile suggesting that the pomposity was a put-on, as did the blue-and-white open-neck check shirt and light brown cords; clean-shaven face hinting by its weathered look a man who spent at least some time in the open air.

I'm sure I've seen you before, Geoff thought, but where?

The woman behind him was half hidden in shadow.

"Morning Mrs Halstead," Frank said, doffing his cap. "No, Charles, this isn't the person who'll be moving in. Allow me to introduce Mr Geoffrey Cousins, another of my tenants as it so happens and a friend of the young lady who'll be living above you. Come to help Miss Birdlip install her worldly goods and chattels."

The woman, who had made no attempt to acknowledge Frank, was now standing beside her husband and studying Geoff through half-lowered lids.

Ah, yes.

But before he could say anything, she spoke. "I have a feeling we've met somewhere before," she said, her voice, with its suggestion of Home Counties drawl, containing the hint of a challenge.

He saw that what at first had looked an unusually long dress of some patterned material was a dressing gown, no, peignoir, he supposed. He met her unsmiling, almost imperious gaze, took in the immaculately made-up face, its smooth contours, the fixed half-smile, auburn hair which surely owed much to the attentions of an expensive salon: he didn't like her.

"The library, perhaps? Where I work."

But he knew differently, and so did she, outsmarting him as she

83

said, grimacing, "I never go to the library. It's such a dreary place." Dreary had at least three syllables. Then, as though a less than pleasant memory was coming slowly back, she asked, and the question sounded more of an accusation, "Are you by any chance some sort of a musician?" Or rat catcher?

The man, who following her words had also been looking at Geoff more attentively, said. "Yes that's it. Of course. You were in the group that played at the golf club, weren't you? I remember now. Saxophonist. I saw you chatting to Peter."

"Peter Cadogan?"

"We were his guests."

"Ah, well, then, that explains it."

Though it didn't explain everything. It didn't for instance explain why on the occasion of the dance Cadogan had said that *he* was the guest, that he'd far rather be somewhere else, but that, after all, one had to be civil. Typical Cadogan. He was, he must have been, touting for business, but he had to make it appear the other way round. The ever-in-demand Peter Cadogan, the sought-after man of talents. All roads and sewers lead to Cadogan. And yet this man seemed on the level. And as if to prove it, he now said, smiling, "If there's anything we can do to help our new neighbour, do please tell her not to be afraid to knock on our door. We'll do what we can to show that the natives are friendly, won't we, love?"

But the woman had already disappeared.

* * *

As they walked round the side of the building, Geoff asked, "So who are they, the Halsteads. I mean, what do they do?"

"Charles Halstead is a surveyor. She – well, I'm not sure," Frank said, looking down the length of garden which to Geoff's eye seemed immaculate even in late winter. Level lawn, no straggle of leafless plants, the flower beds raked over and ready for new growth. As though satisfied by his inspection, Frank nodded before saying, "I understand she has work as some sort of legal adviser. Don't ask me what. They've been with me for several months and before that were, I am given to understand, somewhere south of London."

He looked solemnly at Geoff. "I have the impression they may be birds of passage." Having said which, he took some steps onto the lawn, turned, pushed back the peak of his cap in order the better to scrutinise the house's second storey, said "your Miss Birdlip will have as much privacy here as the heart could desire." Gesturing to the tall bushes that grew either side of the lawn, the bare-forked trees at the garden's high-walled end, and cocking an ear as if to listen out for any intrusive sounds, he nodded with a gentle complacency and a smile which communicated that where they stood was safe from noise pollution. "You'd never know how near you were to the town centre, now would you?"

"You never would," Geoff said, and at that moment they heard a vehicle lumbering near, the sputter of tyres on gravel, slow squeal of brakes, a metal door being slammed.

"Hello, anybody here. Hello?"

Helen's voice was followed by Helen herself, coming into view round a wooden shed that jutted out from the far corner of the house. Below her red coat she was wearing jeans and a pair of scuffed trainers.

"Dressed for action," she said, approaching them. "The men are waiting instructions about how we gain lawful entry with my bits and bobs."

"Can they manage these steps?"

Her landlord indicated the railed-off concrete stairs that led up to what must be the entry to her flat.

"I'm sure they can."

"In that case, I'll accompany you inside Miss Birdlip, remind you how everything works, and Geoffrey, perhaps you'll be so good as to let the removal men know what's what."

"No sweat."

Nor was it. An hour later, all the furniture and an assortment of boxes were in the flat, the men had been paid and gone, Frank, after getting Helen to complete some paperwork, had, in his own words, seen himself off the premises, and Helen had given Geoff a guided tour of her flat.

As they stood in the large, square kitchen whose picture window looked over the garden beyond which he could make out the grey stone of the town hall's rear view, he poured tea from his thermos into mugs she'd dug out of a cardboard box, one of several piled on the draining board.

"Well?" she asked.

"I'm impressed." And he was. As well as the kitchen, there was a good-size bedroom, large lounge, small study which could double as guest-bedroom, bathroom and separate shower unit. Light, he noticed as she took him from room to room, poured through every window of her flat.

"It's the first time I've been up in the air," Helen said, her face showing her pleasure. "Like living in a tree house." She laughed, plainly thrilled at the prospect. "I think I'm going to love it here." She sipped her tea. "I'm really grateful, Geoff."

"When it comes to flask tea, Cousins is unbeatable."

She raised her mug, laughing, happy. "Too true. Though I was thinking of the flat."

"In that case it's Frank you should be thanking." But the touch of her hand resting lightly on his own sang through him.

By lunchtime they'd unpacked most of her kitchen-ware and crockery and were in the lounge sorting through books for the shelves that lined half of one wall.

Among a pile of paperback novels he was trying to find room for, he noticed two of Padgett's. He was making space for them among other paperbacks when she said, "Did anything ever come of your plans to write?"

He turned. She was standing right behind him, on her face a look of genuine interest.

"Afraid not." Then, shrugging as a way of dismissing her question, "But kind of you to ask."

He thought she might be about to enquire what had gone wrong, but instead she murmured, "That's a pity." But as he shook his head in disclaimer of her implied concern, she said, in her normal voice, "I wondered, when I saw that desk of yours. Could it be the anvil on which mighty works were hammered out?" She paused, let the smile die away. "You seemed so certain all those years ago that writing was what you wanted to do. Though you never said what kind of writing."

"Probably because I didn't know. A young man's fancy, that's all. I guess I was trying to impress you."

"Perhaps you did."

"But clearly not enough."

Unable to read the look on her face, he laughed, grimaced, turned back to his task, aware that the words he had blurted out had issued unbidden from his lips, but not knowing what to add to them, nor, scarcely, why he had spoken them. Though he did, of course he did. "Anyway, I satisfy my creative urge by blowing into a sax."

"That's good."

"Yes," he said, turning to her, "it is," and was aware from her silent, almost startled nod, that she registered the emphasis underlining his words.

It made for an awkward moment between them, but before the silence could take hold they heard an urgent knocking and then a man's voice call from the top of the stairs.

"Coming." Helen handed Geoff her mug and almost sprinted from the room.

So she'd remembered the words he'd unguardedly blurted out all those years ago when, at some rehearsal or other, she'd asked him about his work and he'd said that librarianship would do to pay the rent while he tried to establish himself as a writer. Even then, the remark, made after he'd come across a reference to Padgett's first, recently published novel, had, he knew, been prompted by the unformed thought, if him, why not me? Months later he had the answer. It lay in the waste-paper basket which overflowed with abandoned drafts of a novel that was, he had to accept, dead. Not even twitching. Dead. Kaput. By then, though, he didn't need to confess his failure to Helen. She was already in Wolverhampton and would never need to know of his ludicrous attempt to put into words the story of a love affair between an aspiring musician and the woman who, despite the attentions of an older, socially accomplished man, comes to understand the musician's true depth of soul.

"Prat," he muttered to himself, and at that moment she reappeared, carrying flowers wrapped in cellophane. "From Janey," she said, "courtesy of Interflora. Isn't that kind of her. I'd better put them in water."

He followed her out to the kitchen. "This could be the moment for a break" he said to her back as she stood, head bowed over the sink, snipping at the stems of the elaborate, pink-and-white bouquet. "Why don't I go for some sustaining food. Fancy fish and chips?"

"Fish and chips would undoubtedly hit the spot." She turned. The smile was back and he could breathe more easily. "And while you're out I'll rootle around for a bottle. The Birdlip cellar may not be vast but selective isn't the word. And we're entitled to celebrate."

This was becoming almost a habit, he thought, as he stood in the queue at THIS IS THE PLAICE. Talk that brought them near to the edge, from which they retreated into embarrassed silence, a strained flippancy. The edge of what, though? Oh, chaos. Uncharted territory. Transylvania. Here be dragons. To go there would mean having to find words for what was better left unspoken. Words that belonged in the waste-paper basket.

In front and behind him, the queue was noisy with the boisterous affability of those, young men mostly, younger than him, for whom Saturday was the day that licensed pleasure. The brakes were off, they were on the joyride that would for many of them end in the disconsolate, drunken, disillusioned chill of Sunday morning. But for now the excitement was palpable. Listening to their banter, the gusty bellows of laughter, of raucous chit-chat, he thought, Don't let's spoil it all, I thought we were going to be such good friends. But he shouldn't have been so strident in defence of playing of jazz, dammit. Why want to get his retaliation in first? And why assume that her response, "That's good," implied any mockery, let alone condescension? Why couldn't he believe her reply to his remark about blowing into a sax to be as genuine, as unguarded, as her friendliness? Easy. Because it wasn't enough.

"Next please."

* * *

Helen had cleared a space at the kitchen table and, as he came in, she indicated a just-opened bottle of white wine. "How about this?" she said. "Top of the range Chablis, already chilled. An ice-breaker from them downstairs." She poured for them both.

He put down his carrier bag, inspected the label. "Looks good. And," he sniffed then sipped, "it is good, by Jove, what what. Who brought it, Him or Her?"

"Him. Charles Halstead. She stayed below. I did invite them to join us for a glass, but he said they were about to go out. Meeting friends for lunch."

"Probably Peter Cadogan."

"What?"

Wide-eyed, she stopped in the act of shaking out their portions of fish and chips, looked at him as he sat across from her, her look one of troubled enquiry.

"They know him," he told her. "Weren't you aware?" And when she shook her head, he said by way of explanation, "It seems they were his guests at the golf club gig I played at. They noticed him talking to me." He and Frank had been accosted by the Halsteads earlier that morning, he told her. "I'd say he was the friendlier of the two. She looked as if she thought herself the Queen of Sheba, as my mother might have said."

"But *how* do they know Peter – Cadogan?"

"Business, I assume. He prentended not to notice the faint blush that had accompanied her hesitation over the name. "These solicitors get everywhere. Typical of Cadogan to belong to a golf club." And, he thought, typical of the bastard to pretend he was only there on sufferance.

"Perhaps he *likes* golf." But the smile that accompanied her words, the slight tautening of her lips, said something else. It said, yes, I know him, anything for the main chance.

The sardonic edge to the smile gave him a lift, its acknowledgement of Cadogan's true nature, but her next words returned him to the basement.

"I think I *will* try for Rosalind," she said, not looking at him. "I need something to get me out of an evening."

Try me, he wanted to say. I'm here. But the words wouldn't come. Don't make for more awkwardness. Risking speech now would be like stepping out on a sagging tightrope in a high wind. He waited until she chose to meet his gaze, then said, as though he had given the matter some thought, "I probably won't bother, I've got my jazz to keep me warm," and couldn't at all decipher the look that crossed her face. Disappointment? Relief? Vexation?

But she nodded as if in understanding.

"Besides, he offered me the part of Corin."

That light flickering in her eyes, was it anger, amusement, contempt? "AB," she said.

"Corin?"

"Cadogan. Absolute Bastard." And she ducked her head to her food.

They finished their meal in virtual silence and soon after, having been assured that she could now manage on her own, he left.

The sky, which earlier had been patched with blue, was now uniformly grey, and as he drove home scuds of rain pestered the windscreen.

12

Helen's message was bare bones. **sorry u cldnt stay longer. Thanks for help. H x.**

Couldn't? What did she mean by that word? She hadn't asked him to stay and he hadn't said he must go. Was the word intended to put him in the wrong? Had she after all been assuming that he would stay longer, would continue to make himself of further use? Had he failed some test of friendship? But she'd assured him she'd be fine on her own. Or did the words mean more than that? Had he missed some signal or other? There had, after all, been no need to text. So why had she put herself to the bother? Ah, who knew?

He erased the message. After a glum evening in which half a bottle of scotch failed to solace him, he was in no mood, as he sat picking at his Sunday morning toast with Billie in the background lamenting the failure of this year's kisses, to linger over the withheld meaning of Helen's words. Anyway, if she wanted to communicate properly, why didn't she phone or email him. Either way, she could say more than in these text messages. But perhaps she preferred them simply because they were necessarily short, more or less factual, conveniently enigmatic, difficult to answer.

Well, sod that for a game of soldiers. He *would* answer. **Didn't know u wanted me to stay,** he wrote, then erased the words and tried again. **Sorry 2. Hope u had gd evening.** No, that implied either irony or self-pity. While you were enjoying yourself I was here on my own, awash in sorrow and scotch. One more try. **don't u know how I feel abt u still crazy after all these years kill cadogan** He studied the message, nearly yielded to temptation but in the end pressed *clear*. After some consideration, he wrote **whos sorry now. Gx.** Let her work that out.

*   *   *

He was still feeling sore-headed next morning when, toward lunchtime, Colleen came into the staff room where he was trying to complete some paperwork. A woman was at the front desk, asking to speak to him.

"Really, who?" Hope flared.

No idea." Colleen raised an eyebrow with what he guessed was her idea of an arched expression. "Never seen her before. But she's quite a laydie."

"Not my type, then," he said as he levered himself up.

"Though as my old dad used to say whenever he caught sight of any of my boyfriends," Colleen said, going over to the coffee machine and speaking over her shoulder, "there's no accounting for taste."

The woman was not Helen.

Mrs Halstead looked him up and down, her smile in no sense friendly, more a confirmation of the unpalatable truth. "Ah, it *is* you." The manner in which she uttered the words made the young woman part-timer who was issuing books look curiously at him. A hint of disdain, an implied rebuke underlined her next words. "Not knowing your name I was forced to ask for a male librarian who is also a practising musician."

The idea of this woman being forced to do anything struck him as highly unlikely.

"That would have narrowed the field, even if I wasn't the only male member of staff."

He wasn't about to say more. She wanted to see him, so let her explain herself. For a brief moment he wondered whether, given the peremptory tilt of her chin, the way her eyes glanced at and then away from him as though he merited no further scrutiny, she'd come to complain about her new upstairs neighbour. Did Helen play music too loudly? Had she disturbed the Halsteads by throwing furniture noisily about her flat? But no. She'd have taken any complaints straight to Frank, wouldn't she? Or, more probably, made her husband do so.

"I need to ask you a question."

Even an oik like you has his uses. He looked at her, at the grey, tailored coat, top buttons undone to reveal an oyster-coloured silk blouse from which rose a slender, unlined neck, round it a single string of seed pearls, an assemblage that implied both cost and care, as did the black, flared trousers that came into view where her coat stopped at mid-calf, and, below them, black, heeled boots made, he had no doubt, of expensive leather. A pricey lady. Was this always how she dressed or had she put some thought into how best to impose herself on the scuffed, shabby surroundings of Longford library. At all events, her calculated gaze, a kind of moneyed hauteur, certainly didn't suggest that she felt in any way ill at ease.

"Will it take long?"

He might as well let her know he saw her appearance as an unwelcome interruption to his more serious concerns.

She coloured faintly and for the first time looked unsure of herself. "Peter Cadogan has asked me whether I might be interested in joining his play-reading group."

He waited. "And ... ?" He left her to answer the question.

"And he wants me to audition for William Shakespeare's *As You Like It*."

Not Sid Shakespeare, then. He began to feel better. But he said nothing.

Again the faint colouring. "It isn't a play I'm familiar with. I shall have to – shall have to acquaint myself with the part he suggested I might try for."

In other words, for all your airs and graces you're pig ignorant. He was now feeling much cheerier.

"So you need a crash course in Shakespeare," he said. "Not a great deal of use coming here, then. We don't have much that will help you on *our* shelves. You'll have to go to Nottingham if you're looking for commentaries, criticism, that kind of thing. They'll stock what you want." After a moment he asked, "Which part did Mister Cadogan suggest you might try for? Audrey?"

A raised eyebrow indicated that from the slight stress on Mister she'd registered his feeling toward the solicitor. Then, "Rosalind," she said. "I gather she's one of the principal characters." A pause. "Who – who is Audrey?"

"Oh, a rustic tart," he said. "The clown's bit of rumpty."

But even as he watched the colour stain her neck, he thought, Rosalind? What's that sod up to?

"We can supply a copy of the play, but not much more," he said. "Though if, as I *assume*, you're not a member of the library" – she ducked her head in brief acknowledgement – "I shall have to sign it out for you. Or," slight smile to let her know he wasn't expecting her to agree to his proposal, "if you prefer, you can become a user."

To his surprise, she nodded in abrupt agreement.

"In that case, Miss Davis" – indicating the part-timer – "will help you complete the forms." And, enjoying the chance to strike a note of official rectitude, he added, "If I can be of any further assistance – "

"You can let me buy you a drink", she said.

Caught off guard, he stared at her.

"One good turn deserves another, and I *assume*," a smile flickered as she glanced at the expensive-looking gold watch on her left wrist, "that you are entitled to a lunch break."

Still off kilter, he stumbled out words about not drinking during the day.

"Coffee is a drink."

And we have ours in the staff room, he should have said, but some indefinable softening in her manner kept him silent.

A glance at his watch, followed by a squint at the clock above the issue desk confirmed that it was now 1 p.m. "I can spare half-an-hour," he said.

It was graceless enough, but she smiled faintly, back in control. "Half-an-hour. How kind."

* * *

The Black Cat at lunchtime was very different from the bar he knew principally as a place for late-night drinks. The clientele was both older and younger: mothers, some of them no more than teenagers but with small children of their own, older women sharing tables where they leant to each other over plates of serious-looking food and, occasionally, glasses of wine, one or two businessmen in dark suits riffling through the day's newspapers.

He let her choose a table by the window and as the young man in regulation black jeans and T-shirt took their orders – a gin-and-tonic for her, coffee for him – asked, "Your first time here?"

"How *did* you guess?"

And gin might blur the glitter in her eyes. The line from a poem he'd read long years since came back to him as he measured the degree of ironic inflection in her voice. But all he said was, "I've no idea what the food is like. I drop in sometimes after jazz, but for a drink only."

"At which time it's the throbbing heart of Longford."

"Almost too hot to handle."

She glanced about her and he noticed the still taut flesh around her chin, the slim neck with a faint shading of lines, a kind of craquelure the pearls couldn't efface. Mid-forties, he guessed.

When she turned back to him he saw again that she was less sure

93

of herself than she wanted him to believe. Something about the way her eyes met his then dropped to the table, the manner in which she folded her hands in front of her, even the slight inclining of her face away from the light, told him that the woman he'd previously marked down as flawless in her arrogance wasn't, after all, at her ease.

As though to confirm his insight, she said, raising her glass, "I shouldn't really be here." Her words suggested indifference, her look said otherwise.

"Oh?" Then, as she showed no sign of adding to her words, he said, exasperated. "Where *should* you be?" And as she still said nothing, "It's a bit bloody rich, inviting me for a drink and then letting me know you'd rather be elsewhere. *I'd* rather be elsewhere, if it comes to that."

She seemed genuinely startled by his anger. "I put it badly," she said. "I didn't mean to say I *regretted* being here. Only that I was off-limits." A pause, during which she examined her hands, twisted both rings on the third finger of her left hand round and round. "I'm sorry, that doesn't sound much better, does it. Oh, please, sit down." Because, having emptied his cup, he'd risen and was about to put on the coat he'd thrown over the back of his chair. "Please?"

Her smile was troubled, the contrition in her voice genuine.

Reluctantly, he dropped back into his chair.

"I'm not very good at talking to people," she said, watching his eyes, "that's the truth of the matter." Then, "I don't *meet* many, is perhaps what I should say."

Did he believe that? Was she putting on an act? And if so, why? And which part was the act: the self-assurance or the uncertainty? He said, "What about your work?"

She looked at him, puzzled.

"I'm told you're involved in the legal profession." And, when the puzzled look – or was it one of disbelief – remained on her face, he added, "That's what Frank Alexander – our mutual landlord – gave me to understand."

The look cleared. This time her laughter was tinged by bitterness. "Charles no doubt. Doing his best to provide me with a CV that will confer credit on us both." She looked at him, shrugged, looked away and sighed. "No, I've nothing to do with the law, though my father was a top barrister and my brothers, bless their little cotton socks, are all in the game. But not me. Oh, no. Not me."

He tried to take the measure, less of her words, perhaps, than of the manner in which they were spoken, the indefinable mixture of regret, self-contempt – was it? – and the suggestion of holding someone, something to account.

He said, "Then if you don't mind my asking, what do you do?"

"Oh," she said, speaking in a manner reminiscent of an old West-End actress, "actually dahling I do sweet fuck all."

The combination of upper-class drawl and low expletive was so unexpected that he laughed outright.

The youth who'd served them came to remove his cup.

"Another?" she asked, but he said, "No, I ought to be getting back." Then, "Though I'm still not clear why ... "

"Why I offered to buy you a drink? Not because I'm a shameless hussy. And it wasn't even the ready charm of your conversational mode." The note of mockery was back in place. "I did, though, want to hear what you could tell me about Peter Cadogan's troupe – if that's the right word. He asked me to join it. He doesn't know whether I can act – I rather think I can't – or even *read*. I mean read in public. So why me?"

"When was this."

"Last evening." She drank the last of her gin-and-tonic, put the glass down, and, as though to erase any hint of sensuality from the way she'd passed her tongue across her upper lip, dabbed at her mouth with the tissue that had been supplied with her drink before taking a deep breath. "He'd dropped round to see the young woman upstairs – your friend, Helen whatshername – with a flat-warming gift." A smile, more perhaps an ironic pursing of the lips. "Roses and a magnum of Brut I expect. And having performed his act of knight gallantry, he came knocking on our door."

There was a moment's silence during which she looked steadily at him, and this time her smile was almost conspiratorial. Share this one with me. "He and Charles have become chums, so of course he was invited in for a drink, the talk turned to Mr Cadogan's directorial interests, and at some stage in the evening, when I imagine Charles's whisky had begun to soften his brain," the smile now implied the absurdity of it all, "he asked me to audition for the part of Rosalind." Pause. "Which is why you saw me standing before you in the library. Because, cards on the table, I know nothing about the play."

Her eyes were now averted. "In addition to all the other things I know nothing about."

The words, accompanied by a dismissive shrug, seemed

throwaway, not to be taken seriously, like the rest of her story for all he could tell. And yet there was something about her, about her restless eyes, about the constant shifts in the way she spoke, that he found disconcerting. He wasn't at ease with her, he guessed that despite her air of *sang-froid* she wasn't at ease with him, wasn't at ease with herself. Or was it all an act? Who exactly was she?

Deciding honest, plain words would best serve both their needs, he said as he stood, "The Alleyn Players are Cadogan's baby. They've been going for at least fifteen years. Am. Dram., though not bad, and probably all the better for not trying to go for stage productions." What else ought he to tell her. "They're not exactly a 'troupe'," he said, "but there are a number of regulars." Oh, well, she might as well hear this from him. "Speaking of which, I ought to tell you that Cadogan has also asked Helen Birdlip, your new neighbour, to read for the part of Rosalind."

She nodded, once more averted her gaze. "I don't find that surprising," she said, "after all, he doesn't know that I'll be any good."

He couldn't resist it. "But he knows how good Helen is."

"Ah." She raised her eyes to meet what he hoped was a smile of concern. "Men like Cadogan," she said, and did not finish the sentence. "But thank you for telling me."

As he shrugged his way into his jacket, he said, "By the way, how did you know when I take my lunch break?"

She looked up at him. And now the smile was frank, open-eyed, reasonable. "I asked the young woman at the desk," she said. "When I first came in this morning. How else could I have known?"

She was still sitting at the window, staring at her hands, as he left the Black Cat.

Marching past a bakery, pharmacist, and a hair salon, all of them interspersed among the growing number of charity shops along the High Street, swinging his arms to keep warm against the cold wind, he thought, so she's been checking on my movements. What's she up to? And, "Men like Cadogan." What exactly did she mean by those words? All men are like Cadogan. Cadogan is a shit. Therefore all men are shits. No, too easy. Resist all undergraduate syllogisms. Common sense tells us there are exceptions to a priori rules. Name one.

He pushed through the library doors, was grateful for the blast of warm air from central heating that kept the building at the right temperature throughout the year. OK now. Give me a name. Well, present company excepted, he thought as he entered the staff office, what about her husband. Charles Halstead seemed likeable enough.

He stood by his desk. But face it, Cousins, a few minutes' nodding acquaintance are not enough on which to base a sound judgement. Oh, quite, quite, m'lud.

He sat down, pulled his open briefcase towards him. I therefore recommend a closer inspection of the lady's imputation, which will entail both Halsteads being brought within the bounds of enquiry.

Indeed, m'lud.

Very well, case suspended.

13

"Hi. Helen. Geoff. *Pause*

Can you spare a minute? Sure? Not buried under a mountain of marking? Preparing classes? OK. Good. *Slight Pause.*

The reason I'm phoning is … well, I wonder if you'd like to accompany me to a party in three weeks' time. Terry? Terry Marsden. *The* Terry Marsden. He'll be celebrating his fiftieth. He sprang it on us at last night's gig. No, not fiftieth marriage. Not even Terry can boast that number. It's his fiftieth birthday. He wants the group to be there, playing sing-along specials like 'Lester Leaps In' and 'Take the A Train' with everyone joining in the chorus. What night? Saturday, last one of the month. Is that OK? So I can take that as a yes? Great. *Great.* No, it won't be a fancy affair, or rather it doesn't require tiara and crown jewels, though Terry and his latest like to dress up a bit. But the rest of our group can be relied on to lower the tone. Wait till you see Al's idea of casual. No, I've no idea who else will make the cut but Terry has a wide circle of those he likes to call friends. He moves in mysterious ways. As you probably realise. *Slight Pause.*

We'll probably find the Lord Lieutenant lurking in a shady corner while he shares a plate of canapés with Liver-Lips Louie. What, you've never heard of Liver-Lips Louie? He's one of the gangsters in *Guys and Dolls*. Now tell me you've never seen *Guys and Dolls*! If you haven't you should go to the bottom of the class. It's the greatest musical ever. Liver-Lips is a small-time crook, along with Rusty Charlie, Society Max, Benny Southstreet, Harry the Horse, and Nicely Nicely Johnson. I feel I know them all intimately. I should, I've seen both film and the stage version more times than Jeffrey Archer's gone straight. Unlike him, they won't do you any harm but they sing wonderfully. Watch out for Big Juley, though. He's from Chicago. Men like Big Juley are not to be tangled with. Archer could take his correspondence course. *Pause.*

Peter Cadogan? Oh, yes, he'll be at the party, all right. Unless of course something better keeps him away. *Pause.*

Are you still considering his suggestion about *As You Like It?* No, I've not changed *my* mind. No more of the Alleyn Players for me. I ask because – and I hope this doesn't seem like tales out of school – the other day I learnt from the woman who lives below you – Mrs Halstead, no Christian name – that our Mr Cadogan has invited *her* to audition for the part of Rosalind. *Slight Pause.*

Yes, I understand what you're saying. Competition sharpens you up. *Slight pause.* So you know? Who told you, if I'm allowed to ask, her or him? Oh, both. Well, I have to say that it seems pretty odd to me, even if not to you. *Why?* Because as she herself admitted, Cadogan doesn't even know she can act. *Pause.*

I found out when she appeared in the library, not the kind of place I'd associate her with. She was wanting to brush up her Shakespeare. Another good musical, that, by the way. Interesting, when you think about it. The Europeans go in for operatic Shakespeare, *Otello, Lady Macbeth of Mtsensk*, whereas the Americans prefer musicals: *The Boys from Syracuse, Kiss Me Kate, West Side Story.* Would you say this provides irrefutable evidence that late monopoly capitalism has as part of its project the trivialising of art or might you wish to argue for an essentially democratic impulse in recuperating such art for popular consumption. You may turn over and begin. No? *Slight pause.*

Not interesting? *Slight pause.*

Right, leave the room. *Pause.*

Anyway, she was obviously more than a bit taken aback by Cadogan's suggestion, even though I'm pretty sure she didn't know that Rosalind is the lead part. *Pause.*

Yes, I admit, I did vaguely suggest that Audrey might be more suited to her talents. I also admit that I was a bit hacked off by her attitude. *Pause.*

Oh, I see, she's told you all about it. *Pause.* Well, yes, it's true, she deigned to pay me a visit, but I was given the very distinct impression that with her arrival at the front desk I ought to drop my pitchfork, take the straw from my mouth, and put myself at the services of Lady Bountiful. Yes, I know, we *are* a service, but that doesn't make us menials. Besides, I'd say she's not much more familiar with the writings of the Bard than I am with the law of Tort.

Right, nuff said. *Slight Pause*

How's life in the new flat? Oh, good. Yes, you are lucky to have shops on your doorstep, and that garden, too. One thing I'll say for Frank, he gets hold of some ace property. You may quote me. *Pause.*

Well, if I don't see you before, here's to party night. I'll drop round, shall I, about eight o'clock? I suggest we take a taxi. I don't want to drive. How far is it? Oh, three or four miles from town centre, not more. Terry likes to think of himself as at the heart of rural England. Squire Marsden and his Rustic Music. Cow bells and brass serpents. You'll see. Apart from the lack of nearby mountains Misty Manuel would feel entirely at home. *Pause.*

I'm really pleased you can come. *Slight pause.*

Take care. *Pause.*

'Bye, then. *Long pause.*

brrrrrrrr …"

"How not to handle a telephone conversation, eh, Baw," he said as he put the receiver down. "And it's too late to seek advice from Blossom Dearie."

14

"Hey, did you see the programme last night?"

He brought his newly poured coffee over to his desk and, with Josie's eager eyes on him, slumped into his chair.

"I made Mark watch. He doesn't usually like talking heads on telly. But he stuck with it. We both thought he came across really well."

"It" had been an interview in a late-night Arts Programme, a face-to-face between the Presenter and James Padgett which lasted all of ten minutes. Like so many people, Josie seemed to believe that the appearance on TV of someone she knew, no matter how fleeting or in how trivial a context, not only reflected a faint glory on her as well as giving her a kind of proprietorial interest in that person, and by implication an insight into their nature, it more importantly enhanced the worth of both viewer and viewed. Claiming to have met such a person added cubits to your stature at dinner-table or in pub conversation. It wasn't even as though the person had to be in any way attractive or clever or knowledgeable or well connected or even *interesting*. A complete nonentity would do, although having been on telly meant that the person no longer counted as a nonentity. "You know that man who was on the gardening programme last night – the one talking about how to mulch your cobbles?" Probably nobody had seen the programme, which went out on a minority channel at 3 a.m. But still, attention was guaranteed. "I know him. He used to live three streets way from my Auntie Doris." "*Really.*" And the person modestly offering this astounding claim would note a new look of respect in the eyes of fellow-diners.

Weird. Especially as he couldn't imagine who in Josie's circle of friends would be interested in learning that the James Padgett who had been interviewed on the late night *Arts Talk* was a writer she'd recently met, that, as she was almost certainly keen to reveal, she owned a signed copy of one of his books, and that he had impressed her as being, you know, quite human. Almost ordinary. But then, of course, they'd *all* be interested. Josie knew someone who was on the telly. How about that?

"What did *you* think? I mean, you're his friend."

101

"Not friend." Balancing his mug on a pile of publishers' catalogues, he undid his briefcase, began to lift out the papers he'd brought away from yesterday's meeting. But seeing that Josie expected more, he said, "We were students together, but we were never friends. Not enemies, either. Ships that pass in the night. From the day we got our degrees until his visit we'd not even been in touch." How to let her down gently? "Though, yes, I've read most of what he's written and, yes, I thought what he had to say was interesting. On the few occasions he was allowed to get a word in."

"I know what you mean." Josie nodded vigorously. "Mark said he thought that Presenter was a pr— ." She pushed her fingers against her lips in suppressed glee.

"Prick would be my word, too."

"He did go on rather."

"He always does. That's why I rarely bother to watch his show. But as you say, our man came across pretty well. I enjoyed the moment when he got that fat fraud to admit he'd never 'actually' read Henry Green. 'Actually!' As though he'd read him 'virtually' ... "

But Josie was pursuing her own line of thought. "I'll want to see the film, won't you? I said to Mark, well, that's one we can't miss. He's even promised to read the book, so he can show off to all his friends when the film version appears."

"*If* it appears. From all I hear, a good many planned adaptations fall by the wayside."

He was wondering whether Helen had seen the programme. Could he use that as a pretext to phone her? Texting wouldn't do. He wanted to hear her voice, imagined her lips moving, the tilt of her chin, the casual, unselfconscious flick of her fingers as she lifted the fringe of her hair clear of her eyebrows ... Try to do better than last time, avoid the unfunny attempts at comedy, the cod professorial tone, all those things that made only too evident how rarely he could believe himself to be at ease with her.

No, leave it. If she wanted to get in touch she knew how to do it. Since asking her to the party – and that was over a week ago – he'd heard nothing from her. Busy, perhaps, with college life and settling into her new flat ... Perhaps.

"Sorry," he said, aware that Josie, having spoken, was waiting for him to reply.

"I said I'm sure it will," she told him. "The film. Be made. I have faith in him."

Then, noting Geoff's mildly sceptical smile, she added, with a kind of judicious gravity, "What he said about fiction being more satisfactory than life. You know, making sure that it all comes out right in the end. That really made me think. I know he meant it as a joke, but in a way it's true."

"The best jokes are." Forcing himself to concentrate on what she was saying, he picked up his coffee, took a sip. "And yes, he's right. But then, as he himself acknowledged, he's invented the people he writes about."

Preparing to leave the room, Josie said, "So he can decide what will happen to them?"

"More or less."

"Whereas in life things go wrong that you can't explain or predict."

Suddenly her words were tinged with sadness, her earlier, chirpy cheerfulness quite gone. He was alert to Josie's shifts of moods. How upset she'd been when, at least a year ago, she'd told them about a distant relative, a man she admitted she scarcely knew, who had been diagnosed with terminal cancer just as he and his recently-acquired wife were about to move into their new house. "They had their future plans all worked out. It doesn't seem fair." Her eyes had been full of tears.

Now, though, she said, "I mean you can never really understand people, can you? Even the ones you know best can do something that seems … "

She left the sentence unfinished. Perhaps she and her fiancé had quarrelled.

And as if to confirm it, she said, "I only found out last night that Mark prefers going abroad for his holidays. He calls people who stay in England 'Ourgaters'. I asked him what he meant and he said, well, there's Margate and Ramsgate and Southgate, and all the people who go to them and places like them deserve to be called Ourgaters." She spoke in a rush, paused, then said, "I asked him what was wrong with the English seaside and he said, 'Too many English.'"

Not much of a quarrel. "So that's Skegness done for," Geoff said, laughing. "Ah, well, Josie, there's nowt so queer as folk."

She turned to him, her smile partly restored. "My grandfather used to say that."

"Thanks for putting me with the greybeards." But as her mouth opened in abashed apology, he held up both hands in submission.

"Only joking."

He gulped down the rest of his coffee. "But that County Hall meeting yesterday wasn't much fun, I can tell you. Colleen, you and I need to get together to discuss what came up because there are implications for us all." Seeing her look of alarm, he added, "No, not redundancy notices, don't worry. And your exhibition is safe."

"So I should hope," Josie said emphatically. "If they knew the work I've put into that … "

"They don't," he said. "But they will when they get their invitations. I'm looking forward to seeing what you've come up with."

For the past months Josie had been putting together a photographic exhibition of old Longford, a project in which she took great pride. Now nearing completion, it was due to have its opening at the library in three weeks' time.

"But we'll have to put up with more cutbacks, I'm afraid. The shutters have come down good and proper on new stock. At this rate libraries will get brownie points for managing without any books. 'Ah, I see your shelves are quite bare, Cousins. Splendid, splendid. Precisely what we wanted. Expect a knighthood in the New Year honours list.'"

Josie shook her head in concern. "I'd better get out to front desk," she said, "while we still have books to check in and out."

She left, pulling the door shut behind her.

But a moment later she reopened it to say, "Oh, by the way. Someone left a message for you while you were at County Hall. She seemed disappointed you weren't here."

As on a previous occasion, hope flared. Helen?

" She'd come to return a book of Shakespeare's you'd lent her."

As on the previous occasion, hope died. "Mrs Halstead?"

"If you say so." Josie indicated the brown, used envelope on his desk, stapled shut. "I had to give her a piece of paper, *and* lend her a biro, *and* find this envelope for her."

"Good to know that libraries are still of some use," he said as he ripped open the envelope.

The message was brief. *Sorry to have missed you. Another time, perhaps? Verity Halstead.*

Another time? What did she mean by that? One more dame playing you for a sucker, Marlowe. But at least he now knew her Christian name. Verity. Verity and Charles. Meet the Halsteads.

It gave him an idea.

* * *

"Hello, is that Mrs Halstead? This is Geoff Cousins. *Slight pause.* Your local friendly librarian, remember. Yes, I was hoping you would. Oh, I'm fine. *Slight pause.*

Sorry I was away from my desk when you called in yesterday. Unfortunately, I had to be at an all-day meeting in Nottingham. An especially unfortunate meeting for those in attendance. Oh, cuts, cuts, cuts. Too depressing to talk about. *Slight Pause.* Anyway, Josie – Josie Rycroft – gave me your message. Yes, she is a friendly person. I'll pass on your compliment.

I'm phoning to ask whether you and your husband would be interested in a talk that's coming up soon at the library – next week, in fact. Part of our Cultural Events programme. No, it's not as daunting as it sounds. The speaker is a university lecturer called Potts. Don Potts. He'll be talking about Radicals at War with, I think, some new information about a local brigade that fought in Spain in the 1930s. You mean it sounds fascinating as in thank you but I'd rather have earache? Oh, good, well, if you're *sure* you'd like to come I'll reserve a couple of seats for you. I don't suppose the clamour for places will be intense, but it's better to be prepared. *Slight pause.*

The talk starts at 7. 00 pm so allowing for a few questions you'll be out by 8.30 at the latest. Good, that's excellent. I look forward to seeing you both Wednesday week. Goodbye."

Damn, he thought, I never asked her what she made of *As You Like It*. Well, it can wait until next Wednesday.

15

She came on her own.

Because he was up at the front, attending to Don Potts' few requirements – water jug, glass and overhead projector – he could do no more than lift a hand in recognition as she took a seat, unsmilingly, near the back of the sparsely filled room.

Arthur Stanchard was for once in the front row, and after the talk was over it was Arthur who asked the first question, though it took him some time to get there. Arthur wished it to be known that both during and after the war there had been a considerable number of local communists who were an active part of the progressive movement trying to push England onward from or even against its feudalistic instincts. Had the lecturer properly considered the influence of genuine radicalism in shaping post-war attitudes?

Potts thought he had but said cheerfully he was always willing to learn from men and women of Arthur's generation. Because, Arthur said, overriding Potts' words, younger people should know that this radicalism extended to all areas of life. It wasn't just a bunch of 'raving left-wing loonies' as the gutter press liked to call them, who wanted change. He could remember being told by an older woman friend of his that socials organised by the Nottingham East Branch of the Communist League were the only ones where you could hear traditional jazz and watch two men kissing. Now, what had Potts to say about that?

"Impressive," Potts said, smiling amiably. "One in the eye for Uncle Joe. Given that he thought jazz was decadent and gays unspeakable."

"He should have come over here," Arthur said imperturbably. "Got a taste of proper freedom." The pronunciation of 'over' to rhyme with 'hover' added to his laconicism and drew laughter from the small audience. "Anyway," he said, turning to throw a glance over those in the rows behind him before facing back to Potts, "it's a reminder that once, and not so long ago as all that, we had a real socialist movement in this country. Not like the bleddy lot now bringing disgrace on our movement."

One or two nods from those sitting further back.

"Would anyone like to take issue with Arthur? What about those he calls 'younger people', do you agree with him?" But Geoff knew that no one would rise to the bait. The few in the audience younger than himself were almost certainly Potts' own students – several had been taking notes during his talk; the rest was made up of stalwarts who attended Library lectures whatever the subject and to whom he always felt grateful simply for their being present, however awful the weather. They might always ask the same questions, but gratitude for their readiness or anyway determination to speak outweighed irritation. Gratitude even extended to the man who now rose to enquire whether the speaker was aware that, according to legend, an illegitimate son of Shakespeare was buried in an unmarked grave in the town's parish church? He wasn't? In that case, he might like to accept an inscribed copy of the small book the speaker had written on the subject.

Potts indicated he'd be delighted to accept a copy of *Whose Bones Are These?*

With that, Geoff could bring the evening to a close. A scattering of applause, and as he thanked Potts yet again, Arthur and several others came up to suggest the lecturer might like to continue the conversation at a local pub. "Where I'll hope to join you once I'm done with setting the room to rights," Geoff said, shaking Potts' hand, before turning away.

Verity Halstead was still in her place, the grey coat buttoned to her throat, one black-trousered leg crossed over the other, staring without apparent interest at her hands, which rested in her lap.

"Did you enjoy that?"

Only slowly did she raise her eyes to meet his enquiring gaze. Then, as though challenging him, she said, "Did you?"

"Yes, I *did*." The emphasis was, he hoped, unmissable. Potts had spoken well on a subject that was well worth airing. "A shame there weren't more to hear him."

He became aware that Potts, Arthur and the others were now moving past them, one or two throwing curious glances in his direction and, more especially, at the elegant figure to whom he was talking, a stranger to them all.

Behind them, the green-overalled caretaker was noisily stacking chairs before even more noisily dragging them to the side of the room. Time's up, and some of us have got homes to go to.

She stood, unfolded herself rather, rising languidly, and, once upright, pushed her hands into the deep pockets of her coat. But she made no other move.

He stood aside so she could move past him to the exit. "I'm sorry your husband couldn't come."

"Charles wouldn't have been interested," she said without looking back. Then, as he opened the door for her, she passed through into the lobby, turned and looked enquiringly at him, the smile on her lips so faint it might not have been there.

"I'm off to meet the others at the King's Head. You'd be very welcome to join us."

She paused on the library's front step, as though considering his offer, turned up her collar against the night wind, and said, her eyes fixed on a spot over his right shoulder, "I don't like pubs."

On an impulse, he said, "The Black Cat then?"

"That," she said, "might be bearable."

And as they began to walk along the High Street, doing their best to avoid the cracked flagstones that showed under the street lamps' glare, she slipped an arm through his.

"I don't want to risk a fall," she said.

* * *

The first person he recognised as they stood in the crowded bar, trying to locate any available space, was, inevitably, Jade. She was leaning against the counter, a tall glass of dark-coloured liquid at her elbow, listening attentively to the youth who leant over her, staring into her eyes as he spoke. Something he said made Jade draw her head back in mock-astonishment, or so the movement suggested, and as she did so her eyes swivelled, focusing momentarily on Geoff, then the woman standing beside him. She looked away, then back, smiling, and only Geoff understood that the hand she raised in greeting, followed by a thumbs-up, was offered in ironic appreciation of her former lover's pulling power. After which she went back to being impressed by whatever words came from the youth drooping over her.

Verity followed Geoff as he located two free high stools, gesturing to her to sit or, rather, raise herself on one of them. He sat opposite and they waited in silence for someone to come and clear the clutter of glasses and bottles from the shelf by which they'd propped themselves.

Only when their drinks were in front of them, did she say, gazing into her glass of white wine before raising her eyes to meet his, "You're known here, then."

He looked around, then back to her. "Not really. Jade – the one with green hair – is about the only person I could put a name to."

"Is she a librarian?"

"Jade? God, no. She's a part-time jazz aficionado."

"Unusual, given her age."

"Jazz is for wrinklies?"

"Isn't it?"

He laughed, swallowed some Merlot. "Could be. I'm our group's youth policy. The bass player's a retired cop, Al, the guitarist, is an undertaker who's been around for ever, knows all the secrets of the graves, and our noble leader, Terry Marsden, will soon turn fifty."

"Yes," she said, "I know. We've been invited to the party he's throwing to celebrate his big occasion."

"Oh, good."

But the words were a formality. For a reason he wasn't prepared to inspect he didn't welcome the news.

"Don't worry," she said, as though reading his mind. "I doubt we'll be there. Charles doesn't much like parties."

"He was at the golf club thrash."

"Thrash?" She laughed. "Hardly the word I'd have used. Most of those present looked as though they were clients for your guitarist pal – in his daytime job." She paused, began to smile, opened her mouth as though to say something, then, as though deciding against, closed it again.

"A black undertaker, were you going to say? 'How suitable'? About as witty as asking a bassist how he fits the instrument under his chin."

She shook her head reprovingly, laid a hand on his sleeve, withdrew it instantly. "No. I was about to observe that your Mr Cadogan is very pressing, though I imagine you know that. He pressed Charles and me to join him at the golf club and now he's pressing us equally hard to accompany him to the Marsden bunfight 'Oh, *do* come. There are some people I'd *especially* like you to meet.' But I doubt Charles will agree. It's more night life than he's used to. Twice in one year? I don't think so." The shrug which dismissed the thought was without satiric intent.

So the invitation had come from Cadogan. He might have

guessed.

He said, "Would your husband's refusal prevent you going on your own?"

She gazed at him sardonically over her lifted glass. "I do that kind of thing, you mean. Leaving hubby at home while I venture out to hear dangerous subversive talk about socialism. But a party is rather different, isn't it? Soft lights and drinks. The dark corners of rooms. All set for the rumour mill."

He couldn't gauge her tone. Why the contempt, if that was what it was. And if not contempt, then what? Stifled anger? Boredom, even? Concealed petulance? Did she even know what she sounded like? She gave him the impression that what she said was calculated rather than impulsive, but he couldn't be sure. I don't want to risk a fall.

Taking his own risk, he asked, "Why should you care?"

At first she seemed about to reply to his question, then changed her mind and instead enquired, "You'll be in attendance. Guest or playing?"

"Both. Terry's expecting the group to add to the jollity of the occasion by laying down a few numbers."

"Accompanied?"

For a moment he misunderstood. Then, he said, equally indifferent, "I've invited your new neighbour along. Helen."

"Ah." She sat in silence, head lowered, studying the stem of the glass held in her beautifully manicured fingers.

He was wondering how much the expensive-looking rings she wore on her marriage finger cost, as she said, sighing dramatically, "Well, in that case if I *do* decide to be at the party, I shall have to work harder on my dear husband."

He let it go at that, deciding to change the conversation. "How about the Alleyn Players? Have you given any more thought to auditioning?"

She looked blankly at him. "Hasn't your friend told you. I did a trial reading and it was clear that I'd never make the grade. So Miss Birdlip – Helen – will be Rosalind. I rather think Cadogan has been round once or twice recently, offering private rehearsals." The smile was a glitter. "*If* I'm in the production I shall be reading the part of Phoebe. A shepherdess, so I gather, with pretensions to gentility. I rather think the director assumes it will be type casting." The words, so lightly uttered, were sharp as knives.

Sod Cadogan. Sod him twice over. Sod him for worming his way back into Helen's favours, and sod him for turning his attention on the woman now sitting opposite, who Geoff knew was watching him without seeming to do so, her slant look not expecting sympathy but not masking her sense of – of what? Frustration? Self-doubt? Or, he thought, taking a sudden, unanticipatable leap, one prompted by a sudden feeling of inexplicable sympathy for her, might this svelte-looking woman be an example of accidie, that condition which medieval churchmen, he had once read, identified and feared, the state of sloth, torpor, black despair, of malaise beyond hope of redemption? Melancholy. The Black Dog.

He tried to meet her gaze but it slid away from him. There was some unreachable or incalculable element in Verity Halstead, as though, he decided while he watched her half-turn to look around her, she wanted to guarantee for herself an invulnerable place to which she could retreat, yet feared that even there she would be followed.

Not that Cadogan would let Verity's state of mind bother him. She couldn't act, but she could play a part in his getting what he wanted, which was Helen.

Or was all this an act? And if so, why? What was she up to. Pretensions to gentility? A barrister's daughter hardly needed to *pretend*. Verity's way of speaking, her dress, her manner – her *name* – all bore the stamp of a genteel upbringing.

He said, "I don't see you as someone with pretensions."

"Spoken like a gentleman." She swung her gaze back to him. The glitter had gone and now her eyes were fixed unwaveringly on his. "I'm not about to share confidences," she said after a pause, one in which she appeared to consider her next words, "but I think you should know – you've probably guessed – that my education was a waste of time and money. Posh Girls' Academy, Finishing School in Switzerland, Preparing to be a Beautiful Lady." The smile was a down turn of her lips, more a grimace. "I ran away whenever I could, which was quite often."

A pause, while she held up her glass. "I want another," she said. "How about you?"

New, filled glasses in front of them, she seemed at first disinclined to say more. Then, having taken one, two mouthfuls, the words began to come, though her habitual one-speed delivery rarely changed. The overbearing father, the mother who had killed herself when she, Verity, was young, the brothers whom she scarcely knew, the wasted, angry years of private schooling, afterwards the changing, unchanging men, then the meeting with Charles, a school-chum of her oldest brother, marriage, and their life together, shifting every few years, sometimes more frequently, often abroad – Italy, South Africa and Uruguay were mentioned – or, as now, in England, but never settling anywhere for long. If this wasn't sharing confidences, then what was?

"By the way," she said, as she brought the narrative to a close, "I need you to understand that Charles is a good man. A kind man. I wouldn't want him to be hurt. *Ever*."

The emphasis, almost ferocity, with which she uttered the last word seemed as much directed at herself as at her listener. And with that, she slid off her stool, brushed invisible crumbs away from her green, cashmere jumper – or was that the gesture of someone more used to dealing with tobacco flakes – and allowed him to help her into her coat. The discreet scent of expensive perfume was as unsettling as the look she gave him when, turning, she said, "What I told you just now is for your ears only. You understand?"

Dumbly, he nodded, followed her to the door.

Just before he reached to open it for her, she said, "I was talking to your friend Helen the other day about a writer you apparently know. You were at university together."

"James Padgett?"

"She lent me a novel of his, *Masked Owl*. Have you read it?" And when he nodded that yes, he had, she said, "I rarely read novels. I think I lack what's called the required concentration span. But that one … " She broke off when the door was opened by a couple who held it for them as Geoff and she passed through, then waited to finish her sentence until they were outside, standing together on the pavement. "That novel," she said, "is, as they say, food for thought. Though not especially digestible."

"I'll have to reread it," he said, evading her look, "I don't remember much about it."

She rejected an offer to run her home. "I'll be fine by myself. Solitude's my friend. Unless, of course, you're intending to drop in on Helen. No? Well, in that case," she held out her hand. "We may meet at the Marsden mansion, though I somehow doubt it. If not, then who knows where. Or when."

And with that she turned and walked away.

For a moment he stood looking after her retreating figure, the moving silhouette outlined by hazy lamplight. So she'd read *Masked Owl*, had presumably been struck by Padgett's account of a woman who chose to more or less to destroy herself. Reaching the library car park, he bent to scoop his car key from the Fiat's exhaust, and, as he straightened up, found himself wishing that Helen hadn't lent her neighbour that particular novel. "Solitude's my friend." How much of what she said was encased in irony? He unlocked the driver's door, dropped into his seat.

Turning on the engine, he thought, why did she give me that account of her early years? That's the kind of information you share with people who are close to you, isn't it, and I barely know her. *Was* it sympathy she wanted? Understanding?

He steered his way out of the car park. To understand all is to forgive all. But he didn't think she was asking for forgiveness. And supposing she was, why should she think she was in need of it? Was it for something she had done or something she might do? Now that he was away from her, her disconcerting gaze, the steady, almost unrelenting manner in which she had unrolled her story, he was not so much intrigued as discomforted by her words. Something was wrong.

A few minutes later, as he turned into Ewing Avenue, he was still thinking about, puzzling over, the enigma that was Verity Halstead.

16

The studded door, with its ridiculous, fake-medieval iron hinges, was opened by a man, red-faced and rotund, stiff in black-and white and tails.

"We're here for the party," Geoff said.

"Indeed. Sir, Madam." The voice was as fake as the hinges. Rent-a-Domestic.

Geoff and Helen were directed to leave their outer wear in the designated rooms. "Gentlemen first left, ladies upstairs, madam, where you will find the room opposite your arrival on the landing requisite to your needs." The accompanying smirk suggested someone who enjoyed sending himself up.

The room into which Geoff stepped was meant to give the impression of a study. A table with inlaid red leather surface, scroll-top bureau, some high-backed chairs over which coats were thrown, bookcases with a few books and more by way of framed photographs, including black-and-white studies of fighter aeroplanes and warships, guns pointed upward. Above the bookcases were framed black-and-white prints of Hogarth's *Marriage à-la-Mode*.

A man Geoff didn't recognise was studying himself and his dark, immaculately cut suit in the large gilt mirror that hung over a mantelpiece of whitened stone. Left profile, right profile, straight on. Yup. Looking good. As he turned to face the new arrival, the man, patting his breast pocket, nodded unembarrassedly at Geoff, allowing himself a brief scrutiny of his tweed jacket and blue cords – "I'm with the band," Geoff almost said by way of justification – then held the door open for him, and, still without speaking, followed Geoff into the large square hall, where small clusters of mostly over-dressed men and women stood making conversation, though more were passing through glass doors to the right, from where a hubbub of voices came.

On his few previous visits he'd gone straight through to where, at the back of the large room, the group held their infrequent practice sessions, but now, waiting for Helen, Geoff looked around, took in the panelled walls on which hung the obligatory hunting scenes, a large stuffed fish in a glass case above the door on the far side from which a waitress – black dress, white collar, frilly apron and cuffs – now appeared, bearing a large silver tray of what had to be canapés. To the door's right was an elaborately-carved black wood chair above which loomed an oil panting of a man in a ruff. It was like a stage set for some country-house drama.

A woman's hand rested on his arm. "But where's the knight in armour when you need him?"

Without turning, he said, "Given the weekend off, I guess."

"Or waiting his turn in the tilt yard. Or maybe gone to the wars."

He did turn then, met the gleam of laughter, her lips apart, and had to fight off an impulse to lean forward and kiss her. "You look— " he was going to say beautiful, but amended it to "more than— "

And again he stopped.

"I'll take the words as read," she said, mischievously, watching him register the dark-blue dress with its high collar, the curve of her hips, then raising his eyes to the thin gold chain round her neck, those dark eyes, the fringe of hair … "Do I pass?"

He said, when he could speak, "Which wars, by the way?"

"The class wars, of course." She squeezed his arm. "Come on, let's see what lurks the other side of those glass doors."

He picked up his sax case and held the door open, catching a drift of her scent as she stepped beyond him.

"Geoff, over here."

Terry's call came from the far side of the already crowded room.

"His master's voice," he said to her. "Better see what he wants. I'll park the tenor and be right back." And in answer to her question, "A glass of Merlot, if they have it."

Pushing through the press of bodies to where the other musos stood, he found Al and Simon in crisply-ironed white shirts and pressed jeans while Terry was sporting the kind of sunset-and-turquoise blouse with high-waisted trousers that, as Simon said later, Edmundo Ross would have rejected as over the top.

"Soon as you're ready," Terry said, "we'll get the show on the road."

The hint of asperity in the concealed command caused Al to wink at Geoff. The beloved leader reprimanding some perceived lapse in punctuality. Well, well.

"He's a bit nervous," Simon whispered to Geoff. "It's his big night."

A moment later they were off on a fast-paced 'Perdido', which gave Geoff no chance to do more than nod his head in thanks as Helen placed a full glass of red wine by his feet before she retreated into the crowd.

Later in the set, though, as he looked for and located her where she stood among a group who were familiar from his days with the Alleyn Players, he realised that she was watching him, saw her eyes locked on his as he worked his way through a solo on 'Embraceable You', and, as she silently applauded his efforts – had she noticed the quote from Lester? – made her a small bow. Just for you, Helen.

There was no sign of Cadogan.

* * *

Getting on for the best part of an hour had gone by, during which time his glass had been repeatedly topped up by a man in sombrero, fake Mexican moustache, green frilly shirt and tight black trousers – one of several who seemed to be circulating among the guests, bottle in each hand – before they brought the set to a close and Geoff, who had seen Helen slip out of the room a few minutes earlier, unclipped his tenor, preparing to go in search of her.

But before he could move, Terry said, "Wait here lads. Need to get the formal part of the evening over and done with." And off he went.

Damn.

Or rather not. Because as Terry advanced on the glass doors, one of them opened and Helen appeared, glass in hand, and brought it over to Geoff.

"Merlot, my lord," she said, with a mock curtsey.

"Wish I had my own personal assistant," Simon said. "Now then, Geoff, manners. Aren't you going to introduce us?"

But Al was already holding out his huge hand. "Al Stocking, undertaker to the Quality. Saw you a while ago at one of or Wednesday gigs. I never forget a lovely face."

And then, when Helen had retrieved her hand from his, he jerked a thumb at the bass player. "Simon Colston, ex-cop. Used to sit in cars all day and night, chewing on beef burgers. Now he shins up hills. That's why he's lean as a whippet."

Helen looked mock-appraisingly at Simon, who drew in his stomach before saying, "What do you reckon, then?"

"Awesome." She was laughing.

"I reckon Al could do with losing some weight," Simon said, winking as he shook hands with her.

"Nah." Al patted his ample belly. "Keeps you fit enough, hauling bodies up and down stairs. You try marching across a graveyard with one of our teak specials, especially if it's got an eighteen-stone fatty inside."

"Shouldn't make such heavy coffins, then, should he, love?"

"Besides," Geoff said, "you don't carry the coffins. You've got pallbearers for that."

"True," Al said complacently. "But I feel for them. Especially when they've got a special on their shoulders. For them as don't fancy teak we have mahogany, and, top of the range, best-quality oak with brass handles." He paused, said dramatically, "We even had an order the other day for one with bolts and a padlock."

"To stop him escaping?" Helen asked.

Matching her smile, Al said, "He was a locksmith. His family thought it would be appropriate."

"Let's hope you don't ever have to bury a shipwright," Geoff said.

"Oh, he'd go down well enough."

"Like the pianist on the Titanic," Simon said, and they all laughed. Ah, the old ones are best.

"Still," Al was watching as people began to throng back into the room, "you hear some weird stories in my line of business. There was one about some poor sod whose doctor confirmed that he was proper dead. Into the coffin he goes and then six feet under, slate lid over him. Ten years later they lifted it up to pop in his missus and found a message, scratched on the underside. "Help me. I was asleep."

"Oh, I believe that," Simon said. "about as much as I believe that little green men are about to take over the planet."

Geoff exchanged smiles with Helen, watched, he knew, by the others. He felt suddenly, absurdly, happy.

But it couldn't last.

"Well," Al said, as Terry came briskly towards them, "May the bird of paradise fly up your nose."

"Geoff," Terry said, gripping his arm, "give us a blast on the horn, can you, mate. You know. Queen Mary Leaving Harbour."

Perhaps in his haste, Terry had seemingly not been aware of Helen's presence, though she, he noticed, looked briefly at him before she turned away.

Picking up his tenor, Geoff blew a long, wailing note, as near as he could get to a ship's siren, and the conversations and laughter of the now crowded room faded.

Cadogan emerged from the crowd.

Hands held aloft, like a goalkeeper fielding a long punt, he waited for the last of the talk to die before, smiling benignly around the company. He said, "Ladies and gentlemen, may I crave your indulgence for a few moments. Thank you."

From where he stood, slightly to the right behind Cadogan, Geoff could see all the faces now turned toward Cadogan, smiling, anticipatory, acquiescent. But where was the one face he wanted to see? Not visible. Either she'd manoeuvred herself to the back of the room or she'd slipped out.

He took a mouthful from his yet again replenished glass, and with it dismissed a moment of irrational panic.

And then, as Cadogan began to speak, it occurred to him that she'd escaped from the packed room because she couldn't bear to be in Cadogan's presence.

Not unwelcome, that thought. But if she didn't care about Cadogan, hearing what he had to say wouldn't hurt – wouldn't disturb her. Would it?

"Ladies and gentlemen, friends all," Cadogan began, "as I'm sure you're well aware, we are here to celebrate the fiftieth birthday of our friend, Terry Marsden, a man of many parts, though I regret to say he has not as yet deigned to accept any of those I've offered him in productions by the Alleyn Players."

Swivelling his head to glance about the guests, he waited for the few titters to subside. Someone, a man, shouted, "What about Romeo?" which caused heads to turn, frowning, and some of those at the front to turn to each other, eyebrows raised.

But Cadogan was unfazed. "I fear Terry may regard himself as a little too old for so youthful a part. Though," the smile was elastic in its blandness, "he does seem to have the enviable trick of preserving his youthful good looks." Again some laughter, this time more hesitant. "However, to spare his blushes, as well as to obey his injunction to be brief, I intend to say only that I speak for all present in claiming that to know him is a privilege. Terry Marsden is a very special friend."

"Hear, Hear." "Good old, Terry."

"And," Cadogan continued, once more indicating the need for silence, "as he has begged me not to list his good deeds for charity, nor his many accomplishments and successes, I shall mention only one. His achievement in snaring his lovely wife, Lorette."

Cries, though muted by respectful consideration, of "Jolly good," "Well, done, Terry," and "Lucky boy."

"And so I ask that you raise your glasses not merely to our host on reaching this landmark birthday, but to his and Lorette's continuing happiness."

Glasses were raised, Al struck an F major, and they sang 'Happy Birthday to You.'

"And now pray silence for our host."

Having said which, Cadogan vacated his place in front of the musicians and sauntered off to become a member of the public, while Terry unwound his arm from Lorette, with whom he'd stood on the edge of the crowd while listening to the solicitor's words, came forward, thanked everyone for helping to make this a really great occasion, one he and he knew Lorette would always remember, and announced that after performing a number that carried a special message from him to his wife, the quartet would lay down a few more from their songbook before taking a short break, after which they'd play on until all the coaches turned into pumpkins or they were carried out legless, whichever came first.

"OK lads?" Terry bent to the keys and began a long, Erroll Garner-like introduction which eventually modulated into 'There'll Never Be Another You'.

* * *

One of the advantages of playing for social occasions like the present, or, as the group's business card said, *Balls, Weddings and Bar-Mitzvahs*, was that the people who supplied the music were to all intents invisible to those they were entertaining. People might take notice of the music, but they mostly blanked out the musicians. This meant that while the revellers didn't see you, you could keep an eye on them. In Terry's large room, therefore, Geoff could glance around while he played and observe how intently Moira Albert, still trim enough to fit into that green gown which came out once year, was gazing into the eyes of Jack Hateley, who ran a gymnasium, as they talked together, foreheads almost touching, while Moira's husband, Dennis, owner of the town's largest trattoria, and rumoured, despite his girth which the white suit he was in did nothing to hide, to be something of a bed-hopper, had his arm round the waist of the unknown woman – or was she manager of one of the High Street off-licences? – who was flaunting her allure, in black dress with shiny black stockings and black, high-heeled shoes, as Dennis moved her towards the back of the room, nodding as he went to a woman who was looking scornfully (or was it ferociously?) at him, and who was, wasn't she, the wife of that antique-dealer whose business was always about to go bust, though it never did, who, white-haired and lanky, was looming over Jim Potts, improbably of this company, especially as Potts was in his customary uniform of brown cord jacket and crumpled jeans, which was drawing the attention of Molly Chetwynd, the rather large, florid wife of James Chetwynd, local historian and bore unparalleled, who in another corner stood talking to Jim's partner, Stephen Hunter, natty in dark blue suit, while at his back Rupert Airedale, an English teacher who fancied himself as a poet and whose long pony tail hung over the back of his mustard-yellow sports coat, was trying to impress Gabby Houston with, at a guess, a roll-call of impossibly tiny magazines where he'd recently published, although much as Gabby, a successful florist batting her false eyelashes at Airedale, enjoyed flirting – patting the poet's arm, pushing her cleavage up close – he had as much chance of succeeding with her as he did of landing the laureateship. Because Gabby was a happily married woman, and as her husband happened to be Al, to mess with her was to risk finding yourself in one of his coffins, a lead-lined special decked out with funeral wreaths supplied by Gabriella Houston, Florist.

Rupert, Geoff thought, if I were you, I'd back off.

As though he had received Geoff's message – proof, could it be, of the morphic resonance argued for by that other Rupert, Sheldrake wasn't he called? – the poet did just that. He fluttered his hand at Gabby and stepped away. And his making his way from the room seemed to act as a signal for others to do likewise.

Almost alone, Lorette remained at her post. Though by the time, ten minutes later, Terry hammered the final chord of 'I Cover the Waterfront' into position, she, too, had left.

"Right, lads," Terry said. "Take a breather. If anyone wants more we'll supply, Bop till we drop, eh. But I rather think the evening's winding down."

Unclipping his tenor and staggering slightly as he moved to lay it in its open case – too much wine, he thought, which didn't stop him from reaching for and then draining the glass that had stood by his feet – Geoff went in search of Helen.

Where was she?

He'd not caught sight of her since before Cadogan began his speech, and as the room thinned and then emptied during their set, he'd become aware that she wasn't among those who listening to the music.

He couldn't blame her. Jazz, as she'd admitted, wasn't her music of choice.

He went out to the panelled hall but she wasn't there.

Perhaps she'd gone in search of food.

But no, there was no sign of her in the large, black-and-white tiled floor kitchen.

Nor, as a glance was enough to tell him, was she in the study where he'd left his coat and where now several men, none of whom he recognised, were searching for their own coats, preparing for home.

Over by the front door, Terry, his arm around Lorette's waist, was receiving thanks for the party from those taking their leave: lovely occasion, such a charming house, wonderful catering... blah-di-blah.

But no Helen.

And then it happened.

The vast front door was opened from the outside and two people stepped into the hall.

Helen leading was followed by Cadogan, a hand under her elbow, guiding her, on his face that unrufflable, insufferable, what's-all-the-fuss-about smile, the smile of a man who has *of course, what did you expect*, achieved one more triumph. Peter Cadogan. Victor Ludorum.

Geoff stared at Helen, who was looking across at him.

He turned, shouldered his way into the kitchen, stood on the stone-flagged floor trying to get his breath back.

"Have you eaten anything, love? You look as though you could do with something inside you."

A woman behind one of the long tables, dressed as a serving-wench, held up a plate. "What can I get you? Beef? Ham? There's still some salmon, look. Or are you a veggie?"

Behind him, a voice, *that* voice, said, "A wedge of Stilton, I think. One of the smaller plates will do, as long as it bears the Marsden Coat of Arms."

Pause. Then the voice came again, all surprise. "Geoff. Well, well. Sorry I've not had a chance for a chat this evening. Didn't even hear much of the music, I'm afraid. How are you?"

How am I? Terrific, of course. I've just seen the woman I love come into the house with you, you sod, so naturally I'm radiant with joy. Surprised you need to ask.

Keeping his back to Cadogan, he said, thickly, "Could be worse."

"Ah, jazzman's litotes." Cadogan's voice was smooth as a dagger sliding between his ribs. "I think I read somewhere that when Ken Colyer first heard Armstrong, he said, 'He'll do.'"

No reply.

Cadogan said, "Would you mind helping me to gather in some fodder for Miss Birdlip – Helen. The poor mite is feeling a trifle peckish."

And now he did turn, found himself staring at Cadogan's smile, meeting the challenge of those blue eyes.

"Why? Can't she get her own? Faint from exhaustion, is she? Too much night exercise."

He could hear the slurred words. *Egshorshun, Egsershise.*

Cadogan's smile broadened.

"'Scuse me," Geoff said.

He made to push past Cadogan, but a hand, surprisingly strong, gripped his shoulder. "Drunkenness may be forgiven," Cadogan said, "but not rudeness."

"Fuck off, and let go my arm."

Which Cadogan did with such abruptness that Geoff, in the act of pulling himself clear, fell, smacking his cheekbone on the tiled floor.

Getting slowly to his feet, he was aware of the looks on the faces of those few who had witnessed his fall. Contempt mingled with distaste. Another man who can't hold his liquor.

He pushed out into the hall and walked straight into Helen.

"Geoff."

Her eyes registered concern, alarm, and maybe contrition, even, he thought guilt. "What's happened? You've cut your cheek."

She made to put a finger to his cheekbone but he knocked her hand away. "Ask Cadogan," he said.

Then he lurched back to the quartet.

* * *

Later, much later it felt, though no more than twenty minutes could have passed between his exchange with Cadogan and now, he sat beside her in the taxi bearing them away from the party, his tenor case on the seat between them, her face averted as she stared into the unremarkable dark.

He caught her reflection in the glass, saw that her eyes, when not shut, were heavy-lidded, avoiding all possible contact with his gaze.

Eventually, he made himself speak. "I was surprised you waited," he said, his voice, though subdued, loud enough to carry over the night music the cab driver had switched on as soon as they'd climbed into the taxi.

His cheekbone throbbed, his head ached, his throat was dry, his eyes sore. Too much drink. Too much misery. Some party.

"What else was I supposed to do?" she said, her words barely carrying, her head still averted.

"You could have got a lift with someone else. I wouldn't have blamed you."

He spoke softly, not wanting the driver to be witness to his humiliation.

Silence. Perhaps she hadn't heard.

"Helen, I'm sorry. I was drunk."

Further silence.

More loudly now, aware of the driver's eyes studying his in the rear mirror, but no longer caring, he said, "Whatever goes on between you and Cadogan is none of my business."

She did speak then, though she was still turned away and he wasn't sure of her words.

"Sorry, I couldn't hear."

She swung to face him, her eyes sparking fury. "I said, dead right it isn't."

"But ... "

"But *what?*"

Helpless in the face of such anger, he said, "Nothing. No, nothing."

Again she murmured words he didn't at first catch, and when, humbly, he asked her to repeat them, she said, spacing the words as though speaking to a backward child, "*You are a fool.*"

And those were her last words until the taxi drew up outside Hutton Lodge.

Before she got out, she insisted he take money for her share of the cab fare – a ten-pound note was pressed into his hand – said, with a kind of bitter relish, "Well, thanks for *half* a good evening," and was gone.

As they pulled away, the turbaned driver, looking into his mirror, winked and said, "Don't let it get to you, mate. There's plenty more fish in the sea, innit."

"Not nowadays," Geoff said, trying to make a joke of the driver's remark. Don't let him know you're suffering. "Depleted fish stocks. North Sea, Med., the Atlantic, all overfished."

But the driver wasn't to be deflected. "Want to try further off, then. Thailand."

They were now on the High Street, and Geoff decided he wanted to clear his head. "I can walk from here," he said.

"What, to Thailand?"

Waiting until the taxi had turned and headed back for the town centre, Geoff picked up his case and began to tramp the empty streets, past shuttered shop fronts, then down a long tree-lined road to the roundabout that would lead him to Ewing Avenue.

Morosely slamming his feet down, taking savage pleasure in the jolts of pain to his bruised cheekbone, his thoughts keeping pace with his tread, he muttered, "*Blo*ody fool, *blo*ody fool, *blo*ody fool." And then, unable to keep out the thought that he most feared, knew would do him most harm, brought it up. What *was* she doing skulking in the dark with Cadogan. He heard Cadogan's voice, its complacent purr. "The poor mite." What did *that* signify?

He saw in the nick of time he was about to tread in a heap of dogshit and, as he stepped round it, thought, how appropriate, then, no, you're in it, right up to the oxters, Cousins. Because Cadogan is back, big time. He must be.

And yet for all that, Helen hadn't left with him. Oughtn't that to console him. Couldn't he take comfort from the fact that she'd waited for Geoff to finish the group's last, short set, had sat on as the room finally emptied, had uttered civilised goodnights to Simon and Al, as well as Al's wife, Gabby, thanked Terry and Lorette for the party, had to all intents and purposes behaved like the perfect guest, had even seemed, perhaps, to all those, including the musos, unaware of the minor fracas in the kitchen, as though Geoff was her partner, and not merely for the evening.

Was there comfort in all that? No, not a scintilla. Forget it. She'd come to the party with him, good manners required her to leave with him. But her brooding silence in the taxi, broken only by those few, savage words, made all too plain what she thought of him. Cousins, you are, to be frank, an abject prick, a self-pitying, drunken mess. Now, get out of my life.

As he stood in his porch, fumbling for his keys, he noticed a sheet of notepaper wedged in his letter box. Pulling it free before he opened his door, he felt Baw brush against his legs then bound ahead of him, making straight for the kitchen.

Blinking in the hall light, Geoff read the brief message.

Sorry we couldn't get to the party but would welcome an early opportunity to talk. V.

V? Verity. What did *she* want?

17

What she wanted was reassurance.

Not that she told him as much when, early on Sunday evening, with the worst of his hangover behind him, he decided to phone her.

By then he'd given up hope of a reply to the brief text message he'd sent Helen as soon as he fell out of bed that morning, head thumping, dry-mouthed, racked with contrition and a feeling that the look he'd seen in her eyes as she stepped from the taxi signalled not merely contempt but a determination to have nothing more to do with this drunken, self-pitying prat.

v sorry 4 conduct last nite G (= grovel)X

Ha, bloody ha.

A long shower, some vigorous towelling, then, in the kitchen, a few moments of touching his toes while Baw looked sceptically on was followed by a brisk walk to the shops that helped to clear his head, though the almost overpowering sense that overnight the backs of his eyeballs had been brutally sandpapered, scraped, then dried by blow-lamp, didn't finally disappear until mid-afternoon.

He wondered what to say should Charles pick up the phone, but it was Verity who answered. Charles, she said – and it was the first thing she did – was away on business. Knowing Geoff would be at Terry's party, she'd slipped round with the note, and was grateful for his prompt answer. Yes, the Black Cat would do perfectly well. Tomorrow morning. 11 a.m.? Wasn't that early? Oh, well, yes, if he had a lunch-hour meeting then let it be 11 a.m. She was sorry to have missed the party but she didn't feel she could come without Charles. She hoped he'd enjoyed it. Anyway, she'd see him tomorrow, and thanks.

She broke the connection.

Standing by his desk, he played back their brief conversation. He had the impression her voice was less assured than usual, but perhaps she didn't enjoy using the telephone. Plenty, himself included, didn't.

* * *

An unlooked-for problem with the library's fire alarm system – it kept switching itself on and wouldn't be switched off – meant he was late in setting out to meet Verity, and when he arrived at the Black Cat he couldn't see her among the place's few customers. The regular lunchtime crowd would soon be arriving, but for now the bar or café or tea room or whatever it chose to be at this time of day was given over to a few young mothers with their pre-school children and, at one window seat, an elderly man who stared at length and without embarrassment at Geoff before returning to his newspaper.

She must have decided that he'd forgotten about their agreement and left, or for some reason had herself chosen not to turn up.

But then he realised that the woman sitting at a small table in a corner of the large room, half hidden behind a tall glass-fronted cabinet, had her hand raised in tentative greeting.

Feeling self-conscious, and somehow absurd, as though he was in the role of adulterous lover, he made himself call out a cheerful greeting as he threaded his way between tables of watching women until he could drop into the chair opposite her, while she looked at him attentively, but without speaking.

"Sorry to be running late," he said. Then, "More coffee?"

She shook her head, indicating the still full cup. "Well?"

The young woman who took his order for a double espresso having sauntered back to the bar, he was free to give his attention to Verity.

"Well, yes, quite a surprise."

Her hair, close-cropped, had been dyed coppery red, making her face look more angular and, somehow, hungrier, the eyes deeper-set, the lightly carmined lips thinner, vulpine almost. Beneath the grey coat, unbuttoned and eased off the shoulder, she was wearing, he noticed, a black T-shirt and denim skirt and, below its inconsiderable length, green stockings.

She stared at him, white, even teeth gripping her lower lip, before she opened her mouth to speak.

"You don't think it's an improvement."

She wasn't asking him.

He waited until his coffee was set down in front of him, then said, "Different, certainly."

He lifted his cup, lowered it again, watching her prop an elbow on the arm of her chair and, averting her head, lower her chin into the supporting hand, before he said, aiming for humour, "I'm not sure

I'm the best person to advise on coiffure. If that's why you wanted to meet me."

For some moments she kept her head turned away but suddenly swung back to stare at him. "I need some reassurance in my life," she said, her voice low, vibrant – with anger, was it?

Excuse me, he wanted to ask her. How did we get here? But he said nothing. The words, her fierce, unyielding look, shook him. No exchange of pleasantries, no talk of the weather, no idle chat. Cut straight to the chase.

He resisted an impulse to look round, to discover whether her remark had been overheard and, if so, whether they were now being studied by the curious, or more than curious. Instead, he concentrated on meeting her gaze while trying to think how best to answer. He knew what he *wanted* to say. Why me? I hardly know you. But looking at her unwavering stare, the challenge it posed, he thought, perhaps that's the point. Not so much the kindness as the candour of strangers is what she's after. Friends, if she has any, might prevaricate, might feel the need to soften truth to half-lies. She expects me to be honest. But how to do that without hurting her?

Because the truth was that if not mutton dressed up as lamb – she was still a comparatively young, good-looking woman – she'd made herself look as though trying for a role she herself knew she couldn't sustain. Not Rosalind, for sure. Not Phoebe, either. And certainly not Audrey. Audrey would have gone for mascara, false eyelashes, gloss lipstick, and been bottle-blonde. No, a mere glance at that face and the cropped, dyed hair of the woman now staring bleakly at him, and he thought, what you look *most* like is a recovering drug addict. And immediately another thought came to mind. Act your age.

As though the words had transferred to her own consciousness, she said, "It was the young woman who gave me the idea. The one you called a jazz fan."

"Jade? You mean *Jade* suggested you dye your hair?"

"Of course not. We've never spoken." The words came with harsh urgency. Would I ever speak to such a person, she meant. "I only saw her on that occasion you and I were here. But … " She paused, raised a hand, ran fingers through her hair. "If she could dye her hair, why shouldn't I try?"

Because you're older and you come from a different class and … How many reasons do you want? But the angry glitter in her eyes suggested that she'd already anticipated his unspoken answer.

"Anyway, don't think I did it on the off-chance of being bedded by a jazz musician." The laugh was more a snort.

"Ah, yes," he said, stung, "jazz musicians. Lowest of the low. I'm told that even breathing the same air carries the risk of a nasty disease."

She seemed about to answer, then changed her mind, shrugged, lowered her gaze.

He drank his coffee. "Why not ask Charles whether *he* likes what you've done to yourself?"

If she noticed the implicit brutality of those words, she gave no indication of having done so. "Charles doesn't know," she said flatly. "I told you, he's away on business." She paused. "For a week." Another pause. "He won't be back until Wednesday evening." Where was this leading?

For a mad moment he wondered whether, after all, she was letting him know that the coast was clear for a spot of adultery. No thank you.

He said, "Ah, I think I get it. You worry that he won't approve so you need to have a few favourable comments to throw in his face when he tells you what he thinks. 'Well, that nice Mr Cousins tells me it suits me. Shame about his taste in music, but in other respects I trust his judgement.' That kind of thing."

"Charles won't mind. I sometimes think he doesn't give a damn about how I look or what I get up to."

Was it an invitation? But another glance reassured him and at the same time left him feeling deflated. She wasn't calling him to her bed. Instead, she was putting him to the test. Despite what you may think and for all his appearance of caring, my husband is indifferent to me. Call me a liar? Well, yes, he thought, you are a liar. After all, you were the one who not long ago told me how good a man he is and that he's not to be hurt. *Ever*.

He said, "I can't believe Charles won't be better than me – than anyone – at providing the … the reassurance you say you need." Absurd even mouthing such a word. What was this, a session in amateur psychotherapy? Counselling over coffee?

He glanced at his watch. "I'll have to be getting back," he said. Then, aware that the look in her eyes had changed to one of nearalarm – why, because she feared she'd gone too far, that at some moment he might confront Charles with his wife's complaints, if that's what they were? – he said, trying to tamp down the brusqueness in his voice, the irritation he felt, "Sorry I was late arriving, but we've problems at the library. Which is why I have to leave now."

He stood, put down money for his coffee, knew his smile must look more like a grimace. "A librarian's life is not a happy one. Tra-la."

But the attempt at humour was wasted on her.

"Whereas my life is heaven on earth." Her gaze was directed away, as though she was addressing the world at large, though she spoke so softly he wasn't at first certain he'd caught her words.

He knew he was meant to sit down again, ask what was wrong. But he couldn't. I'm the wrong sex for sisterly soul-baring, he wanted to say. He remembered a line from a poem he'd read as a teenager. "There's sorority among whores." No doubt there was. But that wasn't it. He realised that he still didn't trust her. Too much of what she did, what she said, seemed an act. He finished putting on his coat. "No doubt we'll be in touch," he said, raised a hand in farewell, and, made uncomfortable by what he saw in her eyes, left her sitting over her untouched coffee.

No, he thought, walking back to the library, as he did so swerving to avoid the queue of women waiting at a bus stop, shopping bags dangling from their fingers or hugged to their chests as they stared along the High Street; he raised a hand to the Asian ironmonger who stood in the doorway of his hardware shop and who waved cheerfully back – "Morning, you well?" – no, I don't like her and I don't trust her.

Which could, he admitted, be another way of saying that he couldn't begin to fathom her. What on earth made her take the scissors to her hair, then dye it that ridiculous red colour? What was she up to? So much about her performance was hint, innuendo, the withheld remark that might be the trickery of an accomplished actor pretending to gaucheness. And if it *was* the token of someone troubled literally beyond words, what for God's sake was he supposed to do? He hardly knew the woman.

He paused before crossing the road that led into the library's car park. She's playing some game or other, he thought, one whose rules I don't know. Was anything so banal as an unhappy or dull marriage behind her behaviour? Or did she at all events want him to think that? Whatever she might want from him, it wasn't to do with sex. She wasn't any more attracted to him than he to her. Of that, he was certain.

Stepping into the road, he had to jump quickly back to avoid a van that careened towards him, horn blaring. Come on, Cousins, keep your eyes open for God's sake. And keep your wits about you or they'll be spread out on the road.

He stood, getting his breath back before he risked another attempt to cross. If only he could talk to Helen about her neighbour. Fat chance. He couldn't talk to Helen about *anything*. He'd blown that once and for all. You're the one in need of reassurance, Cousins. Oh no, you're not. You've got all the reassurance you need. You've put yourself off limits as far as Miss Birdlip is concerned, and there's no way back. Of that, there's no doubt. Be assured, my friend, be doubly assured, she's finished with you.

Turned into the library forecourt, he thought, well back to the world I do understand, one of slashed book budgets, of the LUCG and Grouser Gleat, of duff fire alarms, of Josie and Colleen, of pleasures and cares a world away from the parish of rich, idle women.

But pushing through the library's front door he made himself recall that, when Verity Halstead momentarily lifted her head in acknowledgement of his farewell, her eyes were full of tears.

18

He was still thinking about her as he chopped onion and green pepper for his evening meal. Her almost ravaged look, the hunger in her eyes, and then the unshed tears – but for what? Would she wash out the dye from her before her husband next saw her? Or was he used to her – her what? Mood swings? Cliché. But she had looked gaunt. Frightened? Was she in fear of Charles? Unlikely. What then?

"Never go without proper food," he said to Baw, who was watching him from her basket. The cat ducked her head and began to wash her front. "And," he added, pointing his kitchen knife at her, "don't let yourself go."

It was another of his mother's admonishments, delivered when he'd helped her settle into the ground-floor flat she moved to following his father's unexpected and fatal heart attack. After getting on for forty years of what the old man called the treadmill, and was in fact a career on the lower slopes of business management, they'd decided to move from their Midlands home to a bungalow in Hove, a move which, given that they'd few friends south of London, Geoff privately thought a mistake. But they were elated at what they were doing. "Our big adventure, it feels as though we're beginning life all over again," his father said when Geoff phoned to ask how they were settling in, his words full of an almost vehement enthusiasm.

Which made it all the harder when, less than a week later, his mother telephoned early one evening from hospital, her voice thick with tears, to tell Geoff that his dad was dead. The old man had keeled over that afternoon while doing nothing more energetic than running his mower over a short strip of grass that scarcely qualified to be called a lawn.

"Don't let yourself go." She was speaking as much to herself as to him, aware, as she told her son, that she was no longer "of use to anyone."

"Yes you are," he replied, listing the work she did for the church, counting off on his fingers the abacus of recurrent activities out of which her days were strung together. But she brushed his words aside. "That's not what I mean," she said, "None of those things depend on me."

The words caught at his heart. He took independence as a matter of course, but for his mother living on her own meant being cut adrift from the meshing of lives to which she was so accustomed that, without her husband's presence, she felt lost in an ocean of indifference.

The last time he'd been down to see her, she made him take away with him a cake she'd baked together with a carrier bag full of tins of soup he knew he'd push to the back of a cupboard and forget. "Don't let yourself go." Deciding for her sake to act the hapless son, he chose not to remind her that he always looked forward to the preparation of his evening meal, that he enjoyed eating what he'd cooked, relished the opportunity to try out new dishes. On such occasions he did let himself go, though not in the sense she meant. He tried out recipes he found in books and magazines, and over the years gained the confidence to prepare ones of his own invention. Having nobody else's taste to consult, he was free to experiment with, for example, pepsicum stewed with neck of lamb (a class-A mistake), roast chicken with a combined stuffing of prune, greengage and apricot (not bad at all) and, a culinary masterpiece, trout packed with sliced almonds, pimento and Gruyère, swaddled in strips of bacon, then baked for twenty minutes in a blisteringly hot oven.

He'd recently been given a recipe for fried tripe, and though he wasn't entirely convinced the friend who'd written it out for him wasn't pulling his leg, had decided that it was worth a try. He wouldn't let himself go.

Now, dicing carrots and quartering field mushrooms from his favourite greengrocer's, he thought how much undeclared, even unintended meaning, that phrase held. Don't let yourself go. Look after your health. But also, be sure to keep up appearances, don't let yourself – and family – down in the eyes of the world. And therefore no emotional excesses, no giving in to temptations of the heart.

Involuntarily, he touched a finger against his cheekbone. It was still tender from Saturday night's contact with the kitchen tiles of Marsdon Grange, though this morning's mirror inspection had revealed that the small cut was all but faded. Scars upon my heart but not upon my face. In a day or two the abrasions would be gone.

"I tripped over the cat," he'd told Colleen when, peering at his face earlier that morning, she raised an enquiring eyebrow. Oh, I believe you, her look said. But she'd said nothing, merely tutted. Such

133

clumsiness. Verity Halstead had said nothing. But then, beyond seeking to know how he responded to what she'd done to her hair, Verity Halstead had barely registered his presence.

He hoiked the olive oil from the cupboard where it lurked with other bottles and measured out for the frying pan he used instead of a wok two good tablespoonfuls and an extra splash for luck. Were her tears genuine? And if so, what did they signify? Wounded pride at his presumed indifference to her? Rage at her act of disfigurement, if that was how she saw it? Exquisite embarrassment at having given herself away, if indeed she thought she had? Or had she had an unfortunate encounter with someone else? Cadogan? Yes, why not Cadogan.

He lit the gas under the pan, adjusted the heat and waited for the oil to smoke. Or was it a dramatic performance, one intended for his eyes only?

And at that point the phone rang.

"Sod it." He turned down the gas. "Yes?"

"Geoff Cousins?" Unmistakable, that voice.

"What do *you* want."

"I need to talk to you. Urgently."

"I'm about to eat."

"I'll drop round in about an hour's time. OK?"

He could have said, he *should* have said, no, it's not OK. To tell you the truth, I very much don't want to see your smug, arrogant face. I'd like you to stay away from me. And here's a thought. Instead of dropping round why not drop dead?

"OK," he said, and went back to his stir-fry.

* * *

Cadogan sat opposite Geoff at the kitchen table.

"I'll come straight to the point," he said, pushing aside the glass of white wine that had been poured for him.

What point might that be? That Helen and Cadogan were now an item and Geoff had better steer well clear? That after his display of teenage petulance on Saturday night, Helen wanted no more to do with him and that he, Cadogan, had come as her emissary in order to tell him as much.

"It's about Verity. Mrs Halstead."

Well, well. "*Verity? What* about her?"

"You saw her today."

And if I did, what's that to do with you. "It was at her request." Why did that sound as if he was on the defensive. He forced himself to look at Cadogan. Yes, he was getting jowlier, though the eyes were as clear blue as ever. As to the man's grey tweed jacket, pale green shirt with generously knotted wool maroon tie, it was the couth outfit of a solicitor.

"I must tell you that she phoned me this afternoon. In some distress."

I must tell you. What was this, some sort of official warning? But he held his peace.

"How well do you know her?"

"Not well, although I don't see it's any business of yours."

"Her husband is one of my clients."

You mean you touted for his favours, he wanted to retort. Instead, trying to control the trembling of his hand as he lifted his glass – don't lose your temper, Cousins, he said, "So? What's that to me? Unless" – the thought, ridiculous thought it was, came to him – "unless you think I'm having an affair with Charles Halstead's wife. Or he does. If so, you both can rest easy. She's no more interested in me than I am in her."

Cadogan's smile flashed on and off. "I quite believe you." Meaning, no woman of her class would give a berk like you the time of day.

Geoff drank some wine. "Frankly, my dear," he said, "I don't give a damn." Then, clearing his throat as he leant back in his chair, he said, "To coin a phrase, what's this all about, officer?"

Cadogan said, "I don't know whether you're aware that Mrs Halstead is – I need to put this carefully – is a somewhat unstable person."

"The thought had crossed my mind."

Cadogan looked hard at Geoff. "This isn't a matter to be taken lightly. As a friend of both of them and as a professional adviser to Charles, I inevitably take an interest in what happens to either."

"Is that why you offered her a part in your next mega-production?"

Cadogan rode straight over the attempted sarcasm. "Yes," he said, "that's *exactly* why I offered her a part. I want to help her."

"By suggesting she might have a talent that's invisible to the naked eye, hers included. Not much of a success, if I may say so. She knew she couldn't handle it."

"No. She *thought* she couldn't. Verity lacks self confidence."

"Which she more than makes up for in self-knowledge."

But as he spoke, he knew that might not be the truth. Not willing to pursue that thought, he said, "Now I come to think of it, it strikes me that her 'distress,' as you call it, could well be down to the pressure you put on her."

"Don't talk poppycock," Cadogan said, evenly.

Poppycock? Where did he get that word from? Was Cadogan doing his best to needle him? If so, he was succeeding. Take a deep breath, Cousins, before speaking.

He took the breath and, as he exhaled, said, "You haven't explained why she … why, after seeing me, Verity Halstead got in touch with you. And you've yet to explain why your need to see me is so urgent it can't wait for another day."

Cadogan leant forward, elbows on table. Here comes the straight talking. "She was afraid she'd offended you."

Geoff laughed out loud. "*Afraid*? *Verity*? Of offending *me*? Now why don't I believe that."

"Perhaps because you're not a very imaginative person."

That stung. He put down his glass without drinking from it. "And now you're going to tell me that I don't understand people."

Cadogan smiled, said, "It follows."

"And *you*, I suppose, do."

He could feel his face redden, the blood beating behind his bruise, saw Cadogan study it, the twitch of amusement on his lips, and was suddenly, violently, angry. "Of course, of course. Peter Cadogan. Balm for the troubled soul. A rock to cling to in stormy times. That's why Verity turned to you, is it? Dear Peter, you alone can see into my heart, can see the desert of emptiness watered only by a fountain of blood."

Cadogan got to his feet. "Now you're being ridiculous. Well, I've said my piece."

Geoff too was standing. "You've not said *anything*. Anything, that is, to explain why you're here, now, this evening."

Cadogan looked long and hard at him. "If you'll stop shouting I'm willing to try again."

Had he been shouting?

"Sorry," he said, then cursed himself for apologising, for being caught again on the defensive, as though he had some guilt to expiate. Mutely, he gestured to the chair Cadogan had vacated and watched as the other man dropped back into it. Pouring himself another glass of wine and settling into his own chair, he said, "As we say in the music world, let's take it from the top."

* * *

Two hours later, having closed the front door behind Cadogan, he retreated to his study where, with a final glass of wine on the floor beside him, he lay fully clothed on his bed, trying to absorb all he'd been told 'in confidence', so the solicitor insisted before beginning his revelations. Revelations? But they weren't so much sensational as squalid. No, that wasn't the right word. Pitiful was nearer the mark. Thinking back, he accepted that he'd not been sure whether to believe the Halstead woman's tale of barrister father and brothers-at-law, and that much beside had been mysterious. But now it was mostly explained, not least the need to be on the move, never to stay for long in any one place. There was something almost saintly about Charles' readiness to put up with a wife who, if Cadogan was to be believed, had been on more than one occasion saved from the consequences of her neurotic impulses only by her husband's interventions.

Correction. Her second husband. The first, present whereabouts unknown, had, according to Cadogan, done time for a number of offences, among them drug dealing and armed robbery, and was a very nasty bit of business. Verity, or Eve, as she was then called, had fallen foul of him when she ran away from foster parents in Swindon and ended up on London's streets. There, or rather in some café, she met a man older than herself, Trevor Lewis. With all too predictable consequences. So Cadogan said, sighing. Lewis gained her trust, offered her a roof over her head and, then, love. The usual story. A hasty marriage was followed by exploitation and some violence, though Cadogan didn't dwell on the details. Details were in fact altogether few – at least Cadogan chose not to reveal many – but in the end it seemed that Eve, as she still was, shopped her brutal husband. At his trial, Trevor Lewis tried to implicate her in all his activities and when that failed told her that once he was out he'd come after her. Hence, the constant changes of address and of her name. Probably not needed, but an understandable precaution, or so Verity felt.

And how did Charles fit into all this? Pure chance, Cadogan said. At about the time of Lewis's trial, Charles Halstead was in need of some office assistance for his London surveyor's business. During her time with Lewis, Eve, or Verity, as she had begun calling herself, had acquired typing and secretarial skills, she applied for and got the job, and romance followed. And no, Cadogan knew nothing more about this. His friendship with Charles only went back a very few years, to not long before the couple moved to Longford, but he not only liked Charles, he respected him as a 'good man', one who, he said sententiously, "is a lesson to us all, myself included".

"Charles. Monarch of all he surveys."

"If that's meant as a joke," Cadogan said, "I have to say I think it's in poor taste. Charles in no way tries to rule over his wife, and as for his work, I can tell you that he acts for the good of the country." With which pomposity, or anyway words made pompous by the way he uttered them, he finally drank down his wine, stood, and announced his intention of leaving his host to consider whether he shouldn't at least contact Verity Halstead to reassure her that he was in no sense offended by anything she had said or done that morning. "Her mind needs to be set at rest, as much for her husband's sake as for hers."

So that was that. Except. "You're not a very imaginative person." It still stung. How on earth was he supposed to understand Verity, or Eve, when she seemed endlessly to vary her roles? Not perhaps stir-crazy but with enough cunning, whether calculated or impulsive, to be a kind of shape-changer, someone whose identity had no more substance than a shadow. Or if not a shadow, then elusive, always out of reach, the story of her life as changeable as everything else about her.

The labyrinth of another's being. Where had he come across that phrase? He couldn't recall but, yes, he thought, I know what it means. Because at the hidden heart of the labyrinth lurks the minotaur, waiting to devour whoever reaches it. Verity. No, don't be melodramatic. Still, those eyes of hers are the eyes of someone dangerous. I'm not imagining *that*. But was she a danger to others or herself, or both? Charles obviously saw her as the one who needed to be protected from danger, and so, it now seemed, did Cadogan; but he himself wasn't so sure. What had she said of her husband? "Charles won't give a damn. He doesn't mind how I look or what I get up to." For a nano-second he had, hadn't he, wondered whether the words were an implicit invitation to him. If you want me, come and get me. But as quickly he knew that that wasn't it. She was declaring a wished-for independence from the husband who, if Cadogan was to be believed, deserved all honour for rescuing her from the misery of her earlier life.

So what to make of her bitter sarcasm. "My life is heaven on earth"? What did *that* mean? It couldn't imply that she was in some sort of domestic cage. On the contrary, as her attendance at Potts' talk surely made evident, she was free to come and go as she willed.

Willed, wilful, willing. There was, he felt certain, a reckless quality in her, one which had led her to do that extraordinary thing to her hair. Trivial enough in the scale of things, yes, but hinting, perhaps, at far more troubling possibilities. Was she capable of real self-harm? Did Charles sense anything desperate in her? He was closer to her than anyone. And yet he was prepared to leave her on his own while he pursued business which, Cadogan implied, was connected to government matters. He acts for the good of his country.

The claim, probably meant to impress, had startled Geoff. "Not armaments?"

Cadogan paused at the front door long enough to shake his head in denial of that enquiry. No, not armaments.

It gave Geoff the chance to ask a question he couldn't prevent himself from blurting out. "How are rehearsals going?"

Cadogan looked coldly at him. "At the moment they're on hold." His tall figure, as he made to leave, was framed in the open door. He said, over his shoulder, "Casting difficulties. One or two people have still to be persuaded."

Recalling those words as he mulled over all Cadogan had said, Geoff experienced a sudden lift of spirits. He swung his feet off the bed, reached for and drained his glass, and went over to his desk.

The phone rang for a long time before the receiver was picked up.

Geoff spoke into the silence. "Is that Verity? Verity Halstead? I'm sorry to be calling at this hour. It's Geoff Cousins … "

"Oh," she said. "Well, you can fuck off."

And the line went dead.

19

"Looks like your one and only's in again," Al said.

The third and final set was nearly done and Terry milking the applause for the three-course meal he'd made out of 'Tea for Two', when the guitarist leant across and, sotto voce, added, "She's got someone with her."

He didn't want to look, but dread as much as curiosity dragged his glance to where Al had motioned.

Yes, it was her all right, sitting at the same table she'd occupied that first time. And beside her? Dare he? He shifted his instant gaze to the figure beside her, and, after a second look, nearly whooped with relief.

No. *Not* Cadogan. *Whooooo.* Thank you, Janey Macpherson. The ginger-red bushy hair which Janey herself had once described, laughing, as "frutescent", the stocky frame, the outline of which he could see against the low lights thrown from the mirrored bar, even the black-frame no-messing spectacles perched on the tip of her snub nose, were all immediately recognisable. He could have raced across the room to hug her, not so much for what she was as for what she wasn't. Instead, he half-raised a hand, although between where he and they sat was the length of the low-lit room, and between them, too, some forty or fifty people, drinking as they listened to music which would soon come to its allotted end. Neither of the women looking toward the quartet gave any sign of having noticed his hesitant salutation.

Terry was now announcing the closing number. "Dedicated to our landlord, an original we call 'Stormin Norman.'" In other words, an up-tempo blues in C.

Two twelve bars intro., solos all round, four and out. Then straight into 'Satin Doll' while Terry did his spiel thanking the audience, identifying the instrumentalists, pleasure to see so many smiling faces, blah blah.

Don't let her leave, please, don't let her vanish before Norman calls time.

She didn't.

She was, however, already standing and about to put on her coat as, without waiting to pack away his tenor, he pushed through the crowd and approached her table.

"Well played," Janey said, as he came up to the two of them. "Or should I say 'well blown'?" She, too, was on her feet, smiling up at him.

"Either's fine by me. It's good to see you again."

"Likewise, I'm sure," Janey said, in passable imitation of stagey, shop-girl gentility. "And now you may tell me I haven't changed a bit in all these years."

"You haven't changed a bit in all these years."

Only then did Helen speak.

"It was Janey's idea," she said, addressing him but not letting her eyes rest on his.

Turning to her friend, Janey, laughing Janey, said, "Don't make it sound as though I dragged you here against your will. My idea it may have been, but you were nothing loath, ducks." Then, to Geoff, "But then where else do you go for a swinging Wednesday night out in Longford?"

"Where indeed?" He tried to match her mood, but Helen's silence, her avoidance of his gaze, was unnerving him. Look at me, look at me, please.

But she wouldn't, nor did she so much as glance at him when Norman hove into view, gathering up glasses and wishing customers goodnight as they made for the door, all professional bonhomie. "Now then, you lovely people, drink up. Plenty of spaces in the front bar, if you want to carry on for a while."

Geoff looked enquiringly at Helen who was looking at Janey. "I don't want to hang around," Helen said decisively. "A long day today, another tomorrow."

There sat down once a thing on Geoffrey's heart, so heavy. Trying to lift it, trying to speak as though Helen's words hadn't been a blow to the solar plexus, he said, "How about you, Janey? One for the road?"

As Janey hesitated, Helen said, "Don't bother about me. I can see myself home."

She turned to leave.

Sheer desperation forced him to say, "Did you get my message?"

She glanced back at him, her raised eyebrows registering the note of panic in his voice, nodded. "I didn't think it needed an answer," she said, her eyes meeting his for the briefest instant.

Then, turning to her friend. "Thanks for suggesting this evening, I enjoyed having the chance to chat."

And she was gone.

There had been no farewell for him.

* * *

As they entered the Black Cat, Janey said, conspiratorily, "I feel too old for this place." Under the heavy, now discarded waterproof, she was in the kind of clothes he always associated her with: polo-neck sweater and jeans, her red hair, now threaded with grey, still a mass of curls. But once they were seated at window stools, a table between them on which they could rest their drinks, she relaxed.

"And I suppose you think that an old fogey like me ought not to be here, either."

"No, not you." She reached over, patted his arm. "You're young, my sweet. Now, what shall we drink to?" she asked, as they clinked glasses.

"We could each make a silent wish."

"No. That's ducking out. Let's drink to the future."

"Is yours bright?"

"Oh, yes," Janey said, emphatically. "It is. It really is." And for the next few minutes she told him about how her work as commissioning editor for a science journal took her to interesting places to meet interesting people. "And in addition to paying the bills it puts money in my purse."

"Oh?"

"You mean, 'Oh', as in seeing that I'm the widow of a banker I can hardly be short of the readies."

"The thought had crossed my mind."

"Then let it go. The fact is, dear Geoff, that after Sandy's death I discovered he had rather more debts than I wotted of. I don't know how he ran them up and I don't want to know, but they were substantial. And then there were the medical bills." She emptied her glass, held it aloft to attract attention from one of the circling waiters. "I'm not saying I was destitute," she said, as their glasses were removed and fresh drinks ordered, "but the coffers weren't exactly brimming. Besides, as I was remarking to Helen earlier, why settle for old age when there's no need to. So, with a degree in chemistry in my dim and distant past, I contacted someone I knew in the university world and, hey presto." She clapped her hands. "This summer I'm off to São Paulo for a week, and come November" – cupping a hand to her ear – "I hear Delhi calling."

"November? Isn't that when Peter Cadogan is hoping to mount his play-reading."

"Do you *mount* a play-reading? It sounds a risky activity." But she interrupted her own laughter to say that she didn't know much about Cadogan's immediate plans. "Except that *As You Like It* is the play of choice. Since Helen's return." Two new, filled glasses appeared at their elbows. "I decided not to be involved with the production, hard though he pressed me. That's a joke, by the way. I don't think my thespian gifts have ever excited Mr C.'s interest. Nor, despite one brief attempt at a pass, have my physical attributes. But anyway my work keeps me busy enough and, to be honest, it's far more entertaining. As I also told Helen."

"And what did she say?"

"Not much. She seems a bit low. Perhaps work is getting her down." She paused, looked at him, as though seeking his view on the matter, then, when he said nothing, added, "Well, the remedy's in her own hands. Get out while she can. I told her that, too."

She clambered off her stool. "And now, dear heart, I need the loo."

While she was gone, he brooded over her words. *Was* work getting Helen down? He doubted it. The cause of her lowered spirits almost certainly lay elsewhere and almost certainly Cadogan was involved. Had seeing him again disturbed her more than she'd anticipated, had it knocked her off balance? If so, she might well decide to clear off. She'd done it before. "The remedy is in her own hands." Not in mine, then. He swallowed the mouthful of the house red he'd held in his mouth. It tasted bitter as gall.

Behind him a voice said, "Well, well, here we are again."

Tonight Jade's hair in the bar's low lights looked steel blue.

He forced a smile, which under her candid gaze slowly became genuine, and said, as he studied her, "Have you got another nose-stud?"

"Have you got another girlfriend? Every time you come in here it's with a different woman. I didn't have you down for a Lonely Hearts, Geoff, but I'm beginning to wonder. It's either that or what newspapers call the pursuit of perfection. Though they've usually got something else in mind."

"Like what?"

"Houses. Cars. Olympic Gold."

"Janey's an old friend."

"Aren't they all?"

"Hey, comments on the ageing process are out of order."

But her presence lifted his spirits. She was so unaffectedly friendly, so – he tried to think of the word – open, untarnished? Yuk. Try again. Try better. He glanced beyond her to where, at the bar counter, those he by now thought of as her crowd lounged, noted that the willowy youth he'd seen with her last time was in attendance, and said, "Are you sure they're old enough to be out after dark?"

"You know you're getting old when all the drinkers begin to look under age."

"Just what I was saying when we effected our ingress to this joint." Janey rejoined them, rolling her eyes in extravagant fashion. "You will please confirm that, Caruthers," she said, hoisting herself onto her stool.

"Glad to do so, m'dear. And, by the way, this is Jade. Jade, this is Janey."

They shook hands, and Jade said, "Well, I'd better get back to nursing the teenies. Nice to meet you, Janey. Look after this old codger, won't you," and she left them.

He said, "Jade is someone I bump into from time to time, usually here," and left it at that. Uncynical, was that what Jade was? Straight? What you saw was what you got. He followed her retreating figure as she swung with easy grace toward the bar and her friends, then turned back to his companion.

Raising her glass of spritzer, Janey looked quizzically at him but held her peace.

How best to bring her back to the subject of Peter Cadogan, he wondered, but he had no need. "Now where were we?" Janey said. "Oh, yes. The Persistence of Peter. I gather our local friendly director has begun to pester Helen about his forthcoming extravaganza. Without her taking the prime part his dream will be torn to tatters." She sipped from her glass. "I seem to be in thrall to alliteration," she said. "A deadly disease. See!"

"But not fatal," Geoff said. "As for Cadogan, he could always try another play."

"Out of the question. She must, she *must* be Rosalind." She clasped her hands in a parody of supplication.

"And?"

"And I don't think Helen's all that keen." The look she gave him had a measured attentiveness about it. Joking apart, it said. "All those years ago, I told you about him, didn't I."

"You told me his wife had left him."

"I did."

"But why did you ask me not to tell anyone where I'd heard it from?"

She looked quizzically at him. "Did you really not know?"

And when he shook his head, genuinely at a loss, she sighed, sad, "God, men are so stupid." Then, after a long pause, during which she gazed about her, she turned back to him, asked, "Is this difficult?"

Meeting her gaze, he realised how easily he felt himself to have slipped back into warm familiarity with this woman, whom he'd not seen for the best part of ten years, but whose gift for friendship was, he now again understood, a quality that unlike youth endured.

"Those are more or less the same words Helen used when she told me about her affair with Cadogan. 'Is this awkward?'"

"Well," Janey asked, "is it?"

At that moment, the bar's loudspeaker music, which until then had been subdued, at least where they sat, suddenly became a thunderous howl before once more subsiding to a level where they could talk without needing to bellow.

"Why should it be?" he asked her, and, laying a hand on his arm, she said, "Because everyone could see you were crazy about her. I mean, everyone involved in that production of – what was it."

"*Much Ado about Nothing.*"

"So it was. In the circumstances, rather an apposite title."

The music level briefly rose again.

"Apposite? In what way?" he asked, shouted rather, making the questions sound more belligerent then he intended.

She opened her mouth as if to shout back, then changed her mind, waited for the music to die down once more, and said, smiling apologetically, "Forget I said that. It was a cheap remark."

"From what Helen told me I gather for her it *was* much ado, though it meant precious little to him. A good actor, though. Helen, I mean. I had no idea what was going on. I had no idea … "

He bit off the words but Jane, guessing, said, "You had no idea of what he was putting her through."

He nodded, said, "No, although later it made sense. 'Kill Claudio.'"

He was remembering the look in her eyes on the night of the public reading, a memory that for so long had lain dormant. "My god, she meant *that* all right."

"Now why do I get the feeling that you're about to tell me something I may want to hear?" Janey said.

"It came back to me quite recently," Geoff said. "Claudio was going to be read by a man whose name I can't now recall, Jeremy something or other. But when it came to the performance he'd gone down with flu, so Cadogan had to read Claudio's lines. I should have twigged, but of course I didn't know what had been going on between Helen and him."

"You didn't?"

"All right, I had my suspicions. But … "

Janey tilted her glass, drank the last of her spritzer. "But you hoped they were wrong. Just think, duckie. If you'd taken her at her word you might have done us all a favour."

She got down from her stool, said "I must go."

Outside, as they prepared to head in their separate directions, he said, "I don't like Cadogan, in fact I can't stand him … "

"But?"

He watched as a few people got off a bus that had pulled up at a nearby stop, then followed their movements as they began to walk away into the dark.

Eventually, he said, "He seems to have behaved quite well to someone else I know. Another woman."

She shrugged, indifferent, and he realised there was no point in trying to tell her about Verity Halstead, not here, not now. He wondered if Helen had mentioned Verity to her friend, decided it would keep.

Janey said, "Perhaps I'll say a prayer for him. But it will be a short one. And now I'm off. No," as he began the offer of walking her home, "I'm fine. I'm not far off the High Street. You should come up and see me some time." Then, standing on tip-toe to plant a kiss on his cheek, she said, "Love without hope, Geoff. Be the bird-catcher."

He looked down at her, tried to read the expression in her eyes, but the gleam of street lights on her spectacles made it impossible.

"What?"

"Robert Graves. The Players did a poetry reading one Valentine's Day, after you'd left us. I was allowed to read that. I suppose Cadogan thought I couldn't do much harm to so short a poem. Highly recommended."

She reached out, squeezed his arm, said, "Good to see you again," turned and began to walk away.

"Janey," he called after her and as she turned back, he said, "What did you mean in there" – gesturing with his head to the bar they'd just left – "that remark about men being so stupid?"

She walked back to him. Putting a hand on his arm, she said, "Guess." She tilted her head back, peered at him in the dark, and when he said nothing, added, "I'd have thought it obvious enough."

"No? No idea? Well, then, I'll have to spell it out. When I told you that Cadogan's wife had left him I was trying to give you a warning and at the same time get you to make a move."

"What? For his wife?"

The way she gripped his arm suggested genuine exasperation. "No, you damned idiot. I was hoping, though goodness knows why, that what I'd had to tell you might, just might, be the spur you needed, might push you into contacting Helen. Don't you *see?*"

From behind them there came a gush of sound and light barred the pavement as the bar door opened and people came stumbling about them, heading off into the night.

"But why was I not to mention your name?"

"*Geoff.*" It was almost a yell of anger, or frustration, maybe. "You really *are* ... well, if not stupid, then I don't know what the word is."

A couple, arm in arm, skirted them as they stood there, looking curiously at them as they edged past, then lengthened their strides as they moved away and the dark surrounded them.

Giving his arm a shake, Janey said, "If Helen knew I'd told you she'd have taken it for granted I was trying to push you into her arms. 'Go on. Boy, the enemy is out of sight.'"

"Would that have mattered?"

"She's as perverse as you are. She'd quite likely have resented my interference. Refused to see you. *I* don't know."

She let go his arm, said, "The best-laid plans ... " once more turned her back on him, and moved rapidly away.

20

Two evenings later, Friday, when he returned from the library, he found among the bills and junk mail in his post box an envelope addressed to him in writing he didn't recognise. The card inside read, *In case you don't have Robert Graves on your shelves I've copied out his poem.* Below this, were four lines of verse. "Love without hope" the poet advised, before going on to instance a young bird-catcher, obviously in love with an unattainable woman, a squire's daughter, to whom the youth paid elaborate homage by doffing his hat as she rode by on what would have been a glossy horse, and whose airy gesture inadvertently released larks he had captured and was concealing in his hat. The freed larks, the poet wrote, flew "singing about her head" as she passed the young man by.

Beneath the poem was written, "Do you have a tall hat? If not, buy one forthwith." It was signed *Janey M.*

He read the lines twice, then put the card down on the table and fed Baw. Glancing at the card again as he poured himself a glass of wine, he tried but failed to understand why Janey had sent him the poem. Bird-catcher? Did that mean someone the wrong side of the law? A stap-me-vitals, merry-as-we-go rogue? Forget it it. He was no bird-catcher, any more than Helen was a squire's daughter.

But then he realised he knew virtually nothing about Helen's background. Parents? Family circumstances? Upbringing? No, nothing. That she came from somewhere down south and had been a student at Sussex University was the sum total of his knowledge of Helen Birdlip's life before they met during rehearsals for *Much Ado*. For all he knew to the contrary, she *might* be a squire's daughter. She didn't sound like one, she didn't behave like one ...

– Or did her being drawn to Cadogan suggest a preference for someone who came from a well-heeled background? Cadogan made no secret of his public-school education, nor of his undergraduate career at Oxford, dropping anecdotes of mild dissolution into the conversation at post-rehearsal drinks while he stood rounds in what he was pleased to call a neighbouring hostelry – which, as rehearsals were held in the civic hall behind the Three Tuns, meant the front bar of Norman's pub. There Cadogan would recall days and, more particularly, nights, featuring the ingestion of wacky baccy and various combinations of alcoholic drink, while cast members smirked, sniggered or smiled as occasion and Cadogan's questing eye seemed to demand. Did Janey know more about Helen's preferences – her prejudices – than he did? Of course, of course. Was that what she'd meant when she had remarked in the Black Cat that men were so stupid? In which case she might be wanting him to read the poem as a covert warning or at least challenge. Love from afar, but getting near to Helen won't be easy. You're not in her class.

Yes, well, thanks for that. Very helpful. Most reassuring. Meanwhile, there was food to be prepared. Geoff rinsed free of salt the sliced aubergine he'd put to drain in a colander before leaving that morning. But as he arranged the softened rounds of vegetable on a baking tray, he realised he'd quite forgotten to buy the black olives and mozzarella he needed to complete the dish.

He took the tray, shook its contents into the waste-bin, poured himself another glass of wine, and, in savage mood, picked up the phone. "Paolo's Pizza Palace," the automated voice said. "We're busy right now, but you can leave your order with us or try again in a while. We're open from … " He slammed the phone down. Love without hope. What did the words remind him of?

Oh, yes. Some lines from a poem he'd read as an undergraduate. "Work without hope draws nectar in a sieve, And hope without an object cannot live." Though he liked poetry – it's soon over but the memory lingers on, he'd told a friend when explaining why he usually had some anthology or other on the go – he'd never thought of himself as much of a student of literature, preferring to play and listen to music rather than sit for hours in the university library, a heap of books at his elbow. Which was odd, given that he was drawn to a career as librarian. But if anyone pointed this out, his reply was always the same: he was looking for a job he didn't have to take home with him, never mind the money, that he'd be happy to earn enough to pay for his needs and his reeds. Because what he cared most about was the tenor sax and even if he never became a more than competent musician – and he doubted he would – competence would, he persuaded himself, be sufficient. He might even be able to make a living as a jobbing sideman, and that would suit him down to the ground. So all in all, and speaking frankly, and having weighed the odds and considered his options, he couldn't wait to call time on his undergraduate years, when, degree in pocket, he'd be qualified for work which would leave him free to devote his nights to music. OK? The desire to be a writer – well, write a novel – had come suddenly and was as suddenly gone. Loss of Helen and lack of talent had seen to that. The love of music was a constant.

Coleridge was the exception to his general rule that any writer recommended by officialdom – that is, his tutors – was well worth ignoring. Some students made a pretence of finding their way unaided through the dark forests of critical theory into which they were lured or, more often, frog-marched – well, most of the theorists were French – though among themselves the majority sent it up. "There's a remarkable porosity about this pint," or "Have you correctly interpellated that roll-up", or "I'm about to deconstruct this sandwich with a view to totalising its gender-inflected basis"; but in class they mouthed the terms with sufficient gravity to allay suspicion. He couldn't be bothered. Let Derrida, or whoever was that week's favoured theoretician, have his swink to him resarved.

But with Coleridge it was different. He read the poetry, loved it. At one wild moment he even considered writing a jazz-rock opera based on 'Kubla Khan' though he got no further than an opening chorus in which, against a background of ethereal, Getz-like blues, Abyssinian maids sang of an acid trip to subterranean grottoes. As if. It was then he accepted that he'd never be a great musician. At first, he decided to be cast down by this, but soon exchanged depression for a sense of liberation, free now from impossible dreams. Competence was what he was after. Competence would be sufficient. Coleridge apparently began to doubt his own gifts as soon as he read Wordsworth. Yes, well, hear Lester or the Hawk and throw away your sax. Hope without an object cannot live.

Except, he thought now, rootling about in the fridge for anything that might serve to make an evening meal, this wasn't how it worked, or at least wasn't how it ought to work. Sweep off the tall hat, rejoice in unconstrained gesture, Cousins, allow yourself to celebrate true carelessness by means of the non-prudential flourish. Oh, yes, yes indeedy, if I may quote Fats.

But peeling off the tin-foil from an opened tin of anchovies lurking obscurely in the fridge's interior, grey-brown membranous strips sunk among gelatinous oil, he remembered how in the pub Helen had said, "It was Jenny's idea," as though to forestall any hope he might have had that her presence meant forgiveness, let alone a readiness to see him again, let alone an *interest* in seeing him again.

Binning the anchovies, he glanced at his watch. Should he try again for a takeaway?

Once more he lifted the phone.

Or ... Oh, hell, why not? Be the bird-catcher.

"Hi. Helen? This is Geoff. Geoff Cousins. *Pause.*

I was hoping for a quick chat but guess you're not in, so I'll try some other ...

Oh, hi. You *are* in. *Pause.*

I haven't interrupted you, have I? Oh, sorry. *Slight pause.*

Look, I'll make this brief. I was wondering if you fancied a coffee tomorrow, if you're free at lunchtime. Why? Well, I have library duties, attending the opening of a home-grown exhibition until then and you'll probably be busy in the morning ... *Pause.* Do you mean why might you be busy or why might we meet for coffee? If it's the latter, let's say because I feel I still owe you an apology for my drunken performance at Terry Marsden's bash. *Pause.*

Well, that's nice of you, but I can't forget what a pig I was. And I'm guessing – to judge from the other evening – you haven't forgotten, either. No, *of course* I don't blame you. Absolutely not. *Pause.*

But ...

No, I realise college must be making heavy demands. In fact Janey wondered whether work might be getting you down. Yes, we went for a quick drink. She's a good friend, isn't she? She's even sent me a poem. By Robert Graves. *Pause.* About impossible dreams, at least I think that's what it's about. But look, if this is difficult scrub round it. It's no big deal. *Slight pause.*

Yes, agreed. Nottingham's better for weekend shopping, wider choice and all that. Still, if you do change your mind I'll be leaving the library at one o'clock. I'll probably make my way to the Black Cat. No, I shan't hang around, a coffee, a sandwich, and if you haven't shown up by half one I'll be off.

Anyway. Right. *Slight pause.*

If I don't see you enjoy your weekend. Thanks, yes, I'll do my best. 'Bye."

No hope there, then. Off to Nottingham. Well, we know how to deconstruct *that*. Spending the weekend in bed with bloody Cadogan.

21

Josie and Colleen were waiting for him, dressed in what his mother would have called their best bibs and tuckers.

"No Mark?" he asked Josie, looking round and seeing no sign of her fiancé.

Josie shook her head sorrowfully.

"His company have sent him chasing off to Gloucester. Apparently there's some problem with a computer system he helped install and getting that sorted out can't wait."

"I'm sorry," Geoff said, meaning it.

This, after all, was Josie's big day. The photographic exhibition of old Longford, which, with his and especially Colleen's help, she had put up in the room set aside for lectures and 'events' and which he now walked admiringly round, was to be opened by the mayor, and already a small group of local historians and regular library users had gathered, chief among them Arthur Stanchard, who was leaning forward intent on hearing the hesitant interview between Josie and a reporter from the *Longford Free Trader*, a young man in an Italian four-button suit remarkable for its creased bagginess. Its wearer, to judge from his barely stifled yawns and bloodshot eyes, didn't seem in much better shape.

Nor did his questions.

Had Josie always been interested in history?

Er, yes.

The reporter nodded, seemingly at a loss for anything further to ask. He stared mournfully about him, then back to Josie, slowly swivelling his head as though taking care not to alert his brain to the possibility of further revenge for the alcohol abuse it had recently suffered.

After some moments of this, his movements slowed to a complete standstill. He closed his eyes, opened them, blinked, as though trying to remember where, or perhaps who, he was, and, staring dumbly at a photograph of a horse-drawn tram, asked Josie whether she thought modern transport was an improvement on those days.

"What days?"

Her counter-question did for him.

"Well, the days ... you know, before improvements."

Without bothering to reply to this, Josie suggested the reporter might like to be talked through the sequence of photographs that featured Longford Mill, whose canal-side, three-storey brick structure with the hundred-foot high chimney stack had for over a hundred years provided work for the town?

Guarding against the possibility of further brain damage, the reporter chose not to nod his acceptance. Josie beckoned Arthur Stanchard forward.

"Our expert," she told the reporter, spelling out Arthur's name and watching as the youth made an attempt to note it down.

Arthur provided a short history of the mill's origins, its glory days, its gradual decline, its eventual closure and the fact that its listed status alone prevented it from being demolished. He also threw in some remarks to the by now glassy-eyed reporter on the ideological strains imposed by a deterioration in management–worker relations in the mid-1950s which had contributed to the emergence of the monopoly capitalist state we now suffered under.

The reporter began to nod, then, as he winced in pain, plainly remembered why he shouldn't.

Another desperate scanning the display boards in the search for inspiration. Ah. How about this?

The photograph was of a substantial two-storey building with loading bay, outside the wide-flung doors of which workers in suits, many of them in caps, others sporting bowlers, lined up, two proudly holding aloft a Union banner.

"Don't recognise that," the reporter said.

"Because it don't exist," Arthur said grimly. "Not any longer. That was a factory as made boilers for industrial use, but it were closed down nigh on ten year ago."

The reporter's version of a smile suggested he knew why. "No one wanted boilers any longer."

Arthur shook his head. "Don't be thinking that, lad. That weren't the reason. There was still orders comin' in, but someone had other ideas for the place, hadn't they."

It wasn't so much a question as a statement, one loaded with dark knowledge. Arthur paused, smiling sardonically, and looked around at his auditors. Several of them were nodding their agreement. They knew what he meant.

Only one man standing towards the rear of the group looked less than sympathetic to Arthur's words. The scornful smile on Gerald Gleat's face was gradually replaced by a look of stiff-backed contempt directed, Geoff knew, at Arthur's shrewd assessment of the factory's last days, the explanation for its closure. Geoff could imagine what Gleat was thinking. Socialist claptrap, the sooner stifled the better.

But if Arthur was aware of Gleat's glowering presence, he gave no sign of being discomposed by it. Satisfied by the response of others, he spoke again. "One day it were a factory," he said, "next day it were shut. Sold off. Sixty men lost their livelihood. Now it's a swish housing complex. Executive style houses. Well, they would be, wouldn't they? 'The Leas'. Know it?"

At which point Gleat turned his back and forced his way through the assembled listeners before disappearing. No more radical propaganda for Mr Gleat.

The reporter, who was now beginning to show signs of life, thought he might know the whereabouts of 'The Leas'. "On the edge of town, near the old railway station? It's a gated community, isn't it? Indoor swimming pool, the lot."

"That's it," Arthur said grimly. "Lived in by those who cost us our jobs."

"Really? Who would that be?"

But before the reporter's question could be answered, Arthur lost his audience's attention. The blast of a car horn announced the arrival of the mayor, and everyone crowded to the library's front doors and watch the capped chauffeur who was holding open the back door of the long, black limousine.

"'Scuse me," the reporter croaked, shuffling toward the foyer as Councillor Moira Clewson, in powder-blue suit and chain of office, steered her substantial body through the door Geoff was holding wide open.

A scattering of applause greeted her entry. Then the usual flummery. Two or three press photographers, among whom Geoff recognised a man from Nottingham's daily, snapped her as she posed beside Josie and Colleen. After that, she agreed to be photographed pretending to study images of the High Street from the early years of the twentieth century, all showing whiskered, straw-hatted traders in ankle-length aprons, arms akimbo, filling their shop doorways, and one, carefully choreographed, of an errand boy cycling toward the camera, a large sack on his metal pannier round which he was forced to peer, his vision dangerously – comically? – impaired by the cap tilted almost over his eyes. The bold cursive scrawl at the bottom of the photograph identified him as *Bayley's (Grocer's) Boy, 1910.*

Councillor Clewson then made a short speech in which she congratulated the library on diversifying its approach to client satisfaction in challenging times, informed her audience that when she was young she rarely had an opportunity to put *her* nose into a book because her parents always impressed on her the need for girls to find work that didn't need all these high-falutin' educational ideas, gave it as her opinion that marriage was still the best way for a girl to find satisfaction in life, and was not to be shaken in her belief that what was wrong with the world today was that too many people got ideas above their station, the fault for which, they were free to infer, lay in books.

She then left, her exit monitored by reporters from the local TV station for whom the opening ceremony would merit the briefest of mentions in the evening's newscast.

"I thought what she said was quite ... interesting?" Josie, dressed in a plum-coloured skirt with acid green blouse, her hair specially done for the occasion, tried for diplomacy as people gathered round the table where soft drinks and bowls of peanuts were laid.

"Interesting? *Interesting?*" For once, Arthur, staring aghast at Josie, was virtually beyond words. When speech returned, he said, "You know what you were hearing from that bloody woman? Advance notice of this bloody council's intention to close down the libraries." He paused, gazed around.

Colleen, who was in the act of pulling a raincoat over sweater and black trousers before leaving, her morning task now done, placed a restraining hand on his arm.

"Don't let it worry you, Arthur. She won't harm us. She has to watch her back. Plenty on her own side can't stand her and, believe it or not, some of them quite like books."

Arthur looked at Colleen. "What do you reckon, then. Tories to save us from Clewson?"

"If necessary," Geoff said. He had been ushering invited guests from the building and, with most of them gone, was free join the other librarians. "Anyway, the budget's set for this year and come next election with luck her lot will get the heave-ho."

"Let's bloody hope so," Arthur said. Then he, too, left.

Turning to Josie, and rocking back on his heels as he clutched the lapels of his jacket, Geoff said, mock-pompous but meaning what he said, "And as for you, Miss Hathersage, you've done an excellent job, even if the lady mayor wasn't up to saying as much. A star is born. I foresee a future in exhibition work."

Blushing, Josie said, "I hope the press photographs come out properly. I'd like to send one to my parents."

"And one for Mark."

"Oh, he sees quite enough of me." Then, hand over mouth, she giggled.

* * *

At 12.45 Geoff went around, reminding the few members of the public still studying the exhibition that the library would be closing soon but that the photographs would be up for a further two weeks and as they left please be sure to record their comments on the forms they'd find in the lobby, comments he hoped would be favourable. "Help to keep our libraries open," he said, nodding to a couple as they made their way to the lobby.

A voice behind him asked, "Are you allowed to say that?"

The shock stilled him.

Then, daring to hope, he turned.

Eyebrow raised in mock-enquiry, the merest of smiles playing about her lips, Helen waited for him to speak.

For a moment he couldn't.

"Just going about my business, officer," he said at last. His heart had returned to its usual place. But his throat still felt in the grip of steel fingers.

"Should I wait for you outside or is it OK if I look around while you close up?"

It wasn't just his throat. Breathing itself was difficult. Silently, he gestured towards the display boards.

"We'll be done as soon as possible."

Aiming for casual utterance he sounded to himself like a malfunctioning speak-your-weight machine.

He noticed that Josie, gathering paper cups, was glancing curiously from one to the other of them. He took the cups from his assistant, crumpled them, and threw them into a waste bin. See, I know how to function.

"No need to hurry," Helen said, "I'm not going anywhere."

* * *

He steered the Fiat up the ramp into one of the city's car parks.

"Let's go to Nottingham." Helen had made the suggestion as they left the library and while he was still wondering whether the coffee bar he'd proposed the previous evening would after all be a suitable venue.

Side by side they walked to his car, and, Geoff, wordless, retrieved his keys from their hiding place, then drove cautiously out of the library car park before turning in the opposite direction from Longford's town centre.

As they drove, she asked him – more out of politeness, it seemed, than any real interest – whether he thought the morning had been a success, and rather to his surprise and, perhaps relieved that the subject she'd broached wasn't one on which he had to be on the defensive, found himself saying with a good deal of emphasis that, yes, it had been, and that he was *very* pleased for Josie's sake that those in attendance had been genuinely interested in the exhibition. "She put masses of work into it," he said. "Research, hunting out old photographs, visiting newspaper archives, interviewing the ancients of days. I'm delighted for her."

"Good for Josie," Helen said. He felt rather than saw her turn to look at him as he drove. "And good for you, too. I assume you planned it or at least made it possible."

His nod was minimal. Yes, he had helped his younger colleague, and he felt a momentary jab of pride at what they'd accomplished between them, modest though the exhibition was.

"But Josie deserves the credit," he said. "She did far more leg-work than me."

Now, as they walked away from the car park he'd chosen and, having followed a pedestrianised street of shops, found themselves emerging into a wide, slabbed square, a water-feature at one end, large Council House at the other, Geoff, gesturing to the square and surrounding three-storey buildings, its pubs and department stores, said, "What does this space remind you of?"

Helen paused, looked around, then at him. "Don't know. Give up. What does it remind *you* of?"

A two-coach tram sidled past, began its clanging run up a street on the square's far side.

"The capital of a small Balkan state?"

"Ah, Nottavia." Her laugh was a flash of warmth, a flush of spring sunshine.

"Exactly." The warmth spread through his body. "The model republic of Nottavia," he said, "where not only fanatics have their dreams."

They began to cross the square, weaving a way through throngs of people, young and old, gathered at the foot of steps that led into the Council House itself, at either side stone lions couchant, unthreatening.

"Do you by any chance know the Nottavian National Anthem?"

"Certainly," she said. "I'm surprised you should ask. As I remember it's set to words by the national poet, Netta Nottscu, and is played on Radio Nottavia every hour on the hour." She seized his arm, made him face her as she sang among people jostling about them, "*Nottavia, Nottavia, 'Tis of Thee we sing*," Then, after a brief pause, "*Thy national food is mushy peas, And all thy folk wear bling.*"

"No that's wrong."

They were past the square now, walking up a concourse at the head of which stood the bronze, life-size statue of a man wearing track-suit bottoms and a sweater as he clutched his hands above his head in victory salute. Posed around him, small knots of teenagers took photographs of each other. "Bling is *so* last year. The final line of Nottavia's anthem is henceforth amended to *And Brian Clough is King.*"

"Of a republic?"

"Oh, all right. *And Brian Clough is hero of the people.*"

"That neither rhymes nor scans."

"That's Modernism for you."

* * *

They chose a small window table in a French-style restaurant, were handed menus, and, as they looked up from them at the same moment, Geoff realised their faces were no more than eighteen inches apart and that it would be easy for him to lean over and kiss her. Her top and bottom lip were connected by a tiny thread of moisture – clitellum, he thought, trying to banish the word when he noticed that he could see the pink tip of her tongue resting on her lower teeth, so lifted his gaze and at once met her eyes, darker and larger than usual, could see at this near distance the tiny gold flecks of her grey-brown irises, the eyelashes' delicate curve above them. The discreet perfume – musk, it surely had to be? – the curve of her neck, tawny in this light as it emerged from her sage-green woollen sweater, the raggedy fringe of hair across her forehead and swept back behind ears from which silver hooped earrings hung shimmering, the flesh of her rounded chin …

As if reacting to a spasm of sudden, physical pain, he jerked his head backwards.

She looked steadily, questioningly at him.

"I was trying to remember the language of Nottavia," he said.

No, you weren't, her eyes told him. But aloud, she said, laughing, "Nottish. Brought over long centuries past by the Norts of Nortway and, through the centuries, adapted into the idiom nowadays used by all Nottavians."

"Ay, yes," he said, breathing more easily. "As in the greeting, 'Cowd mi owd.'"

"Code?" She was mystified.

"No, it rhymes with road but it's spelt c-o-w-d."

"And it means?"

"It's a cold day, my old friend. Nottavians are preoccupied by weather conditions. Take Arthur Stanchard. He may live in Longford, but he's Nottavian born and bred. If he wants you to have a good time, he doesn't tell you to make hay while the sun shines but while the sun *lasts*. With flat *a* of course. You know why?" And, when she shook her head, "Fact. In the days when Arthur was nobbut a lad the sun *didn't* shine over Nottingham, because the air was clogged with industrial soot. You could *see* the sun, like a lit bulb in a steam laundry, Arthur once told me, but you couldn't say that it actually *shone*."

He wondered whether to report Arthur's morning performance, the old man's revelation of how 'The Leas' came into existence, but decided against. The closure of the factory must have happened while Helen was still at Longford but as far as he could recall it hadn't been a matter for much discussion, not, anyway, among people he then knew. Come to think of it, though, hadn't he heard that Cadogan was one of those who bought a house in the new complex? Well, all the more reason in that case to say nothing. He didn't want Cadogan's name coming into their conversation. He shouldn't have mentioned Stanchard.

But Helen wanted to talk about him. "I like Arthur Stanchard," she said. "A man of wide knowledge."

And, as he looked at her enquiringly, she said, blushing a little, "I sometimes meet him for a cup of tea or coffee."

"Really? How come?"

A pause while an aproned waiter took their orders, then Helen said, "He introduced himself one Saturday morning when I was coming out of the library. He was on his way in with an armful of books. Told me one of them was a novel by Padgett, whose talk he'd seen me at. I had the impression he didn't much like it."

But Geoff wasn't interested in that.

"The library?"

Again, the blush. She came in the hope of seeing me, he thought, and then, as the rush of delight subsided, rubbish, she came to the library because that's where you go to borrow books.

He said, "Sorry I missed you. I'm not always on duty on Saturdays."

A carafe of water and glasses were put in front of them. Pouring for them both, Helen said, "We ended up going for a coffee."

"At the Black Cat?"

Shaking her head, Helen laughed. "No. I can't imagine Arthur in there, can you? He took me to a little café off the main street, near where he lives. Do you know it? The Silver Bells, it's called. "No" – seeing his raised eyebrow – "I thought it might be one of Longford's more closely guarded secrets. But it's not bad. Pot of tea and toast, home-made cakes, that kind of thing. Arthur recommended it as a place for lunch if I fell out of love with the college canteen. I gather the vegetable soup is not to be sniffed at and they do an especially lively poached egg on toast."

"Sounds unmissable. Has Jay Rayner been alerted?"

"So cynical and yet so young," she said. "Anyway, Arthur's talk would liven up the deadliest menu."

"You've seen him since, then?"

He was, he realised, envious of their tête-à-têtes.

"Once or twice, yes. If I'm out shopping and we bump into one another, we end up for half-an-hour of coffee and chat. Arthur gives me a run-down on his current reading and I fill him in on the state of education."

And with that she dismissed the topic.

They ate omelettes followed by, for her, *tarte au citron* and a *crème brûlée* for him. Helen, as non-driver, also had two glasses of Sancerre.

Geoff drank water. An acquired taste, he said, draining his glass. "It doesn't suit all palates. But it's good Midland water."

"Do you think of yourself as a Midlander then."

"Oh aye," he said. "Proud of my birthplace."

"You were born here? Nottavian to the core."

"Near enough." He decided not to tell her that he'd been brought up on the outskirts of Ilkeston. A girl can't go on laughing all the time.

Before he could ask about her early years, the waiter appeared to clear their plates and ask if there'd be anything else. Yes, please, anything to hold onto this good mood. Time was away and she was here. Coffee?

Yes, she would have a coffee.

While they waited for it to arrive, he asked if she'd seen anything recently of Verity. She looked at him enquiringly, before saying "I have, actually. Several times. It seems that Charles has been away a good deal of late. She's come up for an occasional chat and I've dropped in on her. Why do you ask?"

"Because the last time I saw her she seemed to me – well … " With extended hand he made the movement of a rocking boat.

She nodded but, dropping her gaze to study the check tablecloth, said nothing.

Had Verity perhaps taken Helen into her confidence? But if so, about what? Or could it be Cadogan who had told Helen to keep shtum on the subject?

Their coffees came. Stirring his, he said, "Actually, Peter Cadogan let me know that I'd helped tilt her off-balance."

Either the name or his words made her look at him keenly. "Why? What do you mean?"

"It's a complicated story. She came round to my flat and left a message while the rest of the world was whooping it up at Terry's fiftieth. She wanted me to get in touch with her. I wondered whether she might have mentioned it to you?"

He paused, but she said nothing, and he went on, "Anyway, I arranged to meet her the following Monday – in the Black Cat." He downed his espresso. "My god. She'd had her hair cut and dyed in some sort of post-punk style. You must know *that*, at least. Said that she'd had it done while Charles was away, but I wasn't to infer that she'd therefore done it behind his back, because the truth was he wouldn't care."

He paused, watched as she spooned froth from her cappuccino into her open mouth, then said, "I *think* she wanted me to understand that he wasn't much of a husband, though on the one occasion I met him Charles seemed a decent enough man, perhaps even more than that. Certainly not – well, I don't know what she wanted me to think. That Charles is unkind to her, perhaps. I could be wrong, but he didn't strike me as at all like that."

Again she nodded, but this time spoke. "Yes, he does his best." A hesitation. "I lent her that novel by your friend Padgett. I thought she might enjoy it. I'm not entirely sure it was a good idea, though." Her laugh ended on a tremor of uncertainty.

"You're not telling me you think she may have taken it to heart? It's just a novel."

"So was *Werther*."

And when he looked mystified, she added, "Goethe. Werther is a youth who's hopelessly in love with a married woman and who commits suicide, and 'The shot was heard all over Europe.' Apparently in the years after it first came out the morgues were stuffed with the bodies of young men who'd killed themselves for love."

"'Now more than ever seems it rich to die.' One of the few poems I can remember from undergraduate days. But I suppose putting a bullet through your brain or heart is rather more dramatic than Keats' idea. Bloodier for a start. And pretty agonising. I don't blame Keats for wanting to give pain a miss. Though come to think of it, I've no idea *how* he was proposing to die. 'To cease upon the midnight with no pain.' How was he going to do that?"

And even as he spoke, he remembered mention of an opiate, but also realised that Keats must have been thinking about death as a kind of orgasm, or was it orgasm as a kind of death? Either way, he needed another topic.

But she seemed not to have heard his question. She was looking out on the street, crowded with Saturday shoppers, young and not-so-young. One couple stopped inches away from where Helen and Geoff sat, turned inward to each other and, arms locked behind each other's necks, kissed.

Instinctively, as though she was loath to seem a voyeur, Helen turned back to him. Meeting his gaze, she said, ignoring his question, "The freedom to be different. The freedom to be the same. My students all bang on about wanting to live their own lives, and then they end up doing the same thing. Clubbing, smoking, popping pills, dress identikit, go to the same pop concerts, follow the same stand-ups ... "

"It's called fashion."

"True." She laughed. "Yes, sorry. A moment of angst I suppose," she said, "that what your James Padgett is writing about used to be fashionable. 'Tuning in, turning on and dropping out', didn't they call it?"

"They did, once upon a while, but that was in a foreign country called the nineteen-sixties. Tuning in was what you did to prevent yourself from being conscripted into the armies of respectability. Padgett's novel belongs to more recent times."

"Not really," she said. "Think of *The Doll's House*. Nora escaping from what you call the armies of respectability by leaving home and slamming the door behind her."

There was a pause while she drank the last of her cappuccino. Then, abruptly, as though to change the subject, she said, "Where does Peter – where does Cadogan fit into this? I mean, what has he to do with what you were telling me about Verity?" She was watching him closely.

"He came to see me that evening. Insisted on paying me a visit. His excuse was that Verity had phoned him after our meeting earlier that day and, so he said, told him she was worried that she'd offended me and wanted some way to apologise." He looked at her, felt the tautness of his smile. "Cadogan took it on himself to let me know that far from owing me an apology Verity deserved one from *me*. I'd let her down, failed to be sympathetic to her because I was unobservant or uncaring, or both." After a moment, he said, "In my own defence I have to say that I didn't notice she was in a vulnerable state. But you probably know that." He paused, dared to meet her eye. "I'm not always very observant." He was thinking of the tears in Verity's eyes.

"Observant? Of women, you mean? No, you're not."

But the rebuke was softened by her smile. She said, "Anyway, he's a fine one to talk. Not that he has – talked about you, I mean." Pause. She looked away, back, met his eyes. "In fact, I've only seen him once since the night of that party. And that was briefly and quite unintended."

As the significance of her words hit him, a rip-tide of feeling poured through his body. Relief, delight, joy even, he wanted to say. He said, "I thought when you told me you might be coming to

Nottingham today it was him you'd be coming with." He paused, then added, "Or for."

"Not bloody likely." She shook her head, vehemently it seemed to him. Then, dropping the Eliza Doolittle voice, "No, I've cut free of him." Her hands went up, chopped down. "He knows that there's no point in him badgering me to be in his production. He tried it on at the party but I made it clear that I won't do it."

"Ah." He paused. "But Janey seemed to think you were still debating whether to be in the production."

Again she shook her head. "*Never*. Geoff, listen." A pause, while she seemed to decide which words to use next. "When you saw us coming back into the Marsden mansion, as you call it, I guessed you probably assumed – well, never mind what you assumed." She waved the words impatiently aside, began again. "He'd wanted me to 'step outside' so we could talk about his plans for the production and as *I* wanted to avoid a scene when I told him the answer was a definite no, I went with him. For the few minutes it took to say No, No, No." There was a glimmer of laughter in her Thatcherite imitation, but it went.

Picking up her coffee spoon, she examined it closely, then returned it to its saucer, before, looking across at Geoff, she said, her voice now low, regretful – was it? – "but avoiding one scene I found I'd inadvertently caused another."

He said, contrite, the tone of his own voice matching hers, "For which you weren't responsible." Making himself look directly at her, he said, "My behaviour then was inexcusable." He wanted to add, *though at least it must have shown you how I feel about you.*

But before he could decide how best to do this she shrugged, looked away, and when her eyes focused again on his, she said, changing the subject, "Can I ask what, if anything, you know about Verity's background?"

How to answer? Cadogan's revelations had been made "in confidence", and though he couldn't stand the man and didn't much like the woman, he had no wish to betray Verity or Eve, or whoever she was. He said, feeling his way, "Cadogan told me a bit about her. He's her husband's solicitor. From what he let on I sense that her life hasn't been entirely straightforward."

"But being full of the milk of human kindness you want to see things from her point of view."

"Despite appearances, we Nottavians are famous for our powers of empathy." But her words stung. She really did think he wasn't very

164

observant. Or that he was careless of other people's feelings? Was that it?

The waiter appeared with their bill but Helen asked for a further cappuccino. "Do you mind," she asked him. Perhaps she wanted him to get back to the subject he yearned to discuss. He, her, them.

"Of course not."

"I have something I need to tell you," she said, slowly, hesitantly even, as she watched the waiter's retreating back. "It's not about Verity. But," she smiled, this time ruefully, "she's certainly been as much help to me as I have to her."

After that she sat silent until her coffee arrived.

"So?"

Once again breathing was difficult. Was she about to tell him that she felt for him as he did for her … ?

She bent her head to the cup, lifted it and then, without tasting it, used both hands to return it to its saucer. Head bowed, she was frowning at the white, crenulated surface of her cappucino. In a decisive gesture she pushed the cup aside. "I need to tell you why I came back to Longford." Then, after the briefest of sighs, "The fact is, I was on the run. I needed to get away from Wolverhampton."

"Who doesn't?" he said, but her only response was an unsmiling stare which was replaced by a flicker of irritation.

Apologetically, he raised his hands. "Sorry. I won't interrupt again."

"Good, because you need to hear this. I was desperate to get away – well, you can perhaps guess. A love affair that didn't work out. Although that's pitching it too high. I mean, it was never all that serious for me. Unfortunately, it was for him. He was becoming a pest, self-pity alternating with threats, and I realised that for both our sakes I had to move, get him out of my life."

Perhaps misunderstanding the confusion he knew must be in his eyes, the confusion that came from words he'd not at all expected, she said, "Don't worry, this isn't going to be a blow-by-blow account of a pretty sordid affair. But you deserve to know that the reason I'm in Longford is simply because it was the first place that came up with a job. As long as there was work I didn't much care where I went."

She left it at that, but the unspoken words lay cold on his heart. I didn't come back because of Cadogan, and I certainly didn't come back because of you.

He said, hoping his voice didn't betray the anguish he was feeling,

"And how has Verity helped you?"

"Because she's a strong person. Cadogan thinks she's off-balance, does he? A pussyfoot way of saying she's unstable, off her rocker, even." A contemptuous wriggle of her shoulders. "Well, she's not."

"Then why worry about her reading Padgett's novel?"

Momentarily startled by the ironic edge of his question, she said, as though exonerating herself, "Because she's impulsive, as ought to be apparent from what she chose to do to her appearance. But the good thing about Verity is that she has the courage to live with the consequences of her actions." She looked at him. "I mean what I say. She's actually a very strong person. She listened to my catalogue of woes, told me hers, and then" – she paused – "then made me agree to put a stopper in my misery bottle."

For all the smile that accompanied her last words, she was studying him, her look earnest, unwavering.

What did Helen know of Verity's early years? Had the other woman told her anything of what he himself had heard from Cadogan or had Helen been told yet another story? Was Verity – Eve – whoever – a fantasist who enjoyed inventing different versions of her life? Was it all smoke and mirrors?

He said, "After Cadogan's visit I decided to phone Verity to apologise for having been less than sympathetic when we'd met in the Black Cat."

"And she invited you to fuck off."

"Oh, she told you about that?"

She drank her coffee in one long gulp. "I was there when you phoned."

"You *were?*"

"I told her she was being unfair, but her reply was that as soon as she heard your voice – its 'melting tones' was how she put it – she guessed that Cadogan must have had a go at you and that you'd decided to go all 'jelly-kneed', whereas it was she who should have been saying sorry. Why should you apologise for what wasn't your fault. She was angry with him, but you were in the way so you got both barrels."

"That's a pretty weird line of attack," he said, easing himself up from his chair. "*She* certainly can't be accused of being awash with the milk of human kindness."

"I did tell you she was a strong woman."

Helen, too, stood, reached for her purse. "We'll split the bill. OK?"

* * *

Out in the street, she took his arm in a friendly enough fashion. "One more word about Verity and then I'll say no more about her. I realise that she isn't what my old gran would have called everyone's cup of tea. But she's had a difficult time of it. Grew up in a hard school. Being suspicious of someone's motives is almost second nature with her."

"Which is why she told me to get lost." He thought about it. Thought about what he'd heard from Cadogan of Verity's early years and wondered what the woman had told Helen. "What hard school was she brought up in, by the way?"

Helen shook her head. "That's confidential," she said, "sorry."

Should he press her? No. After all, he'd not told her all that Cadogan had told *him* about Verity, or Eve's, early years.

The crowds in the square and adjacent streets forced them apart and they wound their way in uncommunicative silence back to the multi-storey car park.

Only as they were once more on the road to Longford did Helen speak again. Reaching to put a hand on his near arm, she said, "I *do* value our friendship, Geoff. I really do."

"Kind of you to say so."

He was staring through the windscreen at the white van they were following out of the city, but sensed her turn to look at his set profile. No, I don't myself know whether I mean to be satirical, perhaps I'm registering genuine gratitude for what you've said. Friendship is after all something.

"In the interest of which," she said, determined it seemed to keep the tone light, "would you mind telling me why you keep your car keys where you do. It's not where most people keep them."

"Ah, you noticed."

The white van, which had slowed to a halt, suddenly shot forward, did a U turn where none was allowed and headed back to the city.

"Wonder what he's forgotten?"

"Well, it can't be his keys," Geoff said, and explained that it was Simon who'd come up with the suggestion of the safest place to keep his key ring. "He says most traffic cops recommend it. Possessions can fall out of your pocket. You could get mugged. A thousand and one things might happen. But when you get back to your car you can still drive off."

"Hmm. There's hot wiring, you know. And suppose you have a

dodgy traffic cop or one who talks out of order. Wouldn't it soon get round among the criminal fraternity?"

The road ahead was empty now and Geoff increased speed in an attempt to lift his spirits.

"If it has I haven't noticed. My car has remained unstolen."

Her hand still rested on his arm. "And that's because of your cunning plan rather than because just as no self-respecting thief would steal your apology for hi-fi so no one after a car would think of going off in your Fiat."

"Top of the range, this car," he said, "the envy of all."

But for all his attempts at matching her banter, he felt as greyly depressed as the sky looming above the bridge that was taking them across the Trent and back to Longford.

22

"Don't often see you in the Tuns of a Saturday," Norman said, as he drew Geoff his pint.

"I've been in Nottingham." Not that it was an explanation. "Fancied a quick one before I took myself back home." There, would that do.

"Understood", Norman said. "Get the dust of foreign parts out of your throat. Shopping, were you? Or on pleasure bent?" But the questions were formal, required no answer. No need to tell the landlord that loving without hope wasn't much fun. As the filled glass was pushed across the counter, Geoff counted out the required money, dropped the coins into Norman's hand and, taking up his pint, turned to look for a seat.

At this early hour the front bar was empty. An air of gentle melancholy shrouded the room, and the dark tables, leather banquettes, stools and scrubbed wooden floor suggested a forlorn abandonment, as though it wouldn't be an outlandish fancy to imagine that the place had been vacated for all time, that it would never again be where people gathered to talk and drink. Even the sound of Norman bottling up in the back bar might be no more than a trapped echo, the clink of glass on glass belonging to a gone life immured in the sepia light slanting dustily through the pub's tall, frosted-glass windows, like an old photograph, one that Josie might have included in her exhibition.

Josie the innocent. Josie the good. A world away from Verity, or Eve, or whoever she was. And perhaps a world away from Helen, too. Josie, with her fiancé and unrufflable plans for a happy, uneventful future. How unlike the home life of …

No, forget it. Instead, he made himself consider how, in an hour or so, the Tuns would be filling with Saturday night drinkers, some, usually the younger ones – the passing trade – stopping for no longer than it took to order and down a cocktail or glass of spirits, others settling in for the long haul, and, as the evening wore on, their laughter turning raucous, voices more assertive, thickening with ale and argument.

But for now, as he stood at the bar and raised the beer to his lips, the Three Tuns was perfect for his mood, as was the taste of the beer itself: the faint acridity, the lingering, musty, sweet sourness that flowed past his gullet and down to his stomach.

He held the glass up to the light, studied the lace-edgings of froth that clung to its sides. A toast. But to whom? Oh, Helen. And at once the memory of her face, so close to his own earlier that day, the intensity of her look, the gold-flecked iris, that scent, was like a physical spasm, constricting his throat. And then came the dull pain, the recall of her words about the former lover from whom she'd so recently escaped. Had it been the truth – that the lover, whoever he was, had not meant as much to her as she meant to him? Probably. Helen didn't shirk from uncomfortable truths. That's why she took pains – ha! – to explain to him her reason for being back in Longford. Well, at least there was no comfort for Cadogan in her return. "I've cut free of him." One step forward. But then by the same token, one step back. Because taking Geoff into her confidence was, wasn't it, also a way of warning him off. I'm here by accident, not design. You're my friend. Meaning, of course, you are *merely* my friend.

He drank some more beer. Face it. For love she looks elsewhere. And is let down. It came to him then, the remark she'd dropped when they first met after the ten-year gap and as they traded memories of the Alleyn Players. Helena, "the love-lorn maid, abandoned by her paramour. The story of my life."

A story in which he himself had only a minor role. The trusty friend. Kill Claudio. But now Claudio turned out to be not one man but two, perhaps more, a Hydra, or rather that many-headed dog, what was he called, yes, Cerberus. So what was the point in cutting off one head? What was to be his reward for services rendered? To be told that she valued his friendship. Oh, thanks. I'll drink to that. He drained his glass, plonked it on the counter, called out a farewell to Norman who didn't answer, and left.

* * *

Frank must have been waiting for him to return because no sooner was he indoors, Baw purring round his legs, than there was a banging on the front door.

"Evening, Geoffrey." His landlord, in suit and tie, and with best cap positioned squarely on his head, explained that he was stepping round to the church for a social occasion and wouldn't come in but, hearing the car, thought he'd pass on some information in which his tenant might be interested.

"Yes?" Geoff asked. Frank enjoyed the drama of revelation.

"The Halsteads will be leaving us."

"*Really?* Why? When?" Then, in a more measured voice, Geoff asked, "When did they tell you?"

"An hour ago." A pause. Then, "So you had no advance warning?"

"Why would I?"

"I wondered whether your young lady, Miss Birdlip, had heard anything."

"If so, she didn't tell me. And I was with her this afternoon."

Something in the way Frank looked at him, a kind of arched, enquiring, speculative look, caused him to add, "The young lady, as you call her, and I were in Nottingham. No big deal." There, let Frank understand from the ironic inflection that Helen wasn't ... wasn't who or what Geoff wished she was.

Reassured, or so Geoff supposed from the way the landlord nodded at that disclaimer, Frank said, "Well, as I may have mentioned, the Halsteads have a reputation for being birds of passage."

He made to go, then, slowly turning back said, "I gather they will be moving out in the next few days. Of course, they've paid until the end of the month. But I must say the information, like their decision, has been precipitous."

"It's fallen on you from a great height."

Frank nodded. "I therefore find myself needing to locate a new lessee. If you happen to know of anyone suitable ... you know my likes and dislikes, Geoffrey."

"I'll keep an eye and an ear open."

As Frank once more turned to go, Geoff asked, "Any idea why the Halsteads are off?"

Over his shoulder, Frank said, "Charles – Mr Halstead – intimated that business matters were involved. Beyond that, he has told me nothing." The words held an implied rebuke. I should have been given more notice. I am not pleased.

Geoff offered what he hoped was a sympathetic sound, half sigh, half murmur, and Frank, taking from this what comfort he could, stepped out of the porch.

In the kitchen, he emptied into Baw's bowl a sachet of what was promised as Cat-o-meat's *Finest salmon. Your pet will* **LOVE IT**, and watched as she crouched to eat.

Well, well, well. The Halsteads were on their way. A surprise, that, or was it? *Had* Helen known about this when she'd talked to him about Verity earlier that afternoon? No, surely not. If she had an inkling of their departure she would have mentioned it to him. So, it would come as a surprise to her, too. Could he risk phoning her to discuss the matter? Yes, why not. But then again …

He reached into the fridge and, having taken a sip of the indifferent sauvignon-blanc, revolved the wine glass slowly between thumb and first two fingers as he considered what he could say to her, what he could ask her. Would she mind him phoning? Would she maybe think he was pestering her? When he'd dropped her off outside Hutton Lodge she'd thanked him for her afternoon, even given him a peck on the cheek, but hadn't invited him in. There was restraint between them, as though an opportunity had been missed or, more likely, he had misjudged her earlier mood, had sensed a promise, a flicker of happiness that in the event proved illusory or too faint to survive, blown out by her words about the lover from whom she'd had recently to escape and as a result of whom she found herself back in Longford. *Back in Longford. Adrift in Longford. Longing for Longford. Lost in Longford.* You've read the book, now see the film.

And Verity. Had she, too, been failed? Suppose, after all, that Helen *did* know the Halsteads were leaving. By her own account she and Verity had seen a good deal of each other, had, so Helen implied, drawn close enough to offer each other the help both needed in coping with problems, nowadays called issues, that had entered their lives. But in that case, and leaving aside the Agony Aunt language he should never have allowed himself, he couldn't imagine that, had a move been in the offing, Verity wouldn't have told Helen. In which case why had Helen not told him, Geoff? Oh, because the Halsteads' move was confidential. Or, more hurtfully, because he didn't need to be told, or, worse, because, having failed Verity, didn't *deserve* to be told. Hmm.

But then for all he knew, Charles might have kept his wife in the dark. Unless the decision had been spur-of-the-moment. Possible, yes, but why?

Why indeed? Business, so Halstead had told Frank. Perhaps *that* was why he'd been away from home. Hunting for somewhere else to live. Or – another possibility occurred to him. Suppose the first husband had shown up or they'd been warned he had wind of their whereabouts? That, too, was possible.

Or else ... Or else what? Many questions, too many for him to answer. Oh, come on, phone Helen What have you got to lose? She'd surely be prepared to say *something,* wouldn't merely hang up on him. Assuming she hadn't been sworn to secrecy.

It was only as he went over to the phone that he noticed the flashing red light. "You were called today at 10. 25 a.m ... " He pressed 1.

"Geoff, this is Simon. Your mobile is switched off so I have to use the answer phone. Whenever you get this message, call me OK? I repeat, *whenever* you get this message, morning, noon or night, just phone me. It's urgent as in super urgent. Capital S capital U. "

Really? What could be *that* urgent? He glanced at the mobile as he retrieved it from his jacket pocket. Yes, of course. He'd switched it off before going into the library that morning and had taken good care it would stay silent while he and Helen were together. A mistake, perhaps, judging from the sound of Simon's voice. Simon, normally the most laid-back of the four, had sounded not merely stressed but in virtual panic mode. The quartet must have been asked to dep for some other group. Probably one booked for this very evening. Illness, break-up, last-minute cancellation, some one trying to arrange a replacement for a party or social event. Can you step in? Please. It's urgent.

He glanced at his watch. 7. 30. Assuming the gig wasn't too far away, there ought to be time for him to get there. But not black-and-white, he'd insist on scruff order. He pressed the recall button, heard Simon's voice.

"Geoff here, Si. What's up?"

23

"You found your way, then."

"Yes, inch-perfect instructions. Everything I'd expect of a traffic cop."

"Ex-cop." Simon's wife peered over Geoff's shoulder and he turned to look with her at the roof of his Fiat showing above the trim front hedge. Beyond it, on the road's far side, willows screened the canal where anglers were already at their stations, rods canted over the sluggish water on which swans, one or two of them, cruised between barges moored all the way up to a nearby lock. Moorhens fussed along the canal's reed-fringed edge.

"Is it safe to leave the car there?"

"That's fine," she said, not meaning the Sunday morning scene, pleasant though that was. "No wheel-clamping in operation hereabouts. And the local car thieves will still be in bed. Come on in. Al's already here, brought by personal taxi." Her conspiratorial smile assumed he'd understand.

"He got one of his staff out of bed?" Al's customary way of getting from A to B, was to go by hearse, thus ensuring, as he pointed out, prompt arrival. Everybody made way for a hearse.

"You know Al." She held the door wide allowing him to step past her into the carpeted, white-painted hallway of their neat semi. He'd forgotten how petite she was, how delicate, almost crushably dainty she'd looked against Simon's muscular bulk on the few occasions he'd seen them together.

"Nice place you have."

"And nice of you to say so." She acknowledged the compliment with a further slight smile and pointed him to a door that must lead into the front room. "Not to everyone's taste, but pipe-and-slippers land suits us. And the natives are friendly. Tea or coffee?"

"Coffee would be fine." The smell of fried bacon came from the rear.

"And a sandwich?"

"I've had breakfast," he said, "but who can say no to a bacon sandwich?"

In the square, comfortably furnished room, Simon and Al were arranged in easy chairs on either side of a glass-topped coffee table. A third, matching chair in lovat green material was pushed up against the inner wall, above it framed photographs of snow-capped hills and one of what had to be police cadets in full fig, lined up and staring into their futures as fully-fledged officers of the law.

Geoff went over to inspect it, greeting the room's two occupants as he did so.

"Which one's you, Si?"

"Second from end, left side, back row. Standing."

"Oh, right. Gotcha, to coin a phrase. Beanpole. You've put on some weight."

He dropped sheets from the *Sunday Telegraph* onto a stool beside the chair which Simon had motioned him to bring up and hauled it across the deep-piled tan carpet to join the others.

"It's what happens when you spend too many days behind the wheel of a car chomping meat pies and burgers."

Al said, "You look lean enough to me. All that sprinting up hills, I guess."

He was in his usual subfusc dress of dark-red cords and leather jacket, leaning back in his chair, thighs spread comfortably, at his ease.

"You should join me," Simon said. "You could do with shedding a stone or two."

"Yeh, like I've got plans to end my days dangling on a rope over some bloody precipice while a police helicopter tries to winch me up." Al patted his stomach. "I'd probably down the 'copter. Anyway, I'm a more of a man for depths. Six feet down does me nicely."

"I don't go climbing, you berk. Derbyshire's got all the hills a man needs for a long day's walk."

Al shook his head in mock despair. "Makes me feel faint, just hearing about it."

There was a pause as Barbara backed into view carrying a full tray: cafetiere, cups, milk jug, large plate piled with thickly cut sandwiches from which tongues of bacon curled, even a bottle of brown sauce. Geoff tried not to look when she leant across the table, cerise blouse open at the neck to show a black, lacy bra. Strands of light brown hair at the nape of her neck were still damp from her morning shower, and as she handed him a cup and plate the scent of perfumed talcum powder created a moment of unlooked-for sexiness. Fresh as a daisy Barbara. Whoever heard of a sexy daisy.

Waiting until his wife, scooping up the newspaper as she exited with the words "I'll leave you to it, then", had pulled the door closed behind her, Simon said, looking a from one to the other of his guests, "So. The question is, what now?" Then, as neither spoke, he added, "I mean, what are we going to do about the quartet?"

His mouth full of bacon sandwich, Al said, "Si, how about some details? I only picked your message up late last night, remember. I'm still gob-smacked."

"Me, too." Geoff poured coffee for the three of them, handing Al milk and sugar.

"If it comes to that," Simon said, "so am I." He chewed on his sandwich, laid it aside. "It was one of my mates that found him. As soon as I heard I phoned you two pronto, but neither of you were around." It sounded almost like an accusation. Where were you in your country's hour of need.

"I was off down south for the day, seeing relatives," Al explained to Geoff. "Didn't get back till past midnight. As I've told Si. I got the message all right but there wasn't a lot I could do from Luton."

"And I'd gone to Nottingham," Geoff said, "though I did get back to Simon mid-evening."

Simon stood, went over to the bay window and drew back the long, dark-blue curtains as far as they would go, as though to let in more light would help.

"There, that's better."

He dropped back into his seat, reached for a sandwich. "It was Charlie Harris who found him. Coming off the motorway after night patrol." He took a bite, chewed, then said, "Charlie had passed the car sometime just before midnight, Friday, in a lay-by near the Longford roundabout, and thought nothing of it."

"Oh?"

"Oh, nothing, Al. Known to the lads as Adulterers' Alley, that particular lay-by, for reasons I guess I don't have to spell out. But seeing as how the car was still there some six hours later Charlie thought he'd take a gander."

He paused for another, larger bite at his sandwich, spent a few moments in reflective silence as he rotated bread and bacon in his mouth, then, having cleared his throat, said, "Charlie knew who it was as soon as he opened the car door. Seeing as how he's teetotal he's been in a condition to clock our faces at the Policeman's Balls we've done, which is more than can be said for some of the tossers I used to work with. Off their faces by the time the Okey Cokey comes round."

The last of his sandwich went into his mouth. "Besides, Terry wasn't exactly Mr Incognito."

Wasn't. Already Terry Marsden was being consigned to the past.

Licking the inside of his wrist – bacon grease was beginning to slide up his arm – Geoff said, "Did your mate have any idea how long he'd been there? I mean, how long he'd been dead?"

Simon shrugged. "That's a question for the pathologist. Charlie played it by the book. Checked that the car was registered in Terry's name, called the ambulance, didn't touch anything once he'd felt for signs of life. According to him, though, Terry – the body – was cold, so he must have been a goner for some hours."

"Was it an accident?" Geoff asked. "Exhaust fumes?"

"That's my guess," Al said, as though it was no guess.

But Simon shook his head. "Charlie said there was an empty bottle of pills on the front seat, together with a quarter of brandy. He reckoned the inside of the car stank like a smashed-up off-licence."

"You're telling us he topped himself. But why?" Al looked at the others, baffled, enquiring. "What the bloody hell did he do *that* for?"

"Besides," Geoff said, as bewildered as Al, "if you're going to swallow pills why take the car? Cars are for driving into brick walls or off cliffs."

"Or fixing a pipe from the exhaust while you keep the engine running," Al said. "We deal with quite a few who've taken that way out."

"Whereas with pills you can see yourself off in the comfort of your own home."

"To be straight, yes, that's about the size of it, Si. I'm telling you, in my line of business you get used to that kind of thing. Nowadays it's usually pills. In bed rather than head in the oven."

"If it *was* suicide," Geoff said.

"Not much doubt about that." Simon was certain

"In that case perhaps he didn't want Lorette to be the one who found him." Al looked at Simon. "I assume she knows?"

"Of course." The former policeman spoke now with brisk reassurance. "By the time Charlie phoned me it was all systems go. Sue Fortiss, she's one of the DCs trained for this kind of work, took a bereavement counsellor out to Terry's place as soon as they were sure who it was that Charlie had found. From what I hear they had to spend some time persuading Lorette to go with them to the morgue. They needed her to make the formal identification. Strictly unnecessary, if you ask me, but it's routine. Got to be done."

Geoff said, "A bit brutal, though, isn't it."

"It always is," Simon said.

The three of them sat without speaking for a few minutes. None of them, Geoff reckoned, much liked Lorette, but still …

It was he who broke the silence. Putting down the coffee cup he'd been nursing, he said to Simon, "After I managed to speak to you, I switched on the telly. There was a bit on local news. Did you catch it?"

"Yes," Simon said, "usual crap. Who writes their scripts?"

"No idea, but whoever it is must take for granted that nobody with an IQ of more than ten ever watches their news programmes."

"Given what they put on, who would?"

" 'Terry Marsden, well-known locally for his music-making skills and contributions to charity.'" Geoff's imitation of the mentally-challenged male newscaster made the other two grimace.

"Contributions to charity?" Simon said, "First I've heard of it."

Al said "That'll be the masons. I guess the TV boys got the info from Cadogan. He mentioned good deeds at Terry's fiftieth."

"Yes," Simon said, emptying the last of the cafetiere into their cups. "I'd forgotten about him."

"If only," Geoff said. Then, as the others looked enquiringly at him, he said more quickly, "So what's to do for Lorette? We'll have to get in touch. Condolences from the group. What else?"

"I've got something here." Simon stood, wiped his fingers on his jeans, went to the white wooden mantelpiece, and came back with a large grey envelope. As he made to prise out the card, he said, "What about next Wednesday's gig? Cancel? Get a replacement on keyboard?"

"Why not do it as a trio?" Al said. "Like the Benny Goodman Quartet without Benny Goodman. Krupa, Hampton, Wilson. One of my favourite LPs, that. When you've got Wilson who needs Goodman."

"And when you've got Geoff Cousins, let alone Al Stocking, who needs … " But Simon let the sentence fade away. Instead, after a moment's silence in which they'd looked awkwardly at one another, he said, as though speaking for them all, "Weird, isn't it?"

"What's weird?" Geoff asked. But he knew what Simon meant.

Simon said, "Weird that none of us has yet … " He swivelled his head, challenging them. "I mean, are we cold-hearted buggers, or what?"

After what seemed an unduly long moment of silence, during which they shifted in their seats and tried to avoid looking at each other, Al, staring at his feet, said, slowly, "Truth is, I don't know what to think." He waited for someone else to speak, then, as though having come to a decision, "All right, cards on the table. I'm sorry Terry's gone, gone this way especially. I'm shocked even." Pause. "But it isn't as though he was a close mate."

He waited, but still the other two stayed silent.

Eventually Simon asked, "Has anyone got a clue as to what lies behind this?" Then, when nobody spoke, he added, "As Al said a few minutes ago, what *did* he do it for? *Why?*"

Geoff said, "Why indeed?"

"It's difficult to work out, to get a handle on. Big house, not to everyone's taste but pricey, new wife, ditto – and he certainly didn't seem short of the readies," Al said.

"Unless it was all show." Looking first at his host, then at Al, Geoff added, "Simon once told me he wouldn't be surprised to hear Terry had done time for murder. That's right, isn't it?" And when Simon opened his mouth to protest, he added, "No, don't worry, I didn't think you were being serious. But there's no getting away from it, Terry is – Terry *was* – a mystery man."

He waited through the silence of their tacit agreement, before asking, "Did he leave a – a note – a message, does anyone know?"

"There was nothing on him. At least if there was, Charlie didn't tell me, and I reckon he would have. I suppose something may turn up – in the house, most like." Simon brushed crumbs from a faded blue T-shirt on which was printed the words COP THIS LOT. "Yes, Geoff's right. I did say that about Terry, though it sort of slipped out. I don't know how seriously I meant the words. Truth is, like Al, I never really thought of Terry as a mate, not one I'd want to meet for a drink."

"Or go walking with."

Simon smiled at Al. "Terry? In those shoes he liked to wear: Italian loafers, weren't they. Can't see him walking far in those. And his suits. Shouldn't think they were off the peg. He'd not want to go scrambling about the countryside in one of them."

"Nor the shirts," Al said.

"No." Simon allowed himself a brief snort of laughter. "They wouldn't be much use to him on Froggatt Edge."

Now they were beginning to open up, Geoff said, "I never even knew whether he much *liked* what we played, did you? He was good, I'll say that for him. He knew his way round the keyboard all right. But it was all somehow mechanical. Looking back I reckon he treated music as a means to an end. A way of meeting people he could do business with, or" – he paused – "or who'd have some proposition to offer him. Golf clubs, Rotary clubs, Masonic lodges, you name it. He was always angling for those jobs. Gave me the feeling that he'd have been just as happy playing Palm Court or cocktail-music or ... " He stopped, remembering Helen's account of how, where and when, she'd first come across Terry. In a hotel bar with ...

Nodding, Al said, "I know what you mean, Geoff. Programme him, set the tempo, adjust the volume, press the button, and away you go."

There was a further silence as the three of them looked at one another, uncomfortable with their words but not prepared to retract them. Conspiratorial, almost. It occurred to Geoff that this was the first time they had ever seriously discussed the man who as of now was their late leader. Strange, you could play together as a group for years and never really get to know each other. Or perhaps it wasn't strange. Perhaps this was how it was with all musos. Music was what brought you together and on good evenings made you more than the sum of your parts, made you *cohere*, gave you a sense that, for as long as the music lasted, you were united in the interest, even service, of what you played, or, to be honest, aspired to play; but once the music ended you fell back into your separate lives.

He looked from one to the other, the ex-cop and the undertaker. Yes, he liked Al and Simon well enough, but he didn't really count them as friends, any more, he knew, than they did him. If the group broke up would the three of them keep in touch? Almost certainly not. He doubted they'd even continue to exchange the cards they ritually handed out to each other at the annual pre-Christmas gig, and as for meeting socially, no, he couldn't imagine it. This was, after all, the first time he'd seen inside Simon's semi, and though he'd driven past Al's large townhouse with its high brick walls and imposing, wrought-iron gates – a lucrative business, undertaking – had even dropped him off once or twice after out-of-town gigs, he'd never been invited in for a drink, had barely spoken to Al's wife on the rare occasions she'd been with Al on a gig, like the night of Terry's fiftieth.

"Seems funny," he said, "for Terry to have put on that big do for his birthday. And then this."

"Just what I was thinking," Simon said, and they sat there.

It was Al who broke the silence. "I wonder what Lorette's making of it all?" And, seeing the enquiring looks on their faces, amended his question. "How's she going to cope?" He shook his head, the expression on his pursed lips one of considerate sympathy. It could be genuine, but Geoff guessed that such an expression came easily enough to someone in Al's line of business.

"To say nothing of Terry's previous wives," Geoff said. "Did anyone present meet either of them?" And, when the others shook their heads, he asked, "And then there are the children? Assuming there *are* any."

"He never mentioned children," Simon said. "Not in my hearing, anyway." Then, turning to Al, and as though answering his first question, said, "As for Lorette, that's another mystery. That time we were round at his place for a practice session. I didn't get the impression there was much love coming from her side of the fence. Did you? I'm not saying she was a trophy wife exactly, but you know…" He stopped. "And as for the birthday party, the Big Five O. That struck me as being – well, I don't know, but it seemed a bit too public, somehow. A big show. Done to impress the hordes."

Al's shrug of the shoulders suggested that he had other ideas. "You could be right, Si, but I don't reckon he called us all together to prove his marriage was in good working order. You don't get flunkeys in for that, do you?"

"You might," Simon said.

"If I'm thinking what I think Al is thinking, then I'm with him," Geoff said. "I reckon that party was more about letting people see Terry had got money in his purse."

The door was opening.

"And it could all have been pretence." Barbara, who had come to clear away the cups and plates, began to redden as the men looked at her. Straightening up with loaded tray, she said, "He wouldn't be the first man – *man*, I'm saying – to play the Big Spender on a pocketful of nothing. You read about it all the time."

They looked at her expectantly.

Al said, "So, what do you reckon then, Barbara? Terry didn't have much money in the bank?"

Simon laughed. "Bank? Terry'd more likely keep his wad stashed under the floorboards."

But Barbara said, "No, he'd not do that. Men who keep their money under the bed or in brown paper bags are street traders or into dodgy corner-shop deals. But they know how to look after themselves."

"Oh? And how do they do that?"

She stood beside her husband, nudged him with her hip. "They don't try to impress people with smart clothes and big cars. They hide what they've got. Pretend to be poor as church mice."

"Bit like me, then."

"Luckily for you," she had scarcely to bend to kiss the top of his head, "you've got me to look after you, keep you on the straight and narrow."

Holding the tray steady, she headed for the door. There she turned.

"From what Si's told me, it doesn't sound as though Terry had anyone who could do that for him."

"How about his solicitor?" Al said. "Peter Cadogan. Judging from his speech at the party, he and Terry seemed pretty close."

"I wouldn't know about that," Barbara said, "but my old dad told me never to trust solicitors. He came into contact with plenty of all sorts who worked in the legal profession and he always said solicitors were the worst. According to him, every man Jack of them was as bent as a three-pound note."

The three watched as she left, using a foot to hook the door closed behind her.

"What was Barbara's dad's line of business?" Geoff asked.

"Surprised you need to ask," Simon said. "He was a copper, of course."

24

Early though he was in getting to the library on Monday morning, Colleen was there before him.

Looking up from the desk where she was sorting through a small pile of order forms, she said, without further greeting, "That Terry Marsden. It *is* his group you play with?"

Surprised, he said, "So you know. How did you hear?"

"It was on the news, yesterday. TV *and* radio."

"Not national."

"He's not *that* famous, is he? The local stations. 'Well-known businessman and musician found dead in car.' I was half-expecting to hear your voice. You know, friend and fellow-musician Geoffrey Cousins says … I'm surprised nobody contacted you."

"They did. That's to say the local rag was on the phone first thing this morning while I was trying to eat breakfast. They'll be ringing round all his contacts, I guess. I didn't tell them anything. Nosey buggers. They only want something sensational to report."

And when she looked at him enquiringly, he said, "They asked me whether I knew of anything 'amiss' in Mr Marsden's personal life. Something that might help explain 'the mystery of his sudden death' as they put it."

Up from her chair and heading for the photocopier, sheaf of papers in hand, Colleen said, "Nine times out of ten when you hear or read of someone found dead in a car or that the death was 'sudden', it means suicide."

"And this wasn't the tenth time." He filled his mug, stood beside the machine sipping the coffee. "Ah, now *this* is the works. Good and strong."

Josie came in, broad of smiles from her weekend in Wales with Mark. Under her ordinary fawn raincoat she revealed a smart new, tight fitting navy-blue skirt and, above it, white button-through shirt. An image of youthful trust, of demure happiness, wanting to share her contentment with them.

"Good weekends, both of you?" she asked. Then, seeing their faces, "Has something happened?"

Colleen looked at Geoff, and when he said nothing, told her. "Oh, how awful."

But the response, genuine though it was, wouldn't take the shine off her own happiness. Why should it? Beyond knowing that Terry Marsden ran the group in which Geoff played, the name meant nothing to Josie. Still, she did think to ask if Terry had 'family'.

"A wife," Geoff told her, "of recent acquisition."

"Poor woman. She'll be devastated."

He could guess what lurked beneath the sudden tremor in Josie's voice. The plans for her own impending wedding were all laid, the church booked, hotel reception and party arranged – "we hope you don't mind, Geoff, if we don't have jazz. We did talk about it, but Mark felt that his friends, and to be honest, mine, would prefer a Rock group, and Stevo, Mark's Best Man, knows one of the Desperate Glories, so we've booked them." And as invited guests, both Geoff and Colleen had heard what the two bridesmaids would be wearing – dark blue dresses offset by orange collars ("Orange is traditional at weddings," she assured them). They also knew about the honeymoon fortnight in the Antilles which would be followed by a settling into Mark's flat near the town centre. They'd been given regular updates on its redecoration prior to the installation of dishwasher and stove, had even been shown photographs of the bargain-basement leather settee and bedroom furniture due to be delivered as soon as the honeymooners were back home. Roses all the way.

And now this news of a death, this wreckage of a life, a marriage. Could some unlooked-for accident, some unforeseeable disaster be waiting to blunder out of the shadows and threaten her own happiness? Josie didn't want a life marked by events, not unless they belonged to the future she saw so clearly for Mark and herself. Marriage, children, growing old together in a haze of tranquil contentment. The Folks Who Live on the Hill. Such innocent egotism. Geoff watched the shake of her head as though she wanted to clear her vision and as she did so he felt to his own surprise a pang of protective concern for her.

"Have you talked to the widow?"

Geoff turned to look at Colleen. "Lorette? I hardly know her."

"I'll take that for a no, then."

Registering the disapproval in her voice, Geoff said "No, you're right, I haven't. been in contact."

Without speaking, Colleen raised an eyebrow.

"It's true what I say. I don't suppose we've exchanged more than half-a-dozen words."

Colleen pursed her lips.

"She won't be wanting *my* shoulder to cry on, is what I mean. I wasn't at the wedding, none of the group were." He remembered how they'd heard of Lorette one night twelve months previously, when Terry told them as they were packing up at the end of a gig. "'Oh, by the way, lads, I've got a new missus.'" And that was it.

But her sceptical look didn't change.

"Not a great communicator, our Terry," he said, "and that's the truth."

"You mean you know nothing about the lady."

"That's it. I've no idea what she did before they met, and as to where she's from – although it's not from round these parts – or *how* they met, not a clue."

"A mystery woman."

Josie, preparing to leave the staff room for front desk duties, paused to share a glance with Colleen. *Men*, the glance said.

Yes, he thought, now you come to mention it, Lorette is a mystery. Like her late husband. Like Terry.

"We sent a card," he said, aware of how lame the words sounded. Then he went back to his desk.

* * *

Midway through the morning when Geoff was on desk duty the phone rang.

"Longford Library."

"I need to speak to Geoffrey Cousins. It's a matter of some urgency." Cadogan's voice, its insistence fruitily magnified by the telephone, was peremptory. Kindly oblige me.

Geoff decided not to know who it was. "Can I ask who wants him?"

"Tell him Peter Cadogan."

"Well, this is Geoff Cousins."

"Hm. I didn't recognise your voice." Touché. "You'll know why I'm phoning." Pause. "I take it you're aware of Terry Marsden's death." And then, without waiting for an answer to what after all was a statement, Cadgan said, "I need to talk to you." The implication was that he wished there was no such need. "In my capacity as Terry's solicitor, that is. When are you free?" When I say jump, jump.

Geoff, on a half-day, was damned if he'd allow Cadogan to interfere with his plans for a leisurely afternoon. There were domestic chores to attend to, and then, feet up, he'd listen to his new Bill Evans CD while reading an early Padgett novel that had so far escaped his attention and which the blurb promised was "an irresistible, comic tale of a young man's entry into life and love". Well, authors weren't responsible for what publishers said about their books. At least, he hoped they weren't.

"I'll be free for an hour after 5.30," he said, having pretended to consider. *I could allow you some time then, you bastard.* "Where do you want to meet? Your office or a bar in town? Or would you prefer me to come to your house? It's in 'The Leas', isn't it? I'm assuming the guards will allow me entry."

Still in *dirigiste* mode, Cadogan said, "I don't think it advisable to conduct business matters at home. You know where I have my chambers?" He named a rather grand street of late nineteenth-century buildings, once private residences for the wealthy but over the years mostly converted to offices for lawyers, private doctors and, so the fitted brass plaques announced, design consultants, although the ground floor of one did service as a restaurant, Hagglers, exactly the kind of overpriced, ridiculously fussy place where the Cadogans of the world no doubt enjoyed wining and dining their important clients.

Still, Cadogan hadn't denied living in 'The Leas'. Geoff wasn't sure why that mattered, but he was certain it did.

* * *

At five o'clock Geoff left off his reading of Padgett's *Starting Out*, pulled on an old lightweight jacket and drove slowly into town. The day being Monday there was comparatively little traffic around, and most of it was heading in the opposite direction from the one he took. But he was in no hurry. Let Cadogan wait. From the library carpark he took his time walking to Clivedon Place. Cadogan would know all about the value of a delayed entrance. The keen edge of a breeze sliced through the afternoon's late-spring warmth, but while he now wished he'd put on a heavier coat, he refused to increase his pace.

His watch told him the time was just on 5.45 when he pressed the intercom button to Newton, Cadogan and Graham. A voice instructed him to enter and proceed to the first floor. Pushing through plate-glass doors he stepped into a large, square, terrazzo-tiled entrance hall, Corinthian-style pillars at each corner, and, at the rear, a wide, red-carpeted marble staircase, branching left and right as it mounted to the first-floor landing. Cadogan stood at the top of the stairs, waiting for him.

"We used to have one of these," Geoff said as he laboured upward, "but the wheels fell off." Ha ha.

Cadogan permitted himself a tight-lipped smile before turning to lead the way through what seemed ten-foot-tall double doors into a room with two computer-dominated desks, behind one of which a young woman was standing as she draped a puffa jacket round her shoulders.

"You'll need that out there," Geoff said. "It's a chill evening." Then, as she turned at the sound of a voice she recognised, "And what's a nice girl like you doing in a place like this?"

"Oh, hi, Geoff," Jade said, her smile one of unaffected good cheer.

"You know each other?" Cadogan was for once off balance.

"Jade's a keen follower of jazz," Geoff said, still looking at her. "Comes to all our gigs. She's hoping for work as a vocalist … "

"In your dreams, grandpa." But the laugh was affectionate. "Right, I'm off. See you tomorrow, Peter – Mr Cadogan."

As she stepped from behind the desk, Geoff saw that she was wearing a blue denim skirt the colour of her hair, black stockings, black court shoes. Every inch the secretary. He lifted his hand to her in a gesture of farewell, said, "Good to see you, Jade," and followed Cadogan into the large room to one side of the office.

The solicitor gestured to a heavy leather armchair in the window bay.

"The things you learn about your own town," Geoff said, crossing the deep-pile maroon carpet to stand before the full-length windows from where he could look down at a railed-off garden space. The garden was screened by laurel bushes, at its centre a small pond with a fountain cast in metal and featuring a dolphin wreathed round a boy, mouth open, ready to spout water which, for the moment at least, was switched off. A few wooden benches were scattered about the grass, none of them in the chill evening air occupied.

"A pleasant place to take refuge in the heat of summer," Cadogan said, coming to stand beside Geoff, "a place where I may pass the fires of the hot day, or," he paused, "hot desires." He smiled. "I brought Miss Birdlip – Helen – here once or twice," he said, as though inconsequentially. Then, turning away, "Can I offer you a drink? Whisky? Brandy? Wine? I don't keep beer on the premises."

And fuck you, too. "A small whisky would be fine."

He watched Cadogan cross to the room's far side, the shelved wall of leather-bound volumes above a dark-wood cabinet where the solicitor, in lightweight, silver-grey suit, was crouching to open the cabinet's doors.

Geoff went over to inspect the books, saw they were indeed to do with law, and switched his attention to the vast desk, the framed photographs on it that showed Cadogan in gown and hood, Cadogan standing among a group of other young men outside what looked to be a country pub, an older Cadogan shaking hands with a greybeard while grasping a plaque, Cadogan in three-quarters profile, head and shoulders only, a black-and-white studio portrait. There were no photographs of Cadogan's children. None of Cadogan ex-family man. No, well.

On the wall behind the desk hung a large oil painting, semi-abstract but with hints of an interior, a table, a small bottle.

"Who painted that?" Geoff asked as Cadogan, having tapped him on the shoulder, handed over a heavy-bottomed glass of what, at a sniff, Geoff knew must be a rare malt. He was taken by the work's compositional balance, the colours, pinks and blues in subtle adjustment, the sense of calm delight the painting gave off.

"A Nottingham artist." Cadogan did not look at the painting. "Rather good, isn't it. I like to support local talent."

"Decent of you," Geoff said, walking away, then dropping into his armchair and resting his glass on the low table between himself and the chair Cadogan now settled into. The table was not so much littered as tellingly arranged with magazines, *Derbyshire Topic*, *The Spectator*, *Telegraph*, *The Literary Review*, one showing a man in green T-shirt and check trousers holding aloft a large silver, elaborately-chased cup he was in the act of kissing, another the Annual Report from what, to judge by the crest spread across the cover, was some public-school Old Boys' Association.

Cadogan raised his glass aloft. "Good health."

Geoff picked up his own glass, took a sip, rested it on a knee, and said, "So, what's this all about, officer?"

Cadogan ran the whisky round his mouth, nursed the glass in both hands, and said, slowly, "As I said on the phone, it's 'about' – " emphasising the word – "Terry Marsden, the late Terry Marsden, the leader of the group of which you are a member, and, more to the purpose, my client."

He looked at Geoff over the top of his glass, the way he no doubt looked at others, calm, judicious, the professional solicitor. "I need to ask you whether you were at all aware of his – of Mr Marsden's – business concerns?"

Startled, despite his best intentions, Geoff asked more sharply than he meant, "Why?"

Having raised his eyes to a point above Geoff's head, Cadogan considered .

"Did he by chance ever discuss them with you or with anyone else in the group."

"Even if he did," Geoff said, "I don't see why you need to know."

Cadogan sighed. "Because, as I have just mentioned, Terry Marsden was my client. Or if you prefer, I was – am – his and indeed his widow's solicitor. And as his solicitor I have to advise her about her late husband's estate."

"Then advise her," Geoff said. *I brought Helen here once or twice.* Yes, I bet you did, and no doubt others. To pass the fires of the hot day. "How did you acquire your new secretary, by the way?"

"Jade?" Cadogan looked faintly amused by the question. "We had a vacancy, she was one of many applicants, and luckily for her – and I hope for us – she was deemed suitable for the position we had on offer. She seems promising material."

There was an ironic inflection in the words. "Since you know her I'm surprised you weren't aware of her current position. Or perhaps your acquaintanceship is of a more intermittent variety."

Cadogan allowed the smile to fade before he drank some more whisky, sat back in his chair, and folded one leg over the other, allowing Geoff a glimpse of white, plump calf above the dark-blue sock with its red diamond pattern. Probably old-school hosiery.

After a moment or two of silence, Cadogan said, "I should tell you, in the strictest confidence, of course, something of what for all I know you may anyway suspect about my client's business affairs."

He paused, inviting Geoff to fill the gap, to nod, to give some sign of agreeing to … To what?

Geoff said, "I don't know *anything* about Terry's business affairs. As you say, I played in the group he ran, and when we talked of anything, which wasn't often, we talked music. We never discussed his professional affairs." Nor his personal life, he might have added, but didn't.

"Hmm." Cadogan put down his glass, leant forward in his chair as though, after prolonged thought, he had decided he could trust Geoff. "I'm taking a risk in saying this, I suppose, though I rely on you not to let my words go beyond these four walls." Presumably taking Geoff's silence for assent, he said, "The truth is, I have good reason to suspect that Marsden's affairs were in considerable disarray."

Having said which, he took up his glass and sat back, waiting for Geoff to speak.

"So?"

Cadogan sighed, said, and now his voice aimed for sincerity, "So if there's anything – *anything* – you know that could help me I'd be grateful to be told about it. Not for my own sake, I hasten to add, but for that of the widow."

"Lorette?" For a moment Geoff allowed himself to wonder whether Lorette *was* the widow. "Will she inherit?" There were presumably other claimants, the first two wives, for instance.

"I can't of course divulge the contents of the will, but, yes, I don't think there's any harm in it being known that Lorette Marsden is the principal beneficiary."

"But?"

"But I doubt that she will become a rich woman. In fact ... " Cadogan stopped, shrugged, said, "I foresee difficulties."

"Did Terry commit suicide – did he kill himself – because of what you call the 'disarray' of his business affairs."

Cadogan looked thoughtful. A practised look. "We don't of course know that it *was* suicide. For that we must await the pathologist's report, and perhaps the coroner's. There was no note."

"But the brandy and pills?"

"Well, yes," Cadogan said, tipping the last of his whisky down his throat. "I don't think there's much doubt that poor Marsden was the author of his own death."

"And you think the cause may have been that his business affairs were in a mess." He paused. "Rather than what people call affairs of the heart."

"Oh, no doubt about that." Cadogan looked across at Geoff, man to man. "My client had, as you probably know, two previous marriages behind him, neither of which, as I understand it, ended at all happily. But you saw him at his birthday party. I'd say he was devoted to Lorette, wouldn't you?"

Geoff drank the last of his whisky, placed the glass on the table in front of him, and shook his head when Cadogan motioned towards the possibility of a refill.

"He put on a good show, I'll say that for him." Should he mention the previous morning's conversation at Simon and Barbara's? No.

He said, "I don't think any of us – any of the group – had a clue as to Terry's business *or* his private life. You may quote me. We – well, I – never clapped eyes on his previous wives, and I met Lorette on no more than two or three occasions." A sudden thought occurred to him. "How did she and Terry meet? Do you know? She's not from round here, is she? Did Terry meet her on his travels? Down in London, perhaps?"

For answer, Cadogan flicked out an arm to look at the slender gold wrist watch that glinted out from under his shirt-cuff. "I'll have to call a halt to this," he said. "I'm due to go to see the lady in question."

He stood. It was clear that he regarded Geoff as being of no further use. "Do you happen to know whether any of the other members of your group were in my client's confidence?"

"I know they weren't."

Cadogan watched Geoff get to his feet. "Then I shan't bother them." A pause. "I apologise for having put you to any trouble," he said, "but you understand that I needed to know whether you had any insight into Terry – Mr Marsden's – difficulties, as I think of them."

"What difference would it have made?"

"Oh," Cadogan shrugged. "Names, places. Who can tell?" Then, as they faced each other, he inclined his head toward Geoff in a gesture of seeming confidentiality. "The third Mrs Marsden," he said, "was, you might say, rather captured by Terry, and at the time when she happened to be the wife of someone he did business with in the London area. Yes, she is from London. The *gentleman* in question – the wronged husband – was not at all happy at her leaving him for another man. For that *particular* man."

He stood aside to allow Geoff to move past him. It was as though, having said this much, he considered their conversation at an end. But something about the way the way he had stressed the two words made Geoff pause in the act of stepping toward the door.

He turned to Cadogan. "What are you not telling me?"

Cadogan, who was just behind him, looked at him, but said

nothing.

"You're not suggesting that this someone is implicated in Terry's death?"

Still Cadogan said nothing.

"*Is* that what you're hinting? London gangland reaches out to the Midlands."

Cadogan shook his head but kept his eyes on Geoff's.

"Then what? Lorette's former husband revenges himself on Terry by screwing his business? You shaft my wife, I'll shaft your – your – well whatever it was that Terry did." He remembered, then. "'Financial adviser' he once called himself. What *is* a financial adviser? Someone who gets his fingers stuck into other people's tills?"

This time Cadogan did not shake his head.

"So Terry was mixed up in dodgy dealings. Is that it?"

Cadogan pushed ahead of his guest and led the way through to the outer office, where he paused as, behind him, Geoff said, "Still, business, financial advisers, I guess it's all pretty dodgy."

Cadogan spun round, chin tilted, his eyes fixed on Geoff's. "Ah, the view from the purer, cleaner air of library services, where nothing so dirty as money is allowed to sully the thoughts or deeds of employees."

The voice was silky smooth, the smile tight, dismissive, as was the gesture, a flick of the wrist as though to dismiss a fly.

But it was Geoff who was being dismissed.

"Remember," Cadogan said, opening the door and gazing left and right before continuing. "If you know of anything … "

"Anything that might help solicitors in their enquiries … "

Cadogan nodded, left it at that.

"To repeat, I don't," Geoff said. "Nor do either Simon or Al. But thanks for the whisky."

"You can find your own way out?"

For answer, Geoff raised a hand and made his way as nimbly as he could down the carpeted stairs.

On the half-landing, he turned to see that Cadogan was watching his descent.

"By the way," he called up, "how's *As You Like It* going. Still on course?"

Cadogan's smile, faint as it had been, disappeared. "How kind of you to ask after the Alleyn Players," he said, "but I have no immediate plans for a reading of the play. It has been, shall we say, postponed."

For all the physical distance between them, Geoff could hear the edge in the other man's voice.

"Sorry to hear that," he said as he turned once more to continue his descent. *Sorry as in Good. Good as in Great. Great as in the more it hurts the better I'll like it.*

He hoped Cadogan didn't see him half-trip on the bottom step, but steeled himself not to look round and up to where the solicitor was probably still standing, watching his exit through the heavy, smoked-glass doors.

25

Back at Ewing Avenue, slicing mushrooms in preparation for a sauce intended to go with pasta, he thought about Terry. Or rather, he thought about how he'd never thought about him – not *really* thought about him – until news of his death came through. How little the news had affected him. Surprise, yes, of course even, perhaps, a sense of mild shock, though that soon passed. But grief? No. Not even a twinge of sorrow. Terry is dead, and what is trumps. Something amiss there. Some guilt, perhaps, that he could fetch up no deeper feelings, that Terry Marsden seemed not to – not what? Not to *merit* them? No, forget that. Merit had nothing to do with it. The truth was rather that Terry had always been a kind of absent presence, a smooth, unscratchable surface with nothing discernible beneath, and faced with such blank impermeability, feelings of any kind seemed unavailing. *That,* he realised, was what he knew to be amiss.

He dropped a handful of pasta into the simmering pan, watched the water cloud over crustacean shapes. How did Terry regard himself? Did he mean to be a mystery to others? Or was he programmed for sets of automatic responses, like his keyboard? Click here for organ, here for honky-tonk, here for spinet. Keep smiling, keep 'em guessing, keep on the right side of the law – and if you couldn't do that then at least make sure you had a smart solicitor. Cadogan. Smart. Oh, yes, Cadogan was undoubtedly smart.

Cadogan. Geoff stirred the sauce, looked at his watch, gave the pasta a few minutes more. Cadogan, bloody Cadogan. Cadogan who oozed assurance. Was it an acquired manner or was he born that way? Nature or nurture? Cadogan had a way of wrong-footing you that went with the territory. He could move from weirdly dated, discomposing slang – that "Don't talk poppycock" still rankled – to formal utterance which was as knowing as it was calculated to throw you. Knowing *because* it was meant to throw you. "A pleasant place to take refuge in the heat of summer."

Look, such words said, *I know I'm acting the part, but what are you going to do about it? Call me out? I don't think so. Playing at being me is not merely what I do, it's what I am. And if it isn't, you certainly won't know where the gap between act and reality occurs. You won't, will you!*

No wonder Cadogan enjoyed directing the Alleyn Players. It gave him power over those who couldn't hope to close the gap, whose modest acting abilities stood apart from their daily lives, whose varying degrees of incompetence as actors allowed him the satisfaction of knowing his own subtle, snug-fitting composure. Cadogan the self-possessed man.

Sin of self-love possesseth all mine eye. One of the sonnets Geoff had been made to learn at school, and which he could still more or less remember. Methinks no face so gracious is as mine. All those photographs on Cadogan's desk. All of himself, because, although others were present in some of the photographs, he was the reason for the display. Other people were incidental, given walk-on parts to support the main actor. Even his words at Terry's party had been a way of asserting his own pre-eminence. "He has begged me not to list his accomplishments and successes." In other words, I know all about Terry. Terry, the mystery man to Al, to Simon and to him, Geoff, was an open book to Cadogan.

Glancing at his watch – the pasta needed another couple of minutes – Geoff tried to remember what Cadogan had said of Lorette. Oh, yes. Terry had "captured" her. At the time that had seemed a casual enough word – as in captivated – but now he could see a hidden meaning in it. Terry had snatched Lorette away from her rightful owner.

Or was that to read more into Cadogan's word than he intended? No, almost certainly not. Cadogan was too calculating a man for that, too self-possessed to let slip words he didn't intend. He knew, and he wanted others to know he knew, that Terry had taken Lorette away from a husband who might, after all, be prepared to act as the outraged landowner behaved to thieves. Set the law on them. What law? Oh, the law of the jungle.

Cadogan, the man whose every word, no matter how lightly uttered, was freighted. Miss Birdlip is back in town. Cadogan knew the old number all right. Lulu's back in town. My lover has returned.

He drained the pasta, tipped it into a bowl, stirred in a splash of olive oil, added the sauce and settled down to eat.

Grating some parmesan over his dish, he said aloud, "But she's *not* your lover, Cadogan. Not any more." She'd said so.

Did he believe her?

He forked up some pasta, chewed and swallowed. Miss Birdlip is back in town.

But they weren't together. "I've cut free of him." Did she mean that? Or was that the nature of the relationship between the two of them: on-off, now brilliantly lit, now plunged into darkness. Cadogan had been telling the truth, hadn't he, when he said that he'd decided to postpone the production of *As You Like It,* implying, so Geoff had assumed, that Helen wouldn't do his bidding? But now, suddenly, he saw the words in a different light. I've got what I wanted without having to bother with all that rigmarole of a play reading.

He pushed his largely uneaten bowl aside, eased Baw off his lap, and, standing, drained his glass in one swallow. He had to hear her voice.

* * *

The answer phone device clicked on. *Hello. Your call cannot be answered now, so please leave your message after the tone.*

Not in. So where was she at 7 o'clock of a Monday evening? With Cadogan? Of course. The lady in question Cadogan claimed he had an appointment to see wasn't in fact Lorette. It was *Helen.* And probably going to Cadogan's office. That was why he was so keen to hustle Geoff off the premises. *I brought Helen here once or twice.* And now she's on her way here, so off you go, sonny boy.

He looked out at the garden where in the dying light of an April evening, Frank, leaning on a hoe as if it was an alpenstock and wrapped in raincoat and scarf against the chill, was bending to inspect a parade of daffodils mustered in rows along the lawn's short length. Beyond, the door of the garden shed swung open in what had to be a stir of wind and Frank, straightening, began to pad across the grass to secure it.

And at that moment the phone rang.

"Geoff? Helen."

Guilt —was it? – froze his lips.

"Geoff? *Geoff?*"

"Sorry." He made throat-clearing noises. "Something went down the wrong way."

"Drink some water."

"It's OK now. How are you?"

"Whacked. I've just got in from a staff meeting, but I saw my answerphone light was on, so thought I'd better deal with it, and up came your number. Are you all right?"

No, I'm not all right, I'm anything *but* all right.

He said, "I'm fine, but I wondered if you'd heard about Terry. Terry Marsden."

"Yes, I have. As a matter of fact I was going to call you later to ask what *you* knew. Janey phoned last thing yesterday evening, too late for me to contact you then, and all she knew was what she'd heard on local late-night news, which left her pretty much in the dark."

Her voice was concerned, friend to friend. Something of his earlier panic was dying down.

"Janey said a policeman found the body."

"An off-duty traffic cop," he told her. "Terry was in his car, in a lay-by."

"And she also told me that the police aren't looking for anyone else 'concerned in the incident'. That means suicide, doesn't it?"

So Cadogan hadn't been in touch.

He took a deep breath and, his heartbeat returning to normal, said, "Yes, it looks as though Terry killed himself. I don't know very much myself." But he told her all he had heard from Simon and Al. Of his visit to Cadogan he said nothing.

"What about funeral arrangements?"

"I'll pass on the info as soon as there is any."

"That's good. I didn't know him at all well, of course, but it seems a horrible way to go. And then his wife … She must be in shock. Would a card be in order?"

"I don't see why not," he said. "Yes, I'm sure it would be a good idea."

"In that case I will. What's the address?"

He told her and she thanked him.

A pause.

"Actually," she said, "I'd been meaning to phone you anyway." Another pause.

Here it comes, he thought. She's going to tell me that – surprise, surprise – she and Cadogan have settled their differences and that from now on they're a pair.

"You've probably heard that the Halsteads – Charles and Verity – are leaving. *Pause.* It came as a complete surprise, they'd not dropped so much as a hint. And off so soon. I've invited them to farewell drinks on Saturday evening and wondered whether you'd like to join us. And *slight pause* as I owe you a meal I though it would be a chance for you to experience the Birdlip cuisine. *Pause.*

Of course, you may have other plans, but if not ... *Pause* Would 6.30 be all right? The Halsteads won't want to hang around for long. Hello? Hello? Geoff, are you still there? Do you need to drink some more water?"

"Yes," he said, "I'm here. And no, I'm OK on the water front."

He took a deep breath. Then, risking further words only when he was reasonably sure he had command of his speech, "Yes, that's fine. Absolutely fine. Saturday. 6.30. Fine. Absolutely fine."

Not water, wine.

26

"Wow," Helen said. She stood in the open doorway, dark red shirt and jeans below which the points of black boots peered out, giving her a deceptively casual appearance. "Flowers as well as a bottle. You're doubly welcome."

She bent her head to smell the roses and one of her pendant earrings became caught in fronds of greenery.

He stepped forward to help her but with a smile she shook her head, already freed of the entanglement. "We're in the front room," she said. "You go on in and I'll put these in water."

Stepping past, he was close enough to her to inhale the unmistakable tang of her scent. There's such an air of spring about it.

The Halsteads, filled wine glasses in hand, were standing side by side before the bay window of the large room, looking as though they might be waiting to interview him.

"Hello," he said, "good to see you."

Fixing his eyes on Charles and speaking for the first time since his arrival, he was relieved to find that he could utter the trite words without sounding as though in urgent need of a tracheotomy. Still, he cleared his throat before adding, "Though I gather that this is hail and farewell. Helen tells me you're about to leave for … Wherever it is." His smile, he knew, was an idiot's rictus. Soon, he would have to look at Verity.

Perhaps mistaking his apprehension for the nervousness of the socially challenged, Charles said, smiling, relaxed, "We're birds of passage. Now you see us, now you don't."

"Here today, gone tomorrow." At least his mouth was beginning to function normally.

"That about sums it up." Plainly unwilling to tell Geoff where they'd be going, Charles was nevertheless entirely at his ease. Hence, no doubt, what seemed to be his perpetual off-duty gear: open-neck shirt and light-brown cords, though in deference to the occasion his ample body was crammed into an old, out-at-elbows tweed jacket.

Risking at last a quick glance at the woman standing by him, Geoff saw the challenge in her eyes, as quickly looked away. But the glance had been enough to show that she was, in appearance at least, immaculate. Her hair had begun to grow out, the red dye was gone, and in her tailored linen dress with careful make-up and remarkably smooth skin – the neck from which the slender string of pearls hung was itself flawlessly white – she appeared the very model of a model Home Counties wife. Only the lips, he realised, never quite at rest, and the eyes he didn't want to meet, deep, glittering, suggested the depths where an unfathomable self lurked.

From behind him, Helen, the anxious hostess, said, "Oh, sit down, *please*, folks. Geoff, what would you like to drink?"

There were open bottles of wine on the narrow table that stood beneath the room's deep bay windows. He went over to inspect them and she came too, poured the white he gestured to while, in the window glass, he watched the reflected images of the Halsteads as they arranged themselves on a low-slung settee. When Helen handed him his glass her smile seemed to contain a question. He sipped, said, "That's fine," looking at her as he did so, and this time the smile was accompanied by a small, affirmative nod. He seemed to have passed some test and felt a sudden upsurge of emotional warmth as he turned to face his fellow guests.

Charles, so as to avoid having his knees up to his chin, half-sat, half-lay on the sofa, legs extended to reveal wrinkled grey woollen socks that sagged above battered brogues, one of them, Geoff noticed as he himself dropped into a chair facing them, making do with a black lace.

Between them was an old wooden trunk, a white cloth thrown over it on which Helen had arranged bowls of nuts and olives. "My one antique," she said, indicating the trunk as she perched on the arm of the settee next to Charles. "It came from my mother who had it from her father who had it from *his* father, who took it with him round the world."

"He was a mariner?"

Verity, knees together, legs tilted at an elegant angle, asked the question with the right degree of polite interest.

"He wasn't exactly a mariner, no." Helen paused over Verity's use of the old word. "But according to family legend he scoured the world looking for a way to make some money. In the end the only money he made was writing about his adventures."

"An author?" Charles said. "Have you read any of his books?"

Helen shook her head. "He didn't write books." She looked across to Geoff, let her eyes rest on his for some moments as though seeking reassurance, before, turning to Charles, she said, "My great-grandfather became what I suppose would nowadays be called a journalist, although I think he wrote mainly for magazines, of which there were apparently plenty. We used to have some at home. *John O'London's, Cornhill, Strand* … I can't remember the others. Anyway, they all went when my dad retired and my parents moved from house to flat."

Verity, eyes tilted towards the ceiling, said, "All this talk of authors reminds me that I managed to finish Padgett's novel, you'll be relieved to know. A fearful trudge, but I slogged on until I could say a last farewell to the bloody thing." She said, directing her words to Helen, and sighing extravagantly, "all about a man who takes off in order to discover his 'authentic self'." She paused, allowed a smile to come and go. "Dreadful stuff."

There was a pause. It was as if she were acting the heroine in some vintage West End farce and might at any moment break into a 'brittle' laugh or search in her handbag for a cigarette-holder while an attendant male leant over her, offering her a light. Well, it won't be me, Geoff thought, knowing what she intended, the performance that was being put on for him, even though – *especially* though – she still wouldn't look in his direction. Being rude about Padgett was her way of getting at him, Geoff.

Charles, crossing one ankle over the other, said, studying the carpet, "I thought it rather good."

Verity laid a hand on the jacketed arm next to her. "I've no doubt it looks different from a man's perspective. But believe me, no woman would be the slightest bit interested in the men he writes about. And as for the women. Unbelievable, *quite* unbelievable."

"Oh, I don't know." Helen stood to hand round the bowls of nuts. "I really liked the novels of his I've read. I believed in the woman in that one you read. I know she behaved badly, but she had her reasons."

Verity glanced swiftly at Helen, who was holding a bowl in front of her guest, shook her head, said nothing. There had been no hidden meaning in Helen's open defence of Padgett.

But there was in Verity's question to Geoff. Looking across at him, as though surprised to find him in the room, she said, "You were a friend of his I gather?"

He took a mouthful of wine, swallowed, then said, "Not so much

201

a friend as an acquaintance. We were students together, had mates in common, sometimes drank in the same company, but not friends, no."

"So you can't explain Georgi Coniscu?"

"*Who?*" Then he remembered. A friend of the main character. But *what* did he remember? And why on earth did she suddenly spring that name on him? He dug around in his mind for the bones of Padgett's story. "Remind me," he said.

"He turns out to be a dud. Fails his friend." She was looking at him with such scorching intensity he had to avert his gaze.

Helen, standing now beside Geoff's chair, said, "I didn't like him, that's for sure. But I thought that was the point." She looked down at Geoff, perhaps hoping for his support. "It never occurred to me that Padgett wanted me to think him particularly sympathetic." Then, finding reassurance in his nod, she said, "That name, Georgi Coniscu. It's Central European, isn't it? He's a displaced person."

Verity said, her smile thinly triumphant, "That still doesn't explain why he lets his friend down."

"*How* does he let him down?" Helen asked, "I've forgotten." She frowned, puzzling over Verity's condemnation.

Charles, making great play of emptying his glass, gestured to his wife, then, heaving himself upright, held out a hand for her to cling onto as she got to her feet.

But she rose unaided, stood apart, half turned away, as Charles said, his smile including both Helen and Geoff, "Sorry to put an end to the book club discussion but we must go. Last minute packing before the van comes to whisk us away."

He took Verity's glass from her, placed them both on the covered trunk and, as Geoff got to his feet, said to Helen, who was standing by the door, "Well, it's been a pleasure to have known you, Helen, and let's hope our paths will cross again."

He looked at Verity, no doubt wanting her to endorse his words, but when she said nothing he reached out to grip Geoff's outstretched hand, then stood back and waited while his wife stepped forward. For a moment Geoff wondered whether to ignore the languid fingers she dangled before him, but, watched by the others, felt impelled to take them in his own.

"Goodbye," she said, her eyes unyielding as she looked at him. "Coniscu. I always wondered whether it was some sort of anagram."

Then, a near-contemptuous smile on her carefully carmined lips, she allowed her husband to usher her out of the room.

He stood, glass in hand, listening to the muffled words of farewell followed by the door to the flat thudding shut, and seconds later Helen re-entered.

She looked at him enquiringly. "Well," she said, "that was a bit sticky, I'm afraid. Did you know what she was on about?"

She gestured to his empty glass and, without speaking, he handed it to her for a refill. She had her back to him, pouring wine for them both, as he said, "She thinks I let her down."

Turning, her look serious, she came over, handed him his glass. "That, if I may say so, m'lud, is obvious. But what the court would like to hear is what's a been goin' on. If, that is, it may be told. And always accepting that it's no business of mine."

And she sank into the settee.

Should he join her there? No, she was occupying centre ground, so that if he sat beside her he would have to squeeze into a narrow space, would have either to press against her or ask her to move a little. He hesitated for a moment, then dropped back into the chair he'd recently vacated, tried to read the expression in her eyes. Now the two of them were on their own, the barriers that had seemed in the presence of the others to have been lowered were re-erected, and he searched about not so much for what to say as how to say it.

Swallowing a mouthful of wine, he said at length, "How well do you know Verity?"

She shrugged, pulling down her mouth. "Not very well. She's quite difficult to know."

"When they left there was no talk from her about keeping in touch."

"No." She looked down at the glass she was nursing in her lap. Without looking up, she said, "Would that upset you?"

"Why on earth should it?" And then he saw, thought he saw, what she might mean. "You aren't suggesting, are you, that there was anything between Verity Halstead and me? Did *she* suggest there was?"

The answer was emphatic. "No." A pause. "But she was giving you a hard time, wasn't she? I'm wondering what it was you did or said to so upset her."

"I think it was more what I *hadn't* done. I hadn't 'been there' for her, or whatever that silly phrase is. Georgi Coniscu to the life." He kept the tone as lightly ironic as he could, but couldn't dispel the barb that gleamed in Verity's final words. *I always wondered whether it was some sort of anagram.* Was it? Had Padgett intended that? Then, realising from the way Helen was looking at him, head tilted back, one eyebrow raised in mute enquiry, that he couldn't leave the matter there, he said, "That meeting she set up with me after Terry Marsden's party. I still don't know what she wanted." He paused. "I'm damned sure, though, it wasn't *me*. When we had our – well, tête-à-tête is hardly the phrase – I couldn't make her out. That post-punk haircut, if that's what it was. To be honest, she looked ridiculous."

"I know what you mean." She sat silent for a moment, considering. Then she said, "When we – when you and I – talked about her that afternoon in Nottingham I didn't tell you – didn't think I should – that she came up here the morning after the party. She wanted to talk. Charles was away, she said, and she needed – was begging for even – my approval of what she'd done. I think she was scared she'd gone too far." She paused, shook her head. "I don't know."

"And what did you tell her?"

"The truth, though as gently as I could. I said that she was an attractive woman but that chopping and dyeing her hair didn't do her any favours. At first she was violently angry, said she knew that, that favours weren't what she wanted. She was pretty wild. I was actually quite worried for her, offered to go down with her, help her wash out the dye, but she said she'd be all right and gradually calmed down. I think she was angry with me for not as it were backing her up. But," she smiled faintly, "as I told you, she's a strong person. She can take the truth. By the end of that morning I was getting as much from her as she was from me."

"About Wolverhampton?" He couldn't bring himself to say "about your love affair."

"Mmm." She was staring into her glass. "I've sometimes wondered whether the story she told about her own past difficulties weren't so as to put mine 'in perspective,' as the saying goes. That may have been why she insisted what she told me was confidential. For my ears only. She was making it up as she went."

And when he looked enquiringly at her, she added, "Well, it's possible, isn't it? She wasn't worried about the truth coming out but about being discovered in a lie. I've no idea how much Cadogan knows about her past, but Charles *must* know. If I'd hinted at anything in their presence the house of cards would have come tumbling down. To coin a cliché."

He said, "When we first met she told me she had a classy background. Father a judge, barristers for brothers. But according to Cadogan she had a lousy upbringing and that was followed by some pretty awful years as a young woman. Her knowledge of the law comes from the other side of the court."

"And we all believe whatever Mr Cadogan says."

But the remark was sardonic rather than bitter. And as though to confirm that, she added, "Still, assuming she and Cadogan didn't cook up the story between them, yes, from what she told me, Charles has rescued her from a bad man and a rotten life."

Geoff finished his wine, said, "Which doesn't entirely explain her behaviour."

Helen smiled, a small, sad, reflective smile. "We're all pretty opaque to each other, aren't we? We do things which are obvious to us, inexplicable to others."

She paused. He looked across at her, but her gaze was withdrawn, eyes fixed on a patch of carpet at her feet. Might she at last be nerving herself to tell him ... Tell him what? He sat silent, holding his breath.

But when she lifted her eyes to his, she said only, "For example, would you have had Terry Marsden down as a suicide?"

Then, looking at his empty glass, and as though not expecting an answer to her question, she gestured to his glass. "More wine?"

"I'd rather wait until we're eating." The moment had passed and they were back in the world of conversational bricolage.

She said, "Good idea" she said. "It's lamb casserole, I hope that's OK. We can eat anytime."

"Lead me to it," he said.

* * *

Over the meal, as they sat facing each other at the kitchen table laid with a dark blue cloth, candle-light glimmering above a bowl of greenery, glinting on glassware and the solid silver cutlery – "part of the Birdlip inheritance," she said when he voiced his admiration – conversation as if by tacit agreement kept clear of the Halsteads. He asked her about college work, and, encouraged, she spoke ruefully about the problems of managing courses for bored teenagers who were, most of them, trying to defer the day when they'd have no alternative but to sign on or accept some dead-end job or other.

"They'd do better to get a grip on the kind of skills Jade has."

She was puzzled. "Who?" Then, expression clearing, "Oh, the girl – young woman – I met at the Black Cat. I thought you told me she was a shop assistant."

Standing, Helen stacked the casserole pot on top of their empty plates and watched as he, too, stood to help her clear the table.

"Not any longer," he said. "She has a new job."

From the fridge she brought a bowl of fruit salad, a jug of cream, then fetched two glass dishes from the shelf that ran the length of the far wall above the kitchen unit. "In the absence of sorbet, which in our case we have not got, citric fruit is ideally suited to cleanse the palate following the ingestion of rich meat. I quote. Cream is optional."

Watching her spoon fruit into a dish for him, noticing the deft certainty of her movements, the curve of her wrist, he said, "Jade's now working in a solicitors' office. Newton, Cadogan and Graham. Secretary to the one and only Peter Cadogan."

She raised her eyes, startled and not, he thought, pleased by his words. "How do you know that? Did she tell you?"

"I saw her there. Cadogan asked me to go to his office to discuss matters to do with Terry Marsden. His client. And there she was, blue hair, nose stud, denim and all. And, I'm happy to report, entirely at her ease."

Dipping his spoon into the cream she passed him, he said, "A swish building, Mr Cadogan occupies. That private garden. I wouldn't mind a slice of that. Who are Newton and Graham, I wonder?"

"No idea," Helen said indifferently, lifting a spoon to her lips.

"But you've seen their place of work."

He tried to speak the words casually, but, putting down her spoon, she said sharply, "Yes, I was there. Once or twice. A long time ago." Then, "Well. Let's hope he keeps his paws off that young woman."

Again she lifted her spoon. Some hope, her pursed lips, almost a grimace, implied.

He said, "Oh, Jade can look after herself."

"She certainly knows how to handle you. Wham, Bam, and thank you, Sam."

It was his turn to be startled. As he opened his mouth to speak, Helen said, "How did I guess? Easy. The way she touched you that evening we met in the Black Cat. Not exactly proprietorial but certainly implying that you and she were more than just good friends."

He shook his head. "Good friends is all we are." He took a

mouthful of fruit salad, swallowed, and said, "Still, if we're 'fessing up, then, yes, Jade and I did spend a few weekends together. But she soon called it off. No tears, no fuss, hooray for us."

"Hardly a confession, then." She was laughing.

"It's the best I can do." He met her gaze, at first mock-defiant, then knew he was staring, but couldn't turn his eyes away from those lustrous irises, the pupils that in softening candle-light seemed to magnify and glow.

I love you, he wanted to say, I love you. You don't have to say anything but I do want to tell you this. I love you, Helen.

He said, "Picking up on your claim that we're opaque to each other. It may be so, but you're pretty good at reading the signs. I mean, guessing from the way Jade touched me that she and I had once been lovers, that's pretty smart."

"It's hardly grade A sleuthing."

"Perhaps not," he said, chasing the last piece of melon round his bowl, "but it's better than I could manage."

He caught the sliver of melon, spooned it in, swallowed. "That first evening you came into the Three Tuns, I wasn't even sure it *was* you."

He looked up to see that she was watching him.

"You hadn't seen me for a long time," she said, her smile, hardly a smile, tugging down the corners of her mouth. "Ten years, Geoff." The words were uttered in a kind of rueful, reflective wonder.

"Did you recognise me?"

"Oh, yes," she said, "but then I knew what I was looking for."

Her eyes, their steady glow lit by laughter, met his.

After a pause she said. "A man of my own age or thereabouts playing tenor sax. Easy. No chance you'd be an apparition to mock my eyes with air."

And when he looked at her wonderingly, she added, and now her laugh was open, "Shakespeare, or rather Antony, explaining that clouds take different shapes. 'Sometimes we see a cloud that's dragonish, A vapour sometimes like a bear or lion.' It's one of this year's set texts." She pushed her bowl away. "I think he's admitting that he can never be sure just who Cleopatra is. The serpent of old Nile. Serpents are shape-changers."

"Someone I used to know at university," Geoff said slowly, "told me that we need very few visual markers to identify people by. I wonder."

207

"Wonder why? Wonder what?"

Encouraged by the warm steadiness of her gaze, he said, "I guess I wasn't sure I could trust the evidence of my eyes that evening."

I wanted it to be you, but, Helen, if only you knew how often in the previous years I'd seen you ahead of me walking down a street, or sitting in a restaurant, or at the wheel of a car, or, once, on the up escalator at St Pancras while I was on the down, and of course I'd catch up with the woman I was sure was you or look again and it was never you, it was a stranger, wrong mouth, wrong hair, wrong gestures, even wrong scent. It was *never* you.

Aloud, he said, his voice dropping to not much more than a whisper, "Dim light and you were sitting at the back of the room. I kept hoping but – yes, ten years is a long time. I think it was the way you lifted your glass that made me know it was you."

When he raised his eyes, he found she was staring intently at him. "The marker," he said, smiling.

She broke her gaze, and as though fearing the words she guessed were gathering on his tongue, stood up briskly. "I'll make coffee," she said. "And why don't you finish the wine. You're not driving, are you?"

"No," he said, "I left the car at home."

The word fell dully among the table things. In fact he'd left his car in the library car park, because, if necessary, if … if … it could stay there all night, because, oh, because you never knew. But he did now. She'd be putting her guest out at a decent hour. Taxi for him, and for her well-earned rest. He watched candle flame spiral upward, yellow and magenta fading into threads of black as the flame elongated, shivered in a wisp of wind.

Her back to him as she poured boiling water into a cafetiere, Helen said, "I do have one confession to make." Her face was turned sufficiently for him to see the curve of her cheek, the edge of her fringe, even the corner of her mouth. It couldn't be merely the candlelight that made her look so beautiful.

"Oh." Irrationally, hope stirred.

She came back to the table, bringing with her the cafetiere, two cups dangling by their handles from fingers of her free hand.

"Verity."

Hope lay down and died. "What about Verity?" I thought further talk about her was off the agenda.

"That evening after she'd been up to see me – the evening after the Marsden party – I thought I should run down to see if she was all right. I knocked on her door and guess who answered?"

"Cadogan," he said, suddenly confident this must have been the brief and unintended meeting she'd referred to that Saturday in Nottingham.

In the act of pouring coffee, she stopped, said, "How did you guess?"

"Because, as I told you, he came to see me the following evening. She'd phoned him after our failure of a meeting to tell him, so he said, that she was worried she'd offended me. I wasn't sure I believed him, and I was even less sure after I phoned her to 'clear the air' you might say and, as you know, she told me to fuck off. End of story."

He pressed his hands down on either side of his coffee cup. A gesture intended to dismiss further talk of Verity and, for that matter, of Cadogan.

But Helen chose to ignore it. "Geoff," she said, looking at him intently, "you can't stop there. You have to tell me what Cadogan said – about Verity, I assume."

He raised his hands, showed her his empty palms. "OK. If you really want to know." But he sipped some coffee before speaking again. Then, "Yes, Cadogan had plenty to say about her – about Verity," Geoff admitted. "But if what he told me is true, you perhaps know it all, probably know more than I do. Either from Verity herself or from – her solicitor." For the moment he couldn't bring himself to speak Cadogan's name.

"Try me," she said.

So he told her the story that Cadogan had told him. That the woman they knew as Verity had originally been called Eve, that her background wasn't one of privilege but a foster home from which she escaped into marriage to a criminal, one Trevor Lewis, a nasty bit of work with violent tendencies, that she was rescued from Lewis by the love of a good man, to wit a businessman, Charles Halstead, who, after Lewis's disappearance into prison and her divorce, found himself in need of a secretary, took on Eve, then offered her love and protection, protection which was needed once Lewis, freed from prison, threatened to come after her. Which was why she had changed her name and why she and Charles never stayed for long in any one place.

All the time he spoke, Helen was looking at him, her face, as his rapid run-through of the narrative went on, registering at first amazement, then increasingly scepticism, then, finally, incredulity.

When, finally, he finished, she said, "And you *believed* all this?"

Startled, he said, "Improbable as it may seem, improbable as the story itself seems, yes." Then, half-defensive, but aware of her expression, the open-mouthed wonder, which, given the narration of so unlikely a story was, he now realised, more than justified, he said, "Who was I to disbelieve it? And after all it made a kind of sense. Squared with the facts as far as I knew."

Her chin cupped in her hands, she was staring into her empty coffee cup. "Yes," she said slowly, raising her eyes to his. "I can see that."

"But you *don't* believe it."

"She told me an entirely different story. "

It was his turn to look sceptical. "And what she told you was enough to make you think she was a strong person?" He paused to let the words register. "That's what you told me when we were in Nottingham," he said.

She looked at him, her expression even in the dim candle-light, plainly troubled, doubtful. "I said it because I believed it. Now, I'm not so sure."

One of the candles was nearly burnt out. Helen fetched a replacement, lit it from the dying flame and squashed its base into the soft wax of the dying candle. The new flame steadied itself in her eyes as she said, "I'm beginning to wonder whether even *she* knows who she is. That story about a foster-home, for instance. She never mentioned that, simply implied that she had an unhappy home life. Parents remote, unloving, sent to boarding school at an early age, Finishing School in Switzerland, few friends … That kind of thing. But no judge. Her father was a successful businessman. As to life on the streets and a criminal husband, it's the first I've heard of any of that. She told me she'd once been engaged but the man had changed his mind and gone off with another woman."

He shook his head. "I give up. I mean, I can see – just – why she might have invented a tale of her own unhappy adolescence for your consumption. Take you away from the black mopes of Wolverhampton. But why should she make up this other tale about street life and crime?"

"The question may be, why did Cadogan." And she looked at him, a faint smile on her lips, in her eyes. A smile that offered him – what?

In the act of lifting cup to lips, he stilled his movements, knew from her own widening gaze that he must be staring at her, said, "Now that *is* a question," and slowly, without drinking, returned cup to saucer.

After a moment or two, he raised his eyes, said, "What's your explanation?" and waited.

"I don't have one," she said, "not a good one, anyway. But wrong-footing people is a tactic Peter – Cadogan – often uses. He enjoys it. It puts him in charge. In the time we were together I saw him do it so often I decided it went with the territory. 'I am a solicitor, watch me in action. This is my Licence to Practice.'"

"Take that. Kerpow."

"Exactly." Again she shook her head, this time as though to clear it, said as though by way of explaining matters, "He treats everyone as a potential opponent." She stared at the table in front of her, remembering. "Once, when we were away for a weekend, in Suffolk, he bumped into a man he'd known at university – Bill something-or-other – and they started talking about student days. We were in a bar and the talk dragged on. A name came up and Bill said 'Oh, yes, a complete shit.' So then came the kerpow." She laughed, looked at Geoff, then away. "Cadogan said 'I think you should know that the man you condemn was badly injured in the Falklands.'" There was no humour in her laugh. "Result, Bill Something had to make his apologies, if he'd known that, then of course etc. End of conversation, we left." Another laugh, even briefer. "Afterwards I asked about the wounded hero. Cadogan smirked at me – *smirked* – no other word will do. 'I made it up,' he said, 'couldn't you tell?'"

She paused there, and, without looking at Geoff said, "If I'd not been so crazy about him I'd have kicked him in the balls and left him there and then. It wasn't so much the lie, it was the way he smiled when he realised that he'd fooled not just his university chum but me. And he expected me to smile back, even to laugh."

"As I said on an earlier occasion, SB. Smug bastard."

"No," she said, "not smug. Or not only smug. He was triumphant. He *loved* what he'd done." Another pause. "AB," she said.

Then, after some moments' silence, she added, "He lives for the prospect of having people endlessly in his power. Beholden to him. Depending on him. Doing what he tells them. "

Watching her, he noticed her shift uneasily, knew that some memory she would not divulge, some humiliation, perhaps sexual, was hurting her, and, seeing that, he was filled with sudden rage against Cadogan. But all he said was, "You think he made up the story about Verity's past – at all events, embroidered it – to humiliate me because I'd been less than sympathetic to her?"

He looked at her, saw she was anticipating his next question. "Do you reckon he was having an affair with her?"

"No idea." She shook her head. "Probably not. He wouldn't have wanted to risk being in the wrong with Charles. And having an affair with someone as unpredictable as Verity would be far too big a risk for Cadogan. He *never* takes risks, not even small ones. Anyway." Pause. "He wasn't much of a lover."

The words, so coolly uttered, were followed by ones that brought him even keener pleasure. "I don't think he cared much about … well, about sex. It was enough to have someone – a woman – in his bed. After that … " Her voice died away.

"Oh, this is so *embarrassing*," she said, violently. "Sorry, it's my fault, I shouldn't have gone back to talking about Verity. Let's change the subject."

But he couldn't, not completely. "What of Terry?" he asked. "Terry Marsden? Did Cadogan ever talk about him?"

Now that he was over the limit his car would have to stay in the car park overnight. He'd need to order a taxi, so why not have another drink. He picked up the empty bottle, tilted it to and fro.

Helen, frowning over her hands, was too absorbed in her own thoughts to respond to his gesture.

It was only when he repeated his question that she jerked her head up, and asked "Why? Why are you asking?" Then, as though to soften the sudden asperity of her question, she said, defensively it seemed, "It was a long time ago, Geoff." There was a note of weariness in her voice.

No wonder at it, either. "I ought to go," he said.

"No. Stay."

The words, their unmissable urgency, left him half-raised from his seat, unable to straighten or drop back down.

"I mean, now we're talking about – about all this – there's something else you ought to know." She stood, looked at the empty wine bottle. "Shall I make more coffee?"

He fell back into his seat. "Not for me," he said, "though if there's a finger or two of whisky … "

Her smile was genuine. "I think the establishment can run to that. Hang on."

She ducked to peer into the lower shelf of a cupboard, her haunches tight against the cloth of her jeans, then brought across a full half-bottle and placed it and a clean glass before him.

"Aren't you having any?"

She resumed her seat facing him, met his eyes, shook her head, smiling apologetically. "You're on your own, pardner. 'Even on the rocks, scotch knocks me off my socks.' An old Northamptonshire saying."

"You're from Northamptonshire?"

"Lancashire, actually. But in Lancashire they couldn't afford socks. Spent all their money on whisky."

"Whereas in Northants everyone wore socks to show off the shoes they made."

"And whisky would have put an end to that. Ruined the shoemakers' trade. Glad you understand." A pause. She gazed at him and in the candle-light her eyes seemed larger, more lustrous than ever, the lines of her face softer. Or was it the drink.

He raised his glass. "Here's to micro-economics," he said. And, inexplicably he added, "and laughter."

Wordlessly, she studied his expression. "Yes," she eventually said, "I do likes a man as makes me laugh."

He bowed his head in mock-acknowledgement of her mock-compliment, then, having let the smoky liquid run over his tongue, he asked, serious again, "So what is it I ought to know? About Cadogan, I assume."

"About him and about Terry Marsden."

He looked at her, but said nothing.

"You asked whether he ever talked about Terry. Did you mean that you guessed what they were up to?"

Geoff shook his head. "No," he said, "I was simply curious. But something tells me I ought to be far more curious. Suspicious perhaps?" And meeting her look, half-sceptical, half-enquiring, he added, "Why do I think you're about to tell me they were into dodgy deals, and why, supposing you are, won't that surprise me?"

"But you don't know what deals?"

"Not a clue."

He drank his whisky, reached for the bottle, raised it and looked enquiringly at her. "Are you sure I can't tempt you?"

"Quite sure. But please, help yourself." Then, watching him pour a more generous measure, she said, "That time I told you about – when Cadogan and I met Terry in the hotel in Nottingham. It wasn't as much by chance as I suggested."

He swallowed some whisky. "I didn't somehow think it was," he said. And when, eyebrow raised, she studied his smile, he added, "I know that coincidences occur, that there are chance happenings, but somehow I never had Terry down as leaving much to chance."

He thought about what to say next, said, "You could tell by the way he played. Every note was calculated, was somehow *learnt*. I don't mean he wasn't a good keyboard man, because he was. But there were no stridings across gulfs of his own leaving for Terry Marsden. That's a quotation, by the way. From an anthology of poems about jazz. The poet who wrote that is an ace jazz pianist. A risk-taker, I guess, which Terry never was. And I don't see Cadogan as leaving much to chance, either. King of the control freaks."

"I don't think he manufactured that meeting with Bill Something-or-other."

"Ah, well," he said, "into each reign some life must fall." But seeing her mock-grimace, "Do carry on, Ms Birdlip."

Was it the drink making him suddenly light-headed? The sombre mood of the past half-hour had lifted and there was a new warmth between them. The flame of one candle had finally guttered to death in a pool of wax, light from the other seemed to be bringing the warm darkness closer. The only other illumination came from a small spotlight above the sink, outlining her head and shoulders as she leant forward across the table, her serious face in which the eyes, fixed on his, dominated, deepened as they were by candle flame.

He reached across, let his fingers stroke the back of her hand that lay, palm down, on the table. She watched his movements but did not remove her hand.

"So tell me," he said.

27

"Geoff, Geoff, come on, wake up. The taxi will be here in ten minutes."

Helen's voice was close to his ear, her hair brushing against his bare shoulder.

Forcing himself from sleep, he yawned, blinked, peered at his watch, trying to see the time by the glow of the bedside light.

"Six-thirty," Helen said. She stood above him, wrapped in an old, blue towelling dressing gown, her face shadowy in the dim light, but her eyes, her eyes ...

"You're lovely," he said, croaked rather, his voice tarred by whisky. "I love you."

"You've got ten minutes," Helen said again. "I'm going to begin clearing up. They'll be here by seven." And, pulling the door shut behind her, she left the bedroom.

He levered himself up, kicked his legs free of the duvet, reached for his clothes, and, bundling them under his arm, staggered into the bathroom.

Ten minutes later, still blinking himself awake, scarcely able to believe what had happened, clinging to the memory of her warm body, the scent of her still on his skin, he climbed into the back of the taxi waiting outside Hutton Lodge.

"Where to, mate?" The turbaned taxi-driver looked vaguely familiar.

Ewing Avenue, he opened his mouth to say, then shut it again. Sod. Apart from some loose change, he had no money on him. As consciousness sharpened he recalled that he'd left home the previous evening without his wallet, had chosen to do so as a sort of dare, a magic trick to ensure he didn't have to go home again that night, the fallback position being that, if Helen insisted on pushing him out he could at least doss down in his car. Like just about every muso he knew, he'd done *that* before, in fact there was an unstated conviction among jazzmen that you weren't truly a member of the community unless you'd spent at least one night in a lay-by or some pub or hotel car park following a far-from-home gig. He even knew a bass player who claimed that, being two-fifths gypsy (two-fifths!), he preferred

215

the bottom of a hedge to a car's back seat, although that, like Lord Melbourne's opinion of prayer in private, was, he thought, going a damned sight too far.

Whereas the taxi-driver, staring into the rear mirror of his cab as he waited for instructions, was about to find out that from his point of view Geoff wasn't going anywhere near far enough.

"So, where's it to be?"

"Just drop me off at Harbin's."

"*Harbin's?* The greengrocers?"

" I live above there."

The driver was incredulous. "You could bloody walk there in two minutes, innit. What you want a taxi for?"

"Bad leg," Geoff said, desperately. "I can't walk far. Doctor's orders."

A very few moments later, he was deposited outside the greengrocer's and, having handed over all the change he had – about £3 – limped across to the doorway beside Harbin's shop front, conscious that his progress was being monitored by the suspicious driver. As he pretended to look for his key, Geoff turned to wave, and with a contemptuous flick of his wrist the cabbie disappeared into the breaking dawn of a wet Sunday.

Should he go back to the library and collect his car? No, better not. Last night's drink – correction, the whisky of the early hours of this morning – was still in his system. He didn't want to risk getting done for being over the limit, and from Simon he'd learnt that cops regularly hit their targets for successful prosecutions by stopping drivers in the early-morning hours of a weekend. "Most of 'em will be on their way home from parties," Simon explained. "It's like shooting fish in a barrel. Why else would you be in a car at that time of a Sunday?"

"You could be on God's business."

"Only if you're wearing a dog-collar."

"Remind me to buy one," Geoff had said.

But in the absence of what Frank would have called that appurtenance, he would have to walk.

* * *

Rain was falling steadily, heavily, as three-quarters of an hour later Geoff squelched his way into the porch of 27 Ewing Avenue. It was only then he remembered he'd left his key ring tucked inside the Fiat's exhaust pipe. There was a spare key to the flat, which he always kept in a kitchen drawer. Unfortunately, he could only gain access to the spare key by gaining access to his flat, and to do that he needed a key.

Sod. And, imprecations aside, what now? He'd have to try to gain entry by prising up one of his own windows.

Given that his front room windows were protected by safety locks against the tea-leaves Frank imagined regularly heading for Ewing Avenue, Geoff scrunched his way round to the back. Rain in his eyes, rain running down the back of his neck, rain chilling his fingers and making him shiver as wet jacket and trousers clung icily to his skin, he dragged over to the wall beneath his kitchen window a box Frank used for starting seedlings off. Made of thin wooden slats, the box felt far from substantial, but perhaps it would bear his weight long enough for him to step up onto the window sill and from there work free the latch of the small, top window he always left tinily ajar.

Right. Let action commence. Cautiously, he put one foot on the box's wooden surround, then raised his other foot so the box now bore his weight.

Except that it didn't.

Cra-ack.

Swearing, he hoped under his breath, he fell awkwardly onto the gravel path, and as he got slowly to his feet could feel pain beginning to flare in his right shoulder. He tried moving it. *Ouch.*

Above him, as he touched his shoulder, he heard his landlord's voice. "Geoffrey! Good heavens. What on earth are you doing?"

Frank, head and shoulders obtruding from his own back window, was peering down at where his tenant stood beside the splintered seedling box. "Do you realise that you're wet through?" he asked.

Good lord, so I am, odd that I never noticed.

"And you've got mud all over your trousers. And my seedling box is broken. And why are you holding your right shoulder? Have you hurt yourself? Well I never."

"I forgot my key," Geoff said. "I was trying to get in through the kitchen window."

"Well I never," Frank repeated. "You haven't surely been standing there all night?"

The question hardly deserved an answer, but anyway Frank was now withdrawing his head, shouting as he did so that Geoff was to hang on for a minute while he came down with a spare key.

Which he did.

* * *

Half an hour later, having stripped off his wet clothes, showered quickly and fallen into bed, desperate for sleep, Geoff became aware of banging on his front door.

Groaning, he hauled himself upright, wincing at the pain that knifed through his right shoulder.

Frank was standing in the porch.

"Your car's been stolen," the landlord said, half turning to indicate the space where the Fiat normally stood. His voice hovered between a certain satisfaction – this is what happens to people who behave as eccentrically, not to say irresponsibly as you, Geoffrey – and concern. This neighbourhood is going downhill and I fear for property values. Blearily, Geoff peered past him, saw that the rain had stopped, and then, swinging his gaze back to the man on his doormat, registered the fact that Frank was in his best sports coat and grey flannels, cap set squarely on his head, and what had to be a bible tucked under his arm.

"Not stolen, no," he managed to say, trying to tamp down his irritation. Why couldn't Frank let him be. "I was at a party. I was forced to leave the car in town. I had exceeded the permitted intake of alcohol." See, I can speak like you. "That's why I had to walk all the way back home."

"Ah," Frank said, "so that was why you were wet through. I wondered."

You mean you wondered where I'd been all night, Geoff thought. Well, keep on wondering. He put a hand up to massage his hurt shoulder.

"I'm surprised you didn't order a taxi," Frank said, "There is, so I am informed, an excellent all-night service." Then, when Geoff said nothing, he stepped off the porch and made to go. "I should get that shoulder seen to," he said as he turned away. "Nasty things, shoulders."

He began to scrunch his way over the gravel and out onto Ewing Avenue. But he turned, came half-way back to where Geoff still stood in the porch. "My seed-box," he called out. "It will have to be replaced. Costs may regretfully be incurred, though I shall endeavour to keep them to a minimum."

As Geoff moved to shut the door, Baw made a sudden appearance from round the corner of the house and brushed past on her way to the kitchen.

"A night on the tiles?" Geoff said. "Dissipation will be the ruin of us all."

But the cat, who was already deep in her saucer of food, took no notice.

* * *

He went back to bed, hoping to sleep. But sleep wouldn't come. Instead, his mind was filled with thoughts of Helen. Helen and him. Helen beside him, Helen beneath him, her skin, her eyes, her mouth, her scent. Making love to Helen. Making love *with* Helen. Not great lovemaking, they were too tired after all their talk – *her* talk, but happy to be together, even for so short a time. She'd warned him he would have to be out of the flat well before seven. Her parents were making a flying visit on their way north from Bedford to Lincoln, where her dad had to be on the first green by 10 a.m. Some sort of golf tournament. "Bedford?" he'd asked. " I thought you said you came from Lancashire?"

"People move around, Geoff." She was beside him, whispering, her breath warming his flesh. "My dad's work took him to Bedford when I was a teenager." In the intimacy of her bed it seemed like love talk.

"What's he do, your dad."

"Did. He's retired. He was a doctor."

He nuzzled up to her bare shoulder. "And your mother was a nurse."

She turned to look at him, her face so close that even in the semi-dark, her eyes, those lustrous eyes filled his gaze. "How did you guess?"

He kissed her nose. "I know plenty of jazzmen who are doctors – in real life, as we say. Most of them have wives who were nurses. Still are, some of them."

"Not my mother." She turned to lie on her back. "She gave up nursing for her children."

"How many?"

"Two. My brother Stephen came first."

He wanted to hear about her family. "And would you say your parents are broad-minded, m'dear?"

She laughed, turned back to him, nibbled his ear. "What kind of pillow talk is this?" Then, "I'm not worried about them knowing I sleep with strange men, if that's what you mean. But I don't often see them, not as often as I should. They've not even yet seen this flat ... " She yawned, turned away. "I must get some sleep," she said, pulling the duvet up over her shoulder

He lay in silence for a few moments, then, "I love you," he said into the dark, but the only response was breathing that told him she was no longer awake.

* * *

After a further shower, dressed now, persuaded by a few manipulative swings of his arm that his shoulder, though mighty sore, had suffered no greater damage than bad bruising, Geoff sat over a pot of coffee and thought about all Helen had revealed. Were Cadogan's business dealings spectacularly nasty? No, he guessed they weren't. Or rather, they were, but they were also business as usual. Terry and Cadogan making money by screwing some people, putting money in the pockets of others, their own included. What was that but business? From all that Helen told him, Terry was the one who did most of the dirty work, Cadogan's chief function being to ensure that whatever they undertook was strictly legal. You bet. No flies on Cadogan. In the worlds in which he moved – social as well as professional, golf club and Masonic Lodges as well as nine-to-five how can I assist you – Cadogan would rub shoulders with bank managers, top policemen, company directors, executives ... all the panjandrums who could drop a word in his ear, not-that-you-heard-it-from-me-old-boy-but-a-little-bird-told-me-that-Smith's-is-about-to-go-belly-up-whisper-whisper, with the unspoken inference that now might be a good time to pull out if you had money in Smith's stock or, of course, stand ready with an offer to buy he couldn't refuse, know what I mean?

That, Helen explained, was how it worked. From time to time Cadogan would get to hear about some business going down the tubes, he'd alert Terry, who would then buy the business out, using bank loans Cadogan guaranteed, Cadogan, as though an innocent outsider, would then be consulted by the parties involved in order to assure all concerned that this was entirely proper and above board, legal fees would be mentioned, and before you knew it the deal would be done, papers signed, the erstwhile owner, even though forced to sell at knock-down price, could at least retire with creditors paid or fobbed off, and the new owners would dispose of the plant at a tidy profit or, increasingly, sell the land to property developers. Office blocks, shopping malls, 'exclusive' town house complexes, even gated communities. Oh, it was easy, easy as falling off a log, it put money in purses, it was within the law. And everybody stood to gain.

Well, not quite everybody. The workers who lost their jobs didn't perhaps appreciate the smoothness of financial operations that for them meant unemployment, sometimes eviction from their homes, sometimes the break-up of marriages, sometimes worse: alcoholism, drugs, the drop into a life of petty and not-so petty criminality that had the *Daily Mail* tut-tutting about sink estates infested by workshy sub-humanoids.

Did Terry read the *Mail*? Probably. Did Cadogan. No. The *Telegraph* and *FT* had been spread in unostentatious display across the table in what he was pleased to call his Chambers. A solid citizen, Cadogan, with his tailored suits and his old-school or was it college tie. But he'd been up to his oxters in the deal he and Terry were discussing on the occasion Helen had been introduced to him. That was the only time she actually saw the man Cadogan had so often mentioned, usually as "my helpmeet" or "the hod-carrier," always in a manner that suggested Marsden was at Cadogan's endless disposal, a bit obtuse, almost at times the fool. He might like to present himself as Mister Sharp, but it was Cadogan who cut the mustard.

Terry, Helen said, had been in London that day she'd met him, arranging the final details of their latest money-making scheme. And Terry had done well. As a result, Cadogan was 'the cat with the cream'. He'd insisted on ordering a bottle of champagne, and, she added, when it came, Terry proposed a health to their enterprise. "'All for one, and one for all, eh Mr C?'" And then, after he had gone back to the piano and announced with a wink in their direction that the first number of his new set would be 'You're the Tops', which he then, Helen told Geoff, proceeded to play in an especially flamboyant manner, Cadogan explained to her the 'operation', as he called it, which he and Terry had just brought to a successful conclusion.

As he emptied the last of the cafetiere's contents into his mug, Geoff played back her account of Cadogan's pleased-as-punch tale about that particular operation. She couldn't know, he thought as she spoke, that he himself was more or less familiar with the story. He'd heard it, told rather differently by Arthur Stanchard. Because the factory which Terry had put in the hands of property developers was the one where Arthur worked, the factory that made boilers for industrial use.

Sipping the tepid coffee, Geoff put together what Helen had told him with stray tidbits he'd heard from Arthur over the years and from local tittle-tattle at the time the factory went to the wall. And what a story it made.

It began with the factory's owner investing in new plant because of some big overseas orders. But no sooner had the plant been installed than one of the orders – from a foreign shipyard – was cancelled. A bad blow, given that the factory had put other work on hold in order to fulfil that particular contract. As a result, the order book for the next twelve months was suddenly looking thin. To be able to pay the bills and the workforce's wages the owner needed a loan to tide the business over until orders picked up again. Creditors were beginning to hammer on the door, but for some reason a loan was proving unexpectedly difficult to come by.

Geoff had long been aware of all that; it was common knowledge in Longford, but now, from Helen, he was learning something else. He was learning about Cadogan's role in all this. As her lover told her about the factory's difficulties, Helen said, she noticed that the slight smile on his lips was replaced by a grave shake of the head intended to imply the uncertain ways of banks. "I didn't give it much thought," she told Geoff, who was listening intently. Then, "No, the truth is, I didn't *want* to. I wouldn't let myself think that the man I was in love with was involved in crooked dealing."

"So they had bankers in their pockets. Bastards."

But swallowing the gritty remains of the coffee and remembering her quick, silent nod, he wondered whether his diagnosis was entirely accurate. Cadogan wouldn't have been that blatant. Leave no fingerprints. A word in the ear did all that was needed, a shared glance, and no doubt in course of time favours to be exchanged. That was almost certainly how it worked. Not that it made Cadogan any less of a shit. The man Helen loved. The man she had once loved.

Anyway, Helen said, going back to the evening of her ten-years-old meeting with Terry Marsden, her face averted as she brought the memories back and not, therefore, seeing in the dim candle-light what Geoff knew had been the look in his own eyes – Helen, oh, Helen – Terry had been in London that day agreeing terms with a buyer who was willing to take the factory off the owner's hands, to settle his debts and leave him free to retire with a modest income. A great relief to all. Because, Cadogan explained, the deal had nearly been stymied by the failure of the prospective buyers to find anyone wanting the factory's salvageable contents, contents which the said buyers had no use for because they were interested only in the land on which the factory stood. They planned to build houses there.

'The Leas,' Geoff thought. Of course. Of course.

But he didn't interrupt Helen's story. Or rather, Cadogan's story, his good-luck story. Because, how lucky can you get, in the nick of time a German manufacturer came forward with a decent amount of money – 'decent' was not further specified – and through Terry's good offices, a shipper had signed a contract to transport the contents from Longford to Düsseldorf. All that remained was to transfer the land to a property developer who, as luck once more would have it, happened to be a cousin of the buyers. So that, as the saying went, was a done deal. And having concluded his tale, Cadogan insisted on more champagne.

Which explains, Geoff thought, as Helen brought that part of the narrative to an end, how Arthur and his mates lost their jobs. How much, he wondered, did Arthur know – or guess – about all this?

But there was more to come. Helen had asked Cadogan who the buyers were.

"And?" Geoff asked.

"He laughed and said, 'A couple of comedians,' and I thought he meant someone who'd been tricked into buying a pig in a poke."

"That sounds about par for the course."

But no, he meant it. The factory had been bought by professional stand-up comics. "Phil and Teddy Summers," Helen said, "remember them?" He did.

Now, sitting in his kitchen, scratching Baw's head as, fed and replete with a saucer of milk, the cat purred contentedly on his lap, he thought about them. Phil and Teddy Summers, a couple of not very likely lads whose motto, 'Summers on the Way', seemed entirely appropriate for their unoriginal brand of stand-up, although for a while they regularly appeared in TV variety shows. Morecambe and Wise they were not, but they had their fifteen minutes in the sun, probably arranged for them by crook agents, he thought now, and it was of course entirely possible they performed for the kinds of club audiences where Terry was a familiar presence. He might even have been their accompanist on such occasions. Yes, it made sense.

* * *

He must have dozed off because suddenly he was jerked into consciousness. That phone wasn't ringing in his dream, it was the phone in his study, and it must have been ringing for quite some time.

Lifting Baw off his lap, he went to answer it.

"You've switched both your mobile and answer phone off." Helen's voice.

"Oh, God, sorry, sorry. I was desperate for some sleep."

"Well, this should wake you good and proper. Your car's been broken into."

"It has?" And then, as his brain began to function, "How do you know?"

"Because," she said, "I'm standing next to it. In the library car park."

There was a pause, during which he desperately tried and failed to come up with an explanation for the Fiat's being where he had said it wasn't. Bloody joy-riders. No, forget that. How on earth did it get there? Yes, brilliant. Entirely convincing. It must have driven itself. He said, "How did this happen? I mean, how did you happen to spot it?"

"Elementary, my dear Cousins. Having seen my parents off the premises, I went jogging. My Sunday routine, if you must know. And I took my usual route through the library car park, saw your beat-up old conveyance, assumed you'd come in to do some work, then found that the place was all shut up." The voice, now suggesting wry amusement, added, "Which is more than can be said for your car."

He took a breath, tried to think. "OK. I'll be right over."

"You'd better, because I'm not hanging around. I aim to finish my run and then get back home. Where I have work to do."

And without even saying goodbye she switched off her phone.

"And I love you, too," he said.

28

A single parp of its horn announced the taxi's arrival.

Hurrying out of the flat, Baw cradled in his good arm, Geoff lowered the cat gingerly to the ground and turned to the driver who said, "Where we goin' then, man." Then, recognising his fare, "Hey, it's you, innit. Peg Leg." He stared at the donkey jacket draped over Geoff's injured shoulder, grinned. "You been tryin' to walk on your hands? Big mistake, by the look of it."

Geoff climbed in, slamming the door behind him. "You want me to drive you as far as the gate this time?" the driver asked into the rear mirror. "What you doin' 'ere, anyway? Bit off limits, innit?"

"I've been visiting a friend," Geoff said.

"'E duff up your arm, did 'e? Some friend."

Without bothering to reply, Geoff said, "Can you take me to where you dropped me earlier this morning, please. Harbin's."

Some fifteen minutes later, when he stepped out of the taxi in front of the greengrocer's, Geoff noticed the driver watching him, a thin smile showing through his wispy beard as he asked for £8 and waited while, with his good arm, his fare struggled to reach the inside pocket of his sports coat. "Lucky for Nelson that he never had this sort of a problem," Geoff said, attempting humour as he finally managed to prise a ten-pound note from his wallet.

There was no answering cheer from the taxi-driver, who took the note and held it up to the light before saying, "If I had Mandela in the back of my cab, man, he'd travel free, innit." Then, without bothering to enquire whether Geoff wanted any change, he drove off.

From Harbin's to the library was a ten-minute walk. Though the rain had long ceased, the sky was overcast, the air dank, and the plane trees, their awkward, arthritic-looking branches still bare of leaves, dripped steadily on him as he trod beneath them, shivering in sudden gusts of wind, his shoulder throbbing, light-headed from lack of sleep, but buoyed up by the memory of Helen's naked body next to his.

And yet in the grey, lowering light of this day, those hours seemed now unreal, belonging to a different world. As if in accord with the depressed feeling Sunday in Longford so often brought, it came to him as he plodded across to the library, head down against the rising wind, that although he'd told her he loved her, she'd said nothing by way of reply.

And from there his thought drifted to another consideration. It was odd, no worse than odd, it was distressing that you could be lying naked beside a woman, nearer than the eye, and, when you next saw her, clothed, she might be distant as the stars. Helen's voice on the phone. Was that the voice of the same woman whose bed he had a few hours earlier shared? The thought, the possibility that in some sense it might not be, unnerved him. Suppose he was no more than a casual, a passing fancy. Is it Grenada I see, or only Asbery Park. No, it was the real McCoy, it had to be.

And yet her brisk voice on the phone, amused though she sounded, must have come from her realisation of his cheap trick. No, I didn't come by car, I took a taxi. What was he hoping to gain by it? Or rather, what was he expecting to happen? Well, actually, what *did* happen. But in light of Helen's discovery there might now be less cause for satisfaction in remembering their love-making. Besides, it hadn't exactly been volcanic. The lateness of the hour and their mutual tiredness had seen to that.

No, but it had been good. Cancel good. Wonderful. Wonderful simply to be in bed with the woman he'd loved since he first set eyes on her all those years ago and who, by a mere turn of the head, he could, by the dim light that came through her half-drawn curtains, see lying beside him in contented – surely it was contented – sleep. The memory of that was enough to make him want to leap into the air.

Instead, he stepped off the kerb, crossed to the front of the library, from there walked round to the car park at the building's rear and headed toward his car. By the time he came up to it he'd decided that Helen must have come to the obvious conclusion: that he'd planned to spend the night with her. Kind of him. And what had he got to show for it? A badly-bruised shoulder and a broken-into car. Nice one, Cousins.

* * *

The passenger window had been smashed. and papers, mostly garage receipts and sweet wrappers, together with a pocket torch and CDs, were scattered across both front seats. Nothing had been taken, probably because there was nothing there to attract the fancy of the youths, as no doubt the wreckers were, who'd used a half-brick to break the glass and who, having rifled through what was stuffed into the glove compartment would have rejected with contempt CDs of the Mulligan Quartet, of Ben Webster, of Dowland, Finzi, Gurney, of Ella singing the Gershwin Songbook The worst damage had been done to the paintwork. Across the bonnet someone had scratched *WANKER* and on the driver's door the same scribe declared his conviction that *TOSERS STINK.*

After walking round the car, inspecting the total amount of damage and deciding that, although he'd need a new window professionally fitted, he himself could paint over the graffiti without bothering to get an arm-and-a-leg spray-job done, Geoff bent to retrieve his key ring from the exhaust pipe.

It wasn't there.

Sod.

He knelt, probed with the fingers of his good hand, but no, nothing. The little bastards must have discovered the keys and made off with them.

Buggeration.

He straightened up, and, huddled in his old donkey jacket, leant against the car. What now? His first thought was that if the person or persons who had smashed their way into his car had also found the keys, then it was odd that they'd not bothered to use them to drive the car away. His second thought was that no joy-rider would want to be seen behind the wheel of his clapped-out Fiat. His third was that joy-riders weren't especially fussy about the cars they rode in. His fourth was that perhaps finding the keys left them without the challenge that came from hot-wiring a car they proposed to drive. His fifth was that it wasn't they who had taken the keys. His sixth was that he ought to phone Helen. His seventh was that he therefore needed his mobile. And his eighth was that he'd left his mobile on charge in his flat. In which case, thought number nine, he would have to walk to her place. Thought number ten followed. Would she want to see him?

Probably not. "I have work to do." His only choice therefore was to go all the way back to Ewing Avenue, where, being a man of forethought, he could effect lawful entry to his own premises with the spare set of house keys he had on this occasion thought to bring with him, and as a result of which he would be enabled to retrieve from his desk drawer the spare key to the car, thence to return to the library car park, after which, assuming his shoulder would permit him to take control of the wheel, he could drive the manky wreck to its rightful home. What better way to spend the remaining daylight hours of this splendidly eventful Sunday. Right, then.

* * *

"Hi," Helen said.

She was in jeans and a dark blue sweatshirt, her hair damp from what he guessed must be a shower. That her face was aglow had probably everything to do with her recent run.

"Sure you don't mind", he said, carefully easing his way past her and into the kitchen.

For a moment her look, when he turned to face her, suggested that she did indeed mind, that she could think of nothing she wanted less than to have him standing here in her kitchen, but all she said was, "Have you come for your keys?" Her voice gave nothing away.

He nodded, grateful that at least she was prepared to talk to him.

"What's the matter with your shoulder?"

She hadn't asked him to sit down, stood, back to the table, staring evenly at him, or was that look one of concern.

"I … er … tripped and fell a bit awkwardly. Trying to effect an entry to my own flat."

"Because you'd left the keys with your car?"

"Because I'd left the keys with my car."

She shook her head, her smile one of frank enjoyment at his discomfort. The daft ways of men.

"Why didn't you go and collect it? Drive yourself home."

"Because I still had enough alcohol in my system to have failed a breathalyser test."

"And perhaps because you didn't want me to know you'd told me a porkie."

"That too." He spread his arms in acknowledgement of his errancy. "Ouch."

Her lips puckered in involuntary sympathy. "Don't wave your arms about so," she said. "Here."

Coming close, close enough for him to inhale the scent of her freshly washed hair, see the faint down on her cheek, she reached behind him and he heard the scrape of keys as she picked them up from the table. "I guessed they'd be where you usually leave them," she said, taking his good hand and dropping the keys into his open palm. "And they were. So I brought them back here, to be on the safe side."

She closed his fingers round the key ring, looking thoughtfully at his hand.

"Thanks. I won't take up more of your time."

There was a pause.

"I'll make you a cup of tea," she said, stepping back a little and, he thought, sighing. "You look as though you could do with something to warm you."

And yes, he was, he realised, shivering, though not with the cold.

"If you're sure. I know you're busy."

"I can spare a few minutes." A faint smile, but still there seemed no way to cross the chasm that separated them from last night. "I'm expecting a friend."

First parents, now a friend. Excuses, he thought, excuses. *Had* her parents paid the flying visit for which she had tipped him out of the flat early that morning?

"The Halsteads' flat looks empty. Have the birds flown?"

She stood by the kettle, watching it boil, face averted. "The removal van arrived even before my parents. It was all pretty quick. I didn't have time for a last farewell. But when I opened my door to see mum and dad off the premises I found this." And now, lifting her head, smiling, she pointed over his shoulder to a magnum of champagne he saw, as he turned, occupied centre stage on the table, a red ribbon around it tied in a fancy bow from which dangled a piece of card.

She motioned him to sit as she handed him a mug of tea and he read the message on the card: *To a perfect neighbour. Good luck with your future projects. C and V.*

Projects? What projects?

"Any idea where they're going?"

Leaning against the sink unit, a mug cradled in both hands, she shook her head. "That wouldn't be their way. Beyond mentioning that it was somewhere down south. No forwarding address, unless they left one with Frank Alexander."

"Could be."

But there was something. Sipping the scalding tea, he said, "I've been thinking."

"Is that a good idea? I mean, for a man in your condition?" She was laughing.

He said, "Probably not, and I suppose it's far-fetched, but I can't help wondering about them and whether in any way they, the Halsteads, were involved with Terry, that they let him down. Or anyway, that's what Verity fears."

"How do you mean?"

From her swift look, he knew that he had gained her interest. But as she spoke she glanced at her watch.

"Don't worry," he said. "Let me drink this and I'll be on my way."

"Not before you've explained yourself." The words came out almost as an accusation. The Halsteads are my friends, her look said. Why are you trying to sling mud at them.

He shrugged, intending a placatory gesture, winced at the pain that thrilled through his shoulder, and this time he was met by a quizzically raised eyebrow.

"It's probably nothing," he said. "Putting two and two together and coming up with seven. The Halsteads know Cadogan, Charles Halstead is a surveyor, which presumably means he deals in land and property, they come up from London, Charles is forever off on business trips, Verity tells Technicolor stories about her past which aren't even consistent let alone plausible … "

He stopped, seeing her look, the sceptical smile that played around her lips. "Well, I did say it was far-fetched." He took a mouthful of tea. "But," he said, wanting to defend himself, "Cadogan hinted that Terry's death, his suicide, might have been connected to his winkling Lorette away from some big cheese in London."

"And from this it follows that Charles Halstead, while not being the big cheese himself, was sent up to act as spoiler for Terry's business affairs?"

"He *might* be Mister Big. Suppose Verity isn't his wife, but acts as cover for him? Not a very good cover, I admit, seeing how much attention she directs toward herself." He was riffing now, picking up suppositions as he went. "And yet that could be part of the master plan, to deflect attention away from Charles. He gets busy, using Cadogan to persuade Terry that such and such a business is well worth buying, so Terry does indeed buy, and then, would you Adam and Eve it, he can't offload said business even though Mr C had assured him it would be a cinch."

Caught up in the plot he'd devised, far from sure how seriously he himself took what he was saying, but speaking with increased urgency, he went on "Two or three of those setbacks and Terry's a busted flush. Businesses on his hands he can't dispose of, no capital, no credit, bills to pay, a property to maintain, plus a wife who takes for granted that she's made a wise career move in throwing her lot in with Terry Marsden. So ... What's he to do?"

She laughed, a short, dismissive laugh. "You and Simenon," she said.

"Simenon? What's he got to do with it?" He put his empty cup down on the table where, the previous evening, he and she had sat facing each other and what was between them hadn't been the unbridgeable distance he would now have to negotiate to get back to her.

Her back was to him as she put her mug in the sink. Turning to face him, she said, speaking as though to explain matters to a not very bright adolescent, her smile one of forbearance, "Simenon thought that because he could plot perfect crime stories he'd be able to solve real-life ones. He also, by the way, claimed to have bedded literally hundreds of women."

"Innocent on both counts."

"I believe you," she said, this time permitting herself a wider smile. "But the point is that on one occasion the French police were stumped by a murder they couldn't make sense of and Simenon boasted that if they invited him to help them he'd point them to the murderer in two shakes of a dog's tail, as my old Gran used to say."

"And?" He was puzzled.

"And he made a pig's ear of it. Missed or muddled clues, confused dates and times, and was left looking a complete idiot. I can't remember the details but I do know the cops had the last laugh."

She paused, looked him in the eye, the smile now plainly one of mocking disregard for his speculations. "The fact is, Geoff, as Oscar never tired of pointing out, art is art because it is not life." She raised an eyebrow, inviting his submission. "I rest my case," she said, "and the jury will now retire to consider its verdict." And again she looked at her watch.

It was the signal for him to leave. He adjusted the jacket over his throbbing shoulder, and got slowly to his feet.

"Christopher Foster," she said.

"Christopher Foster?" He was bewildered. "Who's he? Another crime writer. Never heard of him."

"That man in Shropshire who killed his wife and daughter, then set fire to his mansion, shot his horses and did himself in. Surely you remember? For a while it was all over the papers. Headline news. He'd been living the life of a millionaire, cars, stables, broad acres, wife dripping with jewellery, daughter at posh public school, all to prove that he was rolling in it. Only he wasn't. All lies. He hadn't got a brass farthing. So when he knew the creditors were about to arrive … he wiped himself and his family out."

"Yes. I remember now." He did. "Horrible."

As he moved towards the door, he said, "But I wouldn't have remembered his name. "How come that you do?"

"Because his business dealings took in various people in the Black Country. In every sense of the phrase. More than one person in Wolverhampton was left badly out of pocket," she said. "It was the talk of the town for weeks afterwards. What a no-nonsense man he always seemed, a pleasure to do business with, friendly, personable. Oh, yes, 'personable' was a word that came up again and again." She looked at him quizzically. "In other words, Foster liked to act the Big I Am. But it turned out he was a fantasist, hadn't a penny. At all events, by the time he decided to take his life he was spent out. So he killed himself and took wife and daughter with him."

He said, standing in the doorway, "'The Big I Am.' That's the second time I've heard that term used in the last few days. First Barbara Colston, now you." And, as she raised an enquiring eyebrow, explained. "Barbara is the wife of Simon, our bass player. The ex-policeman. We were round at his place just after we heard about Terry's death, trying to make sense of it, and Barbara came out with more or less the same words you've just used."

"Did she now. Why was that, I wonder." A pause as the smile came back. "Womanly intuition apart, that is."

"I guess womanly intuition explains it. She was suggesting that more than one man's killed himself because he couldn't face financial ruin."

Helen said, holding his gaze, "Or couldn't stand being found out. Couldn't face having his reputation destroyed."

She was right, he knew, just as Barbara was right. Men and their reputations. He tried, without much success, to recall words he'd been required to speak in one of the the Alleyn Players' play readings. Something to do with reputation being got without merit and lost without deserving.

He must go.

But Helen was speaking again, her words now openly questioning, speculative. "Suppose what you say about Terry is true, that he lost out on some deals and that he was broke, you don't really believe the Halsteads could have been involved in what happened to him, do you? You can't. It's poppycock."

"Poppycock." He stopped, looked at her. "Poppycock," he said again. "That word."

"What's so odd about it?" she asked.

"It was the word Cadogan used when I suggested he might be having an affair with Verity Halstead. Poppycock."

She laughed, gently shook her head. "First Barbara, now Cadogan. Coincidence, Geoff, coincidence. Another name for chance."

And, shaking her head at what he knew must be his look of hesitant scepticism, she said, "Chance happens, Geoff. Chance brought me back to Longford. There was no big plan."

"And chance brought you to the Three Tuns in January?"

"No. You know why I was there. I needed a place to live. I was following Janey's advice."

"But you came on your own."

"Yes," she said, "I did."

He tried to read the meaning of her smile.

"Of all the bars in all the world ... " she said. "Well, why not? You must remember this."

She half-sang the words and as she did so came close enough to reach out a hand and hoist the jacket back onto the shoulder from where it had begun to slip. "If that isn't better in the morning," she said, looking directly at him as he stood in front of her, "you should take yourself to the doctor. Or get someone to run you to A and E."

Her voice had softened, her eyes were, he thought, suddenly full of tender care.

Without thinking, without pause, he moved to kiss her; but at the very moment his lips brushed against hers there was a knock at the outer door.

"Oh, you fool." The words were no more than a whispered sigh, then, backing off, she called, "Come on in, Janey, we're in the kitchen."

A moment later Janey Macpherson put her head round the door. "Hi," she said, looking wonderingly from Helen to Geoff, then back to Helen again. "I'm not interrupting anything, am I?"

"Not at all," Helen said briskly, and "I'm just going," Geoff said, adding, "I dropped in to collect my keys. I'll see myself out. Helen will explain." With which words, words that left the women exchanging looks in which Helen's sudden flush of embarrassment caused Janey to look quizzically at them both, he somehow managed to walk out of the kitchen, through the door to her steps, and so crossed back over the bridge and came down to earth.

* * *

But no. All the way home, driving slowly partly to save his shoulder, partly to lessen the cold gusts of wind that came through the Fiat's broken window, he replayed her words, Helen's three little words. "Oh, you fool." Who was the fool? He was. But why? For mistaking one night's passion for love? For waiting so long before he kissed her? For the avoidable damage he'd done to his shoulder? He didn't know, couldn't tell, but all the way home he heard the words, could feel the touch of her lips, inhale, still, the scent of her freshly washed hair.

And later, having swallowed a couple of painkillers that, with the bell of his tenor carefully balanced on his knee, enabled him to sit holding the instrument more or less steady as he ran through the numbers Al had chosen for their next session at the Three Tuns, the memory of that moment in her kitchen stayed in his head. 'My Old Flame', 'This Year's Kisses', 'Lady be Good', 'Don't Blame Me', 'Cheek to Cheek', 'Prisoner of Love' – especially 'Prisoner of Love' – each became 'Oh, You Fool.' The ache in his shoulder all but forgotten, he heard her voice, its husky whisper, he tasted the warmth of her lips, his nostrils were filled with that unique scent, he saw her eyes, the gold-flecked irises so close to his that they filled his entire gaze.

Before putting the tenor back in its case, he blew two choruses of a number not on Al's list, but one he knew that, come Wednesday evening, he'd be sure to ask for. Ellington, who else. 'I've Got It Bad and That Ain't Good'.

How about an alternative title? Love Without Hope.

He snapped the locks of the case and left the room.

Oh, you fool.

But he could feel himself grinning.

29

The body had been released for burial and the funeral fixed for the following Friday afternoon. Al, who phoned early Monday morning to give Geoff the news, told him the ceremony would be held at the town's crematorium, adding that Lorette had left it to him to ask whichever locals he thought appropriate. "Seems like she's semi-detached," he said. Al had put a death notice and information about the funeral in one or two of the nationals. "Just in case some big-timers are interested," he said gnomically.

Glancing across the staff room to where Josie stood holding her ring finger aloft as though searching for possible flaws, Geoff said "We ought to announce it on Wednesday evening, at the gig. Could be a few of the regulars who'll want to pay their respects. What about afterwards? Will there be a wake?"

"Back room of the Three Tuns. Norman's agreed to provide catering and Lorette's given clearance for free drinks on arrival followed by a pay bar. I said we'd play for an hour, OK. We'll fix the details on Wednesday."

* * *

Which was what they did. By then further information about Terry's death and its immediate causes had emerged. Toxicology had been unusually quick in deciding the suicide – as they were certain it was – had been caused by a massive overdose of sleeping pills washed down by brandy. Despite a detailed search of the car and surroundings, followed by an equally thorough going-over of Terry's house and grounds, no note had been found.

"So why he did it is still a mystery?" Geoff asked as they were setting up.

"Hardly." Simon, who was friendly with a number of former colleagues, explained that as Terry worked from home the lads had been given a chance to give his books the once over. "Nothing conclusive, like, but they reckon you don't have to be a Lombard Street Special to see that he was in deep shit."

Al, who seemed to be in the know, nodded, leaving Geoff to ask the bassist to explain.

As he tuned to Al's proffered G, Simon said, "I'm told there were final demands from one or two of the big boys, his bank included, and the word is that Lorette wasn't happy at all. Seems she'd been tailed once or twice and that she was on the receiving end of some decidedly unpleasant phone calls. Threats to her personal safety. That kind of thing."

"She told them that?"

Simon shook his head. "She left all the talking to the family solicitor."

"Peter Cadogan?"

Geoff tried to keep his voice neutral but Simon's quick, indrawn smile suggested that Cadogan's reputation was familiar enough to the police.

"I thought I saw you hob-nobbing with him at that Golf Club gig. A mate of yours, is he?"

"Like brothers," Geoff said. "Cain and Abel, that is."

Simon ran a couple of riffs. "Near enough for jazz," he said. Then, "He was there when the lads arrived. Seems he knew more about the state of Terry's finances than Mrs M. herself did. Anyway that's what they reckoned. According to him, she'd called him in, so there he was, standing by her in her hour of need, acting in her best interests."

"She can't have been happy," Al said, "not with assorted heavies putting the squeeze on her. Not what she'd have been expecting that when she left London for a quiet life away from it all." He was rooting around in a small box, examining various plectrums.

"Dead right, Al," Simon said. "Pack up all your cares and woes and come to tranquil Longford. I don't think."

"My car got broken into over Saturday night," Geoff said. At least Cadogan wasn't behind *that*.

"What did I tell you?" Simon shook his head in mock wonder. "Longford, Sin City of the Midlands. Is there nothing these villains won't stop at. Anything stolen?"

"No. They threw my CDs about but didn't take any."

"Yes, well, your kind of music ... " He left the sentence unfinished. "Speaking of which, Al, what have you got for us?"

They kicked off with 'Rose Room', and while Al took a solo which was at least within hailing distance of Joe Pass, Geoff looked around the more than usually crowded room. As was the way in the jazz world, people who had never been seen before in the Three Tuns were here tonight to show their solidarity with the music. News of Terry's death had soon spread among the faithful. By the time the trio brought the number to a close, letting the last F chord fade away over four bars, nearly every seat was taken and latecomers were already standing, propped against the bar counter.

As he watched Norman struggle through with some more chairs from the front bar, Al took the opportunity to invite all present to join with him and the other two members of what from now on would be called the Al Stocking Trio in celebrating the musicianship of their founder, Terry Marsden, whose memory they would be honouring with an evening that included some of his, Terry's, favourite numbers, starting with 'I'm Beginning to See the Light.' Some, uncertain whether this was jazzman's humour, tittered: others sat in the kind of solemn, attentive silence that made Geoff feel nervous.

"Daren't play a bum note in this atmosphere," Simon said, as they took a break. "Worse than farting in church."

But as the second set rolled on, so they relaxed, and by the end of the evening – during which several of the local musos had come on stand to blow a few choruses – the atmosphere was celebratory, even joyous, and the rip-up 'Chinaboy' that brought proceedings to a close had, as Al said while they packed up, as many of the audience on their legs as had legs to stand on, which was probably at least a third of those present.

"A wonder Norman didn't have to call for the cardiac arrest trolley," Simon said, as he hooded his bass. The room, although rapidly emptying, was still warm from the press of bodies that had been crammed into the back bar, and the higgledy-piggledy scatter of chairs around tables on which empty glasses stood, rim to rim, suggested the hasty departure of celebrants from some discreet bacchanal. "Right, lads, see you Friday. What's the gear, by the way? Black and white?"

But Al shook his head. "Lorette says people to come as they are. No flowers."

"Donations?"

"None. I asked her before I put the notice in the papers, but she said she hadn't had time to consider."

"Really?"

"That's what she said," Al told Geoff.

"Not exactly the grieving widow," Simon said.

In the car park, Geoff said to Al, "What exactly did you mean, Al, about heavies putting the squeeze on Lorette?"

Al watched as one of his employees stowed his guitar and amp in the back of a company hearse, then, when the task was done, sauntered across to the Fiat with Geoff. His bulk outlined against the car park's dim lamplight, he said, keeping his voice low, "OK. I was at Marsden Mansion, trying to finalise arrangements for the funeral, when she answered a phone call. Only a brief one, but," he paused briefly, "it didn't do much for her complexion, that's for sure. By the time she put the receiver down she was red as a Tangier sunset, as a person of my acquaintance would say."

Geoff waited, expectant.

Al said slowly, "According to her it was another of Terry's London pals – her words – but that she wasn't going to let herself be intimidated."

He smoothed his jaw. "Struck me she was a bit more bothered by it than she let on."

"She said that, did she. '*Another* of Terry's London pals'?"

"She did. So, yes, there must have been previous calls. And from the way she said 'pals' I guess they weren't exactly bosom chums. Mind you," Al said, "she soon cheered up. Poured herself a glass of something or other and told me that now she'd got a good solicitor working for her she'd got nothing to fear."

"Peter Cadogan."

"He puts himself about a bit, I reckon"

"He does indeed," Geoff said.

* * *

Driving home, he thought about Al's words and how they linked with Simon's earlier remarks. So Terry had, as they'd all probably guessed, been in financial bother; and Cadogan knew about it. Well, yes, Cadogan was Terry's solicitor. But also, although we don't mention the fact, Mr C. happened to be the fixer behind all their deals. From which it might follow, presumably *did* follow, that he could have been in with whoever pulled the plug on said deals. But why? No answer to that, he thought, as he prepared to turn into Ewing Avenue. And none likely to be forthcoming.

Retrieving his horn from the back of the Fiat, he turned his thoughts to Helen. She hadn't answered the text message he'd sent her on Monday and, more worryingly, she hadn't been in the Tuns. Key in door, he let himself hope that in his absence she'd contacted him, at least let him know why she'd not shown up for the evening's gig. But a few minutes later, having first tried his answerphone and found it empty of messages, then switched on his computer and wiped the few emails waiting for him, chiefly adverts for penis enlargement and executive holidays, he had to accept that his words remained unanswered, and now, playing them over in his head as he busied himself feeding Baw, he thought them hopelessly misjudged. **your fool wants u 2 know shoulder better. Can u make Wed. at 3 Ts. X G X.**

Well, no, apparently she couldn't. Nor could she be bothered to tell that she'd not be there, nor why. Keeping silent was, it seemed clear, her way of telling him to back off.

He poured himself a late-night glass of Merlot and, sitting at the kitchen table, swivelled to look out at the half-moon glimmering above Frank's garden. Love without hope be buggered. *Life* without hope was the real dagger to the heart. What must it have been like to be Terry, alone in his parked car and knowing he was about to swallow all those pills? Terry, Mr Cool, who in his self-contained, self-assured manner always seemed far too streetwise to be anyone's fall guy. And yet it now seemed that was precisely what he had become. In taking on Lorette, Terry had, as the saying went, tried to punch above his weight and as a result had ended flat on his back, out for the count.

And at a guess the one person he couldn't talk to about his problems was the very person who, no matter how unintendedly, had caused them. He had been the smart guy, levering Lorette out of her London life. He could hardly then go on his knees and ask her to save him by calling off the dogs her going had set free. Other men might have done so. But then other men wouldn't have behaved as Terry did, wouldn't have had the brass-neck to lift property belonging to someone else. Not, anyway, when that someone was as much of a threat as Lorette's ex turned out to be. Because if Lorette was getting threatening calls *after* Terry's death, it stood to reason that before he topped himself Terry would have been on the receiving end of more such calls. And they'd have been far nastier, more menacing.

Lifting the glass to his lips, then raising it higher to confirm that the pain in his shoulder survived as no more than a slight twinge, a faint after-shock at worst, Geoff came back to thinking about Cadogan's part in all this. Surely Terry could have expected the man he called Mr C. to help him? Tide him over, perhaps, by paying off one or two creditors, if money, or rather the lack of it, was the problem.

But then, he thought, no, Cadogan was far too clever to come to the aid of a marked man. A case where my enemies' enemy can't be my friend. Cadogan must have known that Terry was beyond help.

At which point a further, darker thought occurred. Could Cadogan have engineered it all? Had he been working with, working *for*, Lorette's ex? Well, anything was possible where Cadogan was concerned. But no, he thought, it was far more probable that the solicitor simply abandoned Terry to his fate. He was too keen on self-preservation to run unnecessary risks. Whatever happened to others, Cadogan was always Mr Clean.

And for a similar reason there was no point in speculating about whether the Halsteads could have been involved in a plot to destroy Terry. In fact, Geoff made himself acknowledge, such speculation was absurd. It was – yes – poppycock. Verity Halstead, or Eve, or whoever she might be, was a mess, but judging from how he behaved, her husband loved her, looked after her, took care of her. Their knowing Cadogan didn't mean that they were in league with him. "After all," Geoff said aloud as he bent to scratch Baw's head, "even *I* know him. He's a known man."

Still, Terry. Staring into the empty wine glass, Geoff wondered about the pills and brandy. Why had Terry done it? Didn't he owe a duty of care to Lorette? He loved her. She'd hardly be welcomed back into the world he'd prised her away from, would she? Or was she the real reason he'd decided to kill himself. He could stand financial humiliation but not her scorn. Geoff remembered then that on the occasion he'd been to Cadogan's office, Cadogan had insisted that Terry was devoted to Lorette. What Cadogan *hadn't* said was that Lorette was devoted to Terry. With good reason. Because she all too plainly wasn't. Whatever lay behind her exchanging a London crim. for Terry, it wasn't love. Infatuation, perhaps, or simply a desire to get away to the country where the grass was greener and the air sweeter than London gangland and where, for all he knew, she'd been bored or worse.

A place in the country. It certainly wasn't beyond Terry to dress up his sweet-talking act as though he was in with the gentry. As if they were worth being in with. God, the rubbish people talked about the country. Pure never-never land. Terry in his converted farm house. Terry Marsden, Squire Bountiful. Cupboard love, Geoff's mother used to call the show of affection which had a purely material motive. But at some time Terry's cupboard became bare. It had been emptied by the London heavies he thought he could outsmart. So, yes, Lorette's fury, her scorn, could be predicted.

No point in feeling sorry for her. But Terry, that was different.

He took his empty glass over to the sink, ran water over it and watched it swirl down the plughole.

Poor Terry. Surprising he should think that, but he did. Poor Terry. And after all, he had behaved better than the man Foster with whom Helen had compared him. Foster took his whole family with him when he went. Terry, on the other hand, though he had done himself in, had spared Lorette, Lorette who by the time he topped himself had presumably made clear that she despised him.

Poor Terry.

30

Geoff took a place at the aisle end of one of the rear pews. A long-established habit, developed from his youth. Sneak out before anyone notices you're missing. Besides, from this vantage point he could spot anyone who came in either front or back door.

A few mourners had already arrived and were sitting ahead of him, but not the one person he wanted to see. He'd decided against contacting her about the funeral. No point in pestering her with messages when she plainly didn't want to hear from him. She could hardly be unaware of either time and place. Everyone knew.

Simon and Barbara were sitting in the middle of a pew towards the front, on either side of them some of the Wednesday night habitués, Norman included, and after a moment Simon turned, saw Geoff and, in the act of turning back to face front, raised a hand in greeting. Geoff watched Simon duck his head and whisper in Barbara's ear and she now turned, smiling, her face under the black beret vivid, *gamin* almost. Lucky Simon.

Other people, the majority of whom he didn't recognise, began to fill the intervening pews, some moving briskly into position, others – the majority of them – taking longer, hesitant, peering warily about them as though the chapel was not so much unknown as feared territory. Here be dragons. Who were they, these men in tailored suits, others in black leather jackets, still others in sports coats, flamboyant ties and defiantly vivid shirts of reds and greens, some young, others greybeards? Where had they come from? They weren't musos, not local ones, anyway. Family? He thought not. Only a few seats at the front had been reserved. The chapel couldn't have been asked to prepare for many official mourners, and these men – and, one or two smartly dressed women apart, they were all men – didn't behave like family. They greeted each other with the kinds of nods and smiles that weren't a million miles from complacency. Business associates, perhaps? Dodgy customers up from London? Some were now exchanging remarks, even laughter, leaning across pews in an ostentatious display of indifference to convention. Well, why not. As you got older you no doubt felt less inclined to pay your respects to

Death. What was the point? He'd soon be coming for you. Then court him, elude him, reel and pass.

Noting the variety of dress, Geoff decided against putting on the tie he had stuffed into the pocket of his dark-grey corduroy jacket.

Recorded music began to filter through invisible speakers; the shuffling, whisperings, coughing died away as the congregation sat, shoulders back, listening to George Shearing play 'I'll Remember April.'

No, wait, that was Terry, doing a more than passable imitation of the Shearing sound. Of course. It was the session they'd recorded last autumn and out of which they'd made a CD: *Four Into Three Will Go, The Terry Marsden Quartet Live at the Three Tuns.*

As he listened to the recording, Geoff began to feel pleasure, even a flush of pride, in the music. Homage to Shearing over, Terry was now taking the number in his own direction, left hand finding a rhythmic energy to push the right into moments of genuine inventiveness. And there, behind the keyboard's sprightly notes, was Al's guitar, chords at once crisp and yet with that steady fullness the best guitarists have, and Si on bass, dependable as always, his firm pulse propelling the number forward, pointing the way for Geoff's solo, delayed entry modelled on Pres, flutter of notes over the closing four bars also owing everything to his hero, but musically adept, even, in its modest way, accomplished. Hey, Geoff thought, feeling that he was hearing the track as though for the first time, *we're not bad.*

The next number, 'Funny Valentine', had hardly begun before it was abruptly cut off, people began to clamber to their feet at the first peal of the chapel organ, and Al entered from the back, black-hatted, frock coat, striped trousers, the man of black in black, as he'd once called himself, leading six pall-bearers, coffin resting on their shoulders.

The pall-bearers were preceded by the chaplain, in surplice and cassock, his feet, Geoff noticing from his vantage point, encased in trainers. Trainers! He thought of the invitations sent to the library staff for what Colleen always called "Posh Dos" at City or County Hall. "Dress: Smart Casual." Some oxymorons were witty, others intriguing. Smart Casual was neither. It was crass. And just what were the chaplain's trainers supposed to be? Smart? Casual? Trendily conservative?

After the coffin came Lorette, her arm linked through Peter Cadogan's. Nobody followed *them*, nobody at all. If there were family members on either Terry's side or hers, they must have decided to stay away. Or perhaps they hadn't been invited. The two former wives wouldn't be likely to attend.

He found himself wondering who might turn up at his own funeral. Both parents dead, no brothers or sisters, two cousins he hardly knew ... Well, he'd never need to know.

The opening hymn, 'Here Hath Been Dawning Another Blue Day', was followed by prayers, then a further hymn, 'The Lord's My Shepherd', which few in the congregation attempted.

As they dropped back into their pews, the chaplain announced that there would now be a 'Tribute' to Terry Marsden, and amid breathy exhalations and muffled coughs, Cadogan, in charcoal-grey suit and maroon tie, strode to the lectern.

He began by looking pointedly at Lorette in order to tell her how deeply everyone felt for her over her sad loss, although he would leave further words of comfort to the chaplain. His own brief was to share with those present some memories of his great friend, Terry Marsden, a man, he knew they would agree, of outstanding talents, not all of them confined to music. About music, indeed, he, Cadogan, could say little, being himself tone deaf and, in the eyes of the jazz fraternity, what he understood was called a Hooray Henry.

Pause for self-deprecating smile. Nor did he propose to enumerate Terry's good work for the many charities and benevolent organisations of which his friend was an enthusiastic and, more important, open-handed if unostentatious supporter, although he would be failing in his duty were he not to mention the Rotary Club, the Midlands Opera Foundation and the John Collins Educational Trust, all of whom had been materially aided by Terry's munificence, and representatives of which organisations he was pleased to see among those attending today's occasion. He did, however, wish to praise Terry the friend, the man on whose judgement and wise counsel he, Cadogan, had so often relied and which he would now miss, as indeed would those many others for whom Terry had been a rock to which they could cling in stormy times.

Pull the other one, Geoff thought.

And yet.

These people packed into the chapel, those organisations to whom Terry had given money. Cadogan's words couldn't *all* be hyperbole. Charitable deeds, friendship, good fellowship. These were facets of Terry's character he hadn't glimpsed, hadn't even suspected.

But they helped to explain the number of people who'd been at the fiftieth birthday party and who now sat, crammed shoulder to shoulder, listening to Cadogan. They must know more about Terry than he, Geoff, did.

He found himself listening more attentively to Cadogan's closing words, their insistence on Terry Marsden's determination to do good by stealth; and he listened, with equal attention, to the chaplain's threadbare words, his offer of the whole chapel's sympathy to the grieving widow, his certainty that she would find among those present many who would be willing to share time with her in the difficult, lonely months to come. Fustian, or, to be more charitable, honest, plain words. Yes, that.

When they stood for the closing hymn, 'Oh, God Our Help in Ages Past', Geoff joined in singing the words, and, as the coffin disappeared through the curtains, was jolted by a feeling that, if it wasn't a pang of loss, was one of uneasiness, even guilt, his scepticism rebuked by the show of support for Terry to which the crowded chapel testified.

* * *

Outside, people shook hands with Lorette, who stood straight-backed but somehow diminished by the black, full-length coat wrapped closely about her, her blonde hair touched by grey, face lined, blank-eyed in the April sun. Cadogan, at her side, let his hand rest lightly on her arm as she replied to those who mumbled their condolences, hoped to see her in the future, assured her they were there to call on in need, that she mustn't hesitate, the whole, awkward, inadequate, necessary routine of grief and mourning, some of it token, some genuine.

Then it was done and the crowd began to disperse. As Geoff stood with Simon and Barbara, Barbara with a tear shimmering tinily on the wing of a nostril, Cadogan strolled over. "I've no idea how many are going back to the pub," he said, "but Lorette's under a good deal of pressure and I doubt she'll want to stay long. You'll understand if she and I slip away."

Simon nodded. "Sure."

"Thank you for your words about Terry," Barbara said. "He was obviously a good man."

Cadogan looked at her as though suspecting irony, but, finding none, said, "Indeed, he was," and walked away.

"I'll see you at the Tuns," Geoff told them, preparing to walk to where he'd parked his car.

He looked around, in case he might have missed her entry to the chapel, but no, she wasn't there. And as though to match his forlorn mood, the sun disappeared behind dirty grey clouds and a gust of wind stung his eyes, making them water.

* * *

Unhooding his bass as the trio set up, Simon said, "So. It seems there was more to Terry than met the eye. Barbara was well impressed by what she heard."

Geoff nodded. "Agreed." He paused, fitting a reed to his mouthpiece. "But he was still involved in dodgy deals. Must have been."

"Speaking of which," Al, who had changed out of his undertaker's gear into jeans and check shirt, waited for a moment, then said, "Heard the latest about Cadogan?"

"What about Cadogan?" Geoff had the reed in place now.

"Knight in shining armour," Al said drily. "Word's out that he's buying Terry's mansion in order to turn it into some sort of Rest Home."

"Make a packet, out of that, the crafty sod." Si said.

"There's more," Al told them. "Guess who he's installing as Manager?"

"Not Lorette?"

And when Al nodded, Geoff said, "How do you know this?"

"Not much us undertakers don't pick up on." Al winked at Simon.

Geoff peered over the heads of the crowd, trying to catch a glimpse of the widow and Cadogan as they stood by the door, welcoming invited guests. Taking a sip of the god-awful plonk Norman had seen fit to offer as the free drink allotted all who came to the wake, he let himself, for one wild moment, consider the possibility that Cadogan had somehow manoeuvred himself into this position. First kill the husband, then take his property and marry the widow. Jacobean tragi-comedy. "Flowers stuck in sand," Coleridge, his hero, had called them. Not real, not real life.

So no, forget it. Or rather, don't indulge the kind of speculation that …

"Behind him, Al said, "Your One and Only's arrived."

"*Where?*"

"No need to blast my earholes," Al said. "There. Look."

He followed the direction of Al's pointing finger and couldn't see her.

And then he could. She had her back to him, but it was her all right, in her dark red coat, close to the bar, surrounded by a scrum of people waiting to be served. She must have come through the front entrance. A surge of joy swept through him.

In one movement he unhooked his tenor, jumped down, and next minute was pushing through a mass of bodies to where she stood, Janey, he now saw, beside her.

"Helen."

She turned and, for a second, he thought, her eyes sparked gladness. It was succeeded by another look, this one wary, withheld.

"You weren't at the funeral."

"Is that an accusation?" She raised an eyebrow.

"No, of course not. But I thought … I thought you'd not be coming at all."

"Well, here I am. And here is Janey."

Relax, her expression said. What's the panic. But there was another look in her eyes, something questioning, was it, something challenging, a look whose significance he couldn't measure?

Behind him a male voice said, "If you're not buying, mate, make way will you. I'm gagging for a pint."

He looked round, saw a wide-shouldered man in black suit scowling at him, muttered a quick "Sorry," then, to Janey, and distractedly, "Good to see you." But it wasn't her he was looking at. "Can I get you drinks?"

But both shook their heads.

They were hemmed in by the crowd, men whose shoulders were wedged solidly against each other, arms raised as they tried to attract the attention of either Norman or the inexperienced youth helping him behind the bar.

Putting her mouth close to his ear, Helen said, "We've been to visit your friend, Arthur Stanchard."

As she spoke, she put a hand on his arm, began to guide him away from the crush at the bar. "Is your shoulder better?"

"Yes, well, almost," he shouted above the hubbub, then found himself wondering at her explanation, if that's what it was, for her

247

non-appearance at the funeral. What did she mean by saying they'd been to visit Arthur? Was Arthur unwell?

"Arthur's fine," Janey said, perhaps guessing his unasked question, looking for confirmation to Helen, back to Geoff again. She opened her mouth to say something else, then swung round as someone barged into her back, catching Geoff's arm as she did so, knocking his glass so that drops of Norman's house red splashed his jacket.

"Sorry," she mouthed to him.

"No need." But he wanted to ask about Arthur.

"Arthur's fine," Janey repeated. "He told us a story which I think Helen is keen to pass on."

This, she implied, is why we're here.

He turned to Helen, pressed up against him in this mass of bodies, breathed in her scent, her fingers still resting lightly against his arm, felt her hair brush against his cheek as she swayed out of the way of a man forcing his way from the bar back to a group waiting, shoulder-to-shoulder round a table, for the music to start. The man glanced at Helen as he passed her, then winked approvingly at Geoff.

Turning back to Geoff, Helen, standing on tiptoe, pressed her lips to his ear, said, "He invited us to lunch."

She leaned back as if to measure the impact of her words. Why? What was she trying to tell him, to get him to understand?

"At his house," Helen said.

Geoff felt a stab of envy. He knew the narrow street of terraced houses where the old man lived, but had never seen inside it.

"And if you want to know, we had baked beans and eggs on toast."

Another pause. The momentary laughter in her voice had dimmed, vanished. She looked down at her feet, then up and away, her words muffled so that, what with the noise all around them, he wasn't sure he'd heard them correctly.

"We thought it was going to be a social occasion. But … " Her next words were blown away by a gale of laughter from the crowd of men immediately behind her.

"Sorry," he said, "I didn't catch that." Then, "Let's get away from the bar," and he hooked his hand under her elbow and drew her toward the back of the room, motioning with a gesture of his head for Janey to come, too.

"This is better," he said, when they were away from the worst of the crush. "Now. You were saying?"

The earlier questioning, no, pained, expression in her eyes now back, Helen said, as she looked unsmilingly at him, "I said, did you know he lost his job because of that deal I told you about the other night?"

So that was it. He nodded but said nothing.

She shook her head. "I feel awful. Sick."

Her eyes locked onto his stare.

He shrugged, then, realising she saw this as an evasion, said, "There were rumours."

"But you didn't tell me." Her face registering distress, she sounded more anguished than angry.

"I suppose I should have. Sorry." I had other things on my mind. I didn't want to spoil the mood, I wanted to go to bed with you, and, yes, I wanted, I'm sure I wanted, to spare you from what you're now telling me you feel. But trust Arthur to have worked it out.

"I wish you *had* told me," she said. Then, her voice taking on a new vibrancy as she looked away from him, she said savagely, "Cadogan. God, he *disgusts* me."

He thought, I ought to be glad and yet, I'm not. Not seeing her like this. Hoping to calm her, he said, speaking slowly, "All over England that kind of thing was going on. There was nothing special about what happened to Arthur." He tried to overlay the rueful words with a thin layer of cynicism he didn't feel.

But she was having none of it. "The truth is," she said, bitterly, "I never let the thought of what he was doing bother me. But now I know about Arthur … " She stared at the ground.

A pause. "It all came out at lunch. Arthur was fussing about getting food on the table and I said there was no hurry, I'd arranged to take the afternoon off because Janey and I would be going to Terry Marsden's funeral. That started Arthur off. Mr Marsden's funeral was one he certainly wouldn't be attending. Not after the dirty tricks he'd been involved in, the damage he'd done to people's lives. And then Arthur told us about how the factory had been sold from under the workforce's feet, and he knew all about Cadogan's part in it. It's just as well that he didn't know Cadogan and I were once … " She stopped abruptly. Then, "Do you know about Cadogan's house," she asked him, with sudden ferocity. "Do you know where he lives?"

"A development of executive-style mansions is how I seem to recall the advertising hoardings described them."

"And you know that development is called 'The Leas'?"

"I do. And I also know that the development is on the land where the factory stood."

"Oh." It was an exhalation of dismay, almost of despair. "So you knew about that, *too*."

"People like Cadogan always get what they want."

She looked at him, furious, but didn't reply.

He said, "You weren't to know about 'The Leas'. It happened after you'd left."

"Still," she said. She ducked her head and when she raised it again her eyes were full of anger. "I feel contaminated, if you want to know."

"And that was why you didn't come to the funeral."

Her reply, when it came, was scarcely more than a whisper. "I couldn't have borne to be there," she said. Disgust, scorn, fury, contrition, they were all in the look she gave him. She reached for Janey's hand, took it, and, speaking more clearly, said, "Neither of us wanted to be there. Not once we'd heard Arthur's story."

Ahead of them, men continued to force their way to and from the bar, as many as four filled glasses gripped in the meaty hands of some who'd made their purchases and who were now treading a slow, elaborately careful way to thronged tables where their mates waited.

"Mind your backs, please."

A man, smelling of stale cigarette smoke, was edging past them, chin tucked in with the effort of concentrating on keeping balanced the full tray of drinks with which he was heading for the yard.

Geoff opened the door for him, then, shutting it behind his retreating, leather-jacketed back, said, "Well, I suppose it would have come out sooner or later."

She waited for a blast of guffaws from the direction of the bar to fade away before she said, "Men like Cadogan … " She made no attempt to finish the sentence.

"Men like Cadogan are all AB," he was about to say, but her shudder of contempt, of self-contempt, of contempt that included them all, abashed him. The words died on his lips.

And yet she'd come to the wake. Of course. She wanted to confront him. He wondered whether to tell her that Terry at least wasn't perhaps all bad, that in the end he'd been as much a victim of Cadogan as had Arthur, a greater victim, even.

But Al's voice came booming over the microphone, battling against the insistent noise of the packed room. "Can we have our tenor man, please. The musical entertainment is about to start."

"I've got to go," he said. "Can we talk later? I'll be clear of the library by six o'clock – seven at the latest."

"Not possible," Helen said. "Sorry. I promised Janey I'd go to the flicks with her this evening." But she did at least manage a quick, apologetic lift of her mouth, though more perhaps of grimace than smile.

"Tomorrow then?"

She shook her head, this time her lips pursed, wry. "Again, not possible. I'm going away."

"*What?*"

He felt his legs begin to shake, his guts slid floorwards.

"May Day, May Day," Al called. "Come in, Mr Tenor Man. Your time is up."

"Going *away?*"

She seemed startled by the anguish in his voice. "Only for the weekend. London."

Then, as he stared, unable to find words – relief, despair? – she said, "Geoff, why haven't you been in touch?"

He was aghast. "But I *have*. I texted you. Monday. Told you my shoulder was better."

Behind him, he heard Al begin to play the blessedly lengthy introduction to 'Honeysuckle Rose'.

And then, as he turned to wave at the stand to show he'd be with them, it came to him.

Perhaps he hadn't sent the damned text. He tried to remember. Having tapped out the message, he'd dithered about whether the words were right, had re-cast them several times. Perhaps after all he simply hadn't pressed **send.**

Oh, you *fool*.

He turned back to her, but as he opened his mouth to speak she put a hand to his chest, gave him a small shove. "Go on, you're needed."

She was smiling now, though he couldn't tell what the smile meant. "You should try a weekend in London sometime," she said gravely, her face close to his, her eyes searching his eyes. "Do you good. The 9.02 from Nottingham. That's the one I take."

"Helen, I'm … what can I say. I'm so … sorry." Sorry. Sorry. Sorry. He was beseeching her. "You're right," he said. "I'm a fool."

"Yes," she said, and now at last her smile had lightened, "you are."

Al's introduction to 'Honeysuckle Rose', extended to thirty-two bars, was coming to an end as he clipped on his tenor. But he was in time – just – for the first chorus.

A few moments later, when he dared to look up, he saw that she was no longer standing where he'd left her. He took his time scanning the room, but no. He could see neither her nor Janey. The two of them had already left.

31

He was home by 8 o'clock.

Hunched at the kitchen table, he poked about among an unsatisfactory pile of battered fish and cooling, soggy chips, while at his feet Baw worked her way through the haddock his fishmonger had assured him was so freshly caught it hadn't woken up to the fact it was no longer in the water.

Were Josie and Colleen right about the Library Users' Consultative Group? When he'd left them an hour previously, the two women had united in claiming that the Group was proving more trouble than it was worth. Gerald Gleat was the problem. Gleat was *always* the problem, Geoff had maintained, but they weren't having that. Or rather, they weren't having any more of Gleat.

"You should have heard him," Josie said, who in Geoff's absence had chaired last night's meeting, "he had something to say about every item on the agenda. On and on he went."

"The old devil won't be happy until he's managed to drive us all into the nut house," Colleen added. "Tell Geoff about his latest scheme."

"I'm afraid you won't like this." Josie looked apologetically at Geoff.

Nor, when she outlined what Gleat had come up with, did he. In fact, he was furious.

"A 'Watch Committee'? *Why?*"

"Because we need to take into account what 'representatives of the public' think. Especially when it comes to future exhibitions."

"And because we're in the clutches of the Maniacs of Political Correctness and it's no wonder decent people won't come near libraries nowadays." Colleen looked at Geoff in mock-despair.

"He can't mean that exhibition of Old Longford."

"Oh, yes, he can," Josie said, her voice trembling with indignation. "He claimed that I'd deliberately promoted 'dissension' by allowing Arthur Stanchard to speak about the hard times at Longford Mill. And then of course the boiler factory. Arthur had a fair amount to say about that."

"Well, there *were* hard times. And there *was* something dodgy about how the factory was closed down. In fact, it was even dodgier than Arthur let on, or than he knew about. It was a crook deal. Why *shouldn't* Arthur be allowed to tell his story? He was one of those who lost their jobs."

But as he spoke he recalled Gleat's behaviour on the morning when the exhibition had opened, the man's obvious fury at Arthur's words.

Colleen said, "Gleat didn't like the fact that the local rag made a good deal of what Arthur had to say. Though there was more about Josie's good work. And quite right, too. Everyone who's been to see the exhibition has had something good to say about it."

"Agreed," Geoff said. "It's a winner."

Josie, blushing at their praise said, judiciously, "Mr Gleat likes to put his own slant on things. He's a bit prejudiced."

"Only someone as kind-hearted as you would call it that," Geoff said.

"The man's a menace," Colleen said briskly. "We're better off without him."

"So what do you suggest? We can't bump him off. Anyway, the old bugger's probably indestructible."

"Either he goes or the rest of the group does, is how I see it," Colleen said. "They won't put up with much more."

"Couldn't Arthur Stanchard put him in his place? Arthur's usually pretty good at shutting Gleat up."

Josie shook her head. "Mr Stanchard wasn't there," she said. "He came to see me earlier in the day, to let me know me he'd not be attending."

Too busy preparing lunch for his female guests, perhaps, Geoff had thought but not said.

"I thought he meant he couldn't get to that particular meeting," Josie said. "But he told me he was resigning from the group. He'd had enough of Gleat's obstreperousness." She pronounced the word carefully, as though it might be a rare medical condition.

"See," Colleen said.

"So what do you suggest?"

"I think," Colleen said, clearly speaking for herself and Josie, "that we use the weekend to mull it over and then next week we come to a decision. Agreed?"

"What a lovely way to spend the weekend."

"At least you've got tomorrow off," Colleen said, with a touch of asperity in her voice. "Josie and I have to be at our posts. Don't expect sympathy from us. Especially as the UCG was your idea. And by the way," she looked at him questioningly, "how come you seem to know so much about the 'crook deal' as you call it, that closed down the boiler factory."

"Things I heard," Geoff said.

"But that you're not prepared to share with your work colleagues."

"I wish I could," Geoff said, "honest. But the libel laws being what they are … "

And on that unsatisfactory note they ended their informal meeting.

* * *

From Gleat, he let his thoughts drift away to the events of the afternoon. Before sitting down to eat he'd put on *Four Into Three Will Go*, but as he chewed on one more tasteless lump of fish, found that instead of listening to the music he was recalling Cadogan's funeral oration for his friend, Terry Mardsen, that generous, good-hearted man. *Generous, good-hearted.* Stroll on. Cadogan and Terry. The unlikely lads. Still, Terry had come off worse. Not that many would know that. He thought of Helen's shame-faced, angry, contrite and possibly accusatory account of all she'd heard from Arthur about the fate of the boiler factory and her realisation of how he and his workmates had been shafted.

Well, no blame to her for that. But her abashed look, the way she spoke, revealed that even while she was sharing Cadogan's bed – or anyway, various hotel beds – she'd known more than she wanted to admit, even to herself, of his devious methods, his snake-like ability to hurt others and then slither out of harm's way. We have scotched the snake, not killed it. Where had he come across that? O-Level. *Macbeth.* But Cadogan wasn't even scotched. No marks on him. Kill Claudio? You must be joking.

And Terry? That was different. Terry *had* been marked, and how. Terry had killed himself.

The music from the CD broke in on him. That was Terry now, providing an introduction to the quartet's arrangement of 'How High the Moon,' laying down the basics, as he might have said. Geoff made himself attend. Good, reliable, semi-pro stuff, worth the applause, neither rapturous nor obligatory, which greeted the final chord. To a background of chatter and the clinking of empty beer glasses, Terry announced the next number, "An up-tempo treatment of 'My Heart Stood Still', so throw away your elastic stockings and zimmer frames, good people, and prepare to live dangerously." Terry, the blandly cheerful front man. Then came the four-bar intro, pale shades of Teddy Wilson, Al and Simon picked up the beat, his own entry followed, its poor-man's imitation of Ben Webster's breathy vibrato, and as he listened he thought, who are we trying to kid. Homage to the greats? Pastiche more like. From Harlem to Longford's Three Tuns was a long, long way, and not a distance to be measured in miles. How do I get from here to Carnegie Hall? Practice. Yeh, yeh.

And yet. Listening, he thought, as he'd thought when, earlier in the day, he'd heard again the group's version of 'I Remember April,' we weren't bad, we really weren't. He bundled his largely uneaten food back into the greasy paper from which it had been shaken, and as he did so remembered a teacher of his who, red-faced and unsmiling, told his class that they shouldn't take for granted that the mechanicals in *A Midsummer Night's Dream* were there simply to be laughed at. There was nothing wrong with learning to master a trade. "Snug the Joiner. Why laugh? Would you want a cupboard door *not* to close, Cousins, a drawer *not* to slide smoothly open?" And then, as the class had sat there, unsure whether to grin or not, the man had added, "Remember the lot of you, an old saying: everyone loves a carpenter, nobody loves a millionaire."

He couldn't at first recall the teacher's name but, opening his back door to take the wreck of his meal to his dustbin, the man's repeated insistence that if a thing was worth doing it was worth not only doing well but *enjoying* came into his head. Ah, yes. *Brewer*. A man of what would once have been called generous girth and inevitably known as Beermug, whose class soon learnt to recognise his praise for a craftsman's skills as the prelude to a denunciation of "bodging", of shoddy goods, of what Brewer, whom the boys privately thought of as a bit of a Red, called "modern industrial capitalism".

Looking up at the night sky as he tipped away the remains of his dinner, registering the scatter of early stars, he recalled that someone at school had started a rumour that Brewer's own father was a carpenter, a "chippie," though he had no idea whether it was true. Probably not. And anyway, why would it have mattered? Only in among the petty snobberies of suburbia, the smug assurances of those for whom the kitchen door was invisibly marked Tradesman's Entrance. Snug but not smug. Beermug had said that, too.

"Everybody loves a carpenter." Brewer's words provided a sort of consolation, even vindication, for the music he played. It might not be cutting-edge (it wasn't), it might not appeal to an audience that preferred breezers to pints (it didn't), but it was still good music, the way a well-made cupboard stayed a well-made cupboard. Not Chippendale, maybe, and not Sheraton – definitely not Sheraton – but serviceable, not to be ashamed of, nor sneered at.

And neither, he thought, as he went back indoors, was library work. Suddenly he saw Gleat's face, the look of contempt that had been on it that Saturday morning when the exhibition of Old Longford was opened, and with that came a sudden anger that the old fool should want to trample on the efforts of someone as innocent and *good* a person as Josie, someone entirely without ego, who simply got on with the task in hand, whatever that was, who never asked or expected favours, who was reliable, and therefore much, much more, was, yes, cherishable.

He poured the last of a bottle of white wine into his glass. "To you, Josie," he said, before drinking. "Have a happy life. You deserve it."

He lowered his glass. Ought he to salute Terry Marsden, musician. Did Terry's keyboard skills excuse his crooked dealings? No, of course they didn't. Then did his suicide exonerate him? Well, no, because it didn't clear him of blame. It did, though, suggest that Terry's decision to swallow a bottle of pills was, among other things, a belated attempt to apologise for the harm he'd done others.

Though who was to know if Terry had seen it that way? An altogether trickier question, and one that turned on *why* he killed himself, a question to which, in the absence of a note, there could be no sure answer. Somehow, Geoff didn't see Terry as acknowledging guilt. Desperation over his probable bankruptcy? Far more likely. Suicide was an act of despair. That, anyway, was what theologians taught. It came to him then that as far as Terry was concerned you couldn't slide a Rizla paper between shame and despair.

But that was followed by another thought. Suppose despair or shame, whatever Terry might call it, was another word for loneliness? For all the show he'd put on at his fiftieth, there didn't seem much love between Lorette and him. She was his reward for being a smart operator, and in the end he'd proved not as smart as he thought he was or made her believe. Which made him a failure, a loser in the eyes not merely of his enemies, but of his friends.

Were there any? Probably not. Not anyone he was really close to, to whom he could talk in confidence. That was the ultimate loneliness. "My great friend" Cadogan had called Terry. Well, if *he* was a great friend it didn't say much for the others. Terry the unknowable. "To be honest, if someone told me he'd done time for murder, I wouldn't be surprised."

He was blundering about in thickets of speculation through which no clear path opened up. Might Terry have hoped Cadogan would help him over his business problems only to discover that Cadogan was less solution than part of the problem, that the solicitor was not prepared to gain him either money or time? And why might that have been? Was Cadogan, perhaps, being leant on by people in London Terry had offended? Or was the solicitor somehow involved with Lorette? Were they lovers, even? But he'd been over that already, and where, apart from Lorette's being installed as manager of the former farmhouse now Rest-Home-to-be, was the evidence? Cadogan was too slippery, too clever to leave any marks. Even if he was in some sense implicated in Terry's death, it could never be traced back to him.

He raised his glass. "Here's to you, Terry," he said, aware from the opening chords of 'Autumn Leaves' that the CD was now on its last track. "You were a good pianist." The music dwindled away on a long-held final chord and then, before any applause could make itself heard, the sound was cut. Melancholy reasserted itself. And sooner or later, he thought, draining his glass, even the best-made cupboard ends up on the scrap heap.

As though in mind-reading protest against such mawkish indulgence, Baw scrambled to her feet, shook herself, stalked to the door, and demanded to be let out.

Peering into the dark before he shut the door behind her, he looked at his watch. Just gone nine o'clock. Helen's words sounded in his head. "You should try a weekend in London some time. Do you good. The 9. 02 from Nottingham. That's the one I take."

Yes, well, perhaps he would. Some time. Meanwhile, being free for once of Saturday morning library duties, he thought of the weekend that stretched pointlessly ahead of him. Apart from considering the problem of Gleat, which he was damned if he'd do, what was there for him? No one to talk with, no place to go, I'm home about eight, just me and my radio.

Rinsing his plate under hot water, he tried to shut his mind to her voice, the way she had looked when she said those words, then, as he held his glass under the tap, caught sight of his face in the mirroring window, and said to himself, "The knight of the doleful countenance? No, a morose prick." Out of nowhere a remark of Janey's came into his head. "She's as perverse as you are."

And he knew what he had to do.

32

"Blimey, you again," the taxi-driver said. "Leg all right? Arm mended? Friend still alive? Where we off to this time? Longford A and E?"

"Nottingham. Midland Station," Geoff said, as he climbed in.

"No way, man."

Geoff, waving to Frank who stood in the porch, holding in both hands the tins of cat food he had been given together with paper instructions on when to feed Baw, wasn't at first sure he had heard correctly.

"What?"

"I said, no way."

"What do you *mean*, no way."

"Cool it, man. I mean, no way. Like, it can't be done. Don't you listen to the news? Big lorry shed its load, innit. The road to Nottingham's closed."

Slamming the door – on his hopes, his resolution? – Geoff said, "But there are other routes in."

"Sure, but that means goin' up the M1 and onto the 610 or down the M1 and up onto the 453. Either way's forty-five minutes least long, probably longer. How much time you got, man?"

Geoff looked at his watch. "Forty minutes. I'm catching the 9. 02 to London."

"Not from Nottingham, you ain't. How about Loughborough?"

Slumped in his seat, Geoff said, "what help's that?"

"Get you there in half-an-hour max. "

The driver was looking in his rear mirror and, as Geoff dully nodded his acceptance, he manoeuvred the cab out between the wrought-iron gate posts.

"The 9. 02. stops there. 9. 15. OK? Belt up, man."

The taxi began to roll. "Eat your heart out, Lewis Hamilton. Ain't nothin' goin' to stop us now, innit."

And, gravel sputtering beneath the taxi's wheels, they were off.

* * *

At a little after 9 o'clock Geoff stood on the London platform at Loughborough, a wad of paper napkins unable to prevent the cardboard bucket of Guaranteed Fresh-Ground coffee from scalding his fingers while he and a swelling number of passengers listened to a tannoy announcement informing them that due to line-side problems in the Nottingham area there would be a delay to the journey of customers waiting for the next train going forward to London and that the company wished to apologise for any inconvenience this might cause.

First the roadblock, then this. Lurching from side to side in the speeding cab he'd asked when exactly the reports of the lorry accident had come through, and been told that the driver didn't know "exactly" when, but that he, the driver, had heard about it on the 8 o'clock news.

Would Helen have heard? Of course. She listened to the local radio. So she'd have been forewarned. She'd have made sure she was in time to catch the train

Wouldn't she?

A keen wind caused him to take refuge in the waiting room where knowledgeable passengers were telling each other that travellers at Nottingham intending to catch the 9. 02 would certainly have been advised to take a connection to Derby from where they could pick up a London-bound train, and that in all probability the 9. 01 Derby to St Pancras would have been held for them. The alternative was to wait at Nottingham for the 9. 21 through-express, first stop East Midlands Parkway, next stop Leicester. Neither train, Geoff was assured, stopped at Loughborough. There was a kind of sombre relish in the way these facts were repeated, a call and response of those inured to their lot.

Bowed with dejection as he turned over in his mind Coleridge's words about a grief without a pang, void, dark, and drear, a stifled, drowsy, unimpassioned grief, Geoff roused himself to ask whether any of the trains clattering through on the southbound line might have included those aforementioned – viz. the stopping train from Derby and the express from Nottingham – and was told, yes, oh, yes, for sure, and that frankly anyone wanting to get to London from Loughborough would be well advised to think again. Well, thanks for that.

At a little after ten o'clock a further announcement apologising for the continued delay of the 9.15 to London was made virtually inaudible by the arrival of the train itself.

Climbing aboard, and noting as he did so that the train was unusually empty for a Saturday morning, Geoff became glumly certain that, as the gnarled, weary veterans of Loughborough had been telling him, many would-be travellers on the 9.02 from Nottingham must indeed have re-organised their journeys and would even now be looking forward to their imminent arrival at St Pancras. Meanwhile he himself was stuck on this jolting, late-running, job-lot of knackered carriages with a clapped-out engine that exhaled cloudbursts of foul-smelling diesel oil.

By the time he'd chosen a seat, moving through two of the carriages before deciding on one where the air-conditioning seemed to operate at slightly above arctic temperature, probably because it wasn't operating at all, the train slowed to a halt at Leicester, where most of those who had boarded at Loughborough alighted, and suspiciously few customers got on. The expresses from Derby and Nottingham had, it was now apparent, hoovered up the majority of travellers from the East Midlands hoping to reach London before nightfall.

The scant numbers who did come aboard were officially welcomed by an eldritch howl on the tannoy which died back long enough for someone who gave his name as Ryan and status as train manager to inform new customers that they were aboard the delayed 9. 02 from Nottingham, – good heavens, so we are – that a trolley service was available and would be passing through the carriages with a selection of snacks, beer, wines and spirits and cold drinks, though due to technical difficulties there was no hot water – good heavens, now *there*'s a surprise – that aisles were to be kept free of luggage in order to allow the safe passage of the trolley, that payment by exact amount was requested due to shortage of change – further surprise – and that anything suspicious was to be reported to the On-Board Team (Who? How?) or the Transport Police (How? Who?).

Ryan further informed customers that on behalf of the company he wished to apologise to customers for the late running of the train which was due to a delay caused by the breakdown of an earlier train in the Bedford area – *Bedford!* that was further down the line, wasn't it? – and finally he wished to let customers know that he himself would shortly be passing through the eight carriages – quiet coach at the front where mobiles were to be switched off – so would they please ensure they had all their travel documents with them, including senior railcards. Customers should also consult the safety information posted at each end of each carriage. A final eldritch noise, this time more scream than howl, and the tannoy became mute.

Leaving the overnight bag on his seat, Geoff levered himself up and began a slow swaying walk to the back of the train, scanning all occupied seats as he did so, then, having passed through the two entirely empty first-class carriage and reached the last, also empty carriage, turned and as slowly walked back to his starting point. A few, not many, passengers looked up as he passed. For the rest, he was free to study each face, and no, hers wasn't among them, wasn't one of the young, old, middle-aged, the black, the brown, the white, the Asian, Oriental, some reading, some in conversation, others shouting into mobile phones – "Hello, I'm on the train" – still others staring intently at open lap tops propped on table or knee, the rest locked into a private world of ear-plug music.

A wave of depression rolled over him. He dropped into his seat. What was the point? What might startle his dull pain, and make it move and live. Only her.

The train juddered to a halt. Market Harborough. No one left and no one came and soon enough they were lurching out into the Midlands countryside. My genial spirits fail.

"Anything from the trolley, sir?"

The question was asked more out of forlorn duty than in expectation.

"No thanks," Geoff said, and as the young woman nodded in sympathetic affirmation of his words – I didn't think you would be tempted – he once more hauled himself to his feet and this time made his way through to the front coach, again inspecting every occupied seat as he went.

Same story. No sight of her.

Of course there were plenty of hiding places on a train.

Oh, where? Well, under the seat or on the luggage rack, or locked in the loo. Very funny. But anyway, she wouldn't be in hiding, would she? So. She must have gone to Derby or picked up the through-express.

Or for some reason simply changed her mind, decided against the London trip, chosen to stay at home. At this very moment she might be calling him, wondering why he didn't answer? It didn't bear thinking about.

But no, she was on her way to London, all right, for a planned weekend that didn't include him. Meeting another man, even. What madness, last night's sudden decision to follow her.

And yet. She had named the train she would be taking. "The 9.02." Last night he had been convinced that she must have intended those words as a signal. Get the train. I'll be on it.

But she wasn't.

Plans for what he might have said to her came and went, plans that had thronged his head for much of a largely wakeful night Most of all, he needed to apologise. Or confess. Or both. Apologise for being a fool. For not understanding how his own envious loathing of Cadogan had blinded him to the fact that, whatever her past feelings for the man, she, too, had finished with him. As for confession. He was a spineless prat. Even love without hope ought to have some gaiety to it, at the very least some self-respect. That she was still prepared so much as to speak to him was cause for wonder. That she might, just might, have been sending him a hint when she told him the time of the London train, was an even greater wonder.

But in that case, where was she? Not on the train, it seemed. Not unless he'd somehow missed her when he went through the carriages. Should he give it one more try?

He stayed in his seat.

Stations came and went. Kettering, Wellingborough, Bedford. He thought of all he wanted to say to her, all he'd imagined they would need to say to each other. So much. It might all have been possible. But now?

If she'd managed to get on an earlier train she'd be at St Pancras soon, might even be pulling in at this very moment, which, he found by consulting his watch, was just gone 11 o'clock. Perhaps he ought after all to use his mobile. He'd fought off doing so, had imagined the perfect coming together, the surprise encounter. Just You, Just Me. Journeys end in lovers meeting.

Well, forget that.

He reached inside his jacket pocket.

No? Try the other pocket.

Now, take a deep breath. Stay calm.

He knew what he'd done. Or rather hadn't done. In his hurry to get out of no. 27, he'd left his phone behind, still on the bedroom floor where he'd set it on charge before going to bed.

Well, that was that then. He'd no way of contacting her.

He found he was strangely calm. Despair suited him.

Ryan was on the tannoy. Having left Luton Parkway the train would now be going forward to London St. Pancras "which will be our final station stop. Please have your tickets ready to exit through the barriers. Once again we apologise for the late running of this service and hope you have had a pleasant journey."

Oh, sure. Couldn't have been more fun.

As the train eased through Kentish Town station he stood, began to make his way to the front, shouldering his overnight bag, outer jacket over his arm.

He entered the front carriage, the quiet coach. "Mustn't stay talking," a man was shouting into his mobile, glancing up at Geoff as he did so. "Get some joyless prick telling me I'm breaking the rules."

"Yeh, don't get yourself into trouble," Geoff muttered, "wouldn't want you … "

And stopped.

Ahead of him, at the far end of the carriage, among the huddle of passengers waiting to leave the train, was a woman, her dark red coat as surely unmistakable as the face in half-profile, the fringe of hair.

Pain – was it – the most exquisite pain, squeezed the air out of his lungs.

Taking a deep, steadying breath, he turned back to make for the nearest door. That way, he could sprint along the platform and perhaps be in time to catch her as she stepped down from the train.

Oh, no, he couldn't. The way was blocked by a stout man, cap jammed full-square on his blunt head, gripping in each hand a large suitcase, a man who not only showed no inclination to clear a passage for Geoff, but who, ignoring his repeated "Excuse me, *please*," stared immovably ahead and would not budge.

Nor, once the doors were open, would the man hurry in lifting his damned cases down. Wedging himself in the doorway, he slowly lowered one case, then, even more slowly, the other, and only then, and after a delay to adjust his cap, stepped oh, so carefully, oh, so deliberately out.

By the time Geoff was on the platform the woman was some fifty yards ahead, already through the ticket barriers and walking briskly toward the escalators that led down to the main concourse.

But even at that distance, the manner in which she moved her shoulders, as though to ward off a sudden blast of cold wind sweeping across the upper station, brought the blood thudding at his ears, anguish turning to a gasp of exultant joy.

It *was* her.

Surely.

He began to run.

Acknowledgements

My thanks to the following for their help in bringing *The Plotting* to fruition: John Dee and Pauline Lucas for reading earlier drafts of the novel and making invaluable comments and suggestions for its improvement; members of staff and Beeston Public Library for answering some technical questions; Henry Maas for his editing skills; and Jude Keen for preparing the text for publication. And, of course, James Hodgson, of Greenwich Exchange, without whom not.

About the Author

John Lucas has published ten collections of poetry, including *Studying Grosz on the Bus*, winner of the 1990 Aldeburgh Poetry Prize. His versions of the Poems of Egil's Saga, an Everyman Modern Classics, has been re-issued as *I, the Poet Egil*. In 2008 *92 Acharnon Street* won the Author's Club Dolmen Award for Travel Literature and three years later *Next Year Will be Better: A Memoir of England in the 1950s* was made a Book of the Year in the *Guardian* and *Times Literary Supplement*. His novel, *Waterdrops*, was published in the same year and was followed by *A Brief History of Whistling*, co-authored with Allan Chatburn. His account of Rebels in English Cricket, *The Awkward Squad*, was short-listed for the 2015 Cricket Writers' Book of the Year Award. Professor Emeritus at the Universities of Loughborough and Nottingham Trent, John Lucas has published numerous critical and literary historical studies. He runs Shoestring Press.